RAMSHACKLE ROW

BLACK CAT BOOKS

Black Cat Books
DaneOwenAuthor.com

Editing: Shayla Raquel, shaylaraquel.com
Publishing Services: MartinPublishingServices.com

ISBN 978-1-7354756-0-8 (paperback), 978-1-7354756-1-5 (epub)

RAMSHACKLE ROW

DANE OWEN

BLACK CAT BOOKS

To the writers who don't yet know you're writers.
May your muse shake you awake one morning
and drag you to your desk.

CHAPTER 1

Patricia Donovan is too far gone. She sits on the back porch of the sprawling ranch in the woods. The warmth of the late fall sun dances gently on her face, never quite settling in. The corners of the forgotten crossword puzzle on the table behind her catch the breeze and softly rise and fall, making it an unsure thing. Should it stand or sit? Should it stay or leave for this? She listens to the birds gab with succinct intelligence out there in the tree line.

Wonder if they're going to try to talk me out of it.

"Please." She feels it. The bad surf she's been wading in has grown tired of holding off what's behind it. She feels an inevitable rise around her belly. Crawling up toward her breasts. Every inch that's submerged will never again see the sun. She knows this. The wave is coming, eating up horizon, and her feet are stuck in the sand.

She thinks of Ellie again. The only cog in the springs of all this. Although she's got that boy now. He's a good man and he'll help her get through it.

"If it's what I decide."

You decided long ago. You've been dead for years.

Over her shoulders now, tickling a cold line up her neck.

A couple squirrels skitter across the narrow yard behind the house, tails twitching and eyes bulging. Shooting around each other in blurry zigzags.

"Talk me out of this," she begs now. Not much more than a whisper in the warm breeze. But she knows it's too late. The bad water is up over her chin now; her whole body, save for her head, is dead. Black things swim around down there, bumping her knees and brushing her thighs, ridden in from the approaching wave.

That voice was right. She *has* been dead for years. Nolan isn't here anymore. Not that he'd ever really been here physically, working like he did. But he isn't *here* anymore. She steals herself for a moment and thinks of that wonderful day they met in the summer of '98. She was carrying groceries in the house from the car with Ellie, back and forth, numerous times since it was only the two of them and neither was dumb enough to try to carry more than a few bags in each hand at a time (like a man would do). A slobbery mess crashed into their scene with a braided leash dragging behind and another slobbery mess right behind that. A small part of her knew he'd planned the whole fiasco and she'd accused him of such on many occasions, with a smirk and pinched eyes. "You were ducking behind that overgrown hosta in the Chapmans' front yard, weren't you? Holding Dozer by the collar and whispering 'Ready, set, go!' in his ear. And if you think *he's* the dog, oh no sirree Billy Bob, *you* were the dog that day and still are, Nolan Donovan. You're still that sly old dog." She'd say this with her nose wrinkled up, inviting him to kiss her. And he most certainly would have, and then they almost certainly would have made love, and that was the norm back then, not the exception. There had been enough bumping uglies to populate a small island. But it was more than that. They were both married and divorced, and there was this new *passion*, a lust for one another in more ways than just fucking.

They yearned for each other's touch and listened intently for each other's needs.

And then somewhere along the way, things began to change. Like a ball of yarn gradually picking up speed down a gentle hill, each day getting closer to revealing what's really underneath all that beautiful frill.

The few times she'd attempted to talk with him about it, he'd do his typical charade, throwing his hands in the air with petulance, then storming off. She'd simply stand there in her little dysthymic bubble and listen for the heavy footfalls to trounce down the hall and into their bedroom *where they don't make love anymore* to get something *probably the keys* then hear the footfalls continue out of their room *hopefully it's just the goddamn keys* and on toward the front door where a reverberant *slam* usually left an exclamation mark hanging in the void behind her eyelids. He'd return usually around three in the morning, collapsing into bed *not even trying to be stealthy* and rolling over to her side, boots clunking heavily together as he did so, and blowing that awful stench of stagnant alcohol across her neck and into her ear as he'd wrap his arms around her. *This is the only time he holds me anymore*, she'd think again. *He'll blow that goddamn fire in my face like Puff the magically drunk-again dragon and smile while doing it. Squeeze me tight while doing it.*

Since Patricia began going to a shrink for her depression, Nolan has been completely absent from her life. He leaves her all alone in this big house all day while he's off doing God knows what. His business has been extremely successful. She'll give him that. But for fuck's sake, he *is* the boss. He can do whatever he wants. Right now, she needs him more than ever, and he's nowhere to be found. You can only be picked last so many times before you just don't want to play anymore.

"I need someone to talk me out of this," she says aloud. Her once-beautiful hair now sticks to one side of her face in a sweaty mop. A realization sweeps through her like an animalistic disease on a mission to drive her mad. Just like Nolan is. Why else would he be doing this?

He knows I've been depressed for years. He knows it's getting worse. Yet he's nowhere.

Nolan and the malicious malady slowly but surely chipping away at her everything, like some sort of fucked-up soul-sucker team.

"There is no cure for this malady."

As she stands up, she becomes aware that her cheeks are wet and her vision blurry. She looks down at the top of her T-shirt and sees a growing collar of tear-darkened fabric.

How long have I been crying?

"You've gone crazy." She glances over at the marble head-stone leaning toward the old maple in the corner of the yard, a splash of crabgrass writhing at its base. "Haven't I, Doze?"

At this, she begins to laugh hysterically. But the sounds coming out of her aren't motivated by hilarity. They are the sounds of insanity. She doubles over, heaving screams, clutching her middle-aged soft middle and spraying saliva around her slippers. "Just like the goddamn dog that day! Rest in pieces, you old fuck! You old snortin', slobberin', sly devil dog you! Just like your master, always staring at me with that stupid face . . . but those sly eyes." She's leaning over the deck railing now, yelling at a mute headstone. An otherwise tranquil scene. "I know there's something in those eyes. Something that's smarter than that dumb face wants me to think." The previously jovial forest critters begin to sense a potential threat in the lunatic on the porch and push deeper into the trees to carry on with their unfeigned existence.

"I'm talking about you, Nolan!" she screams. One final, guttural vocal. She stands there clutching the cherry-stained railing with white-knuckled hands, looking out at nothing in particular but thinking about everything all at once.

Her therapist would define that as acute anxiety, precisely. Her therapist, were she here, would be sitting in the wicker chair in the corner of the porch, rocking back and forth over the worn boards. She'd say this is a typical panic attack, nothing they can't work through. "Focus on your breathing," she'd say. "In through the nose, out through the mouth." She'd demonstrate. "Let the wave of panic wash over you. Just let it. It will pass."

The wave.

The bad water is up over her head.

How am I supposed to focus on my breathing when I can't *breathe?*

The therapist has no answer. Because there is no therapist there to answer. The wicker chair only stares at her. Not stoically, but uncaring. She's probably rolling around in her sheets right now fucking her handsome husband, whispering beautiful notes, basking in the passion radiating from each other's touch.

"Class? Anyone seen Nolan Donovan?" she asks, her pitch higher. "He's sure been skipping a lot lately!" Flakes of old stain rub off onto her hands as she squeezes the railing.

Might as well give me a big ole fuck-you *and toss me a pistol on the way out. A pistol with one in the chamber. One's all I'll need.*

This thought brings up an interesting point. Once your mind comes to the conclusion that it has finally had enough and the only thing left to do is bite the bullet, subconscious thought processes smoothly transition to the question of *how* you are going to do it, with alarming brevity. People who have botched suicide attempts sometimes tend to take their survival as some sort of celestial sign (when in reality, they just sneezed when pulling the trigger or accidentally allowed for too much slack in the rope so their toes were able to touch the ground) and decide to speak about it, to describe their histrionic despair with wild hand gestures, how they marched through the dreck, saw the light, and incredibly came out the other side unscathed (well, sort of, that rope burn on your neck may scar, and that hairless valley running down the side of your head may elicit some gawking, but otherwise, yes). These people sometimes describe this inevitable transition in thought. This is what Patricia is experiencing now.

Just do it already.

But what about Ellie?

She can't stop thinking about Ellie and what would become of her if she went through with this. She's talking to the trees like a madwoman, someone who's trying to justify to their parents why they chose to drink at that party or toilet paper that house down the street. A part of her always knew this day would come—she was right about that. But where she had been wrong was how she'd feel about it. She felt it being forced upon her, something she had no way of controlling. Like lying paralyzed in the sand knowing the tide would eventually creep back up.

The bad water.

Her hands flail above her, but only her fingertips break the surface.

She always pictured this coming moment as an extremely surreal thing, this ennobled feeling of intimacy mixed with a dash of relief. But instead, she feels like she's on a train. She's sitting there chained to her window seat, looking out at the world she's about to leave, all of the important people in her life

crowded around. Ellie is standing front and center with an irrevocable look, asking, *How could you?* And is that Nolan in the
back of the bundle? Is he smiling? The train car lurches forward
and begins to rumble toward purgatory. Silent screaming faces
fill her narrow window, blotting out the beauty of the world
behind. The world she's been trying to see for years.

"Honey." A heavy, callused hand falls onto her shoulder.

Her eyes bolt open. She gulps in a double helping of late
autumn air like a free diver who's been under too long.

Nolan.

Now the hand is squeezing her shoulder a bit too hard. A
reminder.

"You're hurting me." Such a prosaic phrase, yet it reaches
unfathomable depths.

He loosens his grip.

"Just didn't want you falling asleep out here. The sun's
going down soon. Temp's droppin' fast."

She looks up at him with pinched, questioning eyes. Since
when did he give a rat's ass about her well-being? That old
sly-dog smile creeps across his face, but she can't see it. With
the sun setting at his back, he's just a silhouette. A dark, face-
less man.

Suddenly a horrific idea occurs to her.

*He heard me talking. He knows everything. I could've sworn
he was gone, that I had the house to myself. I could've sworn!*

"Where were you?" she asks, shooting for a steady tone,
but the words come out quivering instead.

"Out." He's still standing there over her, blotting out
the sun.

Like he doesn't want me to see his face, she thinks. *I bet he's
wearing that creepy fucking smile again.*

She loathes that smile.

The sicker I get, the more he smiles. Jesus, what has happened to us?

After she stares up at the shadow for a while, not knowing what to say, he decides to expound. "Forgot my wallet. Called for you when I came back in but couldn't find you anywhere. Then heard some mumbling through the screen door." He throws a dirty thumb back over his shoulder. "What the hell are you doing out here anyway, Patty? Shootin' the shit with the robins?" He leans in. She instinctively draws away. Almost imperceptible, but it's there. "Have you been *crying*?"

She turns away and wipes her face with a shirtsleeve, covering it in damp rings and little curds of snot.

What a mess. What a goddamn fucking wreck I am.

At this, fresh tears well up and begin to spill over. The brittle dam finally breaks, and a flood of tears rush through the valley below. She sinks down into a fetal position against the railing, head buried between her knees and arms wrapped around her legs. She looks like a child.

Nolan takes a cautious step back toward the screen door. He winces at her cries. Her *shrieks*. They jab at his chest like frozen daggers. What pain in those sounds. What anguish.

He turns and goes back into the house. He's got to get out of here. It's imperative.

"Nolan." Barely more than a whisper.

He pauses in the doorway and looks back at the woman called his wife. She's looking up at him through mats of wet hair. "Please," she begs. "Help me."

He almost says something, then quickly thinks better of it. Instead, he lets the screen door slowly shut between them, a raspy number followed by a click of the latch. The finality palpable, something you can hold. He sees her through the mesh, once a bombshell with delicious legs and world-class tits, now nothing more than a heap of skin-covered sorrow. Her eyes plead in the silence for moments that seem like eons before her face twists in agony. Her head drops back between her knees, and she continues her fit of icy shrieks. That horrible sound building as she begins rocking back and forth from the balls of her feet to her heels.

Again, he thinks that he's got to get out of here. He turns away for the last time.

CHAPTER 2

Barry Porter feels his iPhone buzz against his thigh, just a quick alert.

Voicemail, he thinks. *Must've missed a call.*

He sees the famous Krispy Kreme sign lit up on the left side of the road, that beautiful ring of neon fire blazing red so everyone can see the donuts are Hot Now, attracting early birds like moths to a flame.

He passes the new LED sign out in front of the old bank, blinking the date, and does a double take at the temp.

Eighty-three already? Jesus.

He swings his F-250 through the entrance and immediately stomps the brake, almost giving the little Civic in front of him a healthy smooch. He sees the driver, a sizable woman with curlers in her hair, throw him an avaricious glance through her rearview. *Me first,* it says.

Barry chuckles and tosses it into park. A young guy pushes through the side door to Barry's left, backward, because in his arms is a small mountain of donut boxes. The kid squeezes between his truck and Miss Me First's rice burner, having to turn sideways to fit through the gap.

Damn, must've gotten closer than I thought.

Another chuckle escapes him, formidable belly hitching over his belt. He's a big man, yet not particularly fat. Although

10

he knows if he keeps wearing down a path through the Krispy Kreme drive-through, that won't be true much longer. He's always been a head taller than everyone else and as solid as an old farmhouse. Barry's been described as a gentle giant as far back as he can remember. Back at Tennessee Tech, his roommates would tease him, calling him John Coffee. *Yessah, Massah*, they'd say when he asked if they paid their share of the light bill or if they wanted to go out for a few beers after class. They'd back away slowly, wide-eyed and hands splayed out in the universal *Don't hurt me!* gesture. He'd laugh it off and scold their stupidity while they'd laugh right along with him, knowing that big Barry Porter wouldn't hurt a fly. Barry was the guy back then who would hit a deer and pull over and tear up. Not for a crushed bumper and a ruined afternoon, but because a life was taken. He's hardened a bit in the years since. Life's inevitable weathering. But at his core is the same tenderness.

The kid sees him laughing through the windshield, blinking into the glare, and looks down at the donut mountain in his hands. Some have now slid here and there, making it look like an oversized Jenga tower that's one bad move away from a cacophonous collapse. He meets Barry's smile again and shrugs in a *What? We're hungry* sort of way. Barry watches him continue through the parked cars, holding the boxes high to avoid catching a corner on a side mirror.

He's probably taking those back to his buddies. A house full of hungover dudes passed out around the living room.

He sizes up the line of cars. *I'm in the wrong business.*

He fancies buying his own Krispy Kreme shop someday. And if it were anything like this one, he'd make beaucoup money. *What a life*, he muses. Instead, he works for his wife's father's company building houses and developing properties. It's not a bad gig by any means, certainly not as fun as running a busy donut shop and raking in the dead presidents, but not bad. He gets to work outside, allowing him to breathe the virgin Tennessee air while cutting wood or laying foundation. He doesn't have to clock in or slide under the boss's office window if he's a few minutes late. If he shows up with donuts (HOT NOW), everyone's happy to see him, even if they had to start without him. Being married to the boss's daughter has its perks, being that the boss usually gives him the benefit of the doubt.

Ellie means more to Barry than anything in the entire cosmos. And number two isn't even close. She's all he's got. He grew up poor. His mother died of an apparently accidental mix of medication when he was nine—although he's never thought that to be true—and his father uprooted to Maine about eight years ago to marry a woman he met on Facebook. They exchange holiday cards and birthday phone calls, but that's the extent of their relationship. If the boss man rides Barry a bit too hard and Ellie tells her dad he needs to lay off a smidge, he usually will. For a few days, at least. Then it's text messages and voicemails concerning his shoddy work or bad attitude all over again. Ellie will chalk it up to "Dad just being Dad." She'll look at Barry through the bathroom pass-through, lying naked under the thin sheet, propped up on an elbow. "No one will ever be good enough, honey."

Barry clicks the stick back into drive and eases a couple car-lengths closer to the speaker. His phone buzzes again. He pulls it out and taps the hold button to wake up the screen. "1 New Voicemail" appears at the top. Below it, "Missed Call: Nolan." And below *that*: "Text Message: Nolan — Where are you, Barry?"

He bucks his hefty hips up so he can slide the phone back

into his pocket.

About twenty minutes later, he pulls into the jobsite. It's a quarter of seven, fifteen minutes after he's supposed to be there. He skids to a stop in the gravel parking area, small clouds of chalky dust swirling up toward the sky, only to be torn away by the early-morning breeze. He pauses a moment before getting out, like he's fiddling with something in the floorboard, an old trick he's learned over the past few months. If someone important walks up and knocks on his window, he can just act like he's busy and he's really not late. He's been there in his truck the whole time. Peering out over the dash, he thinks how much he truly does like this work, and as much as that old bastard Nolan seems to dislike him, sometimes he sure is thankful for giving him this job.

Barry has been employed by Donovan Development & Building Company going on two years now, almost as long as he's been married to Ellie. He'll never forget his surprise and confusion when she told him that her dad was going to give him a job. He first thought it strange that the guy hadn't told him himself, but then he quickly remembered who he was dealing with here. This was Nolan Donovan, a man drunkenly balancing on a fence dividing the land of the marginally wealthy and the land of the bona fide rollers in the dough. He totters back and forth a few times a year, depending on which projects pan out and which ones peter, though never quite tipping over to one side or the other. He's also somewhat of a hermit (though Barry doesn't quite know the extent of it), if that's even the right word. Although he's apparently never home. Quite the paradoxical man. At least he wasn't four years ago when "it" happened. He and Ellie had just started dating around that time. He'd hear Ellie's mother bawling on the other end of the line, Ellie staring with glazed eyes and her cell phone slowly pulling down the side of her face like its weight multiplied the longer she held it, while eggs burned in the skillet on the stove in front of her or while she was sitting on the couch watching early-afternoon reality shows, looking a hundred miles through the TV and breathing big, slow, pain-stricken breaths.

Nolan Donovan, you are not *the father!* he thinks, using his best Maury Povich voice while picturing Nolan jumping around like someone's shooting at his feet, like it's all a game and he's just won the pot. And the trashy crowd goes absolutely apeshit.

A hermit that's never home, that's *what he was.* That's *what he* is.

He pictures a wrinkly crab trouncing across the ocean floor with a pole over his shoulder and a knapsack tied to the end of it. But where does he go? Boss man business, he guesses.

He sees Jordy Danielson now waving at him to get his ass out there. "It's hotter'n two niggers fuckin' in a wool sock," he'd say. Or something of similar charm. Barry doesn't much like Jordy; much less understand his toothless humor. He waves back and points to his cell as if he's busy on it for a moment, checking messages or placing orders for the build (another trick he's mastered).

You do have a message, remember?

A twinge of tightness procures through his gut. If Nolan showed up to a work site, you could safely assume something big was the reasoning, good or bad. Good would be: "There's a fuckin' tornaduh coming. Y'all go home now." Bad would be: "Mistake in the contract. Gonna need y'all to work late tonight." This one would probably be accompanied by a little smirk directed toward Barry. Tornaduhs and mistakes weren't, for the most part, commonplace. They usually had the sites to themselves.

He's heard a few stories about Nolan's late-night bar ventures. There was one time when a guy came at him with a pool cue and, as the story goes, Nolan not only blocked it but ripped it from the bastard's hand and punched it right back into the guy's open mouth. "Dude almost died," Gary Doogan had said while they all sat around in the laundry room of a partially completed single story waiting for a summer shower to mosey on by. "By way of assfishiation." Knee to knee in there, trying to stay dry, he had seen the look on all their faces. Bug-eyed and silent. "But it probly wuhn't that difficult considerin' the old bastard had most of his teeth outta his head already anyhow."

Nolan's a mean son-of-a-buck, that's for certain. You did not want to cross him. He'll lull you to sleep with his seemingly lack of enthusiasm for life in general, but the moment the most minute detail goes awry—something he hadn't planned for and thus had no control over—he comes flying in like a bat out of hell, jumping out of his truck before it's even stopped its skid. Stocky body tramping with purpose, and a hard, deep-lined face painting the expression of someone who's balls deep in a bear trap. That's how Barry's coworkers described the boss man in his first few days on the job: balls deep in a bear trap. He thought they were exaggerating then—scare-the-new-guy sort of thing—but he's seen it himself many times now. It's hard to look that kind of man in the eyes when you know that he knows you're banging his beautiful daughter.

Lately, though, the mumblings about the boss's late-night shenanigans have grown quiet. The normal drunks who sometimes see him out like Gary and Jordy haven't had many new stories for the rest of the guys. Maybe he's keeping it in-house now. Leaning back in his leather La-Z-Boy with those gnarled hands clasped behind his head like a vice and a beer on the TV tray table next to him while he dumbly watches babes in bikinis do jumping jacks and lunges on a beach somewhere on his sixty-five-inch flat-screen. Hell, maybe he's bought himself a Hoveround just to putt around his sprawling, empty house out there in the woods with his shirt off and a bag of buttered popcorn in his lap. Barry chuckles in the cab of his truck at this, still fake fiddling with his phone.

One place he knows Nolan *doesn't* frequent much is his and Ellie's house. Ellie volunteers quite often at various schools and daycares but has no paying job. Nolan refuses so. One evening, during one of only a couple times he's been inside Nolan's home, while Ellie was over in the kitchen doing dishes, Nolan had been explaining his philosophy on the subject. Granted, it'd been after a half dozen or so beers and he was slurring his words a bit as he leaned in to Barry, but he'd said, "The man goes out and makes the bread, and the woman cleans the house and gives the head. That's just how it is, boy." *Such a charmer*, Barry had thought.

Ellie said he never came by during the day while Barry was at work, either. Another thing Barry found a bit strange. Nolan had built the house for them when they got married, he insisted upon it. This was before Nolan had employed Barry. Yes, he owed so much to Nolan. Almost everything, in fact. There is just no feasible way he and Ellie would be in the position they were currently in, which he considered reasonably stable, without Nolan's help. Barry's salary of just over forty-eight thousand was a tick up from everyone else's. And although Ellie didn't work, they still had a lot of help from Nolan's deep pockets on some of the big expenses. He loved his daughter.

Step. Barry reminded himself. *Stepdaughter*.

Even if she was married to someone he didn't much care for. No one will ever be good enough. That fact hung in his mind through their relationship like a familiar jingle from elementary English class.

The house had gone up in a couple months, and he had a new job shortly thereafter. He got to go out and make the bread, then come home to a clean house and the occasional head. And for that, he was truly grateful. There was still that feeling, though, like something wasn't quite true. Something was a hair off. Like a motor that sounds great, but when you pop the hood and put an ear to the moving parts, there's that irregular *click*. Barry often pictured a palpitating heart. Big and strong like their marriage and living situation, but there was always that worry that too many off-rhythm beats would kill it. Every time he was around Nolan, he felt as if he were disabling a bomb. If he stayed by the book, everyone would go home in one piece; but if he wasn't careful, it might go *boom*. So he's careful with Nolan, gentle and unassuming. Nolan is his boss, the only family his wife has, and, in a weird way, their damn landlord. He can't exactly afford for any of those things to change for the time being. Nolan has a way of doing that, see. Before you know it, he's controlled the board. Every move you make is in defense of his attack. Like Bobby Fisher's pluperfect overwhelm of a greased-up dweeb across from him. A silent blitzkrieg.

Barry grabs his belt from the passenger floorboard, slams the door, and begins walking up the short makeshift gravel driveway guarding the entrance to their current work site like a crunchy moat. Donovan Development & Building Company is currently in the process of developing and building a residential neighborhood on the outskirts of town. One that would, when finished, be comprised of precisely thirty-two single-family homes, laid out in a kidney shape with interconnecting streets running through. They're about halfway finished with the neighborhood. In fact, you could already spot a few sporadic minivans and Tahoes nestled up to various homes around the sparkly entrance of the subdivision. Barry doubts Jordy Danielson (who has dropped his saw and started walking toward Barry with that dopey, satirical smile on his face) or even Gary Doogan contain the intellectual capacity to understand that that certain feeling in your gut at the end of a long day isn't your liver beginning preparations for that night's alcohol assault, but actually the feeling of honest-to-God accomplishment. No matter how many times he smashed his thumb with a hammer that day or how badly the back of his neck was burnt (Lord knows it will be today), when he drove by those houses at the front of the neighborhood with Tahoes and minivans and sprinklers and soccer balls, he couldn't help but smile. Maybe one of the Mexicans felt the same way he did about their work. He doubted it, though; for the most part, their communicative skills consisted of plastic smiles at his questions and big *oogah-oogah* eyes at the occasional long-legged white girl walking her dog around her new block, probably chatting on the phone to her best friend in the whole wide world about the cute boy in Spanish class and paying them no mind.

"Nice of you to finally join us," Jordy says. He spits an arrow of dip off to the side, splashing a half dozen chalky rocks, turning them a stringy brown.

"Shut up, Jordy. I'm twenty minutes late. And I'm not dumb enough to think you sacks of shit have actually done anything productive yet anyway."

Jordy eyes him up and down, squinting either against the morning breeze or to add a dash of dramatics. "What were you doin', stickin' it to that girlfriend of yours bright and early?" And then before Barry can reply (much less correct him with *wife*), almost as if he *wishes* that were the case, "I like your style, boss."

"Speaking of the boss, he show up this morning? He's blowing up my damn phone, and I was a little nervous he'd be here when I got to work." And then when Jordy only stares, "You know, like *this*." Barry leans against the nearest truck and holds an imaginary bat in one hand while tapping it in the other. Adding a De Niro-esque scowl.

At this, Jordy bursts into awful laughter. It sounds exactly like you would expect from someone who looked like him. "No," he squeaks. "Boss man ain't here!" He keeps on laughing. Barry pats him on the shoulder, soothing and gentle. Like a sorority girl does to her best friend while she's face-to-face with the shit stains in the toilet because she hasn't yet learned how to say no to the never-ending supply of free shots from avaricious football players at the local spot.

There you go, shhh, he thinks. *Let it all out.* He scoffs at the man, thinking how truly useless numb-fucks like him were in this world of progression and evolution. Now, Barry's no Nobel Prize–winning mathematician, but he at least has a greater sense of self than the family dog. A funny idea occurs to him while he watches Jordy continue to laugh, that it's only the numb-fucks that laugh too long. He's fairly certain the poor guy will never do anything of note in his entire life.

"Pull yourself together, Rain Man. I forgot some donuts in the truck."

Barry makes his way back to the truck. It's now pushing eighty-five, and that sticky film begins to appear on his skin, pulling and folding around the creases of his neck and elbows. He hates that feeling. A couple mockingbirds duel across the trees in their own little *American Idol* finale, one mimicking an angry jay and the other channeling its inner tree frog. Barry notices he's inadvertently taking his sweet time to get back to the truck and realizes he's putting off listening to the voicemail. It's not so much that he's worried about it—it's more to do with the fact that he doesn't want this beautiful day to change complexion with an irate boss's rant or possible *favor*, which could be even worse. Donovan's favors usually consist of running to Lowe's for about seventeen tons of lumber or the hardware store all the way out in Spencer for God knows what. But what God *does* know is that Spencer is likely to take you all day because of the ridiculous thirty-mile-per-hour speed limit and the Mennonite-clad horse and buggies daring your driving skills like it's just one big fucking game of Frogger.

God, he really hopes it's not a favor. He hasn't even thought it could be that till just now. But maybe his inner self has; his subconscious has thought it since the first time he felt his phone buzz back at the Krispy Kreme pickup line window, and has since been stealing his thoughts away from it, causing him to amble and stop and listen to the damn *birds*. Steering his mind through traffic, yawing left and right to navigate through streets clogged with strewn-about cars, all of them with a different version of Nolan hanging out the window holding up his cell and yelling.

He chuckles at the thought of his mind personified. The truck door opens with a creak and a clunk. He conjures up an image of a small man (*He's got to be small if he can fit in my head, right?*) riding the giant wheel of a power-steering-less This apostrophe needs to be facing the opposite direction. '50s Olds, hands and bare feet alike wrapped tightly around the top of the skinny wheel, yanking with all his little might left and right, left and right.

Wonder what Jordy's little mind-guy looks like.

A still shot of the kid plucking the banjo on the porch in *Deliverance* hangs there in front of him. That massive melon, most certainly filled with nothing but a whole bunch of sloshing water, and those beady little eyes looking at you but not, all at the same time.

Barry doubles over his passenger seat, clutching his hitching belly like he's afraid his guts will attempt to push through. He grabs that deliciously warm box of cholesterol bombs (chocolate bombs, sprinkled bombs, glazed bombs, hell even *cream-filled bombs!*), but before he turns around, he catches a glimpse of Jordy back at the site behind him through the side mirror of the open passenger door to his right. He sees him on the phone, standing there, staring at Barry's back with those beady little *Deliverance* boy eyes.

"Shitballs," he says aloud. Donovan has probably grown tired of Barry not returning his texts or calls and has decided to start hounding the rest of the crew till *somebody* answers. Eventually even, if he *has* to, working his way down the hierarchy till he gets to the Mexicans, who eight times out of ten didn't answer their respective cells, and if they did, you were likely to get a long, drawn-out "Uhhhh" as a reply to your question. The innocence of the missed calls and unanswered texts has been sucked away. It's now a thing with teeth and long arms hiding under your bed. It seems too late now to answer the boss; it's grown too heavy in a way. Why is he acting like this? What is the big deal about calling Nolan back?

Barry shuts the door and walks back to ground zero with the box in his hands and a big smile on his face, though Jordy doesn't seem to react to either. He has since ended his call and replaced his cell back into his sawdust-powdered, paint-splattered Levi's. His eyes are trained on Barry.

"That him?" Barry asks, still smiling because *fuck the big bad boss when you got a big box of donuts in your mitts, that's why.*

Jordy seems genuinely perplexed. Barry can almost see his mind reaching for whatever Barry is talking about, knowing all too well that he should know. Barry waits patiently.

Finally, "Oh, boss man Donovan?" He finds it. "Naw, just the old lady. Cam's sick." Then, "Sandy says he's got one shit show of somethin' like a cold."

Is he lying to me? Why is he lying to me?

All of a sudden, the box of donuts feels like a box of lug nuts in his hands, the sound of his mind cranking drowns out the dueling jays and—

Why the hell is Morales eyeing me like he *knows something?*

Now Jordy is the one patiently standing there, grimy hands clasped in front of his belt, waiting for a reply.

"Is there something I don't know?" Barry goes straight for it. He never has been one to partake in the pussyfoot dance, the one both political parties are so damn *dynamite* at. He can't help but imagine a bunch of crusty, turtleneck-clad white wigs tiptoeing around a dance floor of difficult questions. This eases him a bit.

Jordy reaches back into his pocket and pulls out his cell, then holds it out to Barry like an offering. "Want to ask the bitch yourself?"

His job today is roofer. You see, the reason they stay so busy and one of the reasons Nolan has a bank account (probably more than one) that looks like a telephone number is because everyone on the build and develop team can perform every job, thus cutting out many of the middlemen and specialty workers. They have to, otherwise they wouldn't be here. Jordy would be pushing a broom down a tiled hallway in some raggedy-ass school somewhere or maybe even locked up already if he didn't have this job. He's not the brightest crayon in the box, but he's a damn good builder. You sure as shit couldn't trust him any further than you could throw him, but the man knows his stuff when it comes to this. It's something about those *Deliverance*-esque slits in his head for eyes that occasionally cause gooseflesh to propagate down Barry's arms and lower back.

Come to think of it, Gary Doogan isn't much better. He can cut wood like a dam-building beaver and make sweet love to the backhoe shifters and knobs, maneuvering that thing in and out and everywhere in between like it couldn't cause serious damage or even kill someone with just a simple inadvertent turn of a knob or smack of a button. Gary's too old for this, though. Barry often finds himself peering at Gary across the work site through dancing clouds of dirt and sawdust with a certain fondness, like when you order a Whopper from the greasy skater boy at the mic but pull up to the window and out leans Mr. Rogers with a paper crown on his head and a doltish smile frozen across his wrinkly face.

He views the group of Mexicans as a single, breathing entity. Some combination of three or four of them will show up for the workday decked out in their aftermarket cold gear, defying all sensible logic. Whatever the combo is that day will silently work their little brown asses off, doing whatever job is asked of them with unfeigned pleasure and purpose.

Today, it's Hector, who usually speaks English pretty well, Emilio, and another he only knows by last name, Morales. The latter, he recently realized, hadn't in fact been staring a suspiciously canted hole through him earlier. He was eyeing the Krispy Kreme box. Donuts, the sugary bridge of languages. As soon as Barry sets them on the table, Morales slides down the inexorably tall roofing ladder like a fearless fireman, hands screeching against the metal rails, and gobbles up a respectable number before the other guys can get there.

He's roofer with Morales today. He sits at the highest point of their newest creation and surveys which part he should start working on next. With legs splayed, one down the front face and the other down the west face of the roof, he considers his options. He rotates onto roofer about every other week during a home build project and stays with it for a few days before moving on to assisting with electrical (plumbers and electricians are brought in, practically the only jobs the team *couldn't* perform) or installing insulation, which was the norm. But Morales practically lives on the roof. He doesn't mind the heat and seems to enjoy not being on the ground with the others, having to occasionally converse or communicate in some way. So when he's present, it's a general understanding among the build team that he's going to be up here. And if they're not to that stage yet, then something high. Which works for everyone.

So here he sits atop the world on a shingled triune with that blue-white fireball now high in the sky but feeling light-years closer than it was just a couple hours ago. It's hard not to feel somewhat ennobled up here, like a God-King intently watching his worker ants clittering around his castle below. He has completely lost the minute sense of paranoia that stole through his body a couple sweat-stained hours earlier, realizing it was probably just a side effect of the extremely intense yet terrifyingly unsafe sex he had with his wife earlier this morning. He'd rolled over and saw her shirtless (she slept that way, tough life, huh?) body looking more like a drawing than an actual thing, something he could touch, something he could make love to. It had been too difficult for his testosterone-swelled morning body to simply appreciate and carry on. He was usually able to successfully pull it off, that awkward waddle to the bathroom because of the lead pipe in his briefs and that look of longing on his round yet handsome face, hating so much that he had to get ready for work and should just let her sleep. But this morning he couldn't help himself, he couldn't steal himself away. She'd just looked so damn *sexy* lying there, almost like she'd been faking it and striking a pose she knew he wouldn't be able to resist.

Maybe she was?

Unlikely, according to the fact that she loves her sleep and waking her with his heavy body and hard dick in the morning was apt to get him shoved off and a new view of nothing but the back of her sleep-matted hair (which never stopped any man—they could work with any view, any angle, conjuring up the possibilities with any position, no matter how unflattering; oh, the power of testosterone). But this morning was different. This morning she hadn't pushed him away, mumbling dreamy threats under her breath as she did so. She felt his pressing need up against her and rolled over onto her back to accommodate it. Ellie had reached under the haphazard sea of blankets and grabbed his hips, pulling them into place between her soft, splayed legs. He hadn't been expecting this reaction, nor had he been ready for it. Every now and then, they make love in the mornings, but almost always after both have showered and are getting ready for the day. She'll see him eyeing her while she stands nearly nude in the closet doorway, a few lacy square inches of purple, pink, or sometimes black (praise Jesus for the black) fabric barely covering her intimate parts and holding on for dear life in the back, tightly hugging the perfect swell of her ass. She'll glance at the bedside clock, realizing she'll have to choose between breakfast and this early-bird sexcapade before work. Well, before *his* work and before her free work. She's currently volunteering at the local high school's daycare. Isn't that something? Think about what kind of fucked-up world we live in when the local *high school* has to have a daycare. And no, most of the little snot-wads aren't teachers' kids. Eight out of ten children they get have parents who are children themselves, a few rooms away texting their girlfriends while the teacher monotonously enlightens the students on seventeenth century English Puritans, or drooling warm puddles on their cold hard desk behind the fat kid who so graciously uses his girth to block her view when she's supposed to be reading along to *Of Mice and Men*.

But despite the horror stories, she would love to be a real teacher. Someone actively engaging the young adults down the hall, not just making sure little Lucy doesn't suck down a Lego during playtime. At least a substitute. She's heard the students refer to these as "sit-in suckers." She'd love to be a sit-in sucker. If only her father would let her. *Stepfather*, she'll remind herself. He says she's better off making no money to keep the house up than making next-to-no money babysitting those "pimply horn dogs." Despite her dreams, she knows he's right. Especially since her mother passed away, he's been the steady dose of truth and common sense in her life. That old, weathered rock that she's come to trust implicitly, whether he's slid into that parental position by default or not. She doesn't think Barry feels the same. But she knows he wants her to do what makes her happy, and right now, above her own interests, that is making her stepfather happy by taking his experienced advice.

She chose the sex. Besides, there's a Krispy Kreme a few

blocks down. She could just swing by on the way to work and snag some sugary breakfast. He watches her, can see exactly what she's thinking. And most certainly knows the instant she makes up her mind (a man will spend a lifetime honing his skills to be able to discern that look, that wordless acceptance from the body language of a woman who has said yes to what he wants but leaves it up to him to act upon it). Luckily, she doesn't do the dance this morning. She doesn't try to hide her answer and have her own fun at the expense of his Neanderthal brain trying to decipher the woman code.

She licked a palm ever so sensually and reached down, grabbing his throbbing everything. She'd stared him dead in the face with stone-cold wonder, like she was genuinely interested in his subsequent reaction. He'd never seen her quite like that, and they've been in similar situations hundreds of times since their early dating days. That face, he is completely and utterly transfixed by it. The big muscles in his thighs quench almost to cramps by her single, small hand. The expression worn on her face needs no words to communicate—it's written all over it, the two-word phrase that every man fantasizes hearing in the most intimate, blissful moments, melting in response to its atavistic assertiveness. She tells him with her eyes, orders him, what to do to her, and all at once he forgets about not being prepared. He couldn't care less about the damn condom. He wasn't used to one with her anyway, but with her being between birth controls (and him sometimes "forgetting" to pull out, even though they both don't want kids quite yet), he knew it was the smart thing to do. But he wasn't about to be a square and ruin one of the most incredible sexual moments they've ever had together.

And so he didn't. She guided him in with one hand and pressed her other hand against the small of his back, pushing him to her. Into her. She'd tilted her head up then, mouth slightly slack, but kept those soul-piercing eyes locked on his. And they proceeded to make love, with lots of slaps and screams that rarely show themselves so bullishly. He'd been utterly lost, completely helpless to the monster of euphoria and came before he even knew where he was. And *that*, my friends, is why he's been a trifle paranoid since he felt that first buzz in his pants from a missed call this morning.

Or so he tells himself.

That parasitic seed planted deep in the fertile soil of his mind, slowly growing in the wet darkness, shooting up like Jack's beanstalk if you shined just a second of attention light on it. *What if you got her pregnant?* it whispers. Certainly wouldn't be the end of the world, he loves her with all his heart. But he knows they aren't ready for a baby yet. He scolds himself for not being smarter. He attempts to push the fear back down, but attempting to bury it will only place that fear on something less important in the grand scheme of things. It wants to thrive on something. Like the damn voicemail.

You checked the voicemail. All the old man wanted to know was where you were, just like his text said.

Or so he tells himself.

You never replied, and he never tried again, so it obviously wasn't that important. Nothing to get all squirrelly about.

Barry is jolted back to present by Morales.

"Huh?" he asks the dark man squatting near him. He hadn't heard him approach.

"South. I'm west." Talking about the roof faces.

Morales is Barry's least favorite. Not because he doesn't do his job or is a brownnoser or any of the other common reasons employees didn't like other employees. There is a sense about

Morales. Like he's had one hell of a past but hasn't quite experienced yet how hot the flames actually could get. You have to respect the man for it, though. He doesn't mind working up here on the roof with him. He busts his ass; Barry just doesn't like him much is all.

"How far have you gotten? I haven't been up here since last week."

Morales only points to the south side, clearly irritated by his simple question. This house, same as most on this side of the street, is built on a slope. If you're looking from the road, it would appear to be a very nice two-story. But from the backyard, it's a monstrosity. When finished, a three-story wall of windows will look out over a somewhat circular concrete patio (which in the next couple weeks will encase a twenty-five-thousand-gallon in-ground pool). A good-size yard made up of about six hundred square feet of freshly sodded Kentucky bluegrass, and a thin stream, tinkling its way over rocks and limbs, divides the future buyer's property from the common area of unbuildable land behind. A concrete sidewalk snakes its way through the fields of tall grass and into the woods at the far end, where it apparently goes on for another half mile before dumping out into a park on Winchester Avenue. No joggers in sight today. Too hot.

Barry sits on the edge now with his legs spread and heels planted firmly in the gutter. He's fiddling with the unfinished patch of roofing between his legs. It's the only unfinished piece on the whole south side, oddly enough. Morales must've left it by accident; he wasn't one to skimp. This spot is certainly the highest point from the ground on the entire roof, and one of the only spots where that thick bluegrass wasn't waiting below like a purplish sea.

He looks back over his shoulder. Squinting into the sun, he sees an empty roofline. Morales has slid back over to his side. The safe side. Barry's phone buzzes again. He pauses what he's doing, which isn't much, and looks out over the empty field like a lion sniffing the African breeze. It buzzes again quickly. Phone call.

"Shit," he mumbles. *Gotta answer this time. Boss is gonna think I up and quit. Or even worse, slept in.* He chuckles at this while he carefully comes up on a knee. *Waaay in.* He's got his left knee under him now so he can dig into his jeans pocket deeper than fingertip depth, and his right heel still planted in the gutter. He has just enough time to see DONOVAN on his iPhone screen, holding it up close to his face with his left hand cupped around it, fighting the glare, before he feels his weight lurch too far forward, quickly passing that critical point of no return. Too quickly. That foot he had planted in the gutter caught its toe on the lip, violently flipping him from right side up (in which broken legs were certain and a broken pelvis or back was likely, but survival, one would hope, was possible) to upside down, throwing all that hope shit out the window with no remorse whatsoever.

That notion that "it all happened so fast" couldn't have been further from the truth in Barry's case. And had he survived, he could explain it to you himself. His initial unconscious thought upon tumbling over the roofline is something akin to exhilaration, the feeling of flying. But that is forcefully replaced by a very conscious feeling of painful sadness. His entire life with Ellie dances through his head, reminding him of all the beautiful memories they've made, as well as the arguments he wishes he could take back and the things he wishes he could've given her had he been blessed with more time. All this runs through him like a bolt of lightning. But one that he feels every leaden millisecond of. His stomach is clenched, not because of nausea (although that cinder block of digesting donuts in there isn't helping), but because of unimaginable anguish for Ellie. He's leaving her alone in this world and he wishes like hell he could take it all back. As the patio fills his field of vision, her name is all he can say. "Ellie" comes out in a whisper against the rushing wind. The words fling back down his throat. "My Ell—" Then nothing. Barry Porter is engulfed in the Big Sleep.

Morales hears the wet splatter. He dares a look, leaning over the gutter like a child will lean over the edge of their bed praying there is no monster. But there is one, and he has an idea what it will look like. What strikes Morales the hardest is the color of the stuff that came out of Barry's head. It's greener than gray and fanned around a rotten cantaloupe of a head like some sort of aura. Or a fucked-up halo. A dark puddle slowly expands from his ruined body, turning the white concrete crimson. *Well, that's going to be hard to get out*, he thinks absentmindedly. He sees backward limbs, bone fragments, and a shit stain on the seat of Barry's pants. A thirty-foot fall to an immovable surface does ugly things to a human body. *At least he went headfirst,* Morales thinks. *No suffering.*

He's praying to his god that this is what he'd find upon that bug-eyed, dilatory peek out over the gutter, although he will never dare to say such a thing to anyone. He did not want to find a dying man flopping around the soon-to-be pool patio like a fish out of water, twitching and writhing. That would've been much worse. *For everyone.* He looks around. No one has seen, the rest of the guys are working around the front of the house, and there's still no one on the path out back. Morales slides back from the edge and stands up. He pulls his cell out of his pocket, thumbs the "2" key. JEFE comes up on speed dial. He presses CALL.

CHAPTER 3

Cole Harper stands in front of his Ikea bookcase, staring at it but not really seeing it yet. It's too early, but he can't go back to sleep. It's a Friday. And coming up on the one-year anniversary of Barry Porter's big fall. Not that he knows that. He's new here. And even if he did, he wouldn't let it ruin his first weekend of summer break. Those unbelievably magical eight-ish weeks between inevitable high school hierarchies. Well, until about the time the back-to-school commercials start up, then the days begin to shrivel into nervous little slices of what they once were.

The woods behind the house are full of outspoken birds and the sumptuous, endurable smell of sizzling bacon has found its way through the crack under his door. He's up. He and his mother, Stacey, have just moved into this house on Lakeview Heights a few days ago. Boxes full of God knows what are still strewn throughout his room. You never fully get a grasp of just how much stuff you have until you move. To him, his room looks complete. Yet he still has full boxes on his floor. He's decided to leave them be until either he can't find something, in which case he'll suspect the item is in one of them, or until his mother eventually tells him to do something with them.

However, one of the boxes is partially excavated. It sits to the left of his bookcase, nestled between it and the closet door (which now dons a black-and-white poster of Albert Einstein sticking his tongue out at the camera—slightly tattered, but he loves it nevertheless). The box contents are made entirely of paperbacks (new ones, old ones, popular ones, unknown ones), although only ten or twelve remain, packed carefully in the bottom like cobblestones. This was the first box he carried in upon arrival to this new place of residence on this sleepy little street. He had burst through the door, teetering back and forth through the living room and down the hall with his book box (it came with them in their Cherokee, not in the mover's van) wobbling in his arms, through his new bedroom's door (sending a quick hallelujah up to the man for it being cracked instead of shut), and plopped the box down right next to where he wanted his new bookcase to be. Which is exactly where it still sits.

He didn't have a bookcase at his old house, and his mother promised him when they moved, she'd buy him a new one and throw it in the moving van. He had to bribe one of the movers to help him put it together; after a fast haggle, an agreement was reached. Ten bucks and a Sugar Ray CD. The dude wasn't much older than him. So they sat in his room at the back of the house piecing together the black-painted particleboard with wooden pegs and plastic screws while the other two movers did the dirty work (most definitely cussing the new owner of the Sugar Ray CD while they did so, wherever the hell he went, gonna beat his ass, probably off takin' a shit, and so on and so forth, in a candid back-and-forth banter).

Mom was out in the yard, inspecting the crestfallen landscape around the perimeter of the house. Which now wasn't much more than a miniature jungle of twisted vines and overzealous weeds in a race to see who was the tallest. He could've easily put the bookshelf together himself, you see, but he wanted it done *right then, first thing*. He doesn't get excited about much, but this is his prized possession we're talking about here. At his old house, he'd found a few plastic crates behind an abandoned department store and used them as a makeshift bookcase by stacking them on their sides in a porous pyramid and filling them with his favorites, while his other favorites guarded the sides of the pyramid in unsteady towers, their tops making additions almost daily while their bases sat snagging dust bunnies. It's not that they couldn't afford a new bookcase before, he just never asked for one.

His mother had received a small income from doing hair and now graduated to a serviceable income from doing hair at a new place with a broader client base, hence the move. She's a single parent at thirty-six. And has been for thirty-six years. Got pregnant with Cole at eighteen from a guy she didn't know and didn't ever care to. Cole likes it this way, just the two of them; at least he doesn't have to escape into his books to get away from bickering dinners or drunken melees like so many children these days have to deal with. He instead delves into his imaginative worlds because silence is boring. Beautiful, but sometimes certainly boring.

He's a simple kid with a simple life, and that's just how it's always been. Give him his books and some '90s music, and he's good to go. Happy as a tornado in a trailer park, as his mom sometimes says. A few times he's even attempted to write, whether it be short stories or poetry. But he's never been happy with the result. They've always ended up sounding like a kid who's trying to mimic other writers, hijacking prose. Or like someone who's pushing the words across the page instead of being dragged along by them. He muses that one day it may all click for him and he'll be able to make a marginal income from it, but he's not too worried. Whatever happens, happens, man. And what an elegant way to look at the world.

The bookcase is too small. His mother underestimated

his literary prowess. It's about as tall as he is, which is a few inches shorter than the average seventeen-year-old male his age. He has been the baleful recipient of every short joke adolescent boys could conjure up. Hell, even from some of the girls too. Although, he's come to realize the motivation for *their* slights usually derive from flirtation, not malice. A quick jab usually accompanied by a sprout of redness on the cheeks or an inadvertent batting of eyelashes. He's been on the receiving end of many comments from jocks, mainly from the ones who wear uniforms on Fridays through the first three years of high school. But they've slowly tapered off each year. He's learned there's jealously writhing behind there. He's handsome, you see, with naturally tanned skin pulled tightly over well-developed muscles. Shaggy golden-brown hair usually falling naturally in the easy, stylish way some of his mom's clients come in and pay to try to replicate.

But his ascent through the ranks of a flawed school system hasn't been a sob story by any means. Just a kid who keeps to himself, never doing too much or too little, getting through his young-adult life fighting the good fight.

He puts *From a Buick 8* on top of an already-sketchy pillar of fiction on his too-small bookcase. There are two other such pillars. Not to mention the dozen or so still left in the box to his left. He stands there, sleepy-eyed and somnolent, scanning his steadily growing collection. There is not a wide variety of authors in the group, even though the shelves are packed and the top is stacked with upward of a hundred books. He likes to find a style he likes and ride that author out until either he gets bored or a book from another writer screams at him until it's finally recognized. He is currently on his Stephen King kick. *Back on his Stephen King kick.* Over a quarter of his collection is made up of King's work. What can he say? He's always had an unusual affinity for the things that go bump in the night. You can also find some of his son's stuff, Joe Hill, who writes like his hair's on fire and fuck the extinguisher. A couple Jameses share a shelf, Patterson and Rollins. This is the shelf he plucks from when he's suffering from a case of reader's block. Something from either of those guys is guaran-damn-teed to get you out of the funk, when the brain wants a break from all these books. Books from the James shelf make him feel better, give him more confidence about his creativity in general. They each have an ability to completely captivate you, sending you through their dream world so fast your fingers hurt, but never once after flipping the final page of one of theirs did he think, "I'll never be able to write like that." He has a couple Koontzes and a few Michael Crichtons, *Prey* being the best from that bunch. Some Peter Straubs, and Robin Cook has a corner. He has an eclectic group of old books, with their yellowing pages and dark, simple bindings, making them stand out against the others in a non sequitur. Of these are *Gilligan's Island, Lord of the Flies, The Flivver King,* and even Lewis Carroll's *Alice's Adventures in Wonderland.*

He had read somewhere that you could tell everything you needed to know about a man from his watch. He thinks that's bullshit. Surely you can tell much more about a man from his bookshelf. He scans his for his next selection, knowing all too well he's going to be dragged out of his room any second by his nose toward that heavenly smell coming from the kitchen.

I wonder what my bookshelf says about me, he thinks. Then with a smile, *A watch . . . I don't even own a fucking watch.*

CHAPTER 4

"WELL, LOOK WHAT THE CAT DRAGGED IN," STACEY HARPER says. She's standing in front of the stove flipping fluffy eggs around a pan. A southern smorgasbord laid out on the Formica countertops surrounding her.

He takes all this in suspiciously. "What's the occasion, Mom?" he says with a smile.

"Huh?" She turns away from the stove with her hands still over it and sends a little puff of air up, blowing a lock of hair out of her face. "Oh, yes. The occasion," she continues, huffing and turning back to tend to the food. "Well, let's see here. I'm your mother, you're my son. We've got a nice new house. We are both relatively healthy. My credit score is pretty solid, and you're carrying a three-point-five through high school." She turns the burners off. ("If you don't hear the click, don't light the wick" is one of her favorite aphorisms. Their last house had a gas stove—not that the house would blow up or anything, but at least it helped him remember to always turn them off fully. And made him laugh.)

"Do I really need one? Isn't this what mothers do?" she says this with wide-eyed sarcasm, as if she truly doesn't know.

"You're a trip, Mom," Cole says, now sitting at the table with a full plate in front of him. Sizing up the various delicacies like a rapacious tiger shark deciding which ignorant vacationer to pick off first.

"Speaking of trips. I'm taking one this afternoon to the store. Do you need anything?" She sits at the table across from him with her own greasy little breakfast knoll on her plate.

A smile creeps across his face as he thinks, *Yeah, see if you can find a Sugar Ray CD, either "Floored" or "14:59." The rest of the albums kinda suck. And yes, I'm still hanging on to a little collection of CDs even though half the world has an iPod by now. Mementos of simpler times.* "Nope, I don't think so." Then he blurts, "Oh! Suntan oil."

She only stares, working on a piece of bacon, waiting for him to expound.

"I'd like to *not* be mistaken for a ghost on my first day at the new school come August." Then with a straight face, he whispers, "It scares the ladies, Mom."

"Cole, I would die for your skin tone. The last thing you need is suntan oil. People at school would wonder what the new Mexican kid's name was. The inbreds would cut their little chickpea eyes over at you during the National Anthem of the football games. Hell, if you get any darker than you already do during the summer, you could just buy a tool belt and a hard hat and wander over to that big house they're building across the street and just start hammering stuff. No one would say a word."

Cole begins working on a biscuit, smiling through bites.

"For one, I don't think I'll be attending any football games at this school."

"And why not?"

"You know, it's a big school. Lots of kids, none of them I know. None of them I really care about getting to know either probably."

"You'll make some friends," she says out of the side of a jam-packed mouth.

"And for two, I was kidding about the oil. I just know I'll

probably be spending a lot of time out back this summer."

"Doing what?"

"I don't know. Reading, maybe writing a little."

"Knock yourself out, kid. Just know you've got a free ticket anytime you want to join your old lady at the mall or the movies. Or hey, I heard from someone at work that that burger place down on Campbell Street does a trivia night every Wednesday. That'd be neat, huh?" She holds her hands out, palms up, with shrugged shoulders for emphasis.

He rolls his eyes and finishes the last bite of his breakfast, all but licking the plate clean. And had he been in here alone, he may have done that too. He takes his dish to the sink, crossing the linoleum flooring, through a sea of sporadic scuffs from the movers' black-soled shoes. He clicks the Keurig on, then turns his back to the counter and leans against it with arms folded across his chest, waiting for it to heat up. The window over the sink is open, and he can feel the warmth on the back of his neck.

"What do you work today?" he asks. He sits patiently for an answer while she, too, finishes cleaning her plate. She's good at a couple things, and not at a lot, but she is an excellent cook. He thinks that he could sit right here forever, listening to the steady crescendo of the Keurig while that midsummer sun's warmth crawls along the back of his neck, sending fresh patches of gooseflesh down his arms. He can hear the birds back there, the ones that aided so graciously to his awakening this morning, gabbing away in the trees, zinging their terse chirrups and warbles from limb to limb.

"I've got a bit of a day. Kathy said since I'm new she's going to send the majority of new clients my way to help me get caught up. I know I've got an appointment with a lady at ten. That one for sure, maybe a two, and then another with a girl at four I believe, but everything in between—who knows? I should be off after my girl at four. Then I'll go to the store."

The Keurig behind him goes silent. He grabs a cup from the cabinet and puts it under the hood, then grabs a K-Cup from the nifty little lazy Susan K-Cup holder, only a few left, and lifts the Keurig's hood, puts the K-Cup in the slot, and closes it. He loves that muffled little pop. Two blue lights flash on the right of the machine, indicating the size of the cup you want.

"You look like you got hit by a truck, Cole. Must've slept well." She's looking him up and down, really seeing him for the first time this morning.

He clicks the larger of the two.

"You're sweet, Mom. Hey, looks like one thing we do need is some more K-Cups."

She puts her dishes on top of his in the sink and begins running hot water over them, sending the soggy leftover curds and jellies (although not much at all) down the disposal.

"I think we're really going to like it out here. It's beautiful."

"Yeah, it's nice," he agrees. "But it would be *real* nice if whoever is moving into that big house across the street has a hot daughter."

She steals her eyes away from the open window and snaps a peevish look his way. Though Cole doesn't miss the smirk at the corners of her mouth.

He's at the far end of the counter now, stirring a scoop of sugar and just the smallest of dashes of 2 percent into the scalding mug.

"All right, sweetie, I'm going to get ready," Stacey says.

"Okay, I think I'm going to go wander around outside. See what I can get into."

"Okay. I'll see you this afternoon then. If you think of

anything else you need from the store, just shoot me a text. I might not be able to answer a call. Unless it's an emergency! Then just text me that there's an emergency." She plants a peck on his cheek, fiddles with his unruly mane for a moment, and then saunters out of the kitchen.

He smiles as she goes. *Gotta love her.*

He goes back to the window, back into that bath of sunlight, and carefully sips his steaming coffee in occasional slurps. But the backyard has grown silent. A tall, black wooden fence runs behind their house and down one side, then along the road to the end of the street where it connects to an even taller gate, marking the entrance to another house, he assumes. Someone who prefers his or her privacy. He can sympathize with that.

There's a crow back there, perched oafishly on that divider wall between woods and yard. It seems to be looking at him through the window, flitting those beady black marbles around impatiently. He doesn't much care for that look. He has read somewhere that in the ancient Celtic culture, crows were seen as a sign of impending death, and that it was a bad omen when sighted.

You see crows all the time, his mind tells him. *And we're all still kickin'.*

He stares back at the bird on the fence and sips his slowly cooling coffee in longer gulps now. But there's something about those eyes. Black as nothing, but full of knowing all the same. He reaches up and slides the window shut, startled by the dry screech from the warped wood of the sill.

CHAPTER 5

"I DON'T FEEL OLD. I DON'T FEEL ANYTHING TILL NOON. THAT'S when it's time for my nap." Bob Hope said that. The saying rings true of noon at the Harper house, but Cole's nap isn't the sleep kind. His nap is finding a quiet place somewhere to think. Oftentimes, a simple kid has no such mind. But rather one of quare thoughts, constantly quibbling, jockeying for position.

He loves his room, but he enjoys being outside just the same. Behind their house is an attached porch, the wood wasn't stained and a few of the boards are loose.

I'll fix that for Mom before summer's over, he thinks. The porch sits on a good-size backyard, the grass patchy and mismatched, but when mowed short, it looks pretty good. He cut it the day they moved in, but looking at it now, he thinks it could use it again already. They've had a few summer showers since they arrived. He'll put it on his list for today: (1) relax, (2) read, (3) eat, (4) read, and (5) mow.

If you're facing the back fence, to the left is an empty, undeveloped lot that runs up against thick underbrush, marking the boundary of the woods, swallowing Lakeview Heights there and letting it loose about an eighth of a mile away where it empties onto Carlsen Road (if you take a right, Carlsen will lead you into town, hang a left, and aside from a few sporadic neighborhoods, it's farmland for eons). On the other side of Lakeview Heights, the woods tightly hug the two houses. One, the house directly across the street from his, is occupied by a nice-looking black family (possibly a partial family). And the other, the one that's being built, is pushed up against the black fence. To Cole, it seems like they are building a bit too close to that ominous black gate. He bets whoever owns that gate isn't too thrilled about its proximity, being as he doesn't seem like the most sociable guy in the world.

The work trucks over there all have DONOVAN DEVELOPMENT & BUILDING COMPANY plastered on the sides. He saw them the first day he and his mother moved in, while he was out by the road weed-eating the ditch that runs the length of their house. *Bet that fucker behind the gate has them on speed dial,* he thought then. *"You guys are working too loud!"* or *"How am I supposed to bevel the edges of my tinfoil hat through all that racket!"*

From above, you can see the woods surrounding three houses with that black fence dissecting their wooded perimeter almost into halves. You can see Lakeview Heights turning into a long driveway at the ominous gate at the end. You cannot see much of the driveway from above because of the overhanging trees, but you know it's there because it runs into an opening a couple hundred yards from the gate. Nestled in the opening is a big house. From up here, it looks as if the trees hang over the eaves. And even farther back is a creek that curves around the back of the property, eventually joining the lake below. It snakes its way through the forest, running roughly parallel with Lakeview Heights, bending close to where Cole now sits, silently reaching for him like he's got his own gravitational pull. He doesn't know that it's back there and he doesn't know what the house that it leads to looks like. Not yet.

He needs something to prop his feet up. *Desperation,* the book he pulled from the Cole Harper Library shelves this morning, sits open in his lap. Stephen King, of course. Remember, he's back in *that* ballpark; he's a season ticket holder in that one.

The sun is baking the tops of his thighs, but his feet remain in the shadows of them. It's hovering high overhead, causing the overhanging roofline to cut his body in half with a shadow at the belly button. But he needs something to prop his feet up, dammit, so the entirety of each leg can be in the sun while his upper body stays nice and cool in the shade, feeling that persistent summer breeze whipping around the corner of the house.

He gets up and begins across the yard. There's a small tool shed at the back-left corner—maybe he can find something to prop his feet with in there. In the back-right corner of the yard, there is a makeshift fire pit. It consists of an old cast-iron bowl the size of a grill lid that houses a long-dead hibiscus, surrounded by three mini boulders the previous owner used as garden art at the front corner of the house. It took Cole about an hour to drag the items back here one by one the other day, and he didn't even ask his mother first. But it turned out to be a neat little spot. Mom liked it too.

He swings open the shed door, its tired hinges moaning and groaning. A ball of heat pushes past him. It's stifling in the confined space. He has no fear of spiders or creepy-crawlies, but cleaning the shed out the other day tested those neutral feelings. He danced around daddy longlegs and flicked away spasmodic, clittering roaches till he couldn't take it anymore. He finally said fuck it and dragged over the hose, not missing the splendid opportunity to shout that infamous *Scarface* line before blasting them all to hell. "Say hello to my little friend!" he had proclaimed in the best Pacino he could muster, and cranked the nozzle hard, lefty-loosey.

Various yard tools hang from the ply board walls on rusty nails that the previous owner had left. He steps in farther, not completely seeing what he's looking for. Directly in front of him is a push mower that takes up most of the floor space. Around it are a few gas cans and a couple bags of mulch stacked thigh-high. Finally, under the weed eater that's propped in the corner, he sees what he's looking for. A big green bucket that they use for miscellaneous things. It's one of those items that could quietly collect dust for ten years before anyone started asking why the hell they still had that. Cole has a box fan like that. It's been sitting on the floor of his different bedrooms throughout his adolescence and into early adulthood, loyally droning its one note into oblivion. If you were to hold a gun to his head and demand the age of the thing, he genuinely would not know. The couple times he has thought about how long he's had that damn fan, all he can conjure up is that mystical description that elicits no further questions or inquiries, that all-encompassing time frame only defined as "as long as I can remember." More than once, he's humorously entertained the idea of sending Lasko some fan mail (pun intended). Something like, "Just wanted you guys to know that one of your late-'90s models is still going strong. The speed knob's been gone since I was watching *Rugrats* every day after school, so plugged in is ON and unplugged is OFF. But she's still hummin', baby, still hummin.'"

But now, faded old bucket in hand, he can't remember why he wanted the damn thing in the first place.

To prop your feet up, dummy.

To prop his feet up. There's only one chair and table on the deck, and the table is too high. *I'm just a little guy.*

He turns to head out when suddenly the door slams shut with a reverberant *bang*, instantly throwing him into a world of darkness. He jumps and drops the bucket, where it goes clattering to the floor. He stands motionless, not quite scared yet but rapidly approaching it. A faint tickling on his ankles and forearms stands the hair on the back of his neck at attention.

Spiders, he thinks.

He frantically swipes at his arms and legs and lunges for the door. He steps on the bucket, which now lies on its side, with too much forward momentum, and his legs fly out from under him in a textbook cartoon-esque tumble. He lands hard on his back, and all the air *whooshes* out of his lungs. He lay there, temporary paralyzed by an odd combination of fear and embarrassment, looking up at the thin bar of light coming through the space between the door and the frame.

It's not latched, he thinks, not without relief. He lies there, listening for someone, a prankster, a murderer, Bigfoot, anyone. But all he hears is the rushing summer breeze crying around the corners of the shed, parting its flow like a boulder in the middle of a river.

A realization comes over him, and his tensed muscles loosen. He reaches out and pushes the door open. It clears the frame a few inches, causing that bar of light to expand across his face, and then slams shut again.

The fucking wind. He stands up and slowly dusts himself off like an embarrassed rookie who just got picked off first, not wanting to go back in the dugout to face his veteran teammates. He pushes the door hard this time till it passes the angle in which it's pointing directly at the wind. It catches the inside of the door and slings it all the way open, pinning it against the outside wall of the shed. Sunlight once again fills the baking space, throwing bullets of rays against the many metallic surfaces, causing the walls to look like someone paused the disco ball. He suddenly remembers the spiders tickling his ankles in the dark and uncontrollably breaks out in a jig, a high-kneed, tiptoed number that looks like someone trying to avoid a thousand invisible mousetraps. In the light, though, he quickly sees there are no spiders. No daddy longlegs or brown recluses, no rabid rats or bold roaches.

All in my head, he thinks. Then aloud to the hanging tools, "Why am I so damn *jumpy?*" Something has him on edge. Something buried deep in the maze of his brain is cowering in a corner, knocking on the walls.

A few minutes later, he's lounging back on the porch in his previously desired position.

All that for this.

It was a bad idea. He's yanked his shorts down over the top of his fire-engine red quads. But now with his feet up on the bucket, they, too, are beginning to burn. He's always achieved a leapfrog over the burn phase straight to tan with the oil, see. But Mom didn't get it.

He's about thirty pages into *Desperation* when he realizes he has no idea what he's read the last few pages. His eyes have been trudging across the words, but his brain has checked out. "Took the towels and shampoo too," his mom would say. Instead of the delicious story his eyes are looking at, where a psychotic cop is currently leading two out-of-towners into a holding cell in the middle of a ghost town, his brain keeps flashing a big neon sign in the darkness: MY FEET ARE BURNING! MY FEET ARE BURNING! Frustrated, he tosses the book on the table and stands up, thinking, *Just trying to get some even sun on my legs,* then looking up at the hard blue sky with upturned palms, *Is that too much to ask?* He glances down and sees his reflection in the windows of the living room, realizing how ridiculous he looks quibbling with the creator about a couple sunburned feet on a plastic bucket.

He reaches down and grabs the upside-down bucket by

its wire handle and carries it over to the edge of the porch. He doesn't want to leave it on the deck because his mother will just tell him to go put it back in the shed when she gets home, which he doesn't want to do. He scolds himself for laziness, yet he's all too aware of that quivering thing deep in his head, on edge about something, and hiding from it. He walks to the edge of the porch, which runs almost to the end of the house on this side, and leans over the railing, reaching the bucket as close to the ground as he can get. He's holding it by that wire handle, and the bulky body of it is swinging in the wind, having a grand old time. It's about a foot and a half drop, and he's hoping that its flat base hits the yard flush and stays there, obediently continuing its loyal life under the edge of the deck.

It's gonna bounce away, he thinks. *Just walk around and set it there.* But that *thing*. It's banging on the walls in his head, keeping him on the porch. He times the swing the best he can and drops it. Of course, it bounces off an exposed rock or maybe just off the hard-packed dirt leaking out from under the deck, and clatters out into the side yard. *See*, he scolds himself, marching off the back of the deck and around into the side yard.

Here, the breeze is bottlenecked, rushing through with some force. He reaches down for the bucket and pauses, listening. He hears yelling, probably from the building site across the street. It bounces up through the bottleneck, louder in the confined space between the side of his house and the black fence that runs out to the road. He picks up the bucket and starts for the road in a bit of a creep. Keeping close to the fence, so as not to be seen by whoever was making all the racket.

Someone sure isn't happy. He's got his head cocked to one side to eliminate that annoying whine of wind rushing across his ear holes when it's coming head-on. He steals a glance of himself again, this time from his reflection in a cracked window on the side of the house. He pauses, comically reverses feet for a few steps, then proceeds forward while holding a straight face. He looks like Inspector Clouseau closing in on a suspect in one of those *Pink Panther* movies.

Thank God no one can see my dumbass. Over here looking like some sort of psycho. But someone *can* see him. A black boy watches from a nearby window, peeking through the blinds of a dark room. But Cole doesn't know that yet, either. He doesn't know a lot of things yet.

As Cole approaches the end of the fence, close to the road now, some of the words being yelled can be clearly articulated. None of them nice. The bucket is still in his hand, knuckles methodically turning white around its handle, as if whatever monster lay around the wooded corner causes blood to run and hide elsewhere throughout the body. He peeks around the corner, now seeing the epicenter of what can only be described as a full-fledged tirade. What he sees is a stocky man, maybe mid-fifties, presumably the boss of the operation, ripping around the jobsite, pointing at things and yelling, throwing things and yelling, getting nose to nose with some of the builders and *yelling*, man.

Cole watches as the assumed boss gets so close to one worker's face, it looks like their lips are touching. If he had to guess, the guy currently being yelled at probably did something wrong just by the looks of him. Maybe not the other workers, but obviously this guy. Cole conjures up an image from a movie he watched as a kid at Brantley Mavin's house while his mom was asleep and his dad was out banging on a rusty old Mustang and seeing how high the beer can mountain in the corner of the garage could get. The guy that's a sneeze away from making out with the boss right now looks like someone from that movie. He can't remember the name of it for the life of him, but he remembers Burt Reynolds and thinks someone played a banjo. A couple Mexicans are on the roof, peeking out over the edge. An older worker, maybe older than the boss even, stands stupidly by the brick steps leading up to the front porch. Through the noise of the dancing leaves overhead, a wind-disturbed rattling sea of green, Cole can make out snippets of dialogue. Some song about wrong dimensions and a ballad about a bunch of lazy asses.

Cole is fairly certain this guy isn't the homeowner. For one, because of the way they are reacting. They've seen this movie before. Either this is one asshole future homeowner, or it's just another hierarchical meltdown from the guy who writes the checks. And for two, the truck at the end of the driveway, the last one to pull in, is too clean. It has DONOVAN DEVELOPMENT & BUILDING COMPANY on the sides of it like the other trucks do. But it doesn't belong in the dirty bunch. Like the kid on the baseball team who's got a spotless uniform after a hard-fought game. No one likes that kid.

A telephone ring blares from the open window behind him like a slap across the neck. He jerks, banging the empty bucket hard against the fence.

"Shit," he whisper-screams as he ducks out of view. The yelling stops. *I'm caught*, he thinks. *They heard me.*

He sits there for a moment, crouching at the corner of the woods, hiding behind the edge of the fence, and waits for the crazy guy across the street to yell at him. Something like, "Mind your own damn business, kid!" or "Quit hiding like a bitch! Be a man and show yourself!" but none of those things are said. He risks a one-eyed peek around the edge. The yelling most certainly *has* stopped. But only because the guy is trouncing around, measuring some things and just eyeing some others. There's no more ringing through the open window on the side of the house. *Better go check the answering machine*, he thinks. *Maybe it was Mom.*

He walks back into the glorious air conditioning through the back door, pausing only to toss the old bucket under the deck on the way by, thinking that this whole ordeal was the damn bucket's fault as he does so.

Now safe and sound, he's glad no one had seen him. He's quickly becoming a man, sure, but the idea of a fight with someone who's been a grown man for a while—or maybe a couple *someones* who have been grown men for a while—raises a flag of fear, something he wants no part of.

But someone *had* seen him. And that someone had thought it rather hilarious. Laughter fills the dark room.

CHAPTER 6

A FEW HOURS HAVE PASSED, AND COLE HAS DONE A WHOLE bunch of nothing. His mother isn't the type of parent who makes her child slave away all summer, earning something around minimum wage at the local car wash or burger joint till school kicks back in. "Builds character," these parents claim. "Teaches you the value of the almighty dollar." Or the most ridiculous: "Back in *my* day ..." That last one is almost always followed by some ridiculous claim that makes Nazi Germany sound like Central Park. He wouldn't mind a summer job if she had forced one upon him, but it is certainly nice to just relax and have one less thing to worry about during these disconcerting years of his life when lessons will be learned and memories made, both good and bad. Ladies and gentlemen, the Roaring Teens.

Instead of on a bucket in the sun, his bare feet now rest on a coffee-colored ottoman in front of a thirty-five-inch, middle-class flat screen. The ceiling fan pushes cool air down onto his reddish-brown legs. The chain jingles happily against the bulb at this speed. He's watched two episodes of *Catfish*, a few game shows, and one highly entertaining half hour of *Judge Judy*. He thoroughly enjoys watching her intellectually dismantle whatever chump they toss in front of her, usually not without a barrage of colorful and demoralizing insults. He's picked up a pattern with Mrs. Judith Sheindlin. The less you talk, the more she likes you. Maybe "like" is too strong a word. The more she doesn't hate you. Keep your trap shut and let her work through the case in her head, without your banter.

Fortunately, for the viewer, these idiots never seem to understand that completely. They choose to challenge her with their own misinformed interpretations of certain laws or, even better, provide their personal opinions. Then, viewer, you better make sure you got your popcorn ready because Judy is about to start ripping new assholes.

On the kitchen wall behind him, a red "1" stands stoically in the little digital space for the answering machine to display how many messages it's containing. Unblinking, because it's been listened to. It had been his mother, like he'd guessed before pressing play. She was on her lunch break and wanted him to check and see if she needed to add toilet paper to the grocery list. Which she did. He gets up and heads for the kitchen, erases the message on the answering machine, and heads for the fridge. He stands there with the door open, scanning the barren shelves. It's a frozen tundra with random foods sporadically placed throughout. He sees a half-empty bottle of ketchup, a slimy packet of sliced turkey, three slices of cheese, a bag of green grapes that might have a tint of brown, and a six-pack of eight-ounce Red Bulls. He stands in the open fridge doorway deciphering the code, running through all possible combinations of items, trying to determine the couple, which, together, could form an actual meal. The fridge begins to beep, letting him know the door has been open too long. His mother, were she here, would be playfully scolding him for it. He's looking out the kitchen window and into the backyard, which reminds him that he needs to mow soon. Mom will be home with groceries in probably about an hour and a half, and she'd want help loading them in. He learned years ago to never try to outwit your mother when it comes to getting out of bringing in the groceries. They know all the tricks. He finds a couple slices of bread in the pantry (both end pieces, but he's not picky) and makes himself a turkey and cheese sandwich, hold the grapes. He grabs a Red Bull to wash it down with and heads to his room. He wants to read some of his book while he's got a few more minutes of quiet time before lawn duty.

Across the street, a couple numb-fucks are banging in nails and talking shit about the boss.

"I really hate him sometimes," Jordy Danielson says to Gary Doogan over a dip-packed lip.

"Ayuh," Gary replies. "This one sure is a bad one, ain't it?" He's referring to their current build. There have been rumblings around the site about the strange way Nolan was going about this one. They all know whose house it is, but damn, there's got to be something more. Boss man Donovan walks around the site like it's a house made of cards instead of one made of two-by-fours and burnt clay bricks.

"Sandy wants me to quit. She says he treats us like shit and don't pay us any better," Jordy says.

"How's Cam?" Gary blurts out. He knows the answer to that. But he also knows what Jordy will say. Same thing he's said for over a year now.

"Better," Jordy says quickly, without emotion. More of a habit than a meaningful answer. "We got him an appointment with some big-shot doctor at Vandy. Supposed to be one of the best in the Southeast."

"Well, hope all goes fine," Gary says, now starting to clean up. Rain's coming. They've a seasoned eye for weather.

"Me too. We're tired of all the appointments. Tired of it all."

A weighted silence falls over them like a cloak as they both pick up their things and put them in their respective trucks.

The dirty ones. Gary is uncomfortable in these moments. He's hated them since he was a kid, kicking dirt or pretending to tie his shoes when a friend started crying over a scraped knee or got made fun of for leaving his fly open.

Jordy finally breaks it. "If he don't start payin' us more soon, I may just listen to Sandy and up and quit one day."

He tosses a few tools in his truck bed. "Especially if he keeps actin' like this. I dunno what's up his ass about this one, but somethin's off. He's ridin' us about the smallest damned things, like we're a couple loudmouthed slaves."

Gary nods in agreement, also filling his truck bed with dusty tools.

"I mean, what the fuck was that about today?"

Gary remains the same, only changing the direction in which his head is moving. Now shaking it from side to side, he adds a shrug and big eyes for emphasis. "I have no idea."

"Something about the frame being a quarter inch off? He's trying to get us to build the Taj-la-hall in a fuckin' month and he's gonna flip his shit over a *goddamn quarter fuckin' inch?*"

Their trucks are parked behind the others (the shiny one has been MIA for about an hour now). The Mexicans always get here first and leave last. They are taking their time cleaning up their areas. They don't worry too much about the rain, would probably just work on through it if they could.

While Jordy turns right onto Carlsen, contemplating quitting if working conditions don't improve drastically, thunder begins to sound off in the west, announcing its ominous presence.

The thunder shakes Cole out of the world in his hands. He looks over at his bedside clock—it reads 4:08. Time to get a move on. He tosses the paperback aside, grabs his empty plate, and heads for the kitchen, downing the remaining contents of the Red Bull on the way in one big burning gulp of glorious caffeine.

A few minutes later, he is once again standing in the open door of the shed.

Grab it and go, he thinks. He pulls the push mower out by the handle, rolling it backward over the lip of the shed's entrance and out into the backyard. The wind has died down. "Calm before the storm," he says, squinting up into the sky against the glare, sizing up the building thunderhead off to the left. It's beginning to swallow up the late-afternoon sun.

He rolls the mower over to the fence, lining it up against it. This is where he started last time, and he thinks he'll stick to this pattern. He can knock out the backyard fairly quickly; for now, the only obstacles are the fire pit and the shed itself. Then he can move to the side yard, the one against the fence, finishing it in just five or six long strips. After that, he'll get the front yard done, mowing in rows perpendicular to the street so the passers-by can check out those light-and-dark alternating stripes with jealousy. He chuckles to himself as he checks to see if the thing's got gas in it. Also hoping those workers are gone by the time he gets up there. Maybe he'll take his time in the back. He assumes every build crew can sniff the air like a bloodhound and pick up on that electric fragrance of impending rain from miles away. Then they joyfully close up shop and head home to drink their beer or drive over to the local watering hole to do it. Finally, he'll get to the other side of the house, just guessing where the line dividing their property and the open lot is, finishing up right back here at the shed where he started.

He grabs the dead man's switch and pulls it together with the thicker handle, then reaches down and starts yanking on the pull string. He's met with a couple of half-assed coughs.

Great. It'll probably rain for three days and turn the yard into a nature reserve.

He yanks some more, reaching all the way down to the motor and pulling the string high and hard up over his shoulder, attempting to maximize rotations on the flywheel. But again, just a bunch of empty grunts from the engine. He takes a step back, surveying the machine with hands on hips and a perplexed look on his face that is so common among men when they can't get the weed eater or mower started and know that their neighbors can see them. This is the look they go for, that "That's weird, it usually starts right up!" look. Then when the lookie-loos go inside or the road clears of cars, they begin wrenching on the pull rope like a madman in a full-bodied convulsion and kicking the shit out of the mower like it broke into their house and stole all the money.

Then it comes to him. He forgot to prime the motor. The left side of the mower is against the fence, so he pulls it away just far enough to squeeze in there to pump it. Sometimes the bulb doesn't want to fill up right so the little "5x" notifier above it is rendered unless. Sometimes it's a "10x" or even, if it's feeling *really* froggy that day, it's a "whenever I feel like working x."

He kneels down, weight resting against the fence and face close to the bulb. "One," he says to it as he pumps. Nothing happens—it doesn't refill with gas. Just loads up another bulb full of air. A stampede of thunder threatens off in the distance. He tries again. "One ..." There it goes. "Two . . . three . . . four . . . five ..." He starts to stand up; he's got one hand around a two-by-four that's connected to many others for support, running the length of the entire fence parallel with the ground, and the other hand on the top of the motor.

But he hears something. Something off in the distance. There's a very faint trickling sound coming from somewhere.

A creek.

From behind the fence, maybe? He's never been back there, so he's not sure. There very well could be. But the owner of the fence obviously doesn't like the idea of anyone on his property, so Cole stands up and yanks the pull rope again. And this time, it fires right up. All thoughts of potential creeks and even the approaching storm fall by the wayside. Mowing can do that to a guy.

About a half hour later, he's finishing up the fenceless side yard. To his relief, there were no workers across the street there to eye him while he mowed the front. He had the whole road to himself, just how he likes things. That electricity from the impending storm thrives on his skin. He feels like his senses are heightened; things have a certain sharpness to them.

He trundles down the final unkempt row, finishes the last bit, and lets the dead man's switch spring free from his hands, killing the four-cycle motor in a quick hiccup. Something catches his eye off to the right. He looks over and sees the crow. It's once again perched on the fence, but this time in the corner where his fire pit is. A strange sense of violation seeps through him like a virus. He doesn't like that thing anywhere near his house, and where it sits over something he made somehow makes it worse. Like it knows more about him over there. It's too hitchy, like it's not quite right, battling some inner demon or something. Or trying desperately but failing miserably at keeping some secret safe. He peers at the bird unnervingly, then lets his gaze drop to the fire pit.

"Shit," he blurts with trepidation.

He forgot to pull the rocks away from the fence so he

could mow behind them. The mower couldn't fit between them and the fence otherwise. He can't put it off till next time; the tall grass around the rocks and cast-iron bowl looks bad. It screams laziness. Now, he could lie around all day and do nothing but read and stuff his face, no problem, but when it comes to something being nonsymmetrical or haphazard, *that* really chaps his ass.

He has a dilemma, and the bird seems to somehow know this. Those eyes dart around like they see things that he can't, but when they momentarily lock on his, he can feel them reaching, probing his soul. It sits over the high grass, daring Cole to do something about it. He pulls the ear buds that have been serenading him with nostalgia in song form out of his ears and puts them in his pocket, crushing the cords down around his little iPod.

Thunder slowly tears the heavens in two, closer than ever. He can feel the reverberation in his chest. He needs to make a choice now. He's at the age when a grown-up Cole and a kid Cole commonly tussle in situations like these, playing tug-of-war with his mind, battling for reverence. And it's not always the one that weighs the most that wins out—it's the one who's got the best foothold in the sand. To confront the crow and go ahead and finish the job, or to leave it for another day? Moping back into the house in defeat, telling himself it's exhaustion. He could choose C and knock it down with the weed eater, but it's out of oil. Those whining plastic lines would have certainly scared the bird off. The mower may not.

"Fuck this," he says aloud. Ridiculously, he grabs a hammer from the shed and proceeds toward the corner with it swinging from his right hand, while the left does its best to steer the push mower over to the fire pit. He gets halfway across the yard, trying hard to stay in the lines he's made in the grass, when a stunning boom of thunder sounds off behind him. Just a few miles away now. He jumps at the noise, dropping the hammer to the grass in a muffled thump. He bends down and retrieves it, and when he looks back up, the crow has disappeared.

Thunder probably scared him, he thinks, still holding onto it as he approaches. Just for safety measures. That thing could have a disease or something.

There's definitely something not right about it.

The stones sit in a triangle around the bowl. He drags the two that are closest to the corner of the fence away from it and the third one a couple feet toward the house. It gives a sleepy groan as it thumps into the grass next to its usual resting place. There are three disproportionate rectangles of flattened browning grass. Walls of healthy green, which also spread throughout the back corner, surround them. The thunderclaps have become more frequent and are also intensifying. But in between the barrages is tingling silence, thick summer air holding things hostage where they stand.

He reaches down to yank the mower to life once again. His eyes dart over to the hammer resting in the grass clippings behind him, just an arm's length away in case his creepy feathered friend decides to return.

He freezes.

It's that noise again. That far-off trickling sound. But it's louder here in the corner, more adamant and no longer trying to keep secret back there. Trespassing or not, curiosity takes hold. He lets the pull rope go, and it whips back into its coil like an agitated snake. He has a vivid memory of how he used to play with his mother's measuring tape as a young boy, shivering with adrenaline because it could snap a finger pretty good if you weren't careful, whipping back and forth and slamming against walls and floors as it sped toward him.

He steps toward the black fence and jumps up on the sideways support board, peering into the dense woods behind his new house. He can't see anything but thickets of vines and bushes layering deeper into the forest.

Water, he thinks again, cocking an ear to the sound.

He glances over at the menacing clouds coming from the west, estimating their time of arrival. He jumps back down and snags the hammer in the grass, tosses it over the fence, then follows after it. His grass-stained sneakers crunch down on a layer of twigs and leaves covering the ground in this unexplored world. He's immediately aware of the temperature change. The bows of the overhanging maples make somewhat of an unobjectionable roof to the place, bouncing the sun's rays back toward oblivion. Along with the favorable drop in temperature, he notices what is almost certainly some sort of stream back there gabbing away through the trees. But it sounds close. He picks up the hammer and pushes on into the tangled coppice, quickly finding that the tool is also fairly sufficient as a makeshift machete. He moves toward the sound of the creek, consciously creating a bit of a slapdash path.

After a few minutes of bashing down bushes and bending limbs away, he stumbles into an opening. There's a small stream in front of him, gleefully dashing over rounded stones and fallen limbs. Its edges spill over sharply cut sides, forming little pools in the sandy dirt.

Maybe that's why I haven't heard it before today, he thinks. *Water level's up.*

Either from the rain the other day or from the storm that's heading toward him now, the creek is carrying its spillage out in front of it, warning whoever it comes across that the storm's heading straight for them.

"Probably from the other day," he tells the trees. But he pictures a man, his mind's rendition of Paul Revere, with a blond ponytail riding a boat like a surfboard on the head wave of a flash flood, yelling at squirrels and rabbits as he bounces along. He's got on a shirt with billowy sleeves and a buttoned-up vest over it. He's standing on the bow of the boat, feet staggered for support. Those absurd, ball-hugging pants tucked into tall black boots. He's got one hand on top of his three-pointed hat, holding it down, and the other pointing forward, marking his way through the forest flying by. "The storm is coming! The storm is coming!"

"You're a bit soft upstairs, Cole." That's his mother in his head.

Speaking of his mother, she should be home any minute now. Depending on how grocery-happy she was today. He thinks of heading back to the house and saving this exploration for another day. But it's so cool back here. In a weird way, sort of magical, like it's a place made just for him. Now he just really wants to know where it leads. He sends up a hurried promise that he'll head back as soon as he feels the first drop of rain. Or if he hears his mom pull up.

Good one, kid, his mind interjects. *From back here, no one would even hear you scream.*

Not unlike when he was a kid playing in the hall with the measuring tape, careful because it might bite, he proceeds forward with that same sort of adrenaline-shiver. The stream runs down the center of what can only be described as a tunnel in the thick woods. It's cut through like a mineshaft in a mountainside. But up ahead, it bends away, leaving whatever lay beyond to be desired.

Hammer in hand, he follows the flow of muddy water deeper into the forest. He rounds the first bend and sees another fifty yards or so before it snakes away again. He walks on the right side of the stream, sneakers crunching on tiny pebbles like snow, hopping over the occasional tide pool writhing with jealousy, watching the rest of the water rush by. He's bewildered but not complaining about the steady breeze singing through the channel, causing thick leaves to shimmy and shake against each other, cheering him along.

A few minutes later, he reaches the end of the tunnel. It widens and gives way to farmland. If he were standing in the field and facing the woods, it would appear that the creek runs out of a dark cave of trees. On the right side of the stream, the side he's on, the wall of trees continues on for another couple hundred yards. The stream nestles right up to it the whole way, marking the boundary of some farmer's field, then tops a hill on the far side, running down to feed into the lake, he assumes. He can smell the lake out here, the breeze carrying that fishy fragrance across the open field and funneling it into the mouth of the woods that he's standing in.

His road, Lakeview Heights, got its name because it technically rides atop an ancient point that juts out like a swollen elbow into the lake. However, there's no view to speak of. At least not from his side of the street. You can hear the occasional boat hammer down as soon as it crosses out of the No Wake Zone, leaving the dock's placid perimeter in the dust. But that's about it.

This is a pretty neat spot, he thinks. He wonders if Native Americans ever walked on these same rocks that he's standing on. *I bet I could live right here for as long as I needed to.* Nothing answers but the creek, its murky rainwater contents prattling toward an even murkier lake. He once read a book by Euell Gibbons called *Stalking the Wild Asparagus*, which taught the reader how to recognize which plants are edible and which will make you mess your pants before you can make it back home.

He decides that in the event of a zombie apocalypse, this is where he'll flee to. Making sure to grab some matches on his way out the door.

Standing in the clearing, seeing the sky for the first time in twenty minutes or so, he notices the initial line of dark, wispy clouds directly overhead, dancing around as they are being pushed along by the storm front. He feels a few drops of rain on his arms and decides it's time to head back.

He's walked a few dozen yards, rewinding the first bend of the tunnel on the return trip back to his yard and mundane reality, when something catches his eye. Off in the woods to his left, he sees movement, then a flash of rusty orange through the trees. He hadn't noticed it the first time he trudged through this spot, probably because he was only staring ahead, blithely wide-eyed and searching for the light at the end of the tunnel instead of looking around, taking in his surroundings completely. He imagines a Native American again, one who made it through the dreck that was his people's history and still thrives in these dark forests today, crouching behind a tree. Peeking around one side and silently watching Cole with gelid, learning eyes as he stumbles along the creek bed past him like a bumbling, bulky moth to a flame.

His grip inadvertently tightens around the hammer's handle.

Cole steps off into the woods toward the unnatural color. He can't see much yet, just that occasional flash of manmade orange between yards of green. He uses the hammer once again to smash a respectable path through the thicket. An object begins to take shape as he approaches. It looks like an old sign, maybe. Some sort of antique left out here, forgotten. His pulse livens, flitting in his throat. He loves *American Pickers*, learning many things from Mike and Frank as it pertains to what they call "rusty gold." One of them being that extremely collectible, sometimes even invaluable items are often found in forgotten places like this, accumulating dust and rust somewhere off the beaten path.

It's definitely a sign, he thinks.

He pushes on, swinging the hammer left and right. *You're getting a lot of action today, old boy*, he thinks, watching it bash away thin limbs in front of him. *Bet you're not used to all this.* A fence begins to form as limbs and vines fall away.

"What the hell is *this*?"

He approaches the corner of what appears to be a junk-yard. The orange sign is accompanied by dozens more that run along a ten-foot-tall chain-linked fence topped with razor wire. The perimeter of the yard appears to go on for a couple hundred feet to the left. In front of him, he can see maybe fifty feet or so of fencing running perpendicular to the creek behind him before overhanging tree limbs block his view.

"Awesome!" he proclaims to the rusty gold.

But what's even more awesome is what lies beyond the towering jungle of weeds that protects the yard's perimeter. He can see the tops of maybe twenty buses sitting stoically aloof, forming a willy-nilly congregation of metal giants in the middle of the woods.

"Ho . . . ly . . . shit. How cool is this!"

What answers him is a fresh cannonade of thunder, way

too close for comfort. Like a grizzly that sneaks up behind you and roars in your ear. A hot dagger of lightning cracks the sky wide open, bringing an onslaught of quarter-size raindrops down with it. The woods erupt in a raucous chatter of splashes, drowning out what he yells through the fence before dashing back to the creek. "I'll be back!" he promises.

He sprints along the creek bed like a plague survivor being chased through a subway tunnel by the infected. In his head, he hears slobbering and sloshing herds of zombies splashing through the puddles close behind him. He runs faster, hammer pumping alongside in a heavy blur.

He flies over the fence and lands hard on all fours in the swamp that is his backyard. He gets to his feet and takes off for the house. But to his right, he sees the shed door through a blanket of rain swinging violently on its hinges. *Shit,* he thinks. Then remembering, he whirls around to see the mower in the other corner to his left. *Shit!*

He shoves the mower into the shed, crashing it into tools and lawn-care equipment with a hollow clatter, then slams the shed door and slides the hook in the metal hole, locking it up. He turns to head back toward the house, then quickly comes to the realization that he's as drenched as a person could possibly get. No need to run now. He hears his mother's words in his head: "Wetter than an otter's pocket." He allows a laugh. This is all rather funny. Except for the tall grass in the corner, lapping up the rain like steroids to a bodybuilder, seemingly growing as he watches. He strolls back toward the house and in through the back door.

His mother pokes her head out of the kitchen.

"Cole?" she says. "What the hell are you doing? I thought you were in your room reading or listening to that sad nineties stuff." She loves to lay her love for "real music" like the Beatles and the Bee Gees on thick, scoffing at everything else, especially the stuff he loves.

He ignores the good-humored jab. "Out back," he says, tossing off the sodden logs that are his shoes and pulling off the heavy shirt, panting.

She remains in that funny position, head sideways like that, hovering halfway up the hallway opening and looking at him questioningly, waiting for the rest.

"Mom, you'll never guess what I found."

CHAPTER 7

A COUPLE WEEKS AFTER COLE FOUND HIS NEW HANGOUT, JORDY Danielson sits splayed on his front porch. He lives in a trailer park off Carlsen, about ten minutes from where the boss man lives. On the corner of the wobbly wicker table in front of him lies an unfolded medical bill, gently flapping in the tepid summer breeze. If you've got a beer in your hand on a Tuesday morning, which he does, then you're either an alcoholic or you're clearly going through some shit, which he is. Both. He's been on the suds his entire life, not a day gone by when he didn't have a drink, seems like. He controls it pretty well. That's what he tells himself at least, when in all actuality, that dark, slimy monster that goes by Addiction just doesn't bother him too much. People with more to lose are more fun to ruin. He keeps a twelver in a cooler in his truck, taking a minute every hour or so to wander over there and chug one while at work.

Not today, though. Boss told everybody to stay home till they hear from him. From what he could tell, the house was finished, but for some odd reason, Nolan wanted it all to himself for a couple days. God knows why. He wants to believe it's simply because Nolan doesn't feel 100 percent comfortable handing the keys over to his precious daughter till he goes through it alone with a fine-tooth comb. But he doesn't believe that. There's something wrong about it.

Something … territorial.

He did the same thing at her last house. Jordy didn't think much of it then but only because many of the guys on the crew were new. He didn't blame Nolan for wanting to make sure it was perfect before moving her in. But again with this one? They've been working for him for years now, and he knows they don't put out shoddy work. They all bust their asses because they know none of their jobs is secure. *Especially* with this one. Everyone was on edge during this build, but they still somehow managed to finish months before their average on a home of this size. He sort of wishes Barry could have been here with them for this one; he at least could have kept spirits up. But of course, that's impossible—they wouldn't have even built this house if it weren't for the accident.

Nolan had pushed some of the other projects back and made room for his daughter's house as soon as he could swing it. Jordy doesn't know Ellie well, has only talked to her a few times, but from what he could tell, she's one of those girls who believes anything she hears. She just flashes those sexy eyes and nods up and down, saying, "Oh, okay . . . Oh, okay. Okay." Sandy doesn't much care for her. Calls her a hussy. But the real reason Sandy doesn't like her is because Ellie has *actual* beauty. God-given, easy beauty. Not beauty made from hours in front of a mirror and a push-up bra, which is what Sandy's undoubtedly sporting right now over at Moneymakers. Leaning her low-cut shirt over a table of sleazy businessmen on their lunch break. It doesn't bother Jordy in the least bit, though. If he's not making any money today, her tits are going to have to pull all the weight. How else are they going to start chipping away at the growing pile of medical bills on the kitchen table? How else are they going to afford the never-ending doctor visits for their sick kid, lying in the back room right now with three box fans blowing hard at arm's length while he sleeps? The noise that comes out of him sounds like he's breathing through lungfuls of gravel. And it's recently gotten noticeably worse.

He downs a burning swig of Budweiser and spits a rope of dip at a ceramic frog on the corner of the porch. He's usually not a mean drunk, but he's some kind of pissed off this morning. He flicks the dead soldier in the frog's corner and stands up with a groan. He's tired of this shit. The sick kid, the trailer park, the push-up bras, the heat. Everything. One day, he'll grow some balls and do something about it. Something big. He feels it coming like a holiday. Each day, heavier and slower moving.

Maybe I'll quit right in his face, then peel out in a cloud of dust with a big ole "Fuck you!" he thinks. But then what? Then how's he going to help his kid? It's not like he's got any other employment options in this slap-dick town. With a couple DUIs and a felony assault charge (even if it was ten years ago) resting comfortably on your record, you are, by rule, a beggar. Not a chooser. He can't afford to leave, as much as he'd love to. And Nolan knows this. He's like that, see. He'll hire you when no one else will, not because he's a pillar to society, but because he knows he'll have power over you. He'll control you.

"Fuck Nolan," he says aloud, peering through a drunken haze over the crab grass and lawn ornaments. His kid's crying in the back room.

I'll think of something.

Jordy picks up the bill, balls it up, and irritably pelts it into the frog's corner. What an eclectic little place that's becoming.

As he opens the peeling door and heads inside to do nothing for his fading boy besides maybe propping up another box fan at his bedside if he can find one (surely they had another one *somewhere*, every trailer's got more box fans than rooms to put them in), two words illuminate his shallow, murky mind.

SOMETHING BIG.

CHAPTER 8

COLE HAS TURNED THE BUS YARD INTO A PRETTY FANTASTIC hangout. Over the past few weeks, he's led solo exploration missions across different parts of the yard, gradually cultivating a rough map of the area in his head. An Argonaut in a land of forgotten Americana. At the back corner where he originally laid eyes on this place that stormy day, the chain-link fence is still in relatively good shape, those wires still tightly twisted over each other, holding taut, like an undefeated red rover team. But he returned the next day with garden shears and snipped a path along the outside of the fence to the other back corner where he found a fallen limb the size of a basketball goal leaning against it, bowing it inward. The fence had luckily torn the wires away from the corner support post, which created an entryway big enough for him to crawl through.

He discovered that, astoundingly, the yard is chock-full of old buses, many more than he saw originally. To Cole, they resembled what he fancied the ocean floor of the Bermuda Triangle to look like. Except buses instead of boats, enveloped by weeds instead of coral, were all pulled here from different areas to their final resting place. Some of the buses are extremely old and valuable (he's taken pictures with his cell and has gone back to research some of them), but others are just your run-of-the-mill yellow school buses sitting there fat and dead with fading paint and flat tires. Their days of going 'round and 'round long gone. There seems to be no rhyme or reason when it comes to the placement of these buses, most of them just nestled in wherever there's room. Except for one special area, the Main Street of this rusty city.

That's where he's headed right now. He shuffles down the thin path he cut running along the outside of the back fence by the creek, reaches the corner with the secret entrance and the fallen limb, and ducks through. He's got a backpack full of supplies slung across one shoulder and his phone in one hand. It's been running Pandora since he'd stepped foot out of the back of the house. If it's not already playing by the time you reach the bus yard, you'll never get it to connect. So now '90s Alternative Radio bleeds through the speakers, creating a certain ambiance that makes him feel like a young kid again. There's a very short, well-trampled path cut through the thick layer of weeds on the inside of the fence in this corner, butting up to a big pile of small boats. They look like bones in the sun, peeling skeletons of summers passed. He climbs over them; he's got the foot placement memorized. He avoids a couple foot-size punctures on the way over, subconsciously reaching down to rub a spot on his knee that got knurled up one of the times he fell through.

He safely descends the small boat mountain and jumps the remaining couple of feet to the ground, sending up a swirling cloud of dust. There's a large green sign leaning against the bus directly in front of him, telling him where he is. RAMSHACKLE Row, it says. Where all your wildest dreams can come true and you don't even have to worry about the awkward moment when the guy with the pixie nose asks if you want to sleep with him in the big bed because he loves you oh-so much.

He thinks the sign originally said Ramshackle Raceway because you can barely discern a couple hand-painted racecars flying around the turn of a dirt track in the bottom right-hand corner, but all the letters after the "R" in Raceway have been roached off by the elements, exposing the rusty metal surface. He had to sacrifice the lives of two Sharpies to inscribe the dinner plate-size "O" and "W" on that wasted surface. It was heavy too. Took him about an hour one day to drag it over from a pile of old advertising signs he found in an empty space between a few lanes toward the front of the lot. His back barked at him for days after, but it was well worth it.

The sign leans against the end of a string of buses, lined up nose to tail, that runs the length of the lot, ending at the front fence. Another string of buses runs the length of the lot as well, up against the side fence to his left, like decommissioned train cars. The eight-foot-wide, low-cut alley between these two rows is bookended by a wall of weed bushes on the inside of the front fence and the boat mountain behind him. It took him two days to knock down the weeds in the alleyway. He used hoes, shovels, the garden shears, and anything else he could think of to help get the job done. Layers of tall weeds and grass lay flat, resting on top of each other, creating a cushy, woven street of green. He dreads the day it gets tall enough that he'll have to slave through that again. He couldn't bring himself to drag over the weed eater because whoever lives at the end of that long, gated driveway probably owns this. Or at least that's what he assumes. There's a door that rolls open on a small tire at the front-left corner of the lot (front right corner if you're looking from Ramshackle Row). A pathway leads from it off into the woods, in roughly the same general area that the gated driveway at the end of Lakeview Heights looks like it leads to, surely meeting somewhere in the middle.

The newest addition to the yard appears to be a school bus that's parked just thirty feet or so inside the entrance. Most of the school buses in here are newer than the city buses, but none look like they even remember what driving down a street feels like. This one does. Its tires aren't flat, and its paint isn't faded or peeling. It's the bed-wetter in a field of war vets. Even though it looks like it's been months, or maybe even a year, since it was left there, it still gives him pause to be too noisy. Therefore, he didn't think a weed eater would be the smartest choice for the alley between the buses. So he grew some balls and dragged some primitive tools over and got to work.

As the lead singer of Third Eye Blind wails about his semi-charmed kind of life, Cole continues down Ramshackle Row, bopping along with that catchy melody. "*Doot-doot-doot, doot-da-doo-doot*," he mumbles. The row on either side of him is comprised of half a dozen buses each. It looks as if there was an early attempt to be organized with these big antiques, but someone got lazy after two rows. His bus, the second in the row to his right (the one behind the one with the sign leaning against it), is the only bus in the row that's younger than 'Nam, and it's also the only school bus. He walks up to the door, puts the moaning Stephan Jenkins in his pocket, and enters his clubhouse. The door still slides ten or twelve inches on its frame so he's able to open it far enough to slip through (even with a backpack on) and then pull it almost completely shut once he's in. He walks up the steps and turns down the aisle, tipping an invisible cap to the invisible bus driver on the way by.

"It sure is a burner today, ain't it, sir?"

At first glance, the inside of Cole's bus looks pretty normal, aside from the vines crawling over the windows down the right side, constricting the view of the rest of the lot. But as you continue down the aisle, you'll notice that halfway down the right side, four consecutive seats are gone. He's unbolted them from their metal bases and laid them down on their backs and pushed them tightly against each other, forming a rectangular bed on the floor. The actual seat part of the seats stick up in the air around the bed, forming a little barrier, while the backrests make the mattress. He tosses his pack in the seat behind the bed and pulls off the blankets covering it. He walks to the front of the bus and flaps them out; the last thing he wants is a bunch of brown recluses to crawl out of his backpack and up his neck on the way home through the woods. He lays the blankets over the front seat so he doesn't forget them on the way out.

"Won't be needing those today," he says to the bus driver. He pictures a skeleton with a blue and black captain's hat on, skull turned sideways to face him. Right arm resting up on the seat behind him and the left one still holding the wheel. The pointed tips of bones that are his fingers doing that impatient, wavelike movement against the sunbaked steering wheel. *Clickity-clack, clickity-clack.*

Back at the bed, he pulls the two new blankets from his backpack and lays them over the seat mattress. He tries to switch them out every couple days, but that's a tough task when Mom isn't thrilled with this whole idea anyway. He doesn't want her to be able to add "rising electric bill" from the constant blanket-washing to the weighty list of reasons she doesn't like him coming over here.

Number one being that he's trespassing.

"I don't want whoever owns that junkyard to stumble up on you one day, tinkering with his stuff. Guys who own places like that are usually a couple fries short of a Happy Meal. I don't want him to think you're stealing from his stash and shoot you dead right there before you can explain yourself," she had said to him one day. It was the day after he cleared the grass alley in Ramshackle Row. He'd come in through the back door just as the sun was going down, and she was sitting alone at the table with an empty plate in front of her and her head resting on top of her clasped hands.

She knows she always thinks the worst—it's hard not to when your one kid is all you got, but she also knows boys will be boys and remembers back when she was his age, looking around invincibly at life through a sweet, smoky haze. So now she just warns him not to get into too much trouble while she's at work. She knows he won't. Never really has. It's just her job to say it. A formality.

He's a good kid. She got lucky.

His mom's got a point, though; whoever owns the yard seems to be a bit loony. The razor wire on top of an already-ten-foot fence, for example. Yeah, some of this stuff is very valuable, but if someone did somehow get over the fence, how the hell are they going to get back over with a school bus on their back?

This place would be the perfect setting for a horror flick, he thinks, like he has many times now as he reaches to the bottom of his backpack and pulls out the new King he plucked from the Cole Harper Library and drops it on the pallet in front of him. *Lunatic traps kid in bus yard.* He flops down next to it, with a hollow squeak of the old seat's springs. *How will I ever escape?*

Two seven-inch, battery-powered Honeywell fans drone endlessly at his side, pushing thick air toward him, tossing stray locks of hair back and forth in the breeze. It's hot, but not stifling in the bus. The seats in front of him and behind him combined with the side wall of the bus create a little box. So when the fans are set in the walkway, the air that blows toward him has nowhere to go. It dances off the walls of the enclosure, enveloping him in a cool tickle, keeping him comfortable. The vine wall on the outside of the bus covers a good portion of the windows on this side, blocking the sun's rays from penetrating his hangout. On the other side, he's hung old towels like makeshift drapes that cover two windows at a time, then skip one, cover two, and skip one all the way down. He could only manage to take one or two every couple days from the laundry room back at his house—any more than that, and his mom would've noticed. Zealous swirls of dust particles dance in the piercing shafts of light coming through the windows. There's just enough illumination inside to comfortably read a book by (which is how he spends most of his time in there), but enough darkness to procreate a feeling of hiding away. That invigorating sensation that no one on earth knows where he is when he's here, aside from his mother, but even she doesn't know the specifics. When he's here, he feels like an escaped prisoner, laying low while the hordes of authorities sweep through, knowing damn well they'll never find him. Or like a drifter, hiding safely away in a mountainside cave while an invasion of warmongering aliens exterminate civilization down below.

Zombies, his mind blurts, making the synonymous transition from an alien invasion. That's what it's like. Zombies. Like he's locked up tight in a hidden refuge while plagues of zombies dumbly stumble around outside. The Staceyism "sharp as a sack of wet mice" can be applied here. Although he wouldn't make it very long with the supplies he's got. He'd have to risk a trip home or maybe even venture to the grocery store (that's always the happenin' place in those zombie movies) to stock up on some essentials.

He's a couple chapters into his book when sleep envelops him. That's the thing about the hideout, it elicits sleep almost as vehemently as it elicits creativity. With the warm blankets swaddling him and the fans crooning at his side, he slips under. The novel droops in his hands and the dust particles continue their skein in the sun, but there's otherwise a thick stillness. From his cell on the corner of the bed, The Cranberries urge you to let it linger, then fade away, making room for Oasis to serenade their wonderwall with sad eyes and broken hearts.

Cole dreams about the bird. That wrong crow. It's lurching around the bus yard, looking for him. Later tonight when he's back in his room, safely reading under the bedside lamp on his nightstand, he'll reflect on the last time he saw it, that day he found the bus yard, perched on the corner of the fence in his backyard. He'll tell himself, not for the first time, that the bird had just picked a random spot to sit. It wasn't trying to lead him to the stream. That that had nothing to do with him finding it; he would've heard it anyway when he went to move the rocks. Even though he had pulled his headphones out to listen for the crow if it decided to return. He went back a couple days after that storm to finish mowing the high corner but couldn't hear the creek at all. He told himself that he would have found it sooner or later. But deep down, whether he knows it yet or not, he doesn't really believe any of that, does he?

He also tells himself—again, not for the first time—that what caught his eye that day in the woods while he was walking the creek bed back towards home was that sign itself, even if its color was badly faded, not something moving around it like he originally thought. At the time his mind conjured an imaginary Indian ducking behind a tree, and later it told him maybe it had been the big crow jumping around limbs.

And finally, after he clicks off his bedside lamp and rolls over to face the wall, with his room pitch-black and the house making creaks and groans, he'll tell himself that wrong crow is long gone, and it has been ever since the day he found the bus yard. That the thing wasn't creeping around the old buses, looking for him while he slept. But of course, he doesn't believe any of that either. Does he?

CHAPTER 9

IT'S NOW A WEEK INTO JUNE, AND HE'S FINALLY GROWN THE balls to go talk to his new neighbor. She moved in over two weeks now, and he's been watching her ever since.

Not watching, he thinks. *That sounds too . . . creepy.*

But he knows that's exactly what he's been doing. Watching her settle into that big empty house all by herself. Through the front window of his living room (not creepy at all, huh?) he's noticed her demeanor. Throughout the move-in process and now during the lonely strolls around her new home, that drawn, morose disposition consumes her. He can feel it all the way over here across the street. He usually sits with arms folded on the back of the couch and two fingers pulling apart a small section of the blinds in a reverse pinch, knees digging into the cold cushions. Sometimes he wishes she'd close the curtains more.

Not watching her, he says again. *Just noticing her.*

He's staring at himself in the bathroom mirror, thinking this. It's fogged up from his shower, but he's rubbed an area clear with a couple traversing swipes of his hand. His discarded clothes lay in a heap in the corner, covered in grass clippings. He's thought of a way to get closer to the new lady, and his yard must look pristine for it to work. He slowly looks himself up and down, inquisitively taking in every inch of his nude body. He sees what others do, but not to the same degree. He doesn't consider himself good-looking. Just an average guy. His gaze crawls over his well-built frame, covered by more-than-respectable muscles and olive-tinted skin pulled tightly over them.

"Ugh," he says to his reflection. "I need to find a gym."

He slides the towel off the hook on the back of the door (one of the good ones—Mom hasn't yet noticed her towel closet is looking a little sparse these days) and wraps it around his waist. He always sets the overlap to the front, safely covering the above-average bulge he's got down there, which he doesn't quite know the extent of yet, but he will. He turns for the door, catching a sideways glance of his reflection, wrinkling his nose at, in *his* mind, boyish pecs and shoulders. He plants his hands on the edge of the countertop and pumps out about twenty-five incline pushups. He stands up and flexes in the mirror, squeezing as hard as he can until the veins in his upper arms and chest begin to protrude and pulsate, until his face grows purple, trembling in a silent scream. He releases his tensed muscles and stands up straight. Little black dots dance through the air in front of him. He remains in a straight-faced standoff with this reflection for a few seconds, and then he bursts into laughter. He has to grab the countertop again, but this time to keep himself from collapsing into the floor.

"You're . . . a fucking . . . idiot!" he scolds himself between breaths.

"Cole?" his mom yells from the kitchen. "You just see yourself naked for the first time or something?"

It's Saturday. His mom is sitting on the couch now with a bag of pretzels in her lap. She worked the first few Saturdays at her new job when they moved here but hasn't since. She's already built up a larger and more dependable client base here than she ever had at her old place. Ladies like their hair. Cole stands in front of the printer in the corner. It's nestled up against an ancient-looking desktop computer, pushed back into a nook in the wall. The printer is sliding and slamming away, spitting out sheet after sheet.

"What in God's name are you printing?" Stacey asks.

"Just some fliers," he says, not turning away from the printer.

When he doesn't continue, she asks, "What kind of fliers?"

"I think I'm going to start mowing yards till school starts in a couple months. Earn some spending money. Maybe pitch in with the groceries."

At this, Cole's mom recoils away, flailing back against the couch in a panache, Juliet-esque acting job. Pretzels spill everywhere.

Cole tries to stifle a chuckle, but it punches out through his lips, only egging her on. She grabs her cell and jumps up, then runs over to him. She throws the back of her palm against his forehead and asks if he's feeling sick through a fit of crocodile tears. She holds up the phone with the other hand. Her thumb rests on the number pad as if ready to dial 911 at any moment.

Against all his might, Cole is laughing aloud now and pushing her away. "Get off me!" he pleads. "You're freaking nuts, lady!"

She turns and heads back to the couch with a big smile on her face, tossing the cell up and down in one hand, proud of her performance.

"I think that's great," she says, plopping back down and changing the channel. A couple stiff people are sitting around a desk and discussing what's going to happen to the surviving Boston Bomber during next month's trial. "Maybe it'll keep you away from that old junkyard for a while."

"It's a bus yard, Mom. We've talked about this before. It's perfectly safe."

"I just don't like the fact that it's someone else's property.

And I wouldn't be able to get a hold of you if I needed to."

"I can get service there, Mom, if I absolutely *had* to call. It's just the internet that you can't rely on," he says, knowing deep down that that's usually not the case.

"All right," she says, taking the loss and turning back to watch CNN.

He grabs the fliers and heads for the door, pausing for a quick glance at his reflection in a picture on the wall. He flicks his hair this way and that, shooting for a "perfectly messy" look. Not hard for him, remember.

"Cole?" his mom says as she picks an errant pretzel off the sofa cushion and eats it. Her eyes remain locked on the TV.

He pauses in the doorway.

"Don't give one to that man behind the big gate."

Cole waits for more. She chews and stares at Wolf Blitzer.

"I bet he's mean," she finally says.

He hesitates for a moment, staring at the side of her head, then walks out into the heat and shuts the door behind him.

He shuffles across the cracked blacktop with all the professionalism and confidence of a wildebeest wading across a muddy African river. He's got the twenty-some-odd fliers in one hand at his side, holding them like you would a textbook. He feels exposed all of a sudden. Someone is watching him. He can feel it. It's like someone reflecting sunlight into your eye, glinting it off some sort of metallic surface. But you can't find it. Can't see where or what it's coming from. He feels those eyes of something knowledgeable tracking his progress all the way across the street and up to her door. Probably not unlike the wildebeest feels. He knows there are things watching in the water around him. He hopes to God it's not *her*, watching him nervously scamper over here like a little fucking kid.

He climbs the stairs and, at her doorstep, composes himself. He takes a deep breath and presses the doorbell. Half of him pleads to God she's not home. Then he can tell himself he tried and can go back to watching her through the living room blinds. The other half begs that she's here. She is gorgeous, even with that somber aura, and every inch of him wants to meet her. To hear what she sounds like. How she talks. What she's wearing today. What, maybe, she's not.

The door opens about a foot. She peeks one eye around the corner of it.

"Hello," she says. She looks down at the paper in his hand and opens the door all the way. That "new house" smell wafts out onto the porch, surrounding him. Fresh paint and hardwood.

"Hi," Cole manages. That's all he manages.

"Can I help you with something?" A genuine question accompanied by an inadvertent bat of eyelashes.

He's in love. He's gee whillikers, Jesus H. Christ on a bike head over heels. Someday he'll tell their kids that's all it took. This girl who's probably ten years older than him and, judging by the red puffiness around her eyes, is dragging around at least a couple sackfuls of baggage. But none at that matters to him.

After an eternity of only blinking, he finally begins to explain why he's here.

"Uh. Yes. Sorry to bother you. Uh . . . I'm new to the street. I live right there." He turns and points at his house. "I just, you know, wanted to start mowing yards until school starts. It'll give me something to do."

She only bats her eyes and looks down at the printouts in his hand.

"Oh, yeah, here you go." He takes an embarrassing amount of time separating the top sheet from the rest of the stack. But he manages and then reaches it out to her. The paper jitters in his hand, almost undetectably. But not quite.

She takes it from him and begins looking over it.

He uses this opportunity to scan her up and down. It's very hot outside already—he can feel the back of his neck beginning to bicker—but she's wearing sweatpants. Either they once belonged to a very large man or she made them out of a gray theater curtain. They're balled up around her bare feet, and there's a very not-sexy sag in the crotch. Good news is she's got a tank top on. It's ridden up a bit, hugging her tiny waist at the belly button.

He becomes aware of a silence, an awaiting of a response.

"Huh?" he says to her, eyes blinking out of a daydream.

"I said"—she points out the rest of the papers in his hands—"why'd you print off so many?"

"Uh …" He looks down at them as if the answer is written there along with the horrendously half-hearted business name of Cole's Cuts with his name, cell number, and—

What the hell was I thinking?

—a description of his *equipment*. His equipment? His wonky mower and sputtering weed eater? All of a sudden this feels like an incredibly childish and stupid idea. "I dunno," he says. "In case I get that many yards?"

She smiles at him, and his heart practically shits itself, lurching in his chest and causing a rapid loss of breath.

"How are you going to get your"—she holds up the paper, snaps it still, and finds what she's looking for—"twenty-one-inch Troy-Bilt lawn mower with high-powered Briggs & Stratton motor around to all these yards?" He had not foreseen this. He couldn't have. She leans out and looks down the street, at the only two other homes, then at the Cherokee parked in his driveway. "You going to haul it around in the Jeep?"

She's onto him. She knew from the get that all but one flier was a waste of paper. She can see right through his stupid plan to come talk to her. To come *gawk* at her. Just another creepy neighborhood boy, one of probably a trillion she's dealt with in her time on earth. How could he have been so stupid?

He could be balls-deep in a garbage disposal right now and he wouldn't so much as blink. Should he just run now? Punch himself in the sack and sprint back to his house where he sure as shit won't ever leave his room again? He'll go get that old bucket out back and put it in the corner of his room, by his bookcase. He'll piss and deuce in that. Or maybe he'll get lucky and get cartoon-crushed by a car on the way back across the street so he won't have to squat over a bucket for the rest of his life.

"Cole," she says, snapping him out of it. She begins laughing. It's a heartfelt, melodious sound. "I'm joking with you!"

He can only stare.

Throughout a person's life, there are a handful of precious moments, unforgiving forks in the road of time, that can drastically change who, or what, you turn out to be. For Cole's life, this is one of those moments.

"Come inside," she says. "I haven't had any company in a very long time. I'm Ellie." His wooden legs turn to Jell-O, and he stumbles in behind her.

CHAPTER 10

She stands at the kitchen counter, stirring sugar into a plastic jug with a wooden spoon. It's making a *kerplunk, kerplunk* sound as it goes 'round and 'round. With her facing away from him, he can see two small dimples on her lower back. They've already finished a glass each, and she's gone to make some more. Her tight tank top is still ridden up around her waist. He is certain it's not that way on purpose. He tries to be respectful and stare a little higher as if she were facing him, but that's easier said than done. His seventeen-year-old mind is similar to that of an old, senile man's. Not caring at all who knows the shenanigans it's up to, who knows its thoughts. Funny how men do that, regress back to their teenage years later in life. On the timeline of a man's life, you could plot the "horniness" line as a giant capital "U."

He's sitting in a stool at the bar that divides the kitchen and the living room. The ceiling fan behind him *whop-whop-whops* through the air. He's taken inventory since he's been here and has come to the conclusion that the digs are sick. Far too big for just one girl.

They've gotten all the small talk out of the way. Mostly her asking him about himself and his family. She pulls the spoon out, licks it, and tosses it in the sink. It clatters against a small mountain of dirty dishes. Then she comes over and refills his glass first, then hers.

"Need more ice?" she asks.

Every time she looks at him, he feels his knees weaken, the

tendons and ligaments in there thrumming like guitar strings. He's glad he's sitting.

"No thank you," he replies politely.

She takes a long drink of her tea, crinkling her face at the coldness running down her throat.

"So, tell me about you. What have you been up to?" he asks. He suddenly realizes she hasn't even mentioned yet whether or not he could mow her yard. Planned or not, he still wants to.

She sets down her glass. It clinks heavily on the slab of granite.

"Where do I begin?" she almost whispers. She's looking down at her drink, staring into its deep brown contents. Whatever life had returned to her since his arrival is gone again in an instant, shoved back behind a thick brick wall of protection.

Shouldn't have said that, he thinks regretfully.

She takes another long drink and begins talking, like a windup doll with a short cord that's been twisted as far as it can go.

"I lost my husband last year. That's why I'm an emotional wreck, as I'm sure you've noticed."

He shakes his head slowly. "Swear I haven't," his mind says. "Scout's honor." But he doesn't say a word.

"Well, I have been. And I know I haven't been the best neighbor. I'm sure your mom and the family next to me are a bit taken aback by my . . . standoffishness." She takes another sip. "I know I should be over it. It's been a year. That's a long time. But I swear to you, it still feels like yesterday I got that call from Dad. Barry, my husband, worked for my dad. Building houses and office buildings and things. He really enjoyed it." She looks up at him. "He fell off a roof."

Cole winces slightly at this last bit. "Jesus," he says. "I'm really sorry."

"It's okay, really. I feel like I've gotten a little better since moving here. My dad practically dragged me over. He said I'd end up going off the deep end if I stayed in that house much longer. He built that house for us, Dad did. It was still pretty new when . . . it happened. But he's right, I probably would've lost what's left of my marbles. Staring at pictures of him and sleeping with his sweaters. I gave all his clothes away before the move."

Cole glances down at her sweatpants.

She follows his gaze and lets out a quick giggle. "Oh. These?" she says, pulling at the pockets to show him just how big on her they were. "These have actually always been mine. He used to try to take them from *me*." She notices her midriff showing and pulls her shirt down to the top of the sweats.

Cole acts like he doesn't notice.

"Then he built *this* house for me. I'm sure you saw him stomping around over here a few times."

He puts two and two together. All of a sudden, he realizes that that asshole of a boss he'd seen was her dad. The guy who lives behind that big, menacing gate. The one who wants his daughter close. And, therefore, is almost certainly the owner of the bus yard. He feels the blood run out of his face. *Mom was right*, he thinks.

Ellie notices. "What's the matter?"

"Nothing," he says, taking a swig of sweet tea. "Seems like a nice guy."

She tilts her face down, giving him a "don't bullshit me" smirk.

"What?" he says guiltily. "I've only seen him a couple

times. I just didn't know he was the one who lived back in the woods over there."

"Yeah …" she begins. "He's a bit of a hermit. If he's not on a jobsite somewhere, yelling at all the workers, which is becoming less and less frequent I think, getting a little long in the tooth, he's probably at home. Just sitting there enjoying his alone time."

Cole looks at her questioningly.

She answers his unspoken question. "Probably surprised he's not over for dinner every night given how I'm sure he was acting during the building of this house. We are very close. Closer than a father and daughter can be. He just doesn't feel like he needs to be all up in my business. He calls and checks on me every now and then. Sees how I'm doing. Then that's it. He'll leave me alone. Allow me to finish mourning, I guess. As long as I do it here, in a house right next to his, instead of over at the old place, where he couldn't keep an eye on me."

He remembers the clean truck, the boss's truck, parked out front of her house many consecutive nights before she moved in. Sometimes not leaving till the morning.

"Oh," he says. "No, that makes sense." He notices she hasn't yet said a word about her mother, and he's not going to make the same mistake twice by asking her more than she wants to tell.

"Yeah. Well, he's not actually my real father. My mom married him about twelve years ago."

There it is, he thinks. But she doesn't continue, so he seamlessly transitions to another topic. The reason he's here in the first place.

"So, uhh …" he continues, a smile creeping across his face. "About your yard …"

In a brilliant flash, that warmth emanates from her again. She laughs wholeheartedly. "I'm so sorry. I've talked your ear off." She reaches up and touches his hand. He melts inside. "Too much information," she says, still laughing. "Yes, you can mow my yard. Of course! I'll just tell Dad to tell his guy that he doesn't need to do it anymore."

Cole squints, thinking. He's noticed that it's been mowed once, maybe twice, since she moved in but just assumed it was her who was doing it. He hasn't seen anyone else over here.

"It's just one of his workers. I'm sure he hates doing it anyway," she assures him. "He's always got a big, ugly scowl on his face. Probably hates me for being the boss's daughter."

"Oh, gotcha," he says. "Well, awesome, thank you. Just let me know when you need me to do it. My cell's on there." He points to the printout he handed her earlier. It's now lying on the countertop, next to the fridge.

"I know and I will," she says. "But I'm going to pay you much better than twenty-five dollars." (Which was also on the flier.)

He opens his mouth to protest, but she cuts him off. "Ah-ah-ah!" she says, like a mother would say to her baby reaching for the hot stove. "Don't even think about it. I don't work, but that doesn't mean I'm not doing just fine." Because Nolan insists she doesn't. *Stay at home and work on you first*, he says. But she leaves this part out.

When they reach the front door, he turns and thanks her. For the tea, for the job.

"Nonsense." She waves her hand at him. "Thank *you*. It felt good to actually talk to another person instead of myself." She wrinkles her nose at him and giggles. She's had that warmth ever since he saved the conversation by bringing it back to the task at hand, her yard. But during that stretch of her telling him about her dead husband and her father, he saw a coldness that he won't forget.

He smiles back and heads down the steps of her front porch.

"Cole." He turns back with zeal, like she's going to ask him to come back inside or if she can call him later. "You forgot your big ole stack of papers," she continues, rubbing it in. "Don't you need them to give to all the other people you're going to ask?"

"Okay, you're just being mean now," he says, smiling too.

"All the lonely ladies?" she mocks gently.

"I get it! I get it! You caught me, okay? Sniffed my plan a mile away!"

She's giggling hard now. Her hand is up against the door-frame, and she leans to the side, hips cocked. Her firm breasts slightly bounce as she laughs. The bottom of her tank has ridden back up, once again showing her toned stomach and cute belly button. Does she know? Surely she feels it, right? Is she actually leaving it like it is this time? Leaving it for him?

You think you're that special, kiddo?

"I'll just keep them," she says. "Pass them out to all my friends."

For a few seconds, he can only stand there and stare and smile. It's a chore to pull his gaze away from her, but somehow he manages. He gives a little wave that he's never done in his life and continues down the steps and across the front yard. He doesn't hear the door behind him click shut until he's almost all the way to the road. The smile that was already painted on his face stretches further, reaching for his ears.

Was she watching me go?

He's so fucking high on life he completely forgets about

the black family's house. But from it, out of the window in the back corner, someone watches him stroll down across the street, back toward his house. Cole's got his eyes closed and head tilted slightly up. Obviously, about to explode with excitement, but he's trying to stay cool and calm till he gets home. If Cole's eyes were open, he could've easily seen the blinds move in the window at the back of the house to his left. But they weren't.

The figure behind the blinds studies that euphoric look on his face, then glances over at the bedside clock, deducing the amount of time he spent in her house.

"No way. No fucking *way.*"

CHAPTER 11

JORDY'S GOT THE SNIFFLES. A COLD IN JUNE. BUT YOU CAN JUST take the idea of him calling in sick, ball it up, hawk a loogie on it, and chuck it out the window. So, he's here, with a splitting headache and churning stomach, that sweaty cold sensation. He winces at the squeal of a nearby saw blade through wood. He looks haggard, borderline homeless. He's worn the same jeans and T-shirt combo to work for three days now, each displaying stains on top of stains. The ring of sweat around the neck hole of his shirt puts off a pungent, sour fragrance. It matriculates up into his snotty nostrils and makes him very aware of the partially digested donuts in his gut. You know it's bad when your own smell is making your stomach do somersaults. Curds of donut pieces litter the patchy stubble around his mouth, and dark circles surround his beady little eyes from sleep deprivation.

About every other night now, Cam screams straight through. He and Sandy take turns sitting up with him, changing out cool towels for his forehead and rearranging fans to blow on different parts of his body. Sandy's been begging for more hours at Moneymakers, and as of this week, she's been getting them. Probably having to suck off the old manager, but who the fuck cares? Not Jordy. She's also been wearing a "bombshell bra" that one of her little community college co-ed coworkers gave her out of pity. It takes an act of God to get those puppies up around her chin. But hey, she's been bringing home pretty good tips lately. Usually a pocket full of fives and tens, but even with the bra, still more ones than twenties. That's an inherited problem though, see, nothing a low-cut shirt or half-inch-thick mask of makeup can fix. Only pretty girls get twenties, and even at a sleazy, smoke-choked joint like Moneymakers, she's still not one of the pretty girls.

He and Gary Doogan are putting up framing for a large bathroom, big enough for four shitters and five pissers. After almost a week off, everyone looks well rested and fresh. Everyone except for Jordy. Even some of the Mexicans are bopping around, smiling and whistling their country's catchy tunes. Jordy's phone begins buzzing in his pocket. He drops the box of screws in his hands and fishes out his cell. Could be about the kid.

He's dead, his mind tells him.

But it's not about the kid. It's not Sandy. It's Donovan.

"Shit," he says to no one, but Gary hears him and looks up. Jordy meets his gaze. "It's the boss. Wanna answer for me? Tell him I fell off the roof too?" Gary chuckles and shakes his head, returning to his work. "I'll tell you what though, man, every day that sounds a little less bad." Gary continues his measuring and marking, hearing him but pretending he's not. The phone continues to vibrate impatiently in Jordy's hand. Finally, just before the boss man reaches voicemail, Jordy answers.

"Yes, boss?" Just the slightest bit of petulance in his voice. Did Donovan notice? Probably. Did Jordy give two shits? No.

He goes quiet for a moment, listening to whatever the boss has to say. Gary glances up at him out of the corner of his eye. Trying to read Jordy's facial expressions. But Jordy remains completely void of any emotion. He stands there with the phone pressed to his ear, motionless. Like he's just a big plastic toy that no one's cared enough about to change the batteries to.

Finally, the phone slides away from Jordy's ear. He ends

the call without ever saying anything else.

Not good, Gary thinks. Once again pretending not to eavesdrop. *That's not good at all.*

Gary has his back to Jordy on purpose, and his eyes squeezed shut, silently awaiting the inevitable explosion to come.

He's fired him. That's the first thing Gary thinks. *He's fired him, and he ain't gonna have any money to take care of that kid.* Why else would he be taking this long to say anything? Gary knows Jordy's been running on fumes lately, in every sense of the word, but especially physically and monetarily. He feels bad for the guy, he really does. Even though Jordy sure is a leaky asshole most of the time and probably even dumber than Gary himself, he thinks, which is quite the accomplishment, he does have sympathy for the guy. Mostly because the only thing in this world he seems to care about is that kid, and now he's not even going to be able to afford the doctors' visits or the scripts.

Gary slowly opens his eyes. About thirty seconds of silence have passed. Did he walk away? He turns languidly to see if Jordy is still standing behind him, but before he can get all the way around, something explodes on the particleboard floor next to him. It's Jordy's phone. And now it's in a hundred sharp beeping and booping pieces, scattered in a fan around the floor that will someday be covered in a thin, filmy layer of white-collar piss.

Not good.

"That fucking cock-sucking motherfucking bastard." An absurd sentence to utter a couple ticks up from a whisper.

Gary stands up and turns to face him. Proceeding with caution. "He send ya packing?"

"What? No, he didn't fire me," he said. "You know how he

said I could mow his bitch daughter's yard on the weekends to earn a couple extra bucks?"

"Ayuh," Gary replies.

"Well, he took it back. Said he don't need me no more. Said he don't like me that close to his *things*." Jordy spits a laser of dip between two upright two-by-fours on the bathroom's wall frame. "He was laughin', but I sure as shit don't find it too funny. The extra fifty a week was goin' a long way."

A couple minutes later, Gary's relieved to see that the little phone outburst seemed to let off some steam. Jordy's voice wasn't raised at all, and suddenly he doesn't seem too terribly upset. On the outside, at least.

They continue to work for about an hour before Gary finally grabs a broom and sweeps up the pieces of the cell phone. Jordy seems to have forgotten that he had even done it.

As the day goes on, Gary begins to notice a look in Jordy's eyes. He's calmly working, keeping quiet. Hammering, screwing, measuring, and cutting, slaving away for the man with a hint of a grin on his haggard face. Gary doesn't much care for that look. It's the look of a man who's reached that far-and-away realization, like a black cloud gliding avariciously through rarefied air, toward that unfathomable place by any *sane* person's standards, the land of Nothing to Lose.

CHAPTER 12

COLE IS SO ENCHANTED BY THE ENCOUNTER THAT HE completely forgets about stopping by the neighbor's house as well. Yes, he's only mowing yards to get closer to Ellie, and yes, she had sniffed out his plan, but he'd still felt sorry for the lady next to Ellie's having to mow her yard. He's seen her a few times now, out there trudging behind a mower even shittier than his. She doesn't appear to have much help. He's seen a little girl a few times. Mostly just catching glimpses of pink shirts and bopping braids during the sprint inside upon arrival from the store or the mall or wherever. A handful of times, he's seen her playing in the yard. They've got a basketball hoop at the edge of the driveway, but she doesn't seem very interested in that. Cole muses she's more of the Barbies and makeup type of girl. Around ten or eleven, maybe. And being as it looks like they're the only two, the momma most certainly has sole responsibility of all yard work.

He doesn't even try to kid himself that had it not gone so well at Ellie's, he'd still be on his way over to the other house right now. But it had, and here he is. Walking with a little pep in his step. His hands are empty this time, no fliers to hand over. But that's all right. He got the house he wanted. This one's just icing on the cake. A polite formality. He once again crosses the cracked blacktop. It's so hot there's a thin layer of air swirling just above it in a barely visible boiling soup. He strides through the ankle-deep mirage listlessly. He's aware of the smile on his face. It's been permanent ever since he left Ellie's, making it through the hour or so between then and now, while he wandered through his house like a kid in a dream. He's never had sex, just a handful of doubles and the occasional triple in his young career, but when he does, this dopey, blissful look he's wearing is probably pretty similar to the one he'll don after that always memorable, often awkward first time.

As he nears the single-story ranch house, he allows himself to fantasize that magical first time being with Ellie. He sees it like a soap opera. Him finishing her yard, killing the motor, and making his way up to her door. It's a saunter. A walk so full of confidence it bleeds through his clothes and leaves a trail in the grass behind him. Sweat dripping down his shirtless chest and stomach. She answers, gives him the once-over, and yanks him inside, slamming the door behind them.

He's acting like the chubby bookworm that jizzes his cargo shorts when the bouncy cheerleader drops her pencil in front of him in biology class. But he doesn't care; this is what seventeen-year-old boys are supposed to think about, right?

He cuts across the front yard. Had he not been lost in his own fantasy sexcapades, he might've noticed the *Catwoman* comic book pitched over a couple naked Barbies like a slick paper tent in the middle of the yard. With its early '90s version of Catwoman, purple suit practically painted on, sizing up a giant, hairless monster with foot-long claws. He'd have noticed that it's hardly a prissy little teenybopper's plaything.

He reaches the door and knocks without hesitation. He sees a curly-haired doofus grinning back at him in the glass storm door. He runs a hand through his mane and gives a half-assed attempt to wipe that stupid I-got-my-dick-wet-for-the-first-time-today look off his face. He fails.

Screw it, he thinks. Then profoundly declaims, *I'm in love and I want the world to know!*

In his head.

A woman answers the door. It's Saturday, so he assumed the mother would. Plus, he had the four-thousand-pound clue of the midnight blue Explorer parked under the lonely basketball hoop in the driveway.

"Hello," she says, flashing a beautiful white smile. She's got a screaming-orange University of Tennessee football shirt on and stonewashed jeans.

"Hello, ma'am," Cole says politely. "I live across the street."

She nods, still smiling.

"And I was just wondering if you'd be interested in me mowing your yard for the rest of the summer. Maybe into the fall, but I'm not sure on that yet." He sees her mind working, beginning the formation of a polite "no" in her head. "Just trying to make a little extra spending money," he says.

Why didn't you just let her say no thank you and send you on your way, dummy? He doesn't have an answer for that.

She looks him over again, then across the street at his meticulously manicured lawn.

Damn, he thought, seeing her do this. *Ellie didn't even care.* He smiles back.

She looks back at him, her smile beating his in both width and whiteness. "Of course, sweetie," she finally says. "That would help me out a whole bunch."

"I thought it might," he says.

"My husband drives a truck for Mohawk. He's gone for a month or so at a time usually. But right now, he's been away since probably before you moved in, month and a half or so, I guess. I still haven't gotten used to doing all the man jobs." She laughs and shakes her head, showing the strain of wearing all those hats. It's written on her face in new lines, noticeable to even a stranger. They're shallow, spreading from corners and folds, working at going deeper each day within an unrelenting march.

"Well, good, so this will help you out quite a bit then," he says redundantly, not knowing what else to say.

A little girl, the one he's seen a few times in the yard, joins her mother at the front door.

"Who are youuu?" she says, twisting around in shyness and giving him a flirty little girl's sneer.

"I'm Kris, by the way," the mother says. "And this little angel is Brianna." She reaches down and brushes a beaded braid out of Brianna's face.

She sticks her tongue out at Cole and skips away, singing something unintelligible.

"She's our little performer," Kris says, rolling her eyes. "I can't get her to stop singing that new Taylor Swift song. Makes me want to break the radio."

"I know what you mean," Cole says. "That's what most of today's music makes me want to do."

"I KNEW YOU WERE IN TROUBLE WHEN YOU WALKED INNN!" she shouts from the kitchen.

They both cringe at the front door and then begin laughing.

"She doesn't even know the words," Kris says. "It's funny . . . sometimes."

Before Cole can reply, he's startled by a male voice that comes booming out of the hallway to the right.

"Shut up, Bree!" Then, "Jeeesus."

A kid about Cole's age lurches out of the hallway and into the living room. He turns away from the door immediately, not seeing Cole or his mother, and proceeds into the kitchen. Brianna is munching on some Doritos. One hand plunges deep into the red bag and pulls out a wad of artificially flavored triangular chips and jams the whole shebang into her mouth, momentarily stifling her best T-Swift impersonation.

"Can't you just go play outside or something? I'm trying to read back there." He opens the fridge and pulls out a can of Dr Pepper, taps the tab, and pops it open with a mouthwatering, frothy *kuh-shhhh*.

Brianna giggles through a mouthful of empty carbs and points an orange finger at the front door. "Don't be hateful in front of our guest!" she manages.

The boy turns and sees Cole and his mother. Cole senses Kris stiffen in front of him. She's looking back toward her son, trying to use that mother-child telepathy. "Sorry!" She's trying to transmit through the air, wordlessly. "I didn't know you were coming out!"

The boy takes a swig of the soda and walks over to meet them at the door.

He's smiling, so that's good, Cole thinks.

He stands next to his mother and puts an arm around her shoulders. Cole thinks it's more than a buddy-buddy gesture. He thinks it's got more to do with what the dude's dragging around than anything. He's got a prosthetic leg protruding from the bottom of his shorts. He's seen people with fake limbs before, and he's usually good at not staring, making them feel normal, like it's no big deal. It's 2013, nowadays people come home in pieces from a trip to the fucking movie theater as often as they do from some sandy country on the other side of this shitty planet. But the unexpectedness of it all is what breaks his gaze. He wasn't expecting anyone here but the mother and her daughter. And he sure wasn't expecting that unexpected person to be rocking a prosthetic leg.

"I know," the kid says when Cole returns his gaze to his face. He pauses for dramatics. "I'm black." He opens his eyes wide, making an over-done spooky face. "Crazy, right?"

They all laugh a little, and that's good.

Even Bree is cackling in the kitchen through her full mouth.

"I'm sorry, man," Cole says, still smiling. "I just thought it was only your mom and sister here. Just wanted to see if I can start mowing your yard."

"It's all good, man. Not every day you see a kid with a peg leg. I understand."

His mother had stepped back a little. She's watching them talk, her eyes bright, and they shoot back and forth like she's taking in a tennis match from the sideline. She wishes Glenn could see this.

"I'm Cole." He reaches out a hand.

"And I am Gerome. I've seen you out there. Poking around." When he sees Cole's smile fade and cheeks begin to redden a bit with a touch of embarrassment, he quickly adds, "When you are in the situation I'm in, you tend to become more of a watcher than a doer."

"I hear ya," Cole replies. "I'm sure it's tough."

Gerome turns and looks at his mom. "But it didn't have to be, did it, Mom?"

She looks at him questioningly, bracing for whatever joke he's about to deliver next. She's silent, ready to roll her eyes.

He looks back at Cole and continues, "I told the doc I've had three legs my whole life—chopping one off would just make me normal. But he didn't want to hear it. Just wrapped it around my good leg and slapped on this thing on the other side."

He knocks on his thigh. It sounds like he's knocking on a wooden table through tablecloth.

There it is, Kris thinks. The teenage comedian delivers the all-important penis joke. She slaps his shoulder, and he recoils away from her, laughing.

"What?" he pleads. "It's true!"

They all join in laughter again. And again, even little Brianna giggles away in the kitchen, swinging the bag of chips around in big loopty-loops, learning a lesson in centrifugal force. She hadn't understood the joke, but she laughs along anyway. She hasn't seen Gerome like this in a long time. She pesters the living shit out of him, knocking on his bedroom door and asking little-sister questions such as, "Where does water come from?" or "Who would win in a fight, Katy Perry or Hannah Montana?" or even sneaking in his room and stealing some of his comic books while he's in the bathroom and using them as Barbie houses in the yard. But she loves him just the same, so she laughs along.

Because even she knows that laughing is good.

CHAPTER 13

A HANDFUL OF DAYS HAVE PASSED SINCE THAT MEETING AT THE door, and the boys have hung out nearly every one of them. Gerome's mother is elated. She hasn't seen that joyous sheen on her son's face in a very long time. Maybe even since before the red van took his leg. He's always been in good spirits, always wore a big smile and rattled off from an arsenal of jokes, but they've been empty down deep. Like a thick bone that looks sturdy, but at its core lies nothing more than a hollow shaft of spongy, rotten marrow. It's been hard being the wife of a long-haul trucker and the mother of an introverted, handicapped teenager. Not to mention a bona fide, made-for-the-stage diva. In a strange way, Bree keeps her sane, keeps her present. Like a writer who involuntarily lives life in another world; using the suds to keep things real, to feel something, she can always count on Bree to liven up her otherwise mundane existence with some sort of song or dance or elaborate story. Always a performance. Life is a movie to that little girl, and she snagged the lead role.

Kris returns the bread to the cupboard and carries two plates to the bedroom at the end of the hall. She's also got two glasses of lemonade. The disappearing cubes of ice tinkle against each other with each step. She glances at some of the pictures lining the hallway on the way. There's one of all four of them: herself, Glenn, Brianna, and Gerome at the University of Tennessee football game eight or nine years ago. Back when the Vols were actually worth the price of admission. Bree was just a baby then. She wore an adorable orange jumpsuit that

Kris found at Walmart for three dollars. Being that Bree had been nothing more than a tear-filled ball of cheeks and rolls, she looks like a prized pumpkin in Glenn's hands. Gerome was holding on to Kris's arm, needing help to stay upright while standing still. He had quickly learned how to walk with the original prosthetic, loping around with an ever-improving limp, though he had been tired in the picture. UT's campus is all hills and valleys. She remembers when he came into her room late one night, about a year after the accident. She had scolded herself after her half-asleep brain conjured up an image of a drooling monster clanking up the hall toward her. But it had only been her son. Her little boy standing in the open doorway with nothing on but cloud-white briefs and a plastic leg.

"I don't want to go to the therapist anymore, Mom," he had said. "I can walk fine. I don't need them." Truth was he *could* walk fine, all things considered. And the next day, she had called them. Told them thank you for everything.

Every few years, they've given him a new leg, each slightly more sophisticated than the last. But with each leg, she's seen a little more light fade from his eyes. A little less fight in his heart. Moms can see those things. She wishes she couldn't—it kills her. Life dealt him an incredibly shitty hand, and early after the accident, he'd been hell-bent on bluffing his ass off. Bluffing till everyone else folded. But with every new leg, it was like another player sat down at his table, lessening his chances even further. Eventually it stopped becoming something he could show strength toward and overcome. He stopped receiving cards from teachers and parents of classmates. He stopped receiving pity. And little by little, that fire dwindled.

Until the other day when Cole knocked on the door.

"Ta-daaa," she says as she lays down the sandwiches and

lemonades on the floor in front of them. They are transfixed, thumbs moving in clackety blurs as zombies chase their characters through an old theater on the television in front of them.

"Thanks, Mom," Gerome says peevishly.

"Thanks, Mrs. Conley," Cole says, turning and flashing a quick smile toward her before setting eyes back on the growing horde. He's just mowed their yard for the first time and politely left his grass-riddled sneakers on the front porch, but she noticed his socks aren't much better. A fresh sprinkle of her yard flutters to the carpet with every nervous twitch. She reminds herself to go check and make sure he used the weed eater around the mailbox before it gets dark outside.

Probably did, she thinks. *He's a good kid.*

Cole had already been at their house when she got home from work at five, and he'd probably been there all day. No way to know, though—getting words out of their mouths while they played that game was about as easy as getting a straight answer out of a politician. But she doesn't mind a bit. Her son is happy. *Truly* happy. For the first time in too long. Cole could move in for all she cares. Bree can sleep on the couch.

She stands there in the doorway of Gerome's room with her arms folded and a dazed, motherly smile on her face, watching the two boys play. She thinks she could stand here forever. Then a zombie's head explodes in a green, soupy spray, and Gerome gives a high five to Cole and says something about blasting the crawlers to hell. She takes that as her cue and walks out.

Later that night, they're still going strong. They've been playing practically since Cole finished the yard that morning. Cole had sent a text to his mother around 10:30 saying he was going over to Gerome's, and that if she needed him, to try his cell. He'd been in Gerome's room before but never for this long.

Usually they hang out at Cole's place. Gerome loves what he calls "the tower of terror" in Cole's room, often sitting splayed in front of the bookcase and running a finger slowly over the spines like he's missing eyes instead of a leg, and the titles are in braille, calling out the name of some of them with excitement as if Cole doesn't know what he's got in there. Like Cole, Gerome loves Stephen King. But unlike Cole, his affinity for imagined worlds and characters spans far beyond that. You see, where Cole finds solace in his novels, Gerome enjoys inclusion in his comics and video games. He's got a small shelf in one corner that's designated for the novels he's picked up here and there along the way, seemingly the typical amount of good literature every intelligent kid possesses, but his room is dominated by comic books and gaming posters. He's the new-age smart guy. Whereas Cole, even being a year younger than Gerome, is more of an old-school, give-me-a-book-and-my-peace-and-quiet kind of kid. But he enjoys this stuff just the same. The louder, more colorful version of nerdiness. A walk on the wild side with a dude with a limp. He enjoys being with Gerome. Cole's mom sometimes says they're like "peas and carrots," those two, jutting her jaw and furrowing her brow to display her best Forrest Gump face. It's not even close, but it makes them laugh.

It's full dark. Gerome is sitting on his bed flipping through a mint condition 1986 *Daredevil* comic with a smile on his face like he doesn't know the words verbatim. He could probably recite the entire story for you upon request. Cole sits on the flimsy futon that's been dragged about an arm's length away from the old-style, boxy flat-screen, a necessary proximity for optimal gaming experience. A ghoulish melody oozes from the game's pause screen on an endless loop. They're giving *Zombies* a rest. Once you get up around level thirty, each round can last as long as twenty minutes. After a while, your eyes begin pleading for a break, almost clawing at the inside of your eyelids, like a vampire trying his damnedest to pull the shade down on a sunny day. Cole lies on his back, taking in the various posters on the ceiling with genuine interest. Bane is directly overhead—well, Tom Hardy is, peering over that telltale mask with malicious intent.

"I like that one," Cole says.

"What's that?"

"*The Dark Knight Rises.*"

"Oh, yeah," Gerome says. "Instant classic."

"Bane's a badass, man," Cole concludes.

"That he is, Master Wayne." He pronounces this "Mas-tah Wayne," as Michael Caine does. "That he is."

A gentle silence falls over the boys like a misty summer morning, and Cole continues to scan the contents of his new friend's room, more like his new friend's *lair*, and Gerome keeps flipping through stiff comics. Seconds twist into minutes, and minutes pile upward toward an hour before Cole breaks it again. They're tired, though neither will admit it. Those are dangerous words to proclaim at a teenage boys' sleepover.

"So, what brought you here?" Cole asks. Gerome has told him very little about his past and certainly hasn't told Cole how he lost his leg. But Cole assumes that's because he hasn't asked. Gerome seems like the type of guy who would tell you just about anything you'd want to know, if you'd just ask, but maybe also the type not to delve into anything personal without an initial volley from the other side.

Cole hopes this can be that conversation.

Gerome tosses the current comic in his hand back to its forever home beside the bed, landing on top of the pile with a fluttery *fwap*. He calls this pile the "Birthday Fucks." They look good but aren't worth much. He only picks them up when he's bored or lonely.

"Well, when a mommy and daddy love each other very, very much …" he begins, talking slowly and in a painfully demeaning tone.

"Shut up," Cole says. "You know what I mean, you bastard."

"Yeah, I know, man, I know." He paused for a chuckle. "Mom's job."

He sits up in bed and swings both legs over the edge. Cole in his comfy position on the futon, with his hands folded behind his head and his socked feet buried deep in the warm crevice between the armrest and the cushion on the opposite side. Flakes of dried grass cling to the fibers of the faux suede down there around his feet, but Gerome said not to worry about it. "That old thing's fucking gross. Wipe your white ass with it if you want to, man," were his exact words. Cole pretends he doesn't feel strange things down in that crevice, but he does. Feels like a few pizza crusts. Maybe a couple moldy candy bars. But the hungry crevice is so warm. He keeps his feet in there.

"You know she works at the Academy Sports in Baxter."

Cole nods; he did know that.

"Well, she used to work at the one in Nolton, where we lived, but the manager's position became available at the one here, and she applied for it and got it. Maybe it's better than the manager, I'm not sure. But she gets an actual salary and some benefits here instead of the normal seven-thirty-five an hour at a typical, good ole American fuck-me-every-other-Friday job."

Cole chuckles.

Gerome continues. "Dad doesn't care where we live. He's on the road much more than he's here. His truck is more of a home to him than any house is. It's got a bed and a kitchen and a TV. I used to think it was the coolest thing in the world when I was a kid."

"When's he coming back next?" Cole asks. "I remember your mom saying that first day I came over that he's been gone since before I moved in. That's like, what, almost two months?"

"Yeah, I think so. I'm not sure, man. I can't keep up anymore." He doesn't seem the slightest bit resentful; Cole can tell that he just genuinely does not care much whether or not his dad is around. Not necessarily in a bad way, it seems. He's just neutral. He's pretty neutral in general.

"Hey, man, you thirsty?" Gerome asks, perking up. "I need a good smack in the nads."

Cole says that he is and lounges in silence as Gerome clanks down the hall toward the kitchen carrying their two crumb-riddled plates and smudgy glasses from earlier back with him. Not completely silent, though. That morose melody from the TV's pause screen continues to cry. The makers of this edition of *Call of Duty* have really dialed up the scare-o-meter for this one.

He reaches over and snaps the TV off, leaving the console on just in case later they want to continue their zombie slaying deeper into the night. That melody seems harmless until you're alone in the room with it. It's like that movie *Hannibal*. How Anthony Hopkins's character sits in the cage, staring at people in the room who have the comfort of each other. A false feeling of security in numbers. But when everyone files out except one, who's now left alone with the madman, bars or no bars between them, they have to face what's inside the thing inside that cage.

And all comfort flees out the double-pane window with one glance from the black-eyed beast.

For the first time in a while, the crow crosses his mind. Glides, heavy and black, right across that cognitive canyon. And just as Cole begins to wonder how much longer his new buddy will be absent, Gerome kicks the door wide with his prosthetic.

The Mountain Dews certainly were a solid smack in the nads. They're each now working on their respective seconds. Cole offers to be the runner this time. When he was a child, his uncle told him he knew some country folk who used Mountain Dew as their morning pick-me-up. Totally replaced coffee with it. Some swore they couldn't even function without it. He'd said he knew an old farmer named Clut Amberson (Cole will surely never in his life, no matter how many years that is, forget *that* name) who every morning would spike it with cheap vodka. One of the kinds that only comes in plastic with bright caps. Said he'd sip it as he put on his dirty overalls. He would even drink it out of coffee mugs, and he'd be three cups deep before the lazy sun even peeked its head from behind the beyond.

Cole takes another burning swig and feels his pulse flutter. A midnight Mountain Dew for a teen boy can be dangerous. As he sips more and more of that green caffeine, an idea begins to knock through his skull, "sneak out" begins dancing through his head on funny little legs, like one of those ridiculous mascots you see jumping and jiving out front of some restaurant or box store on life support, trying their damnedest to draw more customers in the door. They swallow their ego and pay some pimply Ag major from the local juco about a Subway foot-long an hour to don the bulky, sweat-stained costume and simply hope for the best.

But the jiving idea never makes it out of his head. Instead, they continue their game, quickly approaching their personal best of level thirty-four (having somehow managed to slay six different waves of the demon dogs at this point), and let the caffeine slowly talk its way out of their system.

They briefly talk about Ellie. Mainly her physical appearance and all the areas in which God blessed her, getting the formalities of a testosterone-influenced conversation out of the way. They've talked about her before at greater length. Just the day after meeting Cole, Gerome told him about seeing him leave her house and thinking the unthinkable. "I wish," Cole had said then with a laugh. "I bet I looked like a fucking dweeb, didn't I?" Gerome had agreed that yes, he did, in fact, greatly resemble your prototypical dweeb. Cole had told him that love makes you do the damnedest things, and Gerome cackled until Cole joined in. Laughed until their bellies hurt. "Don't get your tits in a twist," Gerome said. "She's sad and lonely, but there is no way in hell she's letting a teenage dude hit it. I don't care *how* vulnerable she is."

Conversation bent its way to the subject of her father. This, too, they'd covered before. But sometimes when you rehash old questions, new ideas sprinkle out. Like they'd been sprouting up somewhere down in the subconscious when everyone's backs were turned. The main one being what the hell he's up to.

"I've seen mean old Nolan many times since we've been here. But recently he looks more haggard. Like a deer with a bad leg and downwind from a bear or something."

"Probably mob probs," Cole says.

They talk about the week or so that Nolan spent at Ellie's house alone, back before she'd moved in. Gerome had a front-row seat at the time—everyone loves a little stakeout. He'd watched halfheartedly through dozens of episodes of

That '70s Show and probably dozens more pause screens on his game console over that week. Only about a hundred and fifty feet of grass separated Gerome's window from Ellie's house. A linear contrast divides her thick Kentucky blue sod from his melting pot of trash grass at the property line. He watched her father sporadically as he darted through the seemingly finished house doing things. Watched through curtainless windows as he carried things to different rooms, traced steps (sometimes back and forth multiple times), stood too long in certain areas doing nothing. *Like a man making booby traps,* he'd remembered thinking at the time. He needed not a single mote more of evidence that the dude was a bona fide creep show.

"Maybe he's just a loving father." Cole's sarcasm was laid on thicker than Ellie's Kentucky blue.

"Creep show," is all Gerome replies with.

At about a quarter to one in the morning, Cole had a short text exchange with his mother.

> *Hey bby, going to bed!*
>
> *Ok night mom.*
>
> *Key under the mat like always in case you get home after I head out for wrk!*

Gerome's mother had hit the hay hours before. She'd called good night from the end of the hall because she didn't want to see any more zombies get blown to bits. Cole had seen her horrified face out of the corner of his eye when she'd poked her head in earlier and smiled while his fingers fluttered autonomously around the controller toggles. Whatever generation you grow up in, you will look at some of the things your kids are into with a sense of uncomfortable bewilderment and ask yourselves what *you* were like as a kid. Cole didn't blame her a bit—the game was terrifyingly realistic. He'd actually heard of people having night terrors from it. Those are the stories the makers surely sleep soundly because of. Cole imagines those video game masterminds are probably curled up in their six-hundred-thread-count sheets right now, listening to the cold, northern rain patter against their high-rise windows; a misty city skyline can be seen through the water-streaked glass. Colorful lights from restored machines silently strobe over brick accent walls.

As they fend off a dwindling pack of the undead, acquire a couple perks, and proceed to blasting the stragglers with Gerome's coveted Zeus Cannon, sending the boys to a new high-level, Cole is still thinking of Ellie despite all the visually orgasmic carnage.

"Hey, I've been thinking," Cole says.

"Why?" Gerome replies, wide eyes never leaving the screen.

"Remember how I thought surprising Ellie by mowing her yard that first time while she wasn't home, before it needed it, kinda backfired?"

"Uh-huh," he responds, fingers maniacally fluttering.

"*This* time, I'm gonna wait till she really needs it."

"Here we go." Gerome's eyes roll, and a pearlescent smile creeps wide.

"Gonna trudge through the high grass, sex it up a bit with the dramatics. Then I bet she's going to pay me with something better than cash."

"Why do you talk?" Gerome actually pauses the game and turns to look at his new friend. They stare at each other for a brief moment, Old West style, then Gerome resumes. Gunfire and bloodcurdling screams pump out of the TV's speakers as they sit shoulder to shoulder, smiles permanently painted across their faces.

CHAPTER 14

Two hours later, Cole is dreaming of the woman in the house next door. One of those dreams you don't know isn't real until later on, minutes after waking from it, yet you desperately wished you had. He's in her master bedroom. His mind paints an alluring picture of a room he's never seen and never will. She's there. A thin sheet lay over her naked body, leaving little to be imagined. Her golden-brown hair is fanned around her face, perfectly messy. Her smooth arms rest upward under her pillow, legs together and over to one side with her knees drawn up. A small bundle of sheet is trapped between them, covering only her most intimate. The world's finest artist can't duplicate the lines of her body. A childhood memory slams into his head. A memory from a dream. He's back in third grade, sitting on a colorful rug with the rest of his wide-eyed classmates, staring quiescently at Mrs. Thornbough, like a very one-sided kindergarten colloquia. She sings a song that is supposed to be used by children toward other children if somebody's getting a bit handsy. "Stop! Don't touch me there! This is . . . my *no-no square!*" She makes a square with her thumbs and pointers and holds it over the sixty-five-year-old mound of flesh pressing against the inside of her zipper.

Cole squeezes his eyes shut in the dream and shakes the memory out of his head like a madman shaking out the voices. Can't let the image of an old lady's muff-bundle ruin this moment by sending the blood out of where it needs to be, running away screaming to different parts of his body.

Ellie doesn't seem to notice. Or care. She stares at him. Deep into him with campfire eyes. She knows what she wants. And he has never been so sure about anything in his life. He steps toward her, just a boy in a big dream. He's already naked. She slides her hungry, atavistic gaze down his young frame as if she were using hands instead of eyes. She stares at what makes him male, and he notices her swallow down the water that trickled into her mouth because of it. With her knees still bent, she slowly opens them. A pulse-pounding display of complete submission, yet somehow still having a stranglehold on status quo. The little tuft of sheet still covers that covetous area between her legs. She rolls her head back into the pillow and closes her eyes. A hand slides out from under and begins a deliberate crawl over her ivory-colored skin. With just the tips of her delicate fingers, she explores her bare breasts, making playful circles around her pink nipples. She bites her bottom lip as her head lolls to one side. Cole is completely transfixed. He begins not so much walking toward her as he is being *pulled* toward her. Just a boy in a dream. She notices and counters by sending her hand lower, dancing downward in no hurry at all. It slides under the sheet and begins a more sensual dance, like she's gently strumming the strings on a harp. Her head pulls backward again, deeper into the pillow. Her chin is pointing straight up toward the ceiling, and Cole can see the arteries in her throat pounding, pumping beautiful blood through the rest of her. He can see the tendons in her wrist frolicking under the skin. Her body writhes, like she's floating on her back in the ocean, riding low waves of pleasure. Cole reaches the bed. He plants his hands and a knee up and—

A guttural cry rolls through the house. It searches the walls, blindly looking for an exit it can't find. He freezes, one knee still on Ellie's bed. He's wondering if the cry was real, wondering if where he *is* is real. Ellie disappears before him, and a moldy mattress in a black house appears under and around him. He hears it again and this time is instantly yanked awake by the big hand of consciousness before his dream can crumble in on him anymore.

He's on the futon. Yes, of course he is. After a moment, he places himself in Gerome's room. Right again, bud. But it's still dark out. The silver moon sending shards of light through the blinds like frozen bullets. He looks down and sees them slashed across his chest and arms.

But what was th—

Again. From behind him. He remembers he can move and rolls over, quietly as he can, peeking over the armrest his head was on to see Gerome sitting up in his bed, Indian style. Cole can see the shards of moon ice dashed across his friend's legs, only up to his waist. He blinks away the last of the sleep, trying to make out Gerome's upper half, when he sees the eyes. His eyes are two solid white orbs floating in the dark. Cue balls in black water. Cole can make out a set of teeth now below them, adrenaline speeding up his eyes' adjustment process.

Is he smiling?

A cold, malignant terror creeps in. He's seen too many horror flicks and read too many Stephen King stories.

"G-Gerome?" he stammers. He hates the sound that comes out of his throat. A mouse caught in a trap. Cole's eyes float in the dark as well. But his have pupils.

His friend doesn't answer, but the angle of his eyes and teeth change. He's cocked his head to one side. He only stares. Which is impossible considering his pupils are lost in the back of his head somewhere, staring at his own brain matter.

Cole vaguely becomes aware of a cold sweat sprouting across his brow.

The thing in the bed in front of him that looks like his friend, the one he's been hanging out with for the better part of a week straight, unlocks its jaw like a rusty hinge and lets out a long, animalistic shriek. A primitive cacophony of anguish funnels through its yawing mouth and fills the room like rising water. Bad water. Black water.

But it doesn't.

The room is empty and silent. It's in Cole's head. It grows, a pressure playing with his skull's breaking point. He presses his sweaty palms against the sides of his head, hard enough to bruise, simultaneously keeping that sound out and his brains in. He hasn't realized yet the sound is coming from in there too. He's hurting more than helping. He stumbles off the futon and onto the floor, trying to stand on legs that feel boneless. He kicks the remote, and the TV snaps on. The game's pause screen once again displayed, flaunting an impressive number of thirty-eight under the red word LEVEL. A new record.

A soft green glow stains the room. Cole sees sweat glistening off his friend's chest. His mouth is still open, unbelievably wide. The space between the thing's teeth is simply a black hole, large enough to swallow a softball. Its head follows Cole's every drunken move throughout the room. He staggers toward Gerome, hands still plastered to the sides of his head. The scream won't cease. It's like a wail from another world. The sound of black tracks under the train to hell. He can't keep it out. Gerome's face is flat. Void of any evidence of strain.

Dead boy with a broken jaw, Cole thinks. *Sound can't be coming out of that.*

Cole, through clinched eyes, sees Gerome's prosthetic

propped against the nightstand next to his bed. On the night-stand, the clock scolds 3:23.

The shriek is now a *thrum*. His bones vibrate in their soft meat beds like a tuning fork flicked by a giant.

I'm going to faint.

He feels himself giving up, stumbling while trying to stay on his feet. The sound is somehow filling his lungs. He's submerged in the black water now, his body weightless, his vision swimming. He reaches toward where he *thinks* Gerome is, begging him to stop. He finds the leg somehow in the murk, laying a cold hand on its outer plastic just as his blood begins to boil in his belly.

Gerome's mouth snaps shut with a crocodilian *clap*. The noise ceases abruptly. Too quickly. Cole has to squint the pain away as a silence more vicious than the hellish shriek sets in, wreaking havoc like a too-sudden drop in altitude.

Cole's hands fall to his sides. His vision stabilizes, dancing dots fading to nothing. Gerome's eyes roll back forward, gro-tesquely coming from two different directions. He lets out an exuberant exhale, like he's held his breath too long. Like he'd been under the black water too. Cole surmises much deeper than himself, though, almost far enough to never return up into colorful consciousness again. Almost making a forever home with the inhuman things down there below even the black.

Gerome frantically blinks out the confusion across wide eyes as his gleaming chest hitches rapidly up and down.

"You're all right, man," Cole says, panting as well. "What the *fuck* was that?"

Gerome only stares straight ahead for a moment, then shoots a hand over and flips on the bedside lamp. Light showers his face, and Cole can suddenly see how terrified his friend looks. Fright has pulled his face taut. He looks more like a wax sculpture of himself than himself.

"Man, I—"

He takes a couple deep breaths, closing his eyes. Taking his time. "I don't know. I was in your hideout. That place you told me about, the bus out in the woods." He shudders, pulling the comforter up over his lap. "Something was there with us. Me, you, and something else. I couldn't see it, but I could feel it."

Cole finds the remote on the floor and flips off the TV.

"I could feel it walking around those old buses. *Stalking*. So, we left. And then I had *my* dream. My old dream. But it was different, though, even worse than before." He takes a few deep inhales and exhales, steadying himself. "Holy fucking shit."

Cole studies him tentatively. He waits for that too long, too horribly inhuman face to return. It doesn't. He thinks maybe his friend is possessed. Or was, rather. How *else* could a human make that terrible face or that terrible noise? That noise that was all in his head, even though it also was somehow coming from his friend's gaping mouth. But whatever incubus had a hold of Gerome has gone. Or is hidden.

Cole shivers. He doesn't want to believe that something *that* wrong is still here with them, standing shoulder to shoulder yet hiding in another realm so as not to be seen. Like a crowd outside the cage, but the bars are just plastic pieces.

Gerome can see fear in his friend's face but isn't sure why it's there. After all, *he* was the one with the nightmare.

Basking in warm lamplight and cold confusion, he asks, "Was I . . . I don't know . . . saying something?"

Cole decides not to say anything about what he witnessed. He was half-asleep, after all. Plus, they'd been ripping zombies apart for longer than a school day. The brain is an amazing thing, huh? What better trick than to turn your best bud into something straight from the game. Should've made him crawl out of the TV screen and slide leglessly across the carpet! That would've been even *cooler*, right?

That scream.

You know better, Cole, he scolds himself.

His head feels like it's been trapped in an elevator door for about an hour, slamming against the frame on every floor of a fucking high-rise, dinging happily after each blow, straight to the stratosphere, please and thank you.

No part of what just happened wasn't real.

"No," he finally answers, pausing too long.

He wonders if there's any chance Gerome believed that answer as they sit silently, clicking and flicking the buttons and toggles of their controllers. They've switched to *Madden*. A football game. A happy game.

When Cole ejected the zombie game from the console, erasing their record-setting progress in an instant, neither said a word. The idiotic bumbling of John Madden's commentary has a soothing quality, and after a while, they begin to loosen up a bit. Core and back muscles begin to relax, cloudy minds begin to clear. And after a while, a powerful sleep sets in for them both, hitting them at virtually the same time.

At about half past four, as Cole and Gerome plunge temerariously toward stone-cold unconsciousness, a crow cackles itself mad in a nearby bus yard. Cawing painfully through a bone-dry throat.

CHAPTER 15

"Sweet tea or lemonade?"

"Sweet tea, please," Cole says.

"You're doing great on my yard. Sorry I wasn't here to pay you last time. I had a few errands to run." Ellie is standing with her back to him, cold granite pressing gently against her belly.

"Not a problem at all," he says. Almost adding that he'd do it for free, special just for her, but decides against it. He's sure she already knows he has feelings for her. He's old enough to know that women are so much more in tune to things like that than men. He doesn't want to come off as immature. Shooting for close to ten years his senior, guessing as he goes.

"Double this time, dude," she says as she puts the plastic jug of sweet tea back in the fridge.

Dude.

It closes behind her with a magnetic slap, and the motor hums to life as she rejoins him at the bar, replacing the cold air that escaped from the fridge with a certain heat only a teenage boy can feel.

As he begins to argue, she holds up a hand and flashes a look that melts him. That quickly, he forgets the "dude," only shuts his mouth and smiles, smartly taking a long sip of his tea. He closes his eyes and enjoys the taste of summertime and the South.

Quickest way to a man's heart is through his belly, he remembers hearing from somewhere.

"What?" she says, smiling at his smile.

"Nothing," he replies. "This tea is magical."

They enjoy their drinks for a moment, and then Cole breaks the thick silence by asking what she likes to do. Does she enjoy just sitting around all day? He thinks it a safe prod, not too pushy or intrusive. And it's a fair question. He now knows a little about her father. The somewhat wealthy man who probably pays for his daughter's everything. And yet Cole's barely seen him. There was that time he saw him yelling at everyone building this house. But he hadn't known who he was looking at then.

Who is this man who knows this woman more than he does? She seemingly just sits in this bulky brick two-story all day and night. To some, he's describing "the life," true, but he'd like to think he would need more than a shiny four-bedroom with a flat-screen LED hanging on the wall of all of them like kinetic bedroom art. He'd like to think he would need some sort of mental stimuli to stay sane. He thinks of his beloved books and what would happen if he lost them in a fire or some sort of nerd robbery.

There's an ever-so-slight wince. Just barely perceptible, but it's there. He knows the gentle prod hit a soft spot in her, sinking a little deeper than he planned. Cole remembers the stages of grief from a book he'd read a couple years ago. One of those brick-like bathroom readers called *The Story of Psychology* by Morton Hunt. There were five, he knew. Though the first three eluded him, he remembered that just before the final stage of acceptance, there was a sometimes lengthy and extremely malleable stage called depression, which he knows she is currently in the gripping throes of. He's confident he can help this beautiful woman find that consistent smile again. After all, she surely brightens on occasion when talking to him. Each time like a warm knife into his buttery teenage heart.

It's been over a year now, his mind steals. *Move on.*

"I enjoy it," she says. But her eyes can't lie.

Why is she lying?

For Cole, the feeling that something isn't quite right is now completing its process from the fluidity of "yeah buts" and "maybes" to the cold and solid form of a very real danger. Something you don't want to touch your tongue to.

He nods. Trying to fake genuineness. But that knock in the engine, that cog in the wheel somewhere unseen but felt through vibrations won't allow him to accept that answer. Yes, he's fallen in love with this woman (whatever that means when you're barely old enough to buy cigarettes and she's flirting with thirty), and yes, he could talk to her for hours on end, even *watch* her wordlessly for hours on end while she wanders about the kitchen or just sits across from him sipping her tea, but when he's here, there's this piddling little feeling that he's in some kind of sick bay. Or some experiment. Like a low-budget sequel to *The Truman Show*. A hunched overseer taps his chin under a sharp-toothed smile as she scurries around her prescribed premises. He's jotting notes and flipping switches.

"It helps me cope with everything that's gone on. Being alone. Rebuilding your thoughts. It can be nice."

Those your words or your daddy's? he thinks.

He keeps quiet. Only replies again with an understanding nod.

"Maybe one day, when I feel acclimated with everything, I'll persuade Dad into letting me get a job again," she continues.

"Get out of the house a bit more."

As much as he wishes he could describe her as much, she isn't a strong woman. He knows this. He also gets the feeling she's the type of woman that has trouble making decisions for herself. He'd bet his entire King collection that her dead husband had called the shots. That and her dear old dad. Who seemingly still does. It's the way she carries herself. An easy beauty oozes from every inch, unbeknownst to her.

"What would you do?"

"I'd probably get back on track to teaching," she says.

There's that warmth. That all-encompassing warmth.

"Oh, really?" Cole says. "What grade?"

"Any grade! Wouldn't matter to me. As long as it's not college kids. I don't think I can handle that." She looks down into her tea, stirring daydreams of maybes and mights.

"How come?" he asks, knowing the question obsolete because he knows the requirements for secondary education are much more extensive. But he could ask her silly questions till the moon took rise just to watch her mouth move. "I heard it's the best level to teach. The professors do whatever the hell they want, and the students aren't as bad. The only ones who show up are the kids that actually care."

"Maybe, yes," she says. "But they're old enough to challenge you. Well"—she points a finger at him—"even the second-graders challenge a teacher. But college kids are old enough to challenge you and actually be *right.*"

She flashes a "yikes" face, corners of her mouth pulling back and eyes bugging out. "That's terrifying."

A teacher, huh? He fades to a dream. *All the boys would leave class every day just as dumb as they were when they sauntered in if* you *were the one up at the board.*

He can't help the unabashed smile from grabbing hold of his face. And she can't help but return one of her own.

The sun is a few hands lower in the sky now as Cole and Gerome sit in Cole's backyard. Asses on rocks and feet up on the iron bowl between them. Shadows slant across the yard like long monsters. Robins and wrens dance from limb to limb, snacking on early moths. Bulky and slow, they are no match. It's cool for a mid-June afternoon. It's been nearly an hour since they cleaned their plates of Stacey's famous Mexican casserole and plopped down at the fire pit, yet not a single bead of sweat lives on either boy's brow. They chuckle as they notice at the same time how the other is sitting. Legs propped, hands on stomach as if nurturing it back to health. Cole had to unbutton his jeans to make room for the belly he's never had.

"I like your mom," Gerome says, folding a gum wrapper into delicate shapes. Thankful that something reminded him that there are other things to talk about besides that *other* thing. That giant lumbering elephant, bristle-hairy and black-eyed. "She's funny," he continues. "Like in an old lady kind of way, you know? Like she's ..." He trails off, not knowing how to bullshit past those two sentences. "I don't know, I just like her."

He looks up at the trees, angry that he now has this burden.

Cole gives him a courtesy smile. Small and defeated.

A skein of smoke swirls sensuously up from the black leftovers of scalded tinder in the bottom of the bowl. They'd given up on the fire and grown silent, knowing exactly what the other's mind is on. The wind kicks up and tears the top off the vertical gray string of smoke, carrying it eastward. The door to the shed bangs weakly against the side wall. Weak or not, they both start at the noise.

"Okay," Gerome finally says. Cole looks him in the eyes. *Really* into his eyes, for the first time since they've been out here. He knows by the tone that Gerome's about to serve up the meat and potatoes. "What did I say or . . . do in my sleep last night that freaked you out so much, man?" Gerome leans forward now. His prosthetic thumps into the grass. "And don't say nothing, Cole. I saw your face."

You have no room to talk when it comes to faces, bud.

Something turned his friend's face into a ghoul's mask last night. *Something* was inside him, screaming a scream only Cole could hear. And as a result, he feels like he's experiencing his first hangover. Luckily, no one noticed him turn and wince when Gerome flung the fridge open in the kitchen and the white light splashed across their faces. His brains feel mushy. Like that devil sound bullishly ripped around in there, throwing elbows and using claws. Yet the sensible part of him, the measured, I'm-sure-there's-a-rational-explanation-here part, sits prudently on his shoulder and pumps his head full of whispers that make him feel better. Or are, at least, *supposed* to make him feel better. "It was all your imagination," the little man says. "You know all those scary books you read?" But Cole dismisses him.

A for effort, little bud. And, oh, how I wish you were right, but I think we both know you're not.

The little man in his head puffs his chest and tries again. "Your mind was influenced." A little louder now, feeling threatened. "Hours of that game will get to *anyone*." There's an obvious twinge of uncertainty from the man in his head. Influenced in some small way by the game? Possible. Happens all the time.

He's heard of rare instances when a kid has experienced a kind of video game–induced trance, or even what can only be described as a psychosis brought on by the incessant day-in, day-out violence on the TV screen in front of them. A violence they are in control of, in which somewhere along the way, they lose their moral compass because it gets overwritten by a certain game's laws. One kid in Orlando tried to run over a bunch of people standing in line for snow cones because he thought there'd be floating money, spinning lazily over their dead bodies until he came back and collected it, adding to his avatar's growing bank account.

But your head.

Why does it still hurt then? How is *that* possible—

It's not.

—if what he hopes wasn't real actually was?

The little man has grown quiet. And Cole realizes Gerome is still waiting for an answer. Leaning so far forward now that if there were a fire in the bowl, he'd be burning his nose. He's terse, head tilted down and his eyes little more than waning slits. He continues to fold and unfold the Orbit gum wrapper, working it around delicately while his eyes stay on his friend. Cole wonders if *it* is still inside Gerome.

"You weren't saying anything," Cole says. "Or, at least, after I woke up from my nightmare, you weren't saying anything. I dreamed zombies were chasing us through a mall. I had a gunshot wound to the leg, so you were dragging me. It was friendly fire. You blew the head off one that was starting to gnaw at my knee after I tripped like one of those idiots in the movies but in the process took off a pretty good chunk of my thigh. I was yelling at you to let me go 'cause they were right on us, man, I mean *right on us*, but you wouldn't. So then as we were running through the food court and about to make it out the front doors of the mall—you know how it goes in shit like that, so close but yet so far away sort of thing—this red-haired bitch, who had to be pushing three-fifty, jumped out from behind one of those big trash cans. You know the ones that everyone stacks their used trays on top of? She tackled us. She was drooling blood, and her skin was like wax. She bit you in the neck and tore some shit out when she pulled away, and you went flopping around on your side and the horde swallowed you up. Then she turned to me and smiled. She leaned in so close I could smell her dead breath. And that's when I woke up. I jumped up and heard you tossing and turning so I came over and nudged you awake."

Too much, his mind tells him. *Let that imagination run too far, he's not gonna believe that.*

Gerome eyes him. Cole can't tell if those are buyer's eyes or no-deal eyes.

"We were both freaked," Cole adds.

Gerome thinks. Then tosses the wrapper into the bowl. A miniature paper airplane was its final form. The boys watch its engines fail and free-fall to the bottom, disappearing into the ash. "I'm sorry for waking you up."

Realizing there is no more, Cole exhales. "No problem, man." He tries to sound as nonchalant as possible, but the words come out as painful as door hinge squeaks. "What was yours about?" Assuming that he had something to tell.

Gerome visibly bristles. He looks over Cole's shoulder at nothing in particular, prodding the queer feeling that has fallen over them in the last couple minutes with unsure beginnings. Cole's arms break out in a plague of gooseflesh. He crosses them. The evening has grown very chilly.

"You don't have to—" Cole begins, throwing a plastic smile.

"Yes, I do." Gerome cuts him off before he can finish. *He's* not smiling at all. Hasn't all day, in fact. Not even at Cole's mother. Polite, yes. And a warm tone of appeasement with her at dinner, yes. But no smiles. No *real* smiles, at least. Those pearly whites are buried under tightly pinched lips, like he's scared something might come out. Something that's supposed to stay deep and hidden. Far away from the light of day. Those famous knee-slapper zings couldn't be more dead right now.

Cole realizes he hasn't seen him like this yet in their short friendship. They hadn't known each other all that long, sure, but those roots had plunged deep with a quickness a cancer would be covetous of. Cole doesn't know what's going on here.

"It's kind of embarrassing," he continues. "But I sort of have to tell you on account of the fact that it'll probably make me feel better if I do."

Cole lets go of one of his gooseflesh-riddled arms and tips a hand, a "go ahead" gesture. He returns it to its previous position. The sun is now only gasping for breath above the tree line.

"Okay. So when I was a kid, I was hit by a car. Well, a van. I was hit by a man in a red van. One of those big Astro things, you know the ones I'm talking about?"

Cole nods, dragging wide eyes up and down only once.

"Yeah, creepy fucking thing. Anyway, me and my best friend at the time, Jonas, were walking home from school. We lived really close. We were playing this stupid game with an *Eastbay* magazine—remember those? The ones that had all the hottest new basketball shoes and arm bands and stuff."

Cole nods. Something heavy lands on a branch on the other side of the fence, unbeknownst to them.

"He was a few steps ahead of me, and we were doing this thing where he'd toss the magazine over his head and I had to catch it, open it, and wherever my finger landed, that was the thing I had to wear for the rest of my life. Kid shit. Anyway, we were doing this all the way to his mom's, tossing the thing back and forth over our heads like a bouquet at a wedding, crossing streets, diving into peoples' yards. What could go wrong?"

Half-assed or not, sarcasm is sarcasm. Technically humor, Cole will take it.

"We're almost across this street called Ludlow, I'll never forget the name, and he throws it too hard. To this day, me and him both know he threw it over my head on purpose." He motions an over-the-head two-hand basketball shot. "But we never said as much. Just kids being kids. He'd kill to take it back just like I would, so what's the point of bringing up something you can only make worse for someone?"

Cole only nods again. Leaves rustle.

"It sails over my head even though I jumped as high as I could for it. I mean a good, two-footed, max-vert sorta thing. Looking back, it was the last real jump of my life, but shit, I bet if I had been under a hoop, I could've grabbed rim. Maybe with two hands. Anyway, the thing lands a couple feet on the other side of the yellow line. Jonas was already across and into the sidewalk when he threw it, and I was a step or two from the grass myself. I turned and ran back out into the meat of the street, bent down to pick it up." Gerome pauses. Steadies his breath. Cole stays patient. "I even still closed my eyes and jammed a blind finger into one of the pages to see what I had to rock the rest of my life this time. Right then, the man in the red van topped the hill." He's staring at nothing in the fire pit. Maybe looking for the plane in the ash. Somewhat symbolic now. He's silent for a few moments before he finally continues. "Police investigators said he was going the speed limit—they can check those things by measuring the skid marks and doing some math—so it was determined completely accidental. There was nothing the guy could do. He smashed his brakes real good and cut the wheel, so instead of giving the grill a big wet smooch at forty-five, I got the back door on the driver's side at a cool thirty-seven. I don't know where they came up with that, but that's what a bald dude in a dark suit told me on one of my many days in the hospital. I was trying not to puke up the green mush they called vegetables when he was leaned over my bed, so I could be a mile per hour or so off either way. But long story short, that split decision probably saved my life for sure."

Cole's jaw has gone slack. He's involuntarily rubbing his upper arms with his crossed hands like a nervous mom watching her little one's first soccer game.

"All I can remember is lying there in the street, looking up at the sky. There wasn't a single cloud, but a plane slowly made its way across, leaving one of those floating vapor trails. I remember feeling envy. Even a sense of longing, like everyone I ever knew was on that lazy plane, and I was being tortured by watching them float away forever, leaving me alone. That's what it felt like in that moment. I didn't know I had been hit. Hell, I didn't even know I was lying in the middle of the street. But I remember then feeling a sense of something being wrong. I was numb to the pain at first, I know that now. In shock. My bottom half started to take on this hot sensation. I wanted to look, but lifting my head didn't seem possible. Not like it was too heavy, but more like I couldn't remember how. Like that plane full of everyone had taken my thoughts and memories with it. I was all jumbled up. All this only lasted a few seconds, but in my world, right then, it seemed like a half hour. I remember rolling my head to the right. I remember the sound inside my head as it rolled against the blacktop. My right arm was laying across my chest, and I was looking down over the top of my right shoulder."

He snaps out of his trancelike recollection and scares the shit out of Cole by asking him a very random question. "You ever seen what chicken nuggets are made of?"

Cole winces and shakes his head. Hands still rubbing his upper arms for warmth or security or anything at all.

"Well, it looks like a pinkish paste. It's fucking disgusting. But I'd rather bathe in that shit for the rest of my life than have to look down again and see that's what my right leg was made of. It looked like someone had dropped a bag of it down next to me. Except this kind, like, wasn't done or something. Still had the shards of bone sticking out every which way. At the time, my mind told me that was glass. I was starting to sort of piece together what had happened, and a connection was made between the foggy memory of the sound of smashing glass and what I was seeing. I wasn't scared at all. Completely calm. It was an interesting dream."

A muffled sound comes from across the fence. Closer. As if listening. Neither notice.

"I rolled my head on the asphalt and looked back toward where my brain had just pieced together that I'd been hit. The red van was parked about thirty feet away and sideways across the street. There was a large dent on the side, in the back sliding door, and the glass above it was spider-webbed and bowing inward. I saw the guy running in slow motion toward me, action movie style. Like when you're sure the thing's gonna go *kaboom* behind you. I saw Jonas. He was on all fours in the grass by the road. He was screaming hysterically. He looked like he was scared to cross some invisible barrier between him and the road. I only noticed it as something else to look at. Then the magazine caught my attention. It was lying about halfway between me and the van, pages fluttering in the breeze. Which then directed my attention to what was lying next to it. It was my shoe that still had my foot in it. They told me later it probably got 'pulled off,' their words, by the skidding back tire. Caught under, and pop goes the weasel. It all seemed kind of funny to me. Peculiar, in a way. Then I rolled my head back right and looked up at the sky. I was looking for the plane but couldn't find it. The vapor trail led to nothing. I remember being upset that I had lost it. I felt that overwhelming sadness again. That terrible sense of losing something you realized you always took for granted and now would never get back. I remember sounds starting to come back all at once, all jumbled together like they had been paused and someone hit play at that moment to catch them all up to what I was seeing. I was upset that I lost the plane, or my foot, my leg, I don't know. Then I lost it all and passed out."

Cole had never asked how he'd lost his leg. He'd sort of forgotten to ask. It had seemed a moot point thirty minutes ago, so his story is both unexpected and unnerving. In a world of fluff, whatever that meant for Cole's middle-to-lower-class broken family, it's easy to become spoiled. Numbing to the idea that there is death and other even more terrible things lurking around most corners until you hear a story like the one Gerome has just told. It drags that possibility back to the forefront, shining a light beam down the dark alleys of the things we don't like to think about. No, not *possibility*. *Inevitability*. Even though his buddy survived that ordeal, that doesn't mean most people would have. Death drives a red van. And a lot of the crosswalks in life are dangerously close to a hill or a blind curve as if mapped out by morons. You just have to hope that when your paths finally cross, he doesn't square you up too good.

"Now you know," Gerome said. "And thanks for not asking. It gives me a sense of normality when people don't. I know it's a fake sense, but it still feels as good as the real thing. At least I think it does." The corners of his mouth slightly curl up, a small smile. "Although I wouldn't have cared at all to tell you if you had."

"Yeah, I was going to a couple days after we met, but then I honestly just forgot," Cole says with a chuckle. Now Gerome flashes a big one. "It didn't really matter anymore."

"Gotcha," Gerome says. This is the first time Cole has seen him smile all day. But it's gone as fast as it came when he prepares for the rest. "Anyway, that's the backstory. That's not the embarrassing part. Shit happens, and I'm old enough to understand that. No rhyme or reason, it just happens. And there's not a damn thing you can do to prepare for its arrival when it hits too close to home, because you can't possibly predict what form of shit that shit will be in. You know, like the nutty dude who spends all his cash making his house an impenetrable fortress against the Purge or the coming zombie apocalypse or something, who then gets completely fucked when he gets diagnosed with colon cancer at forty-two because he's got nothing left for hospital bills." He takes a deep breath. "The embarrassing part is the dreams I had after the accident. Or nightmares. Mom calls them night terrors. I didn't know what the fuck they were, just that they scared the living shit out of me. It was like a bad belt in a car. The one in my brain went bad, and it was driving me insane. You know, you don't even notice it when it's fine, you just get in your car and drive, but when the belt goes squeaky, you can't even think. You can't do anything till you get it fixed, really. They were the worst right after the accident, obviously, but I had them for years. Almost nightly. My mom got me in to a doctor, and he gave me some meds that helped me sleep, but the dreams always came back. The meds knocked me out, but I realized I became dependent on them for sleep. It quickly became a difficult choice. I could take the meds, which started to feel more and more like tossing a rock to a crackhead, or I could face them. The dreams." He holds up both hands like a scale. "Either staying up all night playing video games, which is precisely when my addiction to them began to flourish, or daring to get some sober sleep and just hope for the best. But it seemed like every time I tried the second one, I'd end up yelling for Mom in the middle of the night like a four-year-old afraid of the fucking monster under the bed."

"I mean, you were just a kid, Gerome. That's nothing to be ashamed about," Cole says with genuine compassion.

"True, yes, I was a kid. When it *happened*. The dreams . . . they kept on. Well into high school. Just as sharp and angry as they were when I was a kid. I learned it doesn't much matter how old you are in real life when you're stuck in a dream like that. You're as young and as scared as it wants you to be."

Cole just sits there, doesn't reply.

"I've just learned to live with them," Gerome says. "I don't scream for Mom anymore."

A short silence falls over them, but Cole waits for Gerome to continue.

"They eventually became far more sporadic. Maybe once every month or so, I'd have it. I still flip shit and practically jump out of my skin when I wake up from the dream, the nightmare, but it's not quite the same feeling. It's like I realize faster it was just a dream or something. Like someone pokes me with a hot iron in my sleep, but when I jump up, no one is there. It's like that. Everything's the same, but I snap out of it faster now."

"It's the exact same dream every time?" Cole realizes he either had missed that important detail or Gerome hadn't yet mentioned it.

A low caw plays on the wind. Followed by a muffled mewling over the fence and through the tree line. The boys miss it. Or does Cole catch it before it's gone?

"Exactly the same. That's what has me so shaken up."

Gerome leans in again. Two eyeballs in the new dark. Too close to what Cole witnessed the other night.

"Not only did I *have* the dream for the first time in probably two years, but it was *different* this time."

Cole realizes what Gerome just said carries much more weight to him than it does to Cole. He waits for Gerome to expound.

"It's always been my grandmother. Nannie, as I grew up calling her. She's been the one handing me the *Eastbay* in my dream since it happened in real life. I don't know why, but that's how it's always been. Hundreds and hundreds of times. She hands it, doesn't toss it over her head. She'll turn and hand it to me, slowly, like some sort of fucked-up offering or something. We're always face-to-face when the van hits. Just staring at each other, like we're both waiting for the next scene in an already-written play. It never hits her, just me. I've always assumed because she's dead."

"In the dream?"

"Both. Real life and the dream. Cancer got her when I was six."

"Oh, I'm sorry," Cole responds. "So how do you know she's not alive in your dream even though she's passed away in real life, and had been gone for, I guess, years before the accident?"

"I'm getting there, boss. She looks alive when she hands me the *Eastbay*. Well, as alive as she was right before she died. Technically considered living, but it shouldn't be. The weeks and/or months before someone dies of cancer, it's just a legal form of torture, man. You're not deep in the safety of the dark dugout of life anymore. You're on deck, and death is on the mound. Some sort of evil version of Randy-fucking-Johnson from some parallel universe or something, and he's pitching a no-no. Then that last little bit before you bite the dust . . . it's like you're up to bat. You can foul pitch after pitch off, I watched her do it. She fought tooth and nail, but really what is the point? He's going to strike you out eventually. He has un-limited life—you can't drain it. He's got all the cheat codes. He just keeps winding up and slinging fireballs right through the zone. After seeing what she went through, I think when it's my time, I'll just leave the bat on my shoulder. Watch three strikes sizzle by, and just take my seat in the afterlife."

Cole just stares.

"Anyway, that's what she looks like in my dream. How she was when she was fighting off those pitches. She's always got a knitted cap over her bald head. She looks me in the eye, and I'm frozen. I know the van is coming, but I can't move. Her face is the color of mushrooms, and waxy like them too. That brown that should be beautiful, but it's not. She's got a couple inch-long whiskers sprouting from each corner of her mouth from the steroids pumping through her. I tried so hard to ignore them when I went to see her there the few times before the end, but I just couldn't. I know now she knew it too, and I feel like shit for it. That's when the bus hits." *Van*, Cole thinks, but doesn't bother correcting. "After a few seconds of looking into each other's eyes. Next thing I know, I'm on my back in the road and everything else is pretty much how it happened. Me seeing the plane, my leg, the van, the dent, the guy running toward me, but I've still got the magazine in my hand instead of it being in the road between me and the van. And of course, it's my grandma on the side of the street. She doesn't cry or anything. Just stands there stone-faced. To answer your question, I know she's dead in the dream because the van just passes right through her when it hits us."

Cole pauses a moment out of politeness. Only delaying a bit the questions he really wants to ask, nodding and keeping his brow tight with concern. The last thing he wants to do at all is diminish the night terror that has been haunting Gerome since childhood.

Finally, after just the right amount of heavy silence, before Gerome can go anywhere else besides where Cole wants to go next, he says, "You said this one was different. You said it was worse."

Gerome doesn't flinch. His thousand-yard stare seems to coincide with a now particularly adamant bout of dry cawing not too far away, making Cole uneasy.

"Yes," Gerome continues. "It was worse. Much."

Cole tries to shove away the unease and asks another important question. "You also said we started in the bus yard. That what happened?"

"No, not me and you. It was me and my grandma. We were in one of the buses. Your music was playing from somewhere. You know, your beloved nineties. I think it was that 'Every Morning' song by Sugar Ray. The one where he says he wakes up to a halo hanging from the corner of his girlfriend's four-post bed. I don't know what the fuck that means, but that's the one."

"No one does. Solid song, though. Go on."

What happens next causes the thin sack of skin around Cole's testicles to crawl. A thousand ants with ten thousand legs clitter across it. The moment Gerome begins describing the rusty guts of the bus yard he has never seen, Cole knows something is wrong. Something is wrong, because everything he says he saw in his dream is exactly *right*. To an absolute tee. Like he visits the fucking thing every day. But Cole knows he hasn't. He knows Gerome would love it, but he also knows his buddy probably can't physically make the trek over there. At least not by himself. Playing near the top of the greatest obstacle list for a friend with one leg being the eight-foot-tall dead black fence looming to his left right now. When Cole had briefly told Gerome about the bus yard, he held out all the details he knew Gerome would salivate over, just as he had when he discovered it. All the magic a teenage boy could handle with its forgotten charm and its rusty gold. The last thing he wanted was to get his buddy too excited about the place he had to see for himself, only to find out the hard way that two fully functioning legs is a prerequisite instead of a preference. He knows Gerome has probably tried and failed at many things in his life since his run-in with the man in the red van, but he really doesn't want to be there to see the bemoaned look on his face when he couldn't make it to the yard. Thus, possibly ending his own love affair with the place, every solo trip after feeling a little dirty. He'd be the dick with two legs. So, he had watered it down. Said it was just okay. A couple grimy buses in a forest of weeds. But the details his friend rips off are spot-on. Impossible to know. He speaks of the cleared tunnel running down along the fence leading to the fallen tree, the pile of small boats, even the cleaned-up alleyway between the rows. The tipping point is the sign. He somehow describes the sign that Cole set up against the front of the first bus. Only, Gerome says he can't read it. He and his Nannie are running. Something chased them in from the woods. They run past the sign and into Cole's bus.

"A couple buses down, there's one that's got its door cracked, so we run up in there to hide from whatever is after us," he says. Cole's mouth is wide open. Under different circumstances, the dumbfounded look on his face would be humorous. "It's like a hobo's house or something. There are a couple fans on the ground next to a slap-dick bed covered in old blankets or towels or something between a couple of bus seats. We hunker down so the thing can't see us through the windows. That's when I hear the Sugar Ray song, but very softly. Just background noise coming from somewhere. Like someone took their ear buds out and set them down but kept it cranked." Cole can only blink at what he's hearing. "But then it's *inside* somehow. The thing. It's in the bus with us. We heard it coming from the back of the bus, so we got up and ran out the front, though the door barely slid open wide enough. Back through the mowed-down alley, past the propped-up sign, and back through the woods. That's when it changed to my old dream. Back on Ludlow." He doesn't even notice Cole's look. He's not really even paying attention as he talks. Just telling the twilit backyard what he saw in his dream last night. He pauses as if something occurs to him in that moment. His brows furrow and his lips condense to a single, short crack in his face. "I wish I could've seen what that sign said. I caught a glimpse, and even though I was dreaming, it seemed important to read. Almost like I was torn between getting out of there and turning back to get a better look. I don't know why. I did notice that it was almost as if it was in Sharpie or something. Scribbled over the original paint."

Cole swallows down what feels exactly like a large, slimy frog and whispers, "Ramshackle Row."

Gerome blinks out of his stupor. "Huh?"

"The sign said Ramshackle Row. *Says* Ramshackle Row."

Gerome cocks his head and stiffens. "How do you know?" he asks slowly. Quietly. Like the darkness muffles the words before they reach Cole's ears.

"Because I wrote it."

CHAPTER 16

THAT NIGHT, THE BOYS SIT UP TALKING. TOO FREAKED TO SLEEP. The trusty Lasko sings its ancient song in the corner of Cole's room. Gerome hasn't said much since Cole explained to him that what he saw in his dream was real. That that is, in fact, exactly what the bus yard is like. In real life. Cole still holds back some of the other interesting things about the place in hopes that his buddy won't want to go see it still. But that's exactly what he wants, and he could give two shits about the piles and rows of vintage gas and oil signs or the occasional antique city bus straight out of a black-and-white film under these circumstances. He wants to go see for himself. Because no matter what his new friend says, he is just that. His *new* friend. Even though they're already close, he needs to see before he believes. And Cole completely understands that. He would want the same. The scariest part is that he *does* believe Cole. He can see it in Cole's face. The implications of that truth open a new door into a room most people wouldn't dare step foot into. How is it possible? And the even heavier question, the one that is feeling more and more like the crux of the whole thing by the minute: What does it all *mean*?

"I'll take you there," Cole says. "But I'm telling you, man, it's hard to get to. We've got a fence to try to figure out how to get you up and over, then there's a sketchy walk through the woods, not to mention the pile of old fishing boats at the entrance. That's probably going to be the hardest part for you."

"I have to go, though," Gerome says.

Cole is sitting up in his bed. Indian style, where his head goes. Gerome is laid out on a pallet on the floor. Stacey helped them get all situated before heading to bed herself. Few things in this world can be done as well as a mom making a pallet for someone to sleep on. It's a strict requirement. Passed down through the genes of child bearers from the hunter-gatherer days.

Cole fingers a few leftover Hot Pockets on a dinner plate in front of him. They've long been cold and thus have grown hard. The whole ones clank around the plate while a couple oozers stick to the ceramic. Cole has a brief yet violent flash of imagery as he's looking at these oozers of a man's head cracked open on concrete as if he's fallen from a great height, green stuff pooled around his shattered skull like rotten seepage.

Too many Stephen Kings.

Cole pushes the plate away. Several of the whole ones topple over the edge and onto his humdrum, faded blue comforter.

"What time is it?" Gerome asks from the floor. They've almost identically swapped sleeping positions from last night, as Gerome is now the one lying on his back with his hands clasped behind his head. But instead of looking up at buff superheroes and curvy heroines, he stares at an off-white sponge-textured ceiling.

"Two-oh-two," Cole replies.

At this, a silence grows bold.

While the boys fight the infantile eyelid battle, across the street a lonely young widow pleasures herself. She writhes beneath the sheets as two delicate fingers strum her pain. Her breathing steadily deepens as she reaches the top. The peak of that mountain where bliss isn't a word but is simply all that *is*. Her moans reach a final, unforgivable crescendo that rocks the cold walls of her capacious bedroom. Walls that were supposed to see lovemaking with Barry, future plans discussed with zeal, and eventually children giggling innocently as they pile in bed with Mom and Dad on cool Sunday mornings.

She suddenly realizes she's crying but doesn't know for how long. She rolls over, giving way to a powerful sadness that engulfs her like a black wave. There, facing the open door of the bathroom, a silhouette looms at the head of the darkness, backlit by the frosted bathroom window out into the night.

"Barry?" she whispers. Childlike, through a throat full of phlegm and a nose full of snot. She knows it's not him. She knows nothing is there. But when you lose all that's left in the world for you to love, built-in logic becomes overwritten. An unsuspecting knock at the door is that person returning from the store, sorry that they got held up at the register. It was all a bad dream. A startling phone call is them calling from work, just letting you know that they have to stay late, babe, the boss has loaded them down and not to wait up. It was all a bad dream. For a moment, it's true. A silhouette in the bathroom doorway is him, returning to bed after an early-morning piss, drained empty and full of that red rage, yearning for his wife. The good kind of rage. His favorite time to fuck. And secretly, it's hers as well.

But then the silhouette fades, and there's nothing there but the humming blackness, almost laughing at her stupidity. The orgasm she felt only minutes ago now feels miles away.

But for a moment, she'd felt *something*. That inkling of eyes on her in the dark. A hair-raising notion. Eyes on her in the empty stillness. That idea that something can see you, but you can't see it. Like a wolf in the woods.

With tears drying on her crimson cheeks, Ellie slips under. The last lucid thought to flit through her head being that something . . . someone . . . undoubtedly had eyes on her here in the dark. That she wasn't completely alone. A staccato heartbeat ever-so slightly tickling the air around her ears when she should hear only her own. A black wolf slinking in the shadows.

The stale silence is torn jagged by Gerome. "Let's go tonight," he says.

Cole looks at him like he's suddenly sprouted a dick on his forehead. "Are you crazy?" he asks. He takes a sip of Mountain Dew and replaces it on the bedside table next to an unread copy of *Lord of the Flies*, his summer reading project. The can clanks heavily, still half full. He closes *From a Buick 8* in his lap with only a few pages left.

"Maybe," Gerome says. His own can of Dew has been empty for a while. It lays on its side, a dead man in a desert of carpet next to his pallet. "But I don't think I can even sleep till I see this place for myself."

"You're not going to be able to sleep because of that soda you chugged."

Gerome just looks at him with pique, not saying anything.

"It's two thirty in the morning, man," Cole says in a half-assed attempt to change Gerome's mind. But he sees the look on Gerome's face and feels inexorable admiration, though he can't let his face show it. He sees the fire. The need to confront the situation head-on, yank back the curtain in a single, violent pull. Cole wonders if he were in the same situation, a severe handicap, hauntings of dreams ever since that terrible day that caused said handicap, and now a telepathic intrusion into the most recent of those dreams, if he would come to the same conclusion. To confront that force face-to-face. That's what it all feels like. Some sort of undead force. Something big hiding just beyond the light of their consciousness. Cole is reminded of a scene in one of the books on the shelf next to where Gerome rests called *The Regulators*, where a barren wasteland lay just beyond the backyard fence of an otherwise normal house on a sleepy little street in suburbia. The wasteland can't be seen until you cross the fence line, in which case if you so dare, you will be confronted by terrifying beasts just waiting for newcomers from the cozy little dimension next door. My oh my, what big *teeth* you have. That's what this all feels like.

Up until recently, this has been an incredibly normal summer. The blinding days full of reading and lounging around have blended into one big fluffy ball of boredom. A quiet break from school for a fairly quiet kid on a painfully quiet street on the outskirts of a pretty quiet town in the middle of Tennessee, the heart of God's country.

Big man can't help us here, I'm afraid.

But now there's this *thing*. A sense of something building. Like that feeling on your skin when a summer storm is approaching, all your tiny arm hairs wake up and walk outside with their tiny arms crossed, chatting anxiously with the neighbors and looking up at the sky in fear. Cole knows deep down that feeling isn't the typical midsummer lull when the devastating realization sets in that it's *already* halfway over, knowing, too, that the back nine rolls by much faster than the front.

No. It's a sense of something working behind-the-scenes. Something *moving* that shouldn't be. And it's getting stronger. At least bolder. Cole wonders if Gerome can feel it too. If so, that would mean he probably isn't going crazy. Which would be a relief. Cole certainly *feels* like he may be going crazy, like that unstoppable transformation of a madman from one of his books. But if he can feel it, that'd also mean that inkling is most likely true. And he doesn't know if he's up for that.

Ten minutes later, they're at the fence in the backyard. The air is warm, coating their throats in sweet summer syrup. The wind gently cries in its sleep, perhaps dreaming dreams of summers past.

Cole again is reminded of *The Regulators* and how they seemed to be crossing a similar threshold as the one in the book, where the very idea of safety is something small enough to squash with your foot. As he boosts Gerome up and over, he wonders what lay beyond for them. This feels more like symbolism than something real. He'd hoped Gerome would have listened and done the smarter thing, which was to wait till morning. Cole explained as adamantly as he could that it would be extremely difficult for Gerome to do it on one leg anytime but *especially* in the dark. And this was completely true, but the more pressing reason behind Cole's plea was simply that he was scared. He didn't want to prod whatever it was that showed Gerome the bus yard in his dream. That's heavy stuff there. Too heavy for two teenage boys to pick up and play with.

"You all right?" he asks Gerome.

"Ten-four," Gerome says. He's got his good leg over and is working on pulling the fake one up and over as well. "Just get your hand out of my ass, Brokeback."

They almost went around. They could've started where the fence starts up toward the main road, Carlsen, but Cole thought it'd be even harder for Gerome to push through the underbrush all the way over to this point instead of conquering the wall.

And he was right; after a few moments, Gerome topples

over unscathed. He lands hard, but the muscles in his good leg are extraordinarily strong and they catch his weight soundly. He sits on the wild side of the fence alone until Cole comes over. Cole has a backpack on. It's the new JanSport his mom bought him the other day. She has a thing about buying him a new backpack every year. To middle-to-lower-class moms, only the affordable Joneses are the ones you attempt to keep up with. Trading hairstyles every other season reigns supreme over upgrading the four-door rust bucket wasting away in the drive-way. But he's thankful; this new backpack has beaucoup room inside. Tonight, it's packed with two long-handle flashlights, the garden shears from the shed, and, since he hasn't been out there in a while, a fresh wad of clean towels to switch out with the old ones on his bus. Cole kids himself that the lazy charm of the bus yard will never be lost. But even now, he already knows it will never be the same.

Cole turns around, and Gerome pulls out the two flash-lights from the unzipped top pocket of the pack. They were too tall to enclose it completely. The handles of the garden shears still poke out like rabbit ears.

They each flick their flashlight to life and follow the beams into the black woods. Gerome follows Cole, not knowing the way.

Or does he?

He aims his light beam directly behind Cole's feet and leaves it there as they push deeper. He doesn't want Cole to notice how terribly shaky his light is, which is a good bit worse than Cole's. He can clearly see the two beams in front of him, probing the ground like a couple blind kids' white canes. He tells himself he'd asked for this. He begged Cole to take him to the bus yard so he could see it for himself. He'd be eaten up inside until he went. He wouldn't be able to sleep until he saw it. But talk is cheap, motherfucker, so put up or shut up. He was Billy Badass back in Cole's room, tucked into his comfy pallet on the floor between Cole's bed and bookcase. But now the wee-hour breeze prickles his gooseflesh alive into a semi-spasmodic living organism.

The moon rides high in the sky, a cold silver dollar floating in a sea of starless black. The trees whisper their secrets to the wind all around. An occasional twig break or bush rattle sends Gerome whirling around, his flashlight beam flying wildly through the underbrush. Every time expecting to see a ghoul's long face set back in the branches. Or his grandmother's dead one. Or who knows what.

A faint trickle switches from background noise to something they can splash in. They've reached the creek, pausing to regroup.

"You good?" Cole asks. He's scared himself, but now he sees that he's not quite as scared as his friend.

"Yeah," Gerome replies. "I'm good." *I'm freaking the absolute fuck out* is what he means.

"Okay, so from here we follow the creek bed. I've never done this at night, and I haven't done it period in a little while, so when we start getting close to where we go back into the woods, I'm going to start slowing down and looking for the spot."

It's sort of an unwritten rule among teenage boys that whenever you're snooping around somewhere at night, albeit somewhere in the middle of the woods, you keep spoken words to an absolute minimum. It's like there's some sort of atavistic ex-soldier deep inside, telling you to keep quiet and tapping into a wide array of ridiculous hand signals. Which they don't use on this particular mission, but it does cross Cole's mind as he's leading through the tunnel, the forest bending over top of them cutting out most of the light from the moon. Silver stripes lay scattered across the creek bed where it does make it through. Gerome watches the splash of battery-powered light behind Cole's feet as they crunch down the tunnel.

The breeze is strong through here. It whips across their faces, causing them to blink back tears. Gerome deduces that straight ahead is the point, and the wind is blowing in from the big lake, up and over its rounded tip of rocky beach and into this natural cutout through the woods. He can't see that far ahead but assumes it opens into the farmland back there somewhere. He's seen old man Garrison pulling his tractor onto Boatdock Road on occasion, holding up traffic on Carlsen as he does so, which is a few football fields to their left. His mom told him once that old man Garrison's kids can't wait for him to die so they can build a big boat storage building on the land right there by the lake. She said they'd probably rake it in too. But he likes it just the way it is. Flat and empty. Something to tend to. Some reason to live.

They round a slight bend, and the breeze picks up. Gerome thinks they're getting close to the opening of the field. Here, the stream trickles away to their left, tumbling toward the point where it empties into the lake somewhere below. In the three years Gerome has lived here, he's never been all the way down to the lake. Well, technically, one time. But he never got out of the car. He went with his mom once when she'd dropped off Bree at the boat dock to hang out with her friend. Jamie, he thinks, was that friend's name. Her family had a boat down there and liked to take it out on the weekends. But he never went out on a friend's family's boat, never went down there to fish or eat at the little mom-and-pop restaurant where they served catfish and rock bass and apparently the best hush puppies in town. The one time his mother had asked him why he didn't have any interest in going, he told her that when you're a black guy, the lake is one of the last places on earth you want to be, and when you're a black guy with one leg at the lake, you're literally a walking punch line. He said this with a smile, but in all actuality, he knew he'd never checked it out because he didn't have any friends. And even though his mother had smiled along with him, he could tell that she knew the true reason too. But things are changing for the better, and he could see from the look on her face recently that she thanked God daily for that. He's been out of his room more in the month he's known Cole than he has in a couple years combined. And even though he is scared shitless as they creep down the dark tunnel of the creek bed, deep down he's glad he's doing it.

But as Cole stops in front of him and points at a barely visible path back into the woods to their right, Gerome is quickly reminded of the possible implications of why they're here. The timid smile that had found its way onto his face now retreats, most certainly not to be seen again for a long while.

"This is it," Cole says. He looks back at Gerome to see what he's thinking. "We can still turn back." It's an offer.

For a moment, Gerome almost does it. He almost spins on his heel and begins making his way back. But that sudden urge is stifled. The look on Cole's face when Gerome was telling him what was in his dream—that's what keeps him strong. He *has* to see what is in the bus yard. He has to see if it truly is exactly as his dream said it was. And if so, they'll go from there. If not, if it's not even close, he'll give Cole a good kick in the nads for a good scare (albeit pretty elaborate) and they'll head back to normality stricken with a nice new pang of relief.

But Gerome knows what he'll find.

"Nah, let's go," Gerome says and nods toward the opening.

It's only a rough circle of black in the murky tree line. Its edges dance haphazardly like a kindergartener's cutout. It had closed up some since Cole had been through last—that's why he had almost led Gerome past it. He shines his light through the vague alley, and the orange sign lights up like a lazy fire on the other side of the fence at the end.

"All right, follow me."

They head through, Cole once again leading the way. Branches slap them with every step. Gerome imagines walking down the middle of a dark hallway as arms of dead people stretch from cracked doors down either side, reaching hungrily for them.

They reach the fence line in a minute or two, and Gerome, for the first time, lays eyes on the bus yard. Moonlight puddles on a few of their hulking tops over the tall moat of weeds on the inside of the fence. He's wary of them, like it's a herd of sleeping giants that might wake if they make too loud of a noise. Quiet enough so far to keep them snoozing, but Gerome remembers the pile of boats. Cole had told him that would probably be his hardest challenge. They make their way down the fence line toward the fallen tree, past the long row of old signs propped up against it.

"How you doing?" Cole calls back over his shoulder, not breaking stride.

"I'm doing," Gerome says with a fake chuckle. He's looking at the thin blanket of fog that hovers over the yard at about eye level. It looks like a stereotypical graveyard scene from a horror flick. There's a thickness in the air, some sort of palpable energy coursing through the bus yard. Gerome tells himself it's the humidity, the underlying curse of a southern summer, but he's not sure he believes that. It's not humid at all. It's chilly. He once read a book on Chernobyl—the nuclear power plant that exploded and leaked a death cloud of radioactive particles into the atmosphere in the northern part of Ukraine in the '80s—and the feeling that researchers describe upon walking around that place reminds Gerome of the feeling he's getting approaching the makeshift entrance of the yard. It's like an almost inaudibly low strum on a guitar that goes on forever, emanating from out in the middle somewhere. As they reach the fallen tree and the ripped, open chain-linked fence, Gerome has a nagging suspicion that that humming, that *energy*, has something to do with whatever chased him out of here in his dream last night. And before he can talk himself out of it, he follows Cole through and into the yard.

Jordy's boy is getting worse. They've completely run out of money, which means no more doctors' visits, no more medicine. Unless you count off-brand Tylenol from Andy's Pharmacy in town. Equate or something. It's in a copycat bottle but at least keeps the headaches and fever behind a thin curtain, sort of like the real thing. Andy and his wife Gail have owned the place probably since Jordy's parents were toddlers. Before Andy died of throat cancer last summer. The old bastard knew Jordy by name. With no insurance to speak of, he's been a steady customer for as long as he can remember. Always trying to wheel and deal for medicines for a kid with a cold, or a wife with a UTI. He'd even been caught stealing a few times. Each of those instances resulting in Andy gently taking whatever Jordy was trying to stash in his coat pocket or crotch of his jeans and replacing it on the shelf with nary a word.

Gail doesn't know Jordy by name. At least, she's never said it. Always calls him Sonny. "Y'all holler, Sonny." "Take care, Sonny." "Y'all come back, Sonny." But this last time, she didn't say a word when she rang him up. Scanned the Equate and tossed in a half-used bottle of Chloraseptic spray from under the desk. Word gets around.

It's Jordy's turn, so he sits next to Cam and watches him sleep. The irregularity of his breathing has become painful to watch. This happened very recently. That awful sound coming from his throat has grown worse too. It's hard to hear. It's tough to take. It seems final. A noise you know shouldn't come out of a person's mouth, especially a young boy. You bow to it. Try to keep it happy. Not knowing when it will grow tired of this boring life and bring the hammer of death down on the Danielson household.

Six box fans surround the bed like a bored crowd. They blow warm air at the boy day and night, the little curl bouncing off his forehead. The fever is rising along with the electric bill. Two dangerous trajectories. They can't afford either of those trend lines to continue much longer. He gives the man upstairs the middle finger. Not that he believes there's something there to receive it, but it feels a little good saying "fuck you" to a little god.

The last doc they saw before calling it quits with the quacks said he thought Cam has some sort of infection, but he didn't know what from or what kind. He'd told the Danielsons that more tests were needed to be performed in order to gain answers. But more tests meant more money. So, they'd wheeled Cam silently out of the big building downtown toward their shitty car in the back corner of the gleaming lot, knowing they were on their own from here on out.

His boy rolls over onto his stomach, wincing painfully as he does so. A road map of blue veins lay pulsing atop a thin sheet of skin the color of raw shrimp. The clock on the wall says quarter of three. Thank god he's got a box full of the suds on the carpet next to him to help him get through this shit. His bare feet slide back and forth over the old mud and soda stains. Flat memories of better times. He's sitting in a rickety chair from the dining room.

"Ha!" he belts to the room. "Every room is the same in this fucking single-wide!" Dining, bed, living, laundry, all the same.

Cam doesn't so much as flinch.

One of the thin wooden spokes on the chair backing snaps at his outburst. He tosses a partially empty to the floor and reaches around to pull off the sharp piece of backrest. He holds it in front of his face, staring wildly at it like a woman shopping for the *perfect* wedding ring while her boyfriend follows behind, holding tightly to her purse but even tighter to his trifold.

For a second, he thinks about ending his boy's pain right here and now. He could drive the sharp end of the spoke straight through his little heart with ease. Like a knife through nuked butter. He watches himself stand up and out of the chair and look down at his boy, weapon in hand. Then Cam rolls over onto his back and opens his eyes. He looks up at his father, trying to squint the blur from his failing eyes. The only light is coming from a small lamp on a TV dinner tray in the corner. A soft glow that gives every corner and sharp edge in the room a dreamlike roundness. A hazy uncertainty.

"What are you doing, Daddy?" he asks, half-asleep. His eyes are crusted almost totally shut, and those words grind against the gravel in the back of his throat, taking their life, their *filling*, before limping out into the open room. They sound like words made of snakeskin.

Jordy shivers and drops the spoke to the floor. It rolls into an empty can with a metallic kiss. He falls heavily back in the chair. "Nothing, son." He reaches over and folds down a tangle of sheet by his boy's head, exposing his sunken chest to the small army of box fans.

Death groupies.

"Just checking on you."

Cam smiles, now waning, and falls back asleep. Jordy lets the tense muscles in his neck loose and catches his head with his hands. A tear in the wall of his emotions forms like a bad spot on a dam. And before he knows it, he's sobbing uncontrollably. Tears trace down his wrists and collect in dark puddles on the thighs of his gray shorts. When was the last time he cried like this? Maybe never. He lets the waves of tears roll over him, free of any trepidation or contention. On and on he wails, next to his dying kid. But Cam doesn't even stir. He's sleeping deeply. Not a good deep sleep, not the kind the docs say you need more of on *Dr. Oz.* This is the kind of sleep you could get stuck in. The kind you may never climb out of.

Sandy never comes over from the room next to them, probably thinking it's Cam who's crying. She lies in there on a pillow covered in makeup stains, having never taken any off after work. In fact, she's still got on her whole getup. Minus the heels. They lay in a pleather heap of flimsy lace, the kind you tie up to your calf. Which, on Sandy, is less like sexy and more like tying twine around a brisket before you smoke it. She'd stumbled in and kicked them off, fell into the bed, and proceeded to cry her own self to sleep.

Jordy cracks open another beer and swallows a big burning gulp between cries.

"He didn't do anything," he says to the otherwise quiet room. The fans drone on in agreement. "He doesn't deserve this." His dark heart rotting toward dead black. He tips up the current can and finishes it off in four wolfing swigs, then squeezes it to a crunching pulp before tossing it to the floor with the others. "Someone's gonna pay," he says. There's a fire in his eyes that his wife would kill to have seen just once in the last few years, and that same knowing smirk on his face that scared dumb old Gary Doogan half to death.

With the fans cheering him on, "Oh, yes. *You're* gonna pay."

Cole was right: the stack of boats was quite a challenge. Cole had to help Gerome the whole way over, standing next to him each step as Gerome ascended and descended. Gerome had swallowed his pride and welcomed the hand. The boats were slippery with a clear veneer of midnight dew, a recipe for a broken ankle for even the most sure-footed individual. But after what seemed like an eternity, and after nearly toppling over numerous times, only to be caught and held steady by Cole, he finally reached the bus yard's hard-packed dirt and trash-grass floor. Ground zero. Where all the magic happens. But this isn't the bedroom of some C-list celeb being displayed by MTV's *Cribs* cameras for all the little teenyboppers skipping summer school to see. No, there's *real* magic in this place. That energy thrumming through the yard is dialed up to a frequency so high it feels like it's making Gerome's one remaining, intact femur itch terribly, deep in its bed of muscle tissue. His blood feels like it's fizzing in the creases of his knees and elbows. He imagines a poor stray pup unknowingly wandering into the bus yard and trying to find its way out while its poor little head swells and swells before it pops and gets green mush all over the hard clay.

They're standing at the end of the long alley between the two rows of old buses. Cole looks over at Gerome and says, "You sure you're ready to see this?"

Gerome nods slowly, not sure about shit.

Cole looks dead ahead and raises his light to a sign that's propped up against the front of the bus to their right. Gerome feels a sinking feeling in his gut, accompanied by a rather adamant pang of fear. The splash of light reveals what Cole said it would.

RAMSHACKLE ROW.

"How did you—"

"Know?" Cole interrupts. "I told you, man, I wrote it. Look." Cole walks over to the sign and lays a finger on it, turning back to Gerome. He looks like a teacher trying to hammer home a point to the scared little student in the back of the class. "I found it in a pile over that way." He points a thumb over his shoulder, out toward the twisted innards of the yard. "Took me forever to get it over here. But look, Ramshackle was already here." He's pointing at the sign again. Gerome can see that the light is trembling a bit as he does so. "I think it said something like 'Ramshackle Raceway' or something, but I changed it to 'Ramshackle Row' with a Sharpie." He turns and looks up at Gerome, who's still standing on the base of Mount Boat. "Actually, it took two. First one shit out on me halfway through coloring in the 'O.' Had to run back and steal one out of Mom's catchall drawer." The fog swirls through the air between them, contorting their faces ever-so slightly. Like a kid took a giant eraser to them but only for a second or two.

Gerome steps forward. His features solidify a bit. "Why?" he asks.

Cole looks at him strangely. "Well, I don't know, really. I wanted to make the place cool, because as you now probably know, I actually loved it here and spent quite a lot of time hanging out in the bus back there. I thought it was a good name. Like its own little street or something. I even cleared the space between the rows all the way to the end. Took me two days." He turns and points down a long corridor of blackness. He'll take Cole's word for it. Cole turns back to Gerome. "I know, it seems kinda kiddish now, but I was bored and I've always been a bit of a loner and things like this—*places* like this—have always appealed to me. Places that I can escape to and sort of forget about everything. I think that's why I love reading so much."

Gerome thinks there's a better-than-nil chance they will, in fact, never forget about this place now. That Cole will get his wish. But it won't be because they had the times of their young lives here. It won't be because they spent endless summer days in this backwoods hideaway where time stood still and the rest of the world outside that vine-riddled fence flung around its axis like a broken merry-go-round at the fair. Kids flinging off left and right into the gravel while the operator is nowhere to be found. On permanent lunch break. No, this place will probably forever be a part of them now, because whatever is happening right here under their noses isn't everyday stuff. The world wavers here. Time runs forward and back. The seams of reality don't quite line up at every corner, leaving holes just big enough for things to come through.

Maybe that's an overreaction.

Or an understatement.

Gerome looks back at the sign. The sign that was undoubtedly in his dream. "Not why did you do all this. It'd be pretty cool under different circumstances. Why was it in my *dream*?"

Both boys stare cautiously at the sign. Like the words might just leap off and sink rusty fangs into their throats. A moment of silence falls over them as the gravity of what is happening occurs to each boy individually. That energy like a living thing now, crawling over their skin, forming a gelid hold.

Just as Cole goes to break the quiet in two by asking his buddy if he's ready to go back, Gerome beats him to it. But he doesn't ask to go back. Instead, he says, "Take me to your bus."

Chill bumps run rampant over Gerome's arms as he clanks his way up the stairs of Cole's bus. He knows it's impossible, but he feels now as if his dream wasn't, in fact, a dream at all. No dream can be this accurate. It's like his eyes are seeing all these things for the second time.

He follows Cole down the row between the busted seats. The only lights in the entire yard coming from their two small flashlights certainly set the scene for a person's worst fears to creep dangerously toward fruition. But Gerome is asking himself questions as they push deeper into the bus. Questions that keep his mind occupied. Was his grandmother trying to tell him something in the dream? Was someone else? Was she just dragged along through it because she's always the one with him in the dreams? He thinks yes. But he can't be sure. The only thing he is even close to sure about is that *someone* is desperately trying to tell him *something*. And that something is directly tied to this old bus yard they're poking through.

Poking the bear.

That canted inkling prods harder against the gray walls of his consciousness the deeper they go.

There's a skeleton arm of vine that has crawled through the

cracked window since Cole's been here last. It hangs lazily over his makeshift bed with nothing to hold on to. Cole slides out of his pack and tosses it on the bed. A billion dust particles erupt upward, dancing in the orange glow of Gerome's flashlight like a microscopic galaxy waltzing through the void of space, the negative blackness around them. Cole pulls out the garden shears. Surprisingly, they haven't really needed them before now. The paths through the woods were still relatively passable. The shears' value unbeknownst.

Cole slices off the vine at the top, then tosses the dead limb to the back of the bus. It clatters dryly to a stop somewhere in the murk. Then he pushes what is left of it back out through the crack and slides the window the rest of the way up. For the first time in years, he's reminded of the time when he was chasing a loose basketball before it went out of bounds at a church camp. He saved it (much to the delight of his then crush, the bombshell blond basketball phenom with the terribly unfortunate nickname of Corndog—unequivocally the best athlete at Northeast Elementary), but as it was bouncing perfectly toward his then best friend and teammate Shandy (who was, in fact, a boy and who was bullied for his name among other things until he eventually offed himself in the back parking lot of the very same church some twelve years later; it took three coats of white paint to cover the crimson fan of blood on the back of the old building, even after a full day of scrubbing from a motley crew of green police officers and senior deacons), Cole slid under the long lunch table that had been set up just out of bounds, probably avoiding a few broken ribs, and accidentally kicking out one of the scrawny legs and causing it to flip heavily onto its side.

Cole's mind is running away from the present, pushing forth an old memory, while Gerome waits in the dark next to him.

The inch-and-a-half-thick maple slab that was the table's top just missing the top of Cole's head as he went under back then, but squarely squashing two of the fingers on his right hand into the hardwood floor as he almost made it completely through unscathed. The meat in those two fingers from the second knuckle up exploded out the tips. He stood up completely in shock as he looked at the guts of his middle and ring fingers hanging unabashed from holes just below each nail. Tears never came. He was transfixed. Like he'd found those fingers and picked them up to study them instead of them being attached to his own hand. He remembers being surprised when his mother ran up screaming and started dragging him to the door and then ultimately to the emergency room as she so subtly professed to the rest of the shocked faces in the church's gym.

Gerome continues to wait.

Cole looked at Corndog and saw big tears dropping onto her white tube top, which chased away any pain that was beginning to set in and replaced it with a rush of blood to certain parts of his young body. He looked at Shandy and thought it funny that when he kicked over the table, a big hearty helping of guacamole dip had somehow flown through the air and found itself splattered down his shirt and onto the ball. Later he realized that that wasn't Mrs. Willow's famous guac dip but instead the remains of whatever was half decomposed in his buddy's belly that day. And later again he realized that that was also probably what his buddy's brains looked like the day he decided to see how the barrel of his dad's Ruger tasted. The day of the table incident, the docs had sliced about half of the ground meat off, declaring it "unusable," and pushed the rest back up into the mushy fingers before sewing them up. He remembered the shots around the base of his fingers to numb the pain hurting much worse than anything else that day, yet he knew it was there. Like he couldn't feel *it* but could feel its *effects*.

Much like right now, standing in the dark in this stuffy bus with a friend he now knows he would do anything for, he knows there's probably pain somewhere buried deep. But it's not his own. He feels like he's crossed the red tape into a radioactive wasteland, and whatever is at its middle is blasting its putrid frequency through the line of consciousness somewhere between him and it.

"Earth to Cole."

"Sorry." Cole snaps out of his stupor and says, "Didn't know I left it down. The window."

"I think those things just need like a quarter of an inch, man, maybe less," Gerome replies. "Like a cat through the crack under a door. You ever seen that? YouTube it, it's pretty incredible."

Focus, Gerome thinks.

He shines his light up in Cole's face to see if he's following. Cole, who was looking at him, throws a hand up against the beam and squeezes his eyes shut.

"Sorry, sorry," Gerome says, lowering the light to the safe zone of Cole's chest to avoid blinding his buddy, but he can still see his face from the residual glow. Gerome answers himself. "Yeah, I hadn't either, but check it out when you get a—

Why am I talking about cats right now?

"—chance. There's a grown-ass cat that slides himself through the crack under a closed door. Now forget the *vines,* how the hell does *that* work?"

After a moment of only staring at Gerome, a confused face floating in the gloom, Cole shakes his head and laughs.

"I dunno, man. But why the hell are you talking about cats right now? We're in the middle of a creepy fucking bus yard, which is in the middle of some creepy fucking woods, at the creepy fucking hour of three in the morning." He bends down and begins to peel off the old towels from the makeshift bed of bus seats, bundling them up between his arms. "And you're talking about cats."

"I'm freaked out, man, clearly. Weird shit comes out."

"Here," Cole says, handing him the dusty bundle. "Shove these in the backpack. Push them down as far as you can 'cause the garden clippers have to fit in there too."

Gerome does as Cole says but doesn't think the clippers will fit. "Uh, okay, but don't you want these clean ones before I put the nasty ones on top of them?"

Cole shakes his head without looking up. He's straightening things up now, pushing the seats all the way against the wall, putting the little battery-powered fans on top. The same fans that were in Gerome's dream. Everything in here is just as Gerome knew it would be. Why did he insist on seeing it? He knew it'd be the same. He's numb to it all at this point. The numbness swept over him like a virus. His thinking changed quickly. Pretty much from the moment he saw the sign.

Ramshackle Row. What a creepy fucking name.

He didn't even react when he saw the fans. He reacted more to the fact that he didn't react. What he saw, ushered into his brain so kindly by his wide eyes when ascending the steps into this thing, just as thousands among thousands of snotty little shits did throughout the decades, was only icing on the proverbial cake. The fans are nothing. The makeshift bed is nothing. But as he stands there in the dark, waiting for Cole to finish doing whatever he's doing, he becomes very aware of the yawing mouth of blackness at the end of the aisle. Remembering all too well what came bursting out, back around the bus's emergency door in his dream last night. Is something moving back there behind that sheet of black? Is something about to find its way through the now-open doorway from his dream to reality and chase them out of here, lurching and gargling behind them as they tear through the yard blind?

"Habit," Cole says.

Gerome flinches and squeaks out, "Huh?"

"I brought the clean sheets, towels, whatever, out of habit. I don't plan on spending any more time out here." He stands up and makes sure the window is shut tightly. Gerome wonders why bother if he doesn't plan on spending any more time out here, but he doesn't say anything. Just keeps glancing down that dark aisle. Waiting for something.

Cole picks up his flashlight and turns to look at Gerome with hands on his hips, the cleanup job done. "You wanted to look around in here?" Cole asks. "You had mentioned seeing the fans—hell, *most* of this stuff—in your dream."

Gerome nods. "Yeah, I see everything I saw." He glances toward the back of the bus again. Cole follows his gaze, face turning pallid after the remembrance of the last part of his buddy's nightmare. "Let's just get out of here," Gerome says.

Cole peels his eyes from whatever is drawing them into the lurking darkness, shifting and weaving around itself back there, and replies, "Don't have to tell me twice."

Gerome follows.

He insisted on carrying the pack this time, so when the garden shears fall out of the top and bounce up under the first bus in the line, the one proudly displaying to whatever creatures espied it that they were about to enter Ramshackle Row, no one is behind him to see it happen.

No *thing*, though ...

Gerome himself was too occupied with the task of trying to pinpoint that peculiar sensation, that radioactive feeling as it swam around them. He felt crazy thinking it (but his mind told him nothing should seem crazy at this point), but it seemed to him that it was stronger out here. *Soupier*, even. Meaning its unstable middle probably wasn't emanating from somewhere in or on Cole's bus, which was both a relief and terrifying all the same. All this mind noise muffled out the sound of the shears' blunt thump as it bounced into the sunburned weeds in front of the bus's back tire.

Twenty or so minutes later, when Gerome pulls the JanSport off and goes to toss it over the wall into Cole's backyard, he realizes they're missing. "Shit," he says to the darkness that had descended over them when they'd flipped their flashlights off before climbing over.

"What is it?" Cole lurches around, clicking his light to life again.

"The clippers fell out somewhere on the way back."

"Oh," Cole replies, relieved. He flicks his flashlight off again and stows it away in the backpack, along with Gerome's. Pausing for a moment, elbow-deep, enjoying the comforting residual warmth from their long trek. The air was syrupy, but Cole's skin had been cold and crawling most of the way back. Probably from the wind. Maybe. He pulls his hands out. "No worries. I'm sure as hell not going back after them tonight."

"Same," Gerome replies tersely.

Cole zips up the pack and flings it well over the fence into his backyard. They follow its dark silhouette until they see it's made it. It lands with a wet *fwap* on the safe side of the fence, slamming down on a sleeping patch of dew-covered grass. Cole helps Gerome up and over again and then follows him. It's much more difficult climbing back over from this side, as there is no crossbar for a foothold, but they improvise by dragging over a couple fallen limbs, propping them up against the fence next to each other to form a fairly stable step ladder.

As they trudge through the wet grass, their paths forming darker dashes in the yard, Gerome says, "That place has to be that crazy old guy Donovan's, you know?"

"Whose?"

"You know, the creepy dude who lives at the end of the road? Ellie's—"

"Oh, yeah," Cole says. "I figured that—the yard's probably not too far behind his house. I guess depending on how long that driveway is."

"I bet it's long," Gerome says wearily.

Cole grabs the faux brass handle of the back door and begins a slow turn, trying best to stay quiet. The only noise out here is the timid chatter of leaves rustled awake by the neutral breeze running away from the west.

"I don't like him," Gerome says. Cole stops just short of a half revolution, not quite far enough for the latch to clear the strike plate.

"You've told me," Cole whispers, wondering if Gerome picks up the implication of the question of *why* in those couple words.

He does.

"What if *he's* got something to do with all this? I'm just thinking out loud."

Cole only stares, mind pushing pieces together, the sweat from his palm beginning to slide the knob back to its resting position. He briefly mulls it over, then his mind flits to Ellie. As he pushes the door open into the dark kitchen, he thinks about how badly he wants to see her again. Completely unaware of the gravity around the transition his mind just made.

And as the sun approaches the long line of the horizon, as he's curled up in bed while Gerome snores open-mouthed from his pallet on the floor, he's still thinking of her.

CHAPTER 17

IT'S SIX IN THE MORNING NOW, AND JORDY'S IN TOWN. HE'S
been sitting in the narrow alley between Angie's Antiques and
Hatter Tactical for an hour or so, waiting for his old friend to
get to work. He's polishing off the second of the two road beers
he brought. It's an overcast Saturday morning; a thick layer of
gray clouds blot out the sun like an old eraser, but the heat is still
unabated. A slimy film wraps Jordy's wiry body, the humidity
drawing out stinking sweat from deep inside of him, every drop
polluted with alcohol.

He's not here for Angie, or Angie's daughter, or whoever
runs the antique place now. Although he'd love to stagger
around, poke through old signs, and run his grimy hands down
the long aisle of dusty books. No, he actually wouldn't. The place
smells like mothballs mixed with a dollop of Preparation H.

He's here for his buddy Bill. His old drinking buddy Bill
Hatter, hence Hatter Tactical, owned and operated since '02.
Or '03. Who gives a fuck. About the time old Bill got his life
together and Jordy kept his rapaciously apart. They haven't so
much kept in touch over the years as they have exchanged the
obligatory quick handshake (in which Bill immediately wipes
his hand on the back of his pants after, thinking Jordy probably
too dumb to notice) and ridiculous small talk that neither of
them cares the answers to, but they do it anyway because that's
what you do when you see someone you've known for a long
time but haven't seen in a while.

Jordy's never been inside Hatter's place. It sells guns. And

being that Jordy has a felony on his record, he's not legally allowed to purchase one. But Bill owes him a favor, so he stands
up and heads the rest of the way down the alley toward the back
of the building where, if he remembers correctly, there is a door
that opens to a little concrete area with a small green dumpster.
Before Cam, he'd bought drugs back here a time or five.

The last time they'd shot the shit, albeit about six months
ago that probably was, he remembered Bill saying Saturdays he
opens up shop at eight but always gets there a couple hours early to clean for the week. This must've been after the presumed
"How's work?" question, branching off into the tributaries of
more uncared-for questions. Turns out he *had* been listening.
He *had* remembered the answer to that stupid question all those
months ago. They had been in the cereal aisle. Bill with a box of
Total in his hands like a fuck.

He's whistling as he gets to the end of the alley, and as he
turns the corner, he sees the back door to the building standing
open, propped wide against a big box of bullets. A loose trail of
fallen trash leading from the open door to the little green dumpster marks his old buddy's path. As he weaves drunkenly toward
the door, he hears grunting from inside, growing louder as he
approaches, then Bill comes stumbling out with a mountain of
garbage in his hands. Empty boxes and plastic wrap piled high
above his head. Jordy stops and watches him carry on toward
the dumpster, its black lid flipped open to form a huge, hungry
mouth. He eyes his old drinking buddy with odd interest as he
drops numerous parcels on the way, thickening the trail of fallen
debris.

"Goddammit," he blurts angrily. He tosses what's left in
his hands up and over the lip and heads back toward the door.
Head down, quietly cussing all the fallen trash as he goes.

"Bill Hatter," Jordy says, now leaning against the wall by the store's back door.

Bill literally jumps at the sound of his voice. His man tits jostle beneath his Columbia button-down.

Ah, the tits of easy living, Jordy thinks.

"Oh my goodness, Jordy?" he says. Jordy sees a twinge of fear coming through the surprise. His heart burns even blacker.

Motherfucker is scared of me, he thinks. *Probably forgot what a drunk looks like.*

"You scared me, bud!" he says. He's smiling a terribly fake smile. He reaches out a hand, but Jordy keeps his distance. Like a gas station clerk trying to be buddy-buddy with the sketchy guy who stumbles in, up to no good, till he can make his way over to the panic button. Jordy doesn't take it.

Jordy feels anger rise up his legs and over his belly, but he has to keep his cool. Only for a few minutes.

"Sorry," Jordy says. A palpably empty apology.

He sees Bill quickly look him up and down, taking everything in from the almost-empty beer can dangling in his hand to his red-rimmed eyes. Jordy smiles at his old friend's awful attempt to hide the disgust.

"Well . . . what can I do for you?"

"Let's go inside, Bill."

Bill visibly cowers away. He's seen plenty of movies; he knows how this thing goes. Crazy guy wants something. Crazy guy gets that something, or else someone is going to get hurt.

"Well," he begins shakily. "Few things. One, I don't open till nine. And two, if you're wanting what I think you're wanting, you know I can't sell one to you, Jordy."

Jordy smiles and looks down at his feet, shaking his head slowly for emphasis. This villain skin feels good on him. "Oh,

Bill," he says, looking back up at his old friend with those red-ringed, dead eyes. "One, the door's open." He nods toward it, Bill noticing quickly how much closer Jordy is to it than he is. "And two, surely you haven't forgotten that favor you still owe me after all these years, have you?"

Back when Bill wasn't a tight-ass and was still drinking, Jordy saved him one night from the worst beatdown of his life. He and Bill were at a bar over in Kenton, drunk as a couple skunks. Bill was newly married, so he wasn't supposed to be there in the first place, but the old lady was out of town. They were shooting shots faster than the bartender could pour them and chasing each with big swigs of Yuengling. A bombshell blonde walked by, and Bill got to staring. Open-mouthed, too drunk to care. She passed by without noticing and made her way to the ladies' room.

"I'm gon' grab her ass when she comes back by," Bill had said. Jordy was almost as drunk as Bill that night—hell, probably even had more than Bill. Bill was a cheap drunk, the nice way to say a bit of a lightweight, but he can still remember that googly-eyed look on his old buddy's stupid face.

"You better not!" Jordy had said with a laugh. But next thing he knew, she was coming back by and sure as shit, when she passed, Bill turned in his chair, lifted up the back of her skirt, exposing her perfectly smooth and tone bare ass to the whole bar, and with his free hand came across with a weighty *smack!* Jordy remembers the jiggle like it was yesterday. And remembers that at the time, it had occurred to him, in that moment the world stopped, that if what had just happened had been in another setting, he'd be about as turned on as one could get; dick might not get hard though considering the gallons of Jameson swimming through his blood, but hey, he'd give it the old college try. But in *this* setting, alarm bells sang throughout the place like the devil himself was about to make an appearance.

Incredibly, Bill had spun back around and faced forward before she even knew what had happened. They sat motionless, staring at the Red Sox game above the barback like a couple stupid teenagers. *About the guiltiest thing you could do,* Jordy thought later. She began berating them, not knowing which idiot it was but knowing damn well it was one of them. She slapped each of them. Hard. Then proclaimed to the entire bar that she was going to get her boyfriend. As she stormed off, Jordy had looked back at Bill and said, "What the fuck, man?!" Bill's drunk ass then proceeded to tear up—yes, *tear up*—in the middle of that shit bar. He rambled something or other about not knowing what he does when he drinks anymore, that his new wife is going to finally leave him, after years and years of empty promises, if he comes home and she sees he's been in another fight, knowing damn well it was at a *baaaar* and knowing damn well who he'd have been *wiiiith*.

So, Jordy took the blame. What he also took was the beating of his life for absolutely nothing other than his friend's shitty papier-mâché marriage from a man who looked like he played middle linebacker for the Pittsburg Steelers.

After that night, Bill had stopped taking Jordy's phone calls, stopped drinking altogether in fact. Jordy never really even got an apology from his old friend.

He hadn't thought about this in years. Hadn't even been upset the times he'd seen Bill around town since then. They were young and dumb back then, so why would he? Yet that pang of anger is here now. It eats at him. Like whatever's got his boy. Some sort of rogue parasite. Or cancer from the clearance rack.

Something you have to deal with alone. Some *thing* you have to *do something* about. The way Bill is looking at him doesn't ease his anger at all. In fact, it exacerbates it. He's looking at Jordy like a big small-town lawyer looks at the guy panhandling on the street corner.

Jordy holds out his hand toward the open door like a *Price Is Right* model showing off a new bedroom suite. Bill Hatter visibly slumps, causing Jordy to have to stifle a smile, and walks through the door. Jordy follows him inside, pulling the door closed behind them.

"Don't try anything funny. This ain't a fuckin' stick-'em-up. I'm just an old friend who needs that favor he's owed." They are walking through the back room of the shop. Bill going on a little too quickly in front of Jordy, eager to get into the open store.

Jordy is dumb as dirt, yes, but not the kind of dumb that gets a hand blown off by a firecracker, or a broken pelvis from walking out into traffic. It's a sneaky idiocy, an *aware* idiocy.

So what's back here he doesn't want a loony alcoholic to see? What's the rush? He scans the shelves as they pass through and notices old Bill making a beeline to another open door in front of them, a power walk that would make the plastic housewives over in Inglewood proud, strutting demonstratively past Porches and Range Rovers through the pristine streets of their little richie-rich neighborhoods. Bill's tits have a lot more jiggle than theirs, though. They'd want him to fix that.

Just before they reach the door to the open storeroom, Jordy sees what he's been smelling for. Like a snake flitting his tongue, tasting traces of things good and bad in the air. What's useful for those animalistic instincts and what's not. He giggles absurdly and speeds up a bit to catch up to Bill.

When they walk through the door, Bill takes a sharp left and settles behind a long glass counter against the back wall. In it is a wide array of firearms lying flat on a dated blue strip of carpet running along the bottom of the case.

Jordy doesn't want any of these.

He locks eyes with Bill and makes his way toward him. He's standing at the far end, next to the register, certainly happy to put something between him and Jordy. Jordy allows it. To him, he looks like a man willing to sell. As he makes up the rest of space between him and Bill, he slides a sweaty hand against the top of the case, leaving a thick, murky stripe of grime as he goes. At arm's length now, he looks back and scans the length of the case.

"What's this, fuckin' Subway?" Jordy says. His beady eyes bright, as his body works double time to burn off the long night of drinking. "Aren't you gonna ask me if I want chips or a drink?"

"What do you want, Jordy?" Bill asks. A stony, defeated look on his face.

Bill's left eye twitches involuntarily. Jordy smiles wide at both the question and the unmistakable ex-alcoholic tick.

"I want a gun," he says. "Not one of these cute ones you got here in the case." He pauses to admire the grimy streak from his hand and then turns his full attention back on Bill. Locking eyes to show his old friend the callous beast behind his pupils. The thing that's got a hold of him.

Bill sees it and squirms. "These are all the guns I got, Jordy. I'm a tactical shop, not a gun shop. I mainly sell body armor, bullets, safety gear." When Jordy doesn't reply, only sits there grinning up at him, he says, "You know, eyewear, ear protection. Things like that."

Still, Jordy only stares.

"If you want, I can get you in touch with a couple big-name gun retailers? I've got a guy who—"

"Shut up." All evidence of a smile wiped clean from his face. That quickly. "Just shut the fuck up, Bill. I know you've got what I want. Now go get it so I don't have to make you." Bill has taken a step away from the case. Which is good, considering that probably means there's no panic button back there somewhere. Otherwise, he'd have instinctually moved toward it as the conversation escalated.

Bill doesn't say a word. Just stands there, left eye twitching and a sort of numb bewilderment on his face.

"How's Karen?" Jordy asks.

Bill's lips squeeze into a dash mark, and he begins to tremble. Anger, fear, whatever. Jordy doesn't care what emotion this reaction stems from. As long as what he is doing is working, he's good with it.

"You guys still together?" he prods, a big crocodile smile once again stretching across his face. "Wow, that's great," he says, replying as if Bill said that yes, in fact, they were still together and happy as a couple fat, flightless larks. "Must've been a doozy though, huh? Making it through that night she found out you went out and drank again after she'd told you she would leave if you did. After she said she didn't marry an alcoholic and wouldn't stand for it all those years ago. She still feel the same way? You still going out every now and again to sip on Gramp's old cough syrup, Bill?"

He's reaching. He knows it. But he also knows Bill is scared shitless right now. At this point, Jordy could probably be in here asking for a game of checkers or if Bill had any spare jumper cables lying around, and he'd still get what he came here for.

"Must've been tough getting past that, huh?" he continues. "Jesus, what did she say about you smacking that bitch's bare ass? What'd she say when you went home with two black eyes and a *broken nose*?"

Bill is trembling severely now.

"Oh, wait ..." Jordy reaches up and touches his crooked nose. "That was *me* that went home all fucked up that night, wasn't it?"

Bill is quiet.

"Wasn't it, you fat fuck?!" he screams, slamming both hands down on the glass case. Bill blinks at the outburst and backs against the cinderblock wall behind him, hands out to his sides like he's Velcroed to it. He looks like a chubby tagalong in a bad spy movie. Chips of old paint rub off in thick flakes against the bristly patch of hair on the back of his balding head.

"I don't—"

"Take me to that fucking box in the back room, or I'll kill you and take myself."

Bill's eyes widen into tea saucers, almost big enough to warrant hilarity. Maybe in another circumstance.

Jordy gets a waft of fresh piss and sees a dark circle on the inside of the right leg of Bill's bootcuts.

"That's right, the one in the corner back there. The thing you were hoping I didn't see."

Bill drops his gaze, on edge yet defeated. "Follow me."

The box had been pushed back under the lowest wall-mounted shelf. It took Bill a few minutes to get it out into the open. His hands worked nervously as he pulled away items that had accumulated around it. Jordy had known it was here somewhere. He'd remembered Bill saying something about it long ago, during one of their bar hops. He'd mentioned the

good stuff being in a box in the back. And that if Jordy told
anyone, Bill would have to kill him. Then they had probably
slapped each other's shoulder and ordered another round. Jordy
knew there was a chance it was long gone. But who really cares,
anyway? It's a gun shop. Sorry, a *tactical* shop. There are plenty
of peashooters under the glass in front of him, lined up on that
strip of faded blue carpet. Those were fallback plans. Plan Bs.
Plan Peas. As in, shooters. He's here for the *froth*, baby, the shit
that costs you extra at the Starbucks window. The shit Betty
Big Tits over in Inglewood would order. She pays extra for that
bubbly moustache and so does *he* now. The old Jordy would've
broken in afterhours and smashed a hole in the glass and stolen
one of the little pistols, then hightailed it out, black mask over
head and black gloves over hands. But not *this* Jordy. *This Jordy's
got somethin'-a-big-a-brewin' by God, and he and old Betty Big Tits
are gonna get their fixes while the fixes are there to get and then ren-
dezvous over in hell, him riding shotgun in her white Range while
they bounce over beggars and burning sinners, laughin' at the top
of their lungs while Betty Big Tits sips that fucking rich-lady drink,
white bubbles collecting on the swell of her injected upper lip and
then running down either side of her hootin' and hollerin' mouth.*

"I'll meet ya there," Jordy whispers. Unaware that he said
that out loud, yet fully aware that he is undoubtedly going mad.

Now the box sits open in a cleared spot in the middle of
the room. In it is a hard pile of very dangerous items. They look
heavy and somehow sharp. Exactly what Jordy is here for. Illegal
shit. Shit that'd slap a Class A, B, C, or E felony, depending on
what he picks out of the goody box, to his record if he were to
get caught.

He looks down, almost drooling at its contents. There are
explosives, switchblades, silencers, brass knuckles, everything a

man with a plan could possibly dream of. But he's not interested in any of that. He wants something that'll leave a mess. He reaches in and pulls out a sawed-off shotgun, illegal in the state of Tennessee and good for a Class E felony if found in the possession of.

"This'll be the one, old Bill," he says. Pulling it out and feeling its weight. Its *potential*.

Bill doesn't look at him, only pushes the box closed. It slams heavily. A satisfactory *thunk*.

Like the doors on ole Betty Big Tits's Range.

Bill follows him toward the door leading out to the dumpster, relieved that this drunken lunatic that used to be his best friend in the entire world is leaving.

But then Jordy whips around, faster than a drunk should be able to move, just short of the door. Bill stops and holds his hands out to either side of his substantial waist in a "What now?" gesture.

"Go get me one of the Kevlar vests."

As Bill fetches, like the little bitch he's become, Jordy leans against the frame of the open back door, the right side of his face warm against the thick summer air and the left side cool against the shop's air-conditioned guts. It's a pleasant dichotomy. Not a word Jordy knows but at least *feels*.

Bill returns with the vest. Jordy takes it and tips an imaginary cap. He thinks of warning Bill that if he tells anyone, he'll kill him, but with one look of the fat little man's face, he knows he doesn't want any part of reaping the benefits that being a rat brings.

He walks out the door, then turns back to look at Bill, who's got one hand on the knob, ready to close it tight. He's got the vest wrapped around the shotgun and holds it under one arm.

"I'm doing this for my boy, you know," he says. A brief flash of vulnerability. Brief yet powerful. Powerful enough for Bill's heart to go out to his old friend. Only for a moment. "Thanks for asking about him."

Bill doesn't say a word. He only stares until the door closes between them. Jordy hears the faint and thick sound of the deadbolt jumping across the doorframe. He turns and heads back down the alley.

A moment later, he's walking across the street toward the car. He's not stupid enough to have brought his work truck. It's got DONOVAN DEVELOPMENT & BUILDING COMPANY plastered on the sides for Chrissake. It'd take him fifty beers to make that blunder. Just a drunk guy coming from an alley with an oddly stiff coat under his arm at six thirty in the morning, nothing to see here.

As he crosses the lot, a flier tumbles across the blacktop, being pushed along by the early and eager breeze. It snags on a lamppost directly in front of him, momentarily flashing its message before being torn away. FIREWORKS! it says at the top. Then under that, JULY 4TH. 8–10 PM. AT THE BOAT DOCK! Then in a friendly farewell at the bottom, SEE YOU THERE!

"Nah," Jordy whispers. A crazy guy mumbling to himself in broad daylight. "You won't." As he continues toward the car, a smile stretches wildly from one ear to the other. There's only one boat dock in this shit-hole town, and he knows exactly where it is. "But I'll be close enough to hear ya, that's for sure," he says as he opens the back door of the sedan and tosses his new toys on the seat. "And you best be loud."

He slides in behind the wheel and shuts the door. It clanks awkwardly as the door and frame meet. He smiles again at the thought of Betty's Range. *His* door only sometimes closes true.

We've all got our fixes.

He takes a deep breath in and exhales stinking air against the yellowing windshield. He leans his head back and looks up at the ceiling of this shitshow they call the family car. A half dozen rips hang down like young stalactites in a cave.

"Thank you, God, for the sign," he says. Then he reaches down and cranks the key. The engine roars to life first try. He laughs wholeheartedly at today's luck. "Fuck you, really," he adds. "But thanks."

CHAPTER 18

A WARM BAR OF LIGHT STABS COLE IN THE FACE, TAGGING HIM awake. As he rolls over and peeks the time on the bedside clock, 11:13, the front of his boxer briefs pull dangerously at the sensitive skin under them. Gerome is gone. He doesn't know why but thanks God nonetheless as he rolls off the bed and waddles out his door and across the hall to the bathroom. He looks like he's overdoing an impersonation of a cowboy's bowlegged saunter. Once safely in the bathroom, he takes a private moment to laugh at himself. He's never had a wet dream before, at least not one that he's aware of, and if they were all like this, surely he'd know if he had. He attempts to peel the crusty fabric from his member.

No good.

He tilts his head up toward the droning bathroom fan with a painfully tragicomic grin and remembers a children's story he used to love about a boy named Alexander who fell asleep with gum in his mouth and woke up with gum in his hair and tripped on his skateboard when he hopped out of bed and then dropped his sweater in the sink while the water was running, and he then knew that it was, in fact, going to be a terrible, horrible, no good, very bad day.

This is actually hilariously bad.

He has an idea. He shuffles over to the shower and twists the water to life. After a moment, he turns to make sure the bathroom door is locked and then climbs into the steaming spray. He stands there, facing the barrage of water beads like the Spartan warriors who stand unafraid in his favorite scene from *300* as a cloud of enemy arrows screams toward them. A cloud so thick, it famously blots out the sun. He could pass for a young Spartan boy. His lean frame and long, dense muscles certainly would be up to par.

But did the Spartans have wet dreams, dumbass?

He chuckles as the warm water bashes against his hard belly and pelts his now-heavy undershorts with a sound of something like rain on a tent's roof. He creeps a careful hand down toward the unfortunate situation, feeling for any improvements. The cement-like front of his underwear eventually turns swampy, and he's finally able to safely separate himself from them. He pulls them down and kicks them to the corner of the tub with a waterlogged *thunk*. Then proceeds to take a normal person's shower, cracking up at his own misfortune as he tells himself it didn't just happen. He envisions Gerard Butler waking up in that open-air suite of his in the middle of Sparta, next to that lady with the hard nipples. But instead of sliding out of bed butt-ass naked, he drags the thin sheet along with him as it's plastered around his holy junk. He pulls it over to the open wall and stares stupidly out into his Spartan countryside splashed in moonlight, obviously in too deep of thought to notice the delicate fabric from his bed puddled around his feet. If the queen's nipples were hard before, they're like too whittled diamonds now. Cole pictures her holding herself in a ball, shivering terribly against the chilly midnight breeze rolling through the Grecian fields. His innocent snickers bounce softly around the foggy shower walls.

When he's finished rinsing all the soap and shampoo from his body, he doesn't get out. Instead, he twists the shower knob a quarter of an inch to the left. He stands in the onslaught of almost-scalding water in something like a trace. It's wondrously painful. He begins to feel something like sexy in spite of the tragically adolescent predicament he found himself in only minutes ago.

A grown-man sexy.

He lets the firewater rush over his body. He feels something primitive and poetic standing there, all just to see how long you can take it. Enthralled in the danger, the burning of his skin, and the blurry vision, his mind opens to Ellie yet again. The very reason he woke up in the situation he did. He sees her in front of him. Sees her perfect white skin through the pulsing cloud of steam between them. She steps forward, taking on most of the water herself. He feels the swell of her breasts against his chest. Her yearning thighs pressed avariciously against his own. He reaches around and slides his hands down her ass until he's got a big enough handful, and squeezes tight. Almost too tight. She smiles. It's hot and tender, slick with water. He closes his eyes as she kisses him. She kisses him deeply. So deep that he feels his heart double-pump and his lungs skip a breath. The kiss that says so clearly with unspoken words what she really wants. She has one hand against the back of his neck as she pulls his face hard against hers, reaching her tongue into his mouth. She brings down her lips gently onto his tongue and begins sucking on it as her other hand slides down his body, undulating fingers teasing on the way down, until she settles on what she wants. He throbs uncontrollably in her hand as she strokes him lovingly, at first. Her supple lips continue to suck his tongue so sensually he feels like his feet aren't on the floor. He's only hovering here in the steam, completely at mercy to her. She holds him. She can do anything she wants with him, and he will say nothing, will only plead *yes* with his eyes. The movement of her hand gradually quickens. Cole loses himself in a pulsing world of bliss and cum. He gyrates with each thrust so hard he has to grab onto the stupid little protrusion where the soap sits in a pink puddle of embarrassment. Each spasm like a shotgun blast. After a moment that could've lasted a thousand years, he looks down and releases his penis, beginning to swim back to the shore of reality now.

Hope Mom's not home, he thinks as he crawls out of the choking steam and into the breathable air in front of the mirror. As he dries off, he listens for anyone out there in the living room, kitchen, or maybe laundry room. He hears nothing.

He comes across the note she left on the kitchen counter.

"Didn't want to wake you! At the store. There's sandwich stuff if you get hungry before I get back. Should be around noon. Gerome was leaving as I was getting ready, said his mom called and needed him home. Said to get your LAZY ASS UP! Love you, sweetie!!"

A few minutes later, Cole is dressed and ready for the day. He's got his mowing attire on. Jeans that are a color known only as "once blue" that fade into thick grass-green cuffs down around the ankles, a pair of sneakers that once again can only be described not as an actual color but instead that of a "once" color, this time white, and a cutoff RHCP tour T-shirt with print so faded you'd have to butterfly kiss the son of a bitch to read it.

He's quickly bored of Saturday midmorning cartoons, growing tired of Spongebob's Fran Drescher-esque pitch. He puts the empty plate and smudged glass in the sink and rinses water over them, something his mother has beaten into his head since early childhood. She'd be at the opposite end of the house and still somehow know he was putting one of his little plastic Spider-Man plates in the sink and the second he'd lay them in there, "Run water over that!" would boom from some room somewhere far away.

Speaking of his mother, it's just after noon. He wonders if he should wait and help her with the groceries when she arrives back from the store.

Nah.

All those years of yelling at him to "Run water over that!" playing a role in the quick dismissal.

He punches the TV off, snapping a scene of Patrick chasing jellyfish around with a butterfly net, and heads out the door and over to the shed where his trusty "twenty-one-inch Troy Bilt lawn mower with a high-powered Briggs & Stratton motor" resides.

God, how stupid, he thinks. *The fucking fliers.*

The embarrassment.

I wonder what she did with the rest of them?

One of the wheels is sticky; the plastic grinds wispy tunes against metal.

Probably tossed them as soon as I left. She knew from the get.

He shakes his head. Maybe he can shake the stupid out.

From the get, *you* nit.

He trundles along toward the street, and Ellie's across it, the first stop of the day, when something catches his eye off to his right. His immediate thought is that it's Mom's car coming down the road, back seat packed headrest-high with plastic bags full of Walmart's finest. But there is no car. A piece of paper protrudes from his mailbox. It does a gentle rock back and forth in the breeze like the flag on the moon set in some Hollywood basement back in '69.

Thick gray clouds now hang low, and a rather fervent chill dances on the wind from the west. Cole tells himself that's what's causing the tiny hairs on the back of his neck to prickle as he watches that piece of paper roll itself hypnotically, but does he believe that?

He slams the feeling shut and heads over to it, leaving the mower at the edge of the road. He slides it out of the mailbox and pushes the door the rest of the way closed, a rusty note too shrill for this quiet, lazy day. It's a flier. FIREWORKS! it says at the top. Then under that: JULY 4ᵀᴴ. 8–10 PM—AT THE BOAT DOCK!

Cole looks up toward the tree line behind his house, the direction of the dock.

That's pretty close, he thinks. Then a random thought flits through his head. *They'll be loud.*

He looks back down at the paper and reads the bottom line aloud. "See you there." He folds it up and stuffs it into his pocket, next to his cell. He'd checked it earlier for a text from Gerome, but there wasn't one. He also sees no flier on his buddy's mailbox, and Mrs. Kris's car is absent from their driveway. Cole surmises Gerome probably isn't enjoying himself right now; there's a good chance he's being dragged along this very moment through the aisles of whatever stores reside on his mother's list of Saturday errands.

He smiles at that thought. "Sucks for you, bud," he says to the wind. *Now that Momma knows you can survive outside your man-boy cave, you'll probably be along for these rides from here on out.* He's still smiling as he pushes his mower across the blacktop and into Ellie's yard, sticky wheel still chanting its scratchy whisper. His smile begins to fade as he pushes farther. Fades at the twinge of . . . something. He notices her mailbox is flier-free as well.

You're being paranoid, he tries to tell himself. *What about a damn Fourth flier has your nuts in your gut? Think it's gonna grow teeth and bite you in the ass?*

But that . . . something.

I'll ask her after I mow. I'll feel better then. I need to sweat some bitch out of me. She and Gerome both got it—they just don't sleep in till almost noon is all.

He rolls over to his normal starting point, the front corner. Next to the mailbox. It's a silent watchman. He primes that sonofabitch bulb until it fills with gas instead of fumy air, then reaches down and yanks the pull-rope hard. A lazy cough from the motor is all he gets.

The dead man's switch, dummy.

He pulls it against the thicker handle and yanks again. It fires to life, the only noise on the whole street. Cole glances over at the house and sees Ellie standing at the front window, waving hello. Something she's come accustomed to doing. He throws a quick wave back and pushes forward before his cheeks begin burning there in broad daylight.

We'll talk after, he thinks.

Roughly an hour later, he knocks down the last strip, the driveway bookend opposite the one he began with. He leaves the mower by the road and heads for the front door. She beats him there, opening it as he's climbing the porch steps.

"Kind of a nasty day out, huh?" she says. She's got on jeans and a long-sleeve T-shirt, sleeves pulled up to her forearms in cute little bundles. She looks like an Abercrombie & Fitch model. One of the ones on those big double-sided posters in the mall, candidly throwing rocks into a lake or riding shotgun in a topless Jeep driven by an equally gorgeous boy.

He surveys the sky as he's taking off his shoes. They look like shoes a three-year-old went after with a couple green crayons.

"Sure is."

"I'm glad you went ahead and mowed—could be some rain coming." She takes a step backward into the house, still holding the door open.

"No problem, lady, it needed it. And of course, if I'd waited, you know it would have rained for three days straight. Always seems to work that way."

She laughs and playfully squeezes his arm as he passes by. She closes the door behind him and locks it. He stands there, off to the side in the foyer. It's too large and too cold. Chock-full of empty space. Space made for bundles of shoes and armies of coats, yet it remains bare. He'd done his best to knock off all the grass clippings that clung to his clothes, but there was always a good deal left, holding on to his shorts for dear life. He minimized the damage at least. She has a beautiful house, despite the coldness and uncomfortable emptiness, and he likes to show that he tries very hard to keep it that way when he comes inside. A gentleman.

He follows her into the kitchen, stopping at his usual spot at the bar like an old townie at name-your-local-shitty-honky-tonk. But this time, she points to the living room behind him, where two glasses of sweet tea already sit, beaded jewels of condensation covering their bottom halves.

To the sofa this time, huh? he thinks. *Maybe the next time we'll try the master bed, what do ya say, ma'am?*

He smiles at the tragically high levels of testosterone coursing through his young-adult body, for the second time this morning. Ellie is fiddling with something on the marble countertop in the kitchen as Cole sits down. The cold leather sends goosepimples down the backs of his arms, also for the second time this morning.

Second time in an hour, he thinks. Then . . . *the flier.* It's in his back pocket. It makes a crunching sound as he straightens up away from that cold leather of the sofa's backrest. Funny how it's always the expensive things that are cold and lifeless. Money itself is cold, like a good chunk of the people who have a lot of it.

"Hey, did you get a flier in your mailbox this morning?" he asks over his shoulder. His eyes flick from one fragile item to the next, items on end tables and fireplace mantles. He thinks, not for the first time, that as beautiful as this place is, it's just not *Ellie*. It's not her at all. He sees her in a single-story ranch (not that he knows what that type of home is called—he simply pictures its low lines and long roof) plopped in the middle of a few forgotten acres somewhere; he sees her baking cookies while a couple little ones waddle around the house and a small stack of bills rests on the kitchen table, bills that won't be paid a day early nor late. He sees himself coming in from work, kissing her busy little face as he takes his coat off and tosses it on the back of the couch behind him. Not a leather couch.

She arrives in the living room and sets a plate of cheese and crackers on the marble table in front of them. She sits down on the other end of the couch. "I did not, why?"

"Just wondering. I got a flier saying the boat dock down there is going to shoot off fireworks on the Fourth."

She's nodding and reaching for her tea. "Yeah, I think they do that every year." She takes a sip, peering at him over the rim of her glass, her upper lip appearing comically large. But her *eyes*. Eyes that can absolutely melt a man's heart. Surely she knows this and does it on purpose, gives him those eyes like that. Probably for the hell of it. Poor girl doesn't have much excitement in her life these days. "Guess I'm not invited," she says matter-of-factly, setting the glass between her legs. She's facing him, sitting Indian style.

She could pass for a teenager, he thinks. *An incredibly blessed teenager. She could play the girl who's barely old enough to drink at the star football player's party in name-your-teenage-summer-smash. The one where the girls all snarl and the boys all gawk. She goes on, moving through water while the rest of the peasants boink around, unbeknownst to her.*

Her golden-brown hair is pulled back in a tight ponytail, exposing the kind of jawline one of those big-name modeling agencies cream their pants for. Someone bigger than A&F. The condensation from the glass turns her jeans dark between her legs. It slowly spreads there, turning the crotch damp one fiber at a time. She doesn't seem to care. And he can't help but gape. She raises her glass for another drink, leaving that softball-size dark circle between her legs in plain view. He finds his eyes wandering back up to her face and sees her staring at him again over the glass's rim. His eyes flit away.

"Guess you're not," he says quickly.

She swallows and puts the glass back down there.

"But why was I?" he continues.

"I don't know. Maybe because you're the new kid on the block," she says, smiling again. Even though *she's* actually the newest.

"I wonder if Gerome got one," Cole says, sort of to himself.

"You guys are cute. I'm surprised you haven't worn a path in the grass between your house and his."

"Oh, you just sit there and creep on the neighborhood guys, huh?" he prods, giving her the most lovable smile he can muster.

"Hey." She's playing along. "I'm a boring lady. I don't have much else to do!"

When the snarky chatting and sweet laughter settle, Cole remembers what his goal for today is. He silently gathers a plan of attack in his head. But he has to be careful. He can't let her know what's going on—not at all because he's scared she might tell her father or even get angry herself at their little expeditions, poking around some property that's not theirs in the dead of night. But instead, she can't catch on because he doesn't want her in on this. He doesn't want her to get hurt. He truly cares for her. Cole has had a handful of girlfriends in his young life, and never had he felt this way toward any of them. It's a kind of primitive instinct to keep her safe. To protect her at all costs. He thinks it's love. And whatever is using Gerome's dreams to try to send some sort of dimension-hopping message to them is certainly doing it for a reason. And then there's that sense of something malicious lurking nearby. Something building its strength, biding its time, slithering in shadows and growing impatient.

How can he start this conversation? What question can he ask to get the ball rolling on his quest to glean some sort of knowledge about what in the hell hijacked Gerome's dream? Or vision. Whatever that was. And what does that old bus yard have to do with it? He thinks for a moment. She watches his mind work and patiently waits. A gleaming mouse in the safety of the light.

"So," he shoots. "How's your dad?"

You fucking dolt.

She tells him that he is good. Same as always. Although it seems like she sees him less and less these days, even though Cole could probably throw a stone and hit his house from where they sit. Her words, not Cole's. Cole does take the opportunity to prod her statement, see how much info he can safely extract from it without Ellie getting suspicious. Again, not that she'd do anything about it. He just wants to keep her as far away from this as he can.

He asks her how far she thinks he can throw a stone. And that her dad's place sure seems quite a ways back there. She says that it is, but she's almost positive a big strong boy like himself could throw a rock all that way. She says this with a demeaning smirk, and it takes everything in him to stay on target. To keep the important stuff dead ahead and not waver at all from a quick, flirty jab from the most beautiful girl he's ever seen.

"Well, I'm definitely big and strong. But a *man*, not a boy," he says with a smile, allowing her only enough time to make a funny look. "What else does he have back in those woods?" He hears how it sounds and makes alterations. "You know, since he's got a big construction business and all. He have some big warehouse or anything? Someplace to tinker with all his toys? Seems like a guy that should have a big building full of big bulldozers and stuff."

He watches her reaction carefully, but she remains nonchalant and indifferent.

"He used to have a dog named Dozer," she says. A nostalgic smile falls across her face. The blissful look of someone touched by the past, the *good* past. The reverie of good old times. "He was a cutie. Bull in a china shop, that pup. But cute came easy. I'm pretty sure he's buried in his backyard under a big tree. But that's the only dozer out there as far as I know. Dad doesn't tinker much."

Cole takes a measured sip of his sweet tea and says nothing, hoping she'll continue. She does.

"There's a barn back there. I haven't been through that gate in years, funny when you think how close it is. I don't know why, either. Well, yeah—"

She pauses. Her eyes literally seem to glaze over for a moment.

There it is, he thinks. *Whatever she's thinking about, that's it.* He knows it. But she continues on, leaving that thing behind. That token of knowledge that could help explain some of this. He chooses not to push it in hopes that it will come back around. Peek back out of the black past.

"There's a barn off from his house. I bet he spends some time in there, but I don't know. I had forgotten about that barn."

She takes another sip, Cole once again taking a peek at that wet spot between her legs, not able to help himself. This time, she replaces the glass quickly. With purpose. Whatever he thought she was allowing him to look at earlier was most certainly all in his horny little head.

"I bet he does too," he adds. "Spend time in there, I mean. I never see the guy."

"Me neither," she says. A sad statement, but she's smiling. "He's slowly but surely backing off. He was so worried about me after the accident. I think he knows I'm getting better, so he's easing off on the visits and things. He still calls me a lot, though. Actually, probably more than ever."

"Just a dad being a dad," Cole says, not really knowing what that means himself.

She smiles in agreement.

"Nice guy," he adds as he takes another swig, finishing off the watered-down bit of tea swirling at the bottom of the glass. He doesn't believe that one bit, for what it's worth. He thinks Mr. Donovan is probably about as nice as a Holocaust guard, pushing bony children away from the gate in annoyance. Heavy, disinterested, half-assed shoves. Away from the gate. Away from freedom. Away from the gate. Not today, little ones.

"Well, better go knock out Gerome's before it rains."

She takes his glass along with hers to the sink, then walks him out.

"You be careful out there," she says as he walks out onto the porch. He turns around, brows furrowed a bit. *Careful?* he thinks.

But she only points to the sky. "Lightning kills more mowers each year than everything else."

A relieved smile spreads across Cole's face. "So uplifting. You just made that up."

"Sure was. And sure did." She flashes that brilliant, heart-stopping smile and shuts the door between them, peeking through the shrinking crack until there is none.

I fucking love that lady, he thinks as he heads over to the mower.

And as he trundles over toward Gerome's tall grass, all he can think about is that crumb he stumbled over. That blank pause. That crumb that's certainly part of a bigger piece. But of what, he does not know. He has a feeling, though, that it's rotten. A bad piece of fruit, smelling of ether and rotting into vestigial gout on the forest floor. Unseen and evil.

The sun is about a hand's width lower in the sky now, and Cole flips free the dead man's switch, killing the motor for the last time today. He looks up and sees that it's burned away the clouds from earlier. Instead of being hidden, now it's heavy and bright. Only a summer sun can feel so thick, like you can sense that it's as deep as it is wide, pushing you into the dirt with its mass. As he walks toward Gerome's door, he begins thinking how nice a fall sun would be today. A fall sun is just a paper cutout glued to the crisp blueness. Thin and quiet.

But fall meant school. Maybe he's okay with a heavy sun for a while longer.

Gerome's mother's car is back in the driveway. He hadn't seen them pull up. He was probably lost in thought, replaying his conversation with Ellie on a loop in his head, listening attentively for any clues previously unheard. He'd found nothing.

Bree answers the door, not saying hello to Cole but simply, "Gerome's in his room. He just took a poop in the hall bathroom, so if you got to go, I'd hold it if I were you." She giggles at her scandalous announcement. "Mom says something's dead inside him."

A few minutes later, Cole is sitting on Gerome's futon and wildly thumbing the controller in his hands. Gerome thinks over Cole's conversation with Ellie. He's lying on his stomach on the floor, flipping through an early '90s Marvel comic. He thinks about all the main points of Cole's meeting with the chick who's too close to it all. The chick who somehow seems to be the center. Yet the chick who also seems oblivious. The dog, the barn, but especially that interesting little pause that Cole told him about. That *something* that was obviously not *nothing*, something painful and hard for her to think about. That something that was the reason for her not visiting her father's house in so long.

Gerome mulls it over, and Cole continues to flick and punch on the controller while he waits for Gerome to come up with something. He doesn't.

"So weird," Gerome finally says. True confusion laced in both words.

Cole clicks pause and swivels in his seat so they're

face-to-face.

"Right?" Cole cocks his head.

"So she didn't say anything about the bus yard at all?" Gerome asks, just making sure he's got that part right.

"Not a word. I really didn't get anything out of her but that strange glazed-over look when she almost told me why she hasn't been over. That's really the only meaty thing I got."

"Maybe she just doesn't know about it," Gerome says. "The bus yard, I mean."

"Yeah, or maybe she just didn't really think it was noteworthy enough to bring up—"

Bullshit, he tells himself.

"—I mean, even though it does have some cool shit in there—old shit people like the dudes from that *Pickers* show would go batshit for—it really is just a glorified junkyard."

Bullshit again, cowboy.

"And she's a woman," Gerome adds. "Women don't care much about that stuff. My mom has never even paused on *American Pickers* when she's flipping through the channels." He dramatically shakes his head. "No respect for the past. Damn shame."

"You're an idiot. But could be somewhat true. Plus, man, it's not like I asked her for an inventory of her dad's assets. It was a pretty casual convo."

"But in the end, we didn't get any closer to figuring out what's going on," Gerome says. He looks at Cole squarely. The frightened boy inside Gerome sometimes peeks through his spongy wall of humor. So tall it casts a shadow over everything else, but if you punch hard enough, your fist will come through the other side. Gelid air swirls over there.

"Nope," Cole says. "But we will."

Gerome joins him on the sticks. Both boys keeping their minds off what happened the last time they were in this room together. *Madden* was the clear choice today. *Zombies* had been tossed behind the stack, safely hidden against the wall. A good old-fashioned football game is about as scary as an episode of *The Suite Life of Zack & Cody*.

The boys play for a couple hours before Cole starts getting antsy. He looks out Gerome's window and can tell that the sun is hanging low and heavy out there. He doesn't necessarily want to still be here when it finally slips below the tree line. Not yet at least. That image of whatever had a hold of Gerome's face is still fresh in his mind. Like a fading sunburn that hasn't yet begun to peel.

"Where'd you guys go this morning?" Cole asks between games (Falcons 42, Titans 27). Matt Ryan's goofy, grinning face is displayed on the screen, his game stats scrolling next to it.

"My dad's supposedly coming home next weekend. Just for the weekend. So Mom took us to Hobby Lobby to buy some streamers and stuff to set up before he gets here."

"Damn, just for the weekend? That blows," Cole says, genuinely bummed for his buddy.

"Yeah, it does. Quick turnaround this time."

"Super quick after having been gone for so long. I still haven't ever seen him! That's nuts."

"He says it's a big money year. Economy is getting better, and the company's orders are sky-high. It's a good thing. I don't mind it." Gerome picks up his controller, the good one. It's a rule among boys that whoever's house they're at gets first dibs on the controller of their choice. Home-field advantage. "Another one? I'm gonna beat your ass this time."

Cole tosses his controller, wonky joystick flopping stupidly, over to the side. White flag thrown. "Nah, man. Better act like a dick and head."

"Suit yourself. I don't blame you anyway. I'd be scared too," Gerome says.

For a moment, Cole thinks Gerome is talking about what happened the other night, but after a cursory glance at his expression, he could tell he was just shit-talking about his *Madden* skills. Which were, for the record, almost nonexistent. *Madden* wasn't his game. Wasn't really Cole's, either, but he was at least competent.

Cole chuckles like a bad guy in a bad movie. "Maybe someday, champ."

And just as he's about to leave Gerome's room, he turns and asks, "Hey, you get a flier in the mail this morning?"

"Sure did. Fireworks at the boat dock. Why?"

"Just wondering. I did too. But Ellie didn't. Doesn't that seem odd?"

Gerome thinks about it for a moment. His own clear-cased controller blinks adamantly next to him. Blue boops and beeps dance dully in the slanting late afternoon sunlight. "I guess. Yeah, yeah, that is kind of strange. Not like she lives with anyone else who could've gotten it without her knowing."

Both boys ponder over this for a brief moment before Gerome breaks it. "Maybe whoever passed them out knows the babe's old man is nutso." He walks over and twists the blinds shut. The bright stripes across Cole's chest fade away. "I bet the old man didn't get one, either."

Little did either of them know that one of those statements was true. And the reason for it is maybe a stone's throw away. Maybe a bit farther. Not too far for a big strong boy, though. Lying in wait. Growing impatient with an unknowable hunger.

CHAPTER 19

THE ONLY PLACES YOU'LL FIND OPEN FOR BUSINESS ON A SUNDAY morning in a small town in the South are mom-and-pop restaurants and the local feedstore. Occasionally, a couple of those hipster coffee spots. Cole's grandmother always said that atheists sleep in late, and that's why they never see God. Cole always gave her a polite chuckle.

Cole and his mother, Stacey, sit across from each other at a small plastic table wedged in the corner of one of these mom-and-pops. The ladies who come to get their hair done up by Stacey told her this one's the best in town, so she likes to drag Cole over every now and again for a warm, salty meal. He can feel his arteries tightening just by looking around at other people's plates. It's called Gibbly's, and on Saturday and Sunday mornings, it turns more tables than the Hooters over in Oak Ridge. Mr. Gibbly himself has host duty these mornings, sending the usual off to the kitchen to help fight the tsunami of tickets. He's a bony old man with a nose cocked about three healthy clicks to the left and breath like his lungs are basted in bile. He wears a permanent frown on his leather face. Even as he boldly stared at the swell of his mother's tits while he tossed down a few yellowing menus before shuffling back to his post at the front of the house, the frown remained like a plastic thing, unable to move even if he wanted it to. Cole saw his mother blush against the onslaught of the old fuck's liver-colored eyes and had a quick and heavy urge to punch him square in the gut, surely breaking something loose in there and eventually ending his life, like Houdini. But that anger passed as soon as he turned away; he never said a word.

The clock on the wall says 11:38. It's one of those ridiculous cat clocks where the eyes and tail flash to and fro with each passing second. The only people in Gibbly's this morning are churchgoers and farmers, as has been the case for the few other Sunday mornings they've been here. Although these people call it "Sun-dee." Cole scans the dusty crowd and wonders where the big businessmen who work in those shiny buildings Ellie's father builds eat their Sun-dee brunch.

They probably eat their meals in Spring Hill or Columbia, where they probably live. Where most of those buildings probably are. Around things that are going somewhere and people on the same path. Places where there's Starbucks and street trashcans and street trashcans full of Starbucks cups. Not this place. Places with Uber and actual company ladders. Slathered in grease, sure, but they're there nonetheless. At least they're able to climb if they're so inclined, those people who live in places like that.

Not places like this. Everything's a sin here. It's all hairspray and walking canes.

Cole wonders where Nolan eats. Wonders if he ever actually eats outside of his home. The guy seems to be a special kind of hermit. The kind that can not only function when he does venture out into public but can also apparently run a very successful business. One of Cole's friends in elementary had a mom who worked at the prison over in Pikeville. She'd come home and tell them scary stories about foam that grows on the black guys' mouths in there and big mean guys who like to make other little guys (like them, come to think of it, they'd always realize, then exchange a terrified look) bend over and wash the floor while they put things inside them. She spoke of drug kingpins who ran whole neighborhoods on the outside from *inside* the prison. They had more money than all their buddies out running the streets combined. One of them—his name escapes Cole, Shane or Shank or Shade or something—she said would casually ask her every Monday for a can of dip in exchange for six hundred dollars. He wanted one can a week. And he wanted to pay her six hundred dirty dollars each time. She claimed she refused weekly, but even then, Cole was smart enough to know she wouldn't tell them if she hadn't.

Nolan's like that.

At least, he *thinks* Nolan is like that. A mastermind within the confines. Not for the first time, Cole wonders what his recent obsession with this man stems from. A tiny, unearthed part of him is adamant that he's wasting his time. It's calling up through the dirt in muffled whines, telling Cole to move on and enjoy being a kid while he still can. But he cannot. The rest of him screams that little whiny part of him back down and controls Cole to press on. There's something there. He spins his water glass in his hands, droplets rolling down the back of his wrists, and thinks of Ellie.

A phlegmy cough breaks Cole's concentration, a booming noise that only someone who qualifies for AARP can produce.

"How are your eggs, honey?" his mother asks. She's pretty in her green sundress. A couple pea-size curds of mulch cling to the valley under her bosom. They'd been at the feedstore earlier, which also sold flowers, mulch, and, strangely, coffee mugs. Cole let the little clingers be. They somehow gave him comfort, protecting him from the pretentious eyes of the smelly farmers and the even smellier church crowd, which he and his mother were despicably apart of neither, but the little mulch clumps let everyone know they weren't out-of-towners anymore, that they were gonna plant some flowers today, by God, and just keep gumming that bacon, Grams and Gramps, mind your own business.

"They're good," Cole says. And they were. As plain as this place is—simply a hodgepodge of blue and white plastic chairs, even a few random brown metal ones speckled throughout like liver spots, tossed haphazardly atop a peeling yellow laminate floor—the food is divine. A salty gift from a plump, overall-clad god.

She takes a bite of her omelet. It's the size of a newborn. "You going to help me with those flowers when we get home?"

"Of course, Mom. Love to," he says with a sideways smile as he plows another forkful of greasy eggs into his mouth. "Aygs," the waitress had said when he ordered them. A mole the size of a cockroach from Madagascar was plastered above her left eyebrow. If she'd looked up from her notepad even once, she'd have seen him staring at it. A single hair as thick as a dog's whisker sprouted from it. To Cole, it looked like a hand reaching from a fresh grave.

On the way out, old Mr. Gibbly simply grunts at them, taking another unabashed glance at the swell of his mother's breasts beneath her dress. As they walked toward her Cherokee in the second row of the parking lot that flanks a crumbling string of closed storefronts and a couple others on life support, Cole notices a few beer cans in the alley between Hatter Tactical and some antique shop that he couldn't read the sign to. Its scroll-like cursive was too thin and gangly to be seen from where they are.

People are such pigs, he thinks as he plops down in the

passenger seat. A smell as airy and green as his mother's dress wafts up to his nose. He certainly wasn't against beer. And he'd certainly had his fair share on a handful of occasions (all of them followed by a morning of pounding headaches and laborious breaths through a throat scorched and coated with a thin film of stomach bile). Not since he and his mother had moved, though. He just never understood how someone could litter so blatantly.

As they pull onto the road and accelerate toward home, he pictures a drunk sitting splayed in that alley, drinking his sorrows away right there in front of God and everybody. He remembers being a boy and passing a wino sleeping on the street downtown, sun glinting off millions of windows and acrid notes of rot and exhaust churning in the air, and his mother had seen how he was looking at the man. Later in the car, she'd said from the driver's seat, back over her shoulder, "When life goes down, so do the suds, bud." Cole ponders the possible life of the man with the cans. Then the thought is gone.

A few minutes later, when they come out into the opening of their street, through the overhanging trees that run all the way to Carlsen Road behind them, Cole knows something is wrong. He can see a huddled form sitting on his front porch and knows at once that it's Gerome. A virus of dread quickly steals through his body. His initial thought is that something happened to Gerome's father. Maybe his big rig slipped off a mountain road somewhere on the way home.

"Is that Gerome?" It takes Stacey until they are slowing down to turn into the driveway before noticing he's there.

"Yep," Cole says. Gerome's got his head in his hands. "Sure is."

Gerome hears them pull in and does an incredibly poor job of putting on a face like everything's okay. Hunky-dory, right as rain. He waves a hand at them in an awkward hello.

The Cherokee comes to a squeaking halt in front of the garage. "I'll get the flowers. You go see what's wrong," she says matter-of-factly, no questions asked. Cole loves her for it. He hops out of the car and walks over to Gerome, who has now stood to greet him.

Stacey carries flowers in each hand around the side of the house, away from them, to the place in the backyard where they'll soon be planted. Once she has disappeared around the corner, Gerome looks at Cole flat and cold, ditching the effort at a false face now.

"I had it again last night," he says.

"Had what?" Then Cole knows. "The *dream*?"

"The dream. Only worse. Worst I've ever had in my life. I woke up in the floor on my back. Mom was shaking my shoulders, and Bree was standing in the corner screaming."

"Jesus, man." It's all Cole can think to say. Then when Gerome doesn't help him, only glances down at his feet and works at all that's on his mind, Cole suggests, "Let's go inside."

As they pad single file down the hallway toward Cole's room, with plates of cheese and crackers and soda cans in hand, Cole silently scolds himself for leaving Gerome last night. He'd ditched his friend, left him all alone to deal with this himself even though they are very much in this fucking thing together. Gerome just happens to be the vessel. He didn't ask for it. Cole can't help but wonder if he'd never found the bus yard if any of this would be happening. But as he jumps up on his bed and Gerome at his spot in front of Cole's little library, deep down the quiet, mewling coward inside him is wiping the cold sweat off his microscopic brow, thankful he wasn't there in Gerome's room last night to witness whatever ugliness took place.

"So, tell me," Cole says. "Everything you remember."

"I remember it all. That's the problem." He stares a thousand miles away at the splotchy carpet between his feet. "I don't think I'll ever forget this one, either." He cracks open his soda, and a fan of mist erupts from its tab, a miniature firework backlit by the light coming through the window. "It's Nolan, Cole. Whatever is going on has to do with Ellie's dad. Whoever, *whatever* he is."

"Tell me how you know. I mean, besides the fact that he's creepy as hell and it sounds like he's been doing a great job of staying out of the public eye as of late."

"He was in my dream. I know it was him. I couldn't see his face; Mom shook me awake before he got to me, but I know it was him. He was running for me. Running like he was angry. Coming to kill me as I lay there in the street." Gerome spoke in a staccato rhythm, each sentence a synopsis of something larger and scarier. "Not like he was coming to help. I just know it was that fucker." Gerome's not even looking at Cole as he says this. He's looking straight through Cole's bedroom wall like there's something interesting out in the hall closet. He's rocking slightly, back and forth, with nervousness or anger or fear, something. All three.

"Whoa, whoa, whoa," Cole says, holding his hands out like a lawyer. A bad lawyer who knows his client is a stone-cold murderer but keeps a beautifully stern face for a yearlong case. "Start from the beginning."

Gerome literally shakes his head clear and takes a big swig of his soda. His Adam's apple jumps high in his throat, then falls back into place. "Okay," he says. "From the beginning. From the beginning." He searches for it. Cole can now see with painful clarity just how much all this is affecting him. For a black kid, he looks pale. More yellow than brown, the color of a catfish. He doesn't look good.

We've got to figure this shit out, Cole thinks. *And quick. He can't keep having these dreams. They take too much out of him.*

Gerome finds it. "Okay, it started like the other one did."

He explains how it once again began in the bus yard. He and his grandmother hid from something in Cole's bus. It had been just outside. He could hear it breathing through the walls. He said they were huddling on the seat-bed, the little fans buzzing behind them. Then the thing was at the back of the bus. It had gotten in somehow. Gerome and his Nannie ran. They ran as fast as they could, but it didn't seem like it was fast enough. Gerome asks Cole if he knows what it feels like in a dream when you're running, but it's like your boots are drying pies of concrete and the scary thing can always haul ass? Cole says he knew. He'd had a few terrifying dreams himself as a kid, usually having something to do with that famous cat-and-mouse game for your life, but you never get to experience what it's like being the cat. Years later, he'd looked up the meaning of such dreams, as an inquiring young mind is wont to do. He found a website that said he was avoiding something or someone. Having an "idle attitude about the issue helped it manifest," it had proclaimed. Provided was a four-step process to help break down the dream that ended with an examination of the attacker. He'd laughed and shut his laptop.

Gerome describes the utter hatred that thing had for him being there. Trespassing. A tick on the thing's sack. As he and his grandmother leaped from the bus and ran for the boat pile, both struggling mightily with their own particular ailments, he with his one leg and she with her brittle old body lurching along beside him, closing on gold and silver in a fucked-up clodhopper dash. On a whim, he'd spun and grabbed the RAMSHACKLE ROW sign and hurled it behind him toward the bad thing crashing through the brush. The sign was way too light. He'd flung it like a big Frisbee, but it struck the thing in the chest and the thing let out a booming *whoosh* of noxious air. They pulled away.

Cole asks if Gerome saw the thing's face.

"Like a shadow," he replies. "It was broad daylight, but the thing was a shadow."

Cole can clearly see the fear in his friend's eyes as he describes the bad thing.

"It hated me." Gerome says they escaped, and once again the dream seamlessly transitioned to a re-creation of the accident. He was following his grandma across the street at that terrible spot. He'd heard the slap of the magazine on the blacktop. "But this is where it gets weird. This is what shook me up so bad," Gerome says. To Cole, he looks too frightened to continue. Like he's scared something will hear him and shoot an arm out from the darkness under Cole's bed, dragging him away and into another place where scary things live.

"Tell me," Cole all but pleads. His shoulders are square. He's locked in.

"It wasn't the *Eastbay*. It was a letter, Cole. A letter in an envelope." He shifts his legs along with his eyes. "It said Nolan on the front. Blue, faded ink."

There are a few unfortunate moments in everyone's life when a brusque fear becomes real. It's no longer a thing you hope won't happen but something that has teeth and has to be dealt with head-on. Like a flimsy tent trying to keep out a bear. Once the damned trestle snaps, shit, as they so eloquently say, hits the proverbial fan.

This is the first of those moments in Cole's young life.

The moment he hears Gerome utter the name on the letter, he knows like he knows his own nuts that this thing is bigger than them. Whatever it is. There's something real here. Something somehow yelling at them through the conduit of dreams. Cole thinks of Ellie. Why is he so worried for her?

Maybe 'cause her dad's the monster? his mind says.

What's dad hiding?

"I'm standing there in the road holding it. Frozen, like it's a winning lottery ticket. There's a big bird Kamikaze-ing my head. It's swooping down, diving at me as I'm about to open this letter to Nolan. I look up, and then everything's in slow motion. It's not my grandmother. It's a lady with half a head. All I can see is one eye and her mouth, and the rest is mush. She's still holding on to the *Eastbay* magazine because it was never thrown. What was thrown was the letter—"

The bird. The bird was a crow, and it dropped the letter in front of Gerome.

Cole doesn't say this aloud. It sounds crazy even in his own head, but nonetheless he knows it's the same bird he has seen many times in *real* life. That thing that's not right.

A ghoul in a crow costume.

"—and she's mouthing something to me. Then the van hits. Same as always, I open my eyes and take everything in. See if I'm hurt. But this time, the lady is in front of me again. She's bending over me. Black blood is pouring from the hole in her head onto me. Her eye is crying. I can't hear anything, so I'm trying to read her lips. The letter is still in my hand, and she points at it and begins to scream. At the same time, she's trying to tell me whatever she's trying to tell me, but I just can't hear her. It looks like she's saying 'Run, my son, go!' over and over. Pointing at the letter, she starts looking back over her shoulder.

The driver is coming, and she starts crying harder from that good eye. She just keeps saying it—'Run, my son, go! Run, my son, go!'—till he gets close, then she literally disappears. I roll my head farther to the right and watch the driver run toward me. Only it's not the driver. It's him, Cole. It. Whatever it is. The thing from the bus yard. It's black and evil, striding hard and heavy across the blacktop for me. The last thing I remember is that bird. I think it was a crow, diving at his head as he came for me, just as it had mine. Only it was angrier. Just before I woke up, I saw it take one final dive, just as the black thing was reaching for me. It flung itself at the thing's face and sent its beak deep into one of its empty eyes. Its blacker holes where eyes should have been. It howled, Cole. An inhuman *shriek*, man. Then I woke up. Mom said I was screaming."

Cole sits on his bed, befuddled. Only staring stupidly at Gerome. What a strange and terrifying bear they've stumbled across. A bear with a throat full of bones. Swinging from its dewlaps in crass delight.

"The thing is Nolan," Cole finally says. The words bounce through the room like Super Balls.

Gerome almost winces at them. "I know that now."

Cole takes a deep breath, then says, "Gerome, mouth the words 'Run, my son, go.'"

Gerome does so, then sits and stares, not understanding.

"Watch me," Cole says. Then does it. Slowly.

Ramshackle Row.

Cole sees it hit Gerome like a blast wave. If you don't stare at the talker's tongue, the syllables are undeniably similar. Gerome turns the same color he described his late grandmother as having in the first dream. The color of mushrooms. The color of contagion.

"When do we go?" Gerome asks. Gaze set on the floor. *Through* the floor. An old soldier who's just come to grips with the idea of another deployment.

Cole again thinks of Ellie. She's too close. "Now. We go right fucking now."

CHAPTER 20

HE WATCHES HER. A BLACK-AND-WHITE WRITHING FORM dancing in silk sheets. He got lucky this time. A midmorning check-in between early beers. She dances a hand playfully under the sheets as the other squeezes and relaxes the pillowcase in pulsing fists. The only sounds in the small room are the low hum of electrical equipment and the animalistic rapid exhales between clenched teeth. From the big room comes sensual moans, though they go unheard. As she loses herself in the tendrilled meadow of bliss, the sheet falls off one side, exposing milky skin pulled tight over perfect curves. Gooseflesh breaks out over her stomach, where a warm stripe of lucky sunlight falls across her. Her convulsions come in waves, increasing in both frequency and intensity. This is matched by a new sound in the small room, which also quickens and intensifies. He won't use the thing in the corner this time. The thing that looks like her. Not today. Today, right here will do. As she begins a vocal display that would rattle the basement bones of any God-fearing man, the beer on the table trembles rhythmically. Jolting slightly with each strike in the crisp light from the monitor. He notices and moves his foot. Can't have *that* spilling over now, can we? The big room's black-and-white walls do their best to stifle the sound, but an unabashed climax pulses through the otherwise empty and silent house. Of both rooms. The big one and the small one. Though neither can be heard.

CHAPTER 21

EVEN WITH THE SUN SITTING HIGH AND MIGHTY ABOVE, THE path out to the bus yard seems colorless, like everything's covered in a skein of dust. Soft and cold instead of vibrant and cheerful—what a summer sun usually provides. The air is thick with murk. To Cole, it's like they're trudging through a low pool of pennies. A faint breeze dances down the streamed alley around and past them, tickling skittish leaves. The water babbles lazily beside them, rolling monotonously toward the big lake below. A faraway cawing stops them simultaneously. They share a wordless, wide-eyed stare. But when Cole breaks gaze and continues on, Gerome reluctantly follows, his fake leg mashing rounded pebbles a bit louder than its organic counterpart.

The boys reach the opening to their right. Another caw. Much louder this time. Not lacking fervor, like it's answering a question the boys didn't ask. At least, not aloud. They haven't said a word since hopping the backyard fence when Cole's mom knocked on the kitchen window with soapy hands and mouthed "What are you doing?" to which Cole had replied, "Bus yard!" She'd shaken her head—not in an angry way, but the way a mother of a teenage boy often does. Not a bad kid at all, but certainly all boy. She saw Cole flash her a quick smile through the foggy glass and turned to help boost Gerome.

"Wait," Gerome says, pulling at Cole's shirtsleeve as he starts to head into the opening toward the bus yard.

Cole notices that his friend's knuckles are the same color as his.

"What?"

"What if we *do* find it? I mean …" His harried gaze is set ahead down the streambed. "What does that say about *me* if we find that fucking letter, man?" He looks at Cole with pleading eyes. Cole remembers how wide and wrong they were that first night. They're not that wide, but close. Too close for comfort.

"What do you mean what does it mean? It means that we will be right. We'll be right about something trying to …" He trails off and searches for the word. One that won't scare him out here in the open more than he already is. "Reach us. It'll mean that something is so important that it's somehow being transmitted into your head like a fucking lighthouse for a lost ship."

"A ghost ship," Gerome mutters, eyes still wide but fixed in a stare at nothing in particular on the ground.

"Maybe," Cole says. "But at least we can help somehow. Something is so wrong that this crazy thing is somehow happening to you and whoever, or whatever"—Gerome whines slightly at this—"thinks that we can do something about it."

Gerome realizes he's still got his hand clamped onto Cole's shirtsleeve. He releases a crumpled fist of cloth and raises his eyes to meet Cole's. "This isn't one of your books, man. There's no hero out there who's going to fly in and save us from whatever we're messing with. Whatever that thing with no eyes was. That thing is real. I know it. I think you know it too, but I don't think you're fully aware of how fucked up that is or how so astronomically far above our pay grade that is. I mean . . . think, man, a few months ago, my mom couldn't get me out of the house long enough to get the mail. *Now* look at me. About to go searching for some letter in some horror-movie bus yard."

Cole rolls his eyes (they're tight and timid, not able to

perform the usual loose loop around riding on a true feeling of humored annoyance) and grabs his buddy by the shoulders. A hand on each. He tries as hard as he can to soften his face but doesn't know if he's successful. "Look," he says. "We're going to be fine. I know this isn't one of my books. I know we can't cheat and skip and check out the ending before we continue, and I know there's no character who can swoop in and save us if shit hits the fan. But I also know that there's some kind of letter in there." He throws a pointed hand off Gerome's shoulder and aims it behind him. Never letting go with his eyes, though. "And whatever it is, is some sort of key to all this. All these weird things that have been happening. And I want to find out what that key unlocks. I'm scared shitless too, man, trust me. But we *have* to do this." He thinks he sees a little fire start to emerge in Gerome's eyes. Maybe a little rallying flame. A little fight. "We can't let whatever this is continue on."

Gerome stares into Cole's eyes for a small eternity and then gives a single, terse nod. Cole turns and heads in, and Gerome follows.

It doesn't take as long as one might think. As long as it *should've* taken. Needle in a hydrangea instead of haystack, which makes no sense. But what does now? There's a previously unexplored bus near the back of the yard (one that can be seen clearly when walking along the back fence to and from the entrance opening—one Cole has seen many times). Its peeling two-tone white and shit-green sides encase twenty or so dusty and broken windows. None of them large enough for a big bird to fit through. It's quite clearly an old city bus and is probably one of the founding members of this forgotten fraternity. The boys had split up upon entering the yard and began searching the buses along the perimeter. They planned to work their way inward until they met somewhere in the tangles of the middle. But Cole and Gerome had independent thoughts about what would happen if some sort of enveloped letter were actually found. Both had quiet hopes that they'd finally meet out in the middle with empty hands and pounding hearts and trudge back to Cole's house and back to normalcy and begin formulating a plan B. However, neither is at all surprised the moment the letter goes from something dreamed up to something very, very real.

"Cole!" Gerome yells.

Cole pictures a kid yelling for his dad while carefully keeping an eye on a snake in the corner of the garage.

"You got it?" Cole yells back, already almost to the shit-green and faded white bus. It had taken Gerome both hands to pull the door open. He can see Gerome through one of the windows. A dark, jagged form through spiderwebbed glass standing over something. He looks up and meets Cole's harried eyes.

"Unfortunately."

Cole doesn't notice the hitchy crow dancing a devil's jig on top of the bus Gerome is in. The thin layer of dirt and leaves muffle what would have been the sound of squealing talons. But when he reaches his black friend in the bus's black innards and sees what Gerome is staring down at, they both jerk in fright at the loud barking caw overhead.

There is a blue plastic milk crate under the spiderwebbed window sitting on its side in a calm sea of dust and twigs. In it is an envelope lying facedown so they can see the previously opened triangular tab had been stuffed inside the envelope to keep it closed. Gerome still hasn't moved, so Cole picks it up and flips it over. Gingerly, like the thing might blow them all to hell if two of the wrong wires touch. NOLAN claims the front in a blotchy blue ink. It seems to have been scratched on rather than written. Clearly scrawled rather hastily. A blurry dot deforms the bottom half of the first "N."

"Tear," Gerome whispers. Still not moving. A teardrop had fallen from the writer.

Cole undoes the tab and pulls out the note. It's a single page of lined paper unevenly ripped along the perforation. Toward the bottom, the rip reaches far into the middle of the page. On it is an explosion of ink, underlines, and scratch-outs. Some marks are so deep that they've actually punctured the page.

Gerome takes a step back and plops down on the brown leather seat behind him, one of the few inside the bus. Its backing is torn open, and yellow foam hangs out of the hole like a dead tongue. But Gerome doesn't notice the dry lick on his shoulder. He's staring intently at Cole, who takes Gerome's seating as a sign to start reading. He turns and faces Gerome. Suddenly it's as if all the air is sucked out of the bus like a puncture hole in a spaceship. Hot, acrid air pushes against Cole's forehead, causing beads of sweat to materialize. It fills his throat and nose. He takes a deep breath and swallows down spit, feeling it crawl toward his stomach like Play-Doh, doing nothing for the dryness. But he looks up at Gerome, who still sits there, just waiting for him to do something, for the next step in this fucked-up story that is unfolding, eyes wide and ears open. Cole slides down the bus's inner wall and sits on top of the now-empty milk crate. And as the yellowing paper clatters softly in Cole's trembling hands, he begins.

CHAPTER 22

SUMMER THUNDER BOOMS OUT IN THE WEST. SHE'S HAD enough. Enough of it all. She'd looked him in the eye and begged for him to help her. And what did he do? Just shut the screen door in her fucking face. It's been too long since the last time she's lived, and now there's nothing left for her here. The rancid blossom of a very final realization spreads from a dark, wet place deep inside her with the fervor of a hungry cancer. She doesn't know when it goes from just a small thought tickling the back of her brain to something real, from an almost-laughable last resort to something she can touch, something not very funny at all.

But it has.

And it's happened fast. She suddenly feels almost weightless. No, that's not quite right. She feels like she's in a chair in the same room and also a thousand miles away watching herself play herself in an autobiographical film. She moves with a fluid, prescribed purpose that she can't remember the last time she possessed. She's thought about this moment many times over the years and envisioned many different scenarios since her marriage transitioned into the final act.

Ha! Marriage?! she thinks as she watches herself float through the screen door Nolan closed in her face moments ago.

Marriage is between a man and a woman. A man *and a woman.*

He hasn't been her man in a very long time now.

We're talking years, jack.

He's done nothing but feed her black fire of depression, but in his very own, very Nolan, no-good, very bad way. He works behind-the-scenes. That's one thing about him she's come to know and come to hate. He's a button-pusher from a dark room, trying to play God. He'll never be found with blood on his hands.

She watches herself pull the .38 from his bedside night-stand and toss it on the bed. She floats over to the little desk in the corner of the room and sits down. This is the resting place for bills and important documents. *Don't bother,* he'd tell her. *You're liable to fuck somethin' up and lose me money.* It occurs to her that her husband probably spent more time at this desk when at home than with her.

The money is what he's married to. I'm just the maid and the psychological punching bag.

"Well, *fuck him!*" she screams at the stale air in the room and slams her small, trembling fists down hard on the pile of papers. A tingling flare of pain erupts in her wrists. The sweat is now drying but giving her skin a sort of *steamy* feeling. She pulls a ringed notebook down from the little cedar shelf over the desk and rips out a blank page and watches herself snag a pen from the brown mug, knocking it over in the process and spilling its guts out into the sea of papers. She begins writing.

> *Nolan . . . why? That's all I want to know. Why have you not helped me? It almost seems as if you're against me now instead of in my corner. Not almost. You* are *against me. It's been this way for a long time. You assist in the worsening of my depression, not do what a good husband does and help his wife who needs him. You've made me feel so insignificant. Your quiet abuse and non-*

*chalance about anything that involves my feelings
after all these years have put me in a place where
I feel like I can't even go get help from someone
else. I'm too far gone now to come back. I don't
even want to come back. I suppose it's my fault.
I should've left a long time ago. But I stayed for
Ellie. I truly thought we could make it work and
be a happy family. A normal family.*

The thought of leaving Ellie in this world without a mother
sends fresh tears spilling down old tracks, some dripping to the
page under her trembling hands. The frustration of not being
able to eloquently convey the true pain and anguish eating her
from the inside in these final moments causes her to become
angry on top of everything else. There is no sad music playing.
There is no audience on the edge of their seats. There is no
writer scribbling these scenes as his heart races and thoughts of
awards swirl around his beautiful mind. There is none of that.
It's just her in this empty room. No one there to give a shit what
she does. If a gunshot rings out in the forest, but no one is there
to hear it, does anyone really even die?

*You're a murderer, Nolan Donovan. A fucking
coward and a murderer. You haven't been a
husband in years. The one thing I pray, my final
prayer to a God who's not there, is to simply ask
him to help you be a good father to my sweet Ellie.
I'm already regretting this decision like it's already
been made. Because it has. I can't stop myself this
time. I feel like a puppet in a terrible, never-ending charade pulled by strings around and around
for all eternity. But now I have an out. I'm not*

myself. I'm not the woman you married or the
woman Ellie needs as a mother anymore. I have
no place here. I'm done, Nolan.

Then scrawled at the bottom of the page, written almost as if someone is pulling her away as she tries to get one final thing down …

Tell Ellie I love her more than the world and that
she is the only thing that kept me from doing this
long ago.

And finally, scribbled quickly but with a palpably thick layer of accusation: *If you were in here right now, would you even stop me?*

She doesn't know why she puts it in an envelope, but she does. She even licks the back and seals it like it's about to partake in a long journey with the United States Postal Service instead of never leaving this awful room. All the beeps and boops of electrical synapses that made Patricia *Patricia* are now dormant. A deep, seething inner self is running the show, and the sad little woman can do nothing but watch. She tosses the envelope on his side of the bed, the side with his tear-blotched name printed on it facing up so there would be no way to miss it. She crawls up onto her side. There is no moment of second-guessing or dramatic recalling of the precious moments that composed the good memories in her life while violins lazily cry in the background and audience members cover their mouths and gasp—none of that.

From across the room, she watches herself lie on the bed and look up at the ceiling and grab the revolver lying between her and the letter to her fuck of a husband and puts it to her head, and as she pulls the trigger, one final memory lights up the yawing darkness. It was the moment they met. That beautiful day when she and Ellie were unloading groceries and a big, slobbery bulldog came barreling up to them that began a dialogue between her and its owner. Her future husband. As the hollow-point tears through her head, splattering a chunky wet soup onto her nightstand and the wall beside the bed, the image of the way Nolan had looked at Ellie in that first moment played on a loop over and over, never and forever. And as some of the thicker chunks begin a race down the wall next to Patricia Donovan, what's left of her dead brain in her opened-up head thinks an unknown thought: "He never looked at *me* like that."

But there's nothing there.

Less than a minute after he sees the flash through the bedroom window from where he sits (in the old barn in the woods next to the house) waiting, he's standing next to his dead wife with a hard-on. He'd skimmed the letter and saw nothing of note. Yes, yes, he planned to be *very* good to Ellie. Yeah, yeah, you're sad and lonely. He admires the little fire she had, though—that was cute.

The first step is done.

He's a smart man in a dumb sort of way and knew from years of watching *Cops* with his afternoon sixer that he should call immediately. They could time that shit.

True, all I'd have to say is I didn't find her till right before I called if I wanted to wait, and I could go eat a fucking Popsicle and have a cold one, but they'd know that shit too and might find it a bit odd on account of my wife's brains are all over the walls and all.

Plus, he's excited that the first piece of the puzzle is securely in place. And it's a *big* piece. He glances at his wife's hideous face (the half that's there) and thinks that yes, this piece isn't going anywhere.

"It's done," he says aloud to a room thick and warm with spent sulfur. A grin creeps across his face, pushing deep lines together. "Hell, you look purdier than before!" He's still laughing as he walks into the kitchen and dials 911. Thank God the bitch at dispatch picks up on the second ring because he's still chuckling softly well after he mashes the numbers.

As he sits in front of the living room TV watching tits dressed up as a weather lady bend and point, bend and point, it occurs to him that he should probably do something with the note. He knows legally no guilt can be obtained from it, but it still makes him look pretty bad. He'd worked hard to point her toward suicide. Did everything in his power to kill her without touching her. Do you know how hard that is? If it got out, it would most certainly disrupt future reveries with his stepdaughter. This gets him going.

He's not sure why he doesn't just toss the letter. Maybe because part of him knows there's a chance they could look pretty hard for clues on his wife's—

Ex.

—recent demise. *What could have caused her to do such a horrific thing?* the hairsprays in town would ask tomorrow in between bites of cardboard sandwiches (but it's gluten-free!) and glances at the young boys running food at Which Wich, the cool little sandwich dive in town. *You'd never think something like that could happen in this little town,* they'd whisper to each other while sitting under hairdryers at the beauty salon, thumbing through trashy rags with full pages devoted to Zac Efron's airbrushed abs while a milky wetness blossoms between their fat, crossed legs. *What a terrible husband!* Housewife One would say. *He didn't even help her at all!* Housewife Two would reply.

Did you see the copy of the note on Facebook?

Before he knows what he's doing, Nolan is walking through the roll-open chain-link gate at the head of the bus yard behind his house. He walks past an open chunk of brown grass near the entrance that will, a few years from now, be occupied by the last member of his dead collection. A too-new-to-be-valuable, good old-fashioned yellow school bus, Miss Frizzle style. A loser cruiser. *The Big Yellow Dragon Wagon,* he'll think as he's pulling it into this spot a couple years from now, which will be just about a year before a three-legged, interracial friendship stumbles upon what is currently in his hand.

A favor for a friend—

Acquaintance, I got no friends, he'll think.

—over in Sparta that will buy a plot of dead land and then will discover the cheese wagon under a rusted covering at the back of the field, then ringing Nolan.

He speeds up a bit at the sound of a siren in the distance.

They don't fire those up for barrel-suckers, do they? He thinks not. Although he should hustle regardless. It wouldn't be a good look to take forever answering the door when your wife is dead inside. *Hell, most people probably wait for the boys in blue on the front porch.*

"Well, I ain't most people!" he says aloud, leaping over thorn bushes and various piles of junk. He feels ten years younger already.

She ain't a barrel-sucker, though, it didn't seem. She blew that shit all over the wall.

"Probably didn't want to get the pillows dirty!"

He's still laughing as he picks a bus way in the back. He doesn't remember snagging a little blue milk crate on the way, but apparently he had, because it's now swinging from a hard, tan hand like it's having the time of its plastic little life. He yanks the door hard and boards the old bus. Grandma shit-green and sunbaked dog shit-white. He picks a spot about halfway down to put the crate and then the letter inside, not knowing why he's doing any of this. He's working on autopilot. As he jogs back through his old hobby (it started to die around the time he met the dead lady in his bed and her gorgeous daughter—certain things sorta started taking up more space in his mind than others), there is no sound but his heavy footfalls on dry underbrush. A monster munching a salad. The siren is now gone.

Probably some drunk kid drowned at the lake down there, he thinks, hoping it true. The still scene and vacuous silence allow him to shift his focus to the second part of this hellish puzzle. It will be a tough one, but not nearly as difficult as the one drying in his California king currently. He already has someone in mind who will gladly do his dirty work. For a nice wad of green, that is (most certainly not the color of anything in this man's wallet), and subsequently keep his mouth shut. A hell of a roofer with quite the checkered past. Nolan knew he might need him sometime. He could find good roofers anywhere (take a drive down to the local flea market any Saturday and scoop up a whole country of them if he wanted); this is the South, after all. But a guy who will do his dirty work also? A dime a dozen. The majority of them are proud workers without an ounce of defiance in them. Working to feed their families and nothing else. But every now and then, he meets one with something in him similar to what's inside Nolan. Something behind the eyes. He can see it as clear as day when it's there.

Morales.

"But I'll have to wait," he says as he jogs along the side of the house toward the front. "Maybe even a couple years." It hurts, but it's true nonetheless. He can't afford to get caught, especially now that his prized possession is right there for the taking, nothing in between.

As he climbs the steps to the front porch and sits on the edge of a Cracker Barrel–style rocking chair—

Guess I will wait out on the front porch for the blue suits like most people, after all. That's good. Blend right in.

—his mind flicks back to the first time they all met. Unbeknownst to him, this was exactly the same thought that last fluttered through his dead wife's mind. That old Dozer had run up to Ellie and her mother as they were unloading groceries from the back of their car. He sees Ellie now, standing there all by herself. Her mother is gone from the picture. From the memory already. She's staring at him with those big, beautiful "fuck me, please!" eyes. Dozer sits between them, looking back and forth like he's drooling at a tennis match being played with a raw chicken bone. She reaches up to seductively unbutton her shirt.

Right here in the open? he thinks, unaware that his eyes are closed and he's massaging a warm spot between his legs. *In broad dayli—*

Suddenly he starts awake and bolts upright from the crunching sound of a vehicle rolling up the gravel driveway.

Wait, the gate, he thinks. *How did they get through?*

"Fuck," he says to the porch. A passing squirrel stops to look at him and then bounds into the woods that surround the house. "I left the gate open."

An oak tree of a man who steps out of the police cruiser is Jared Bumbalough. Born and raised here in this shithole town. He was a star O-lineman back in high school half a decade ago and even got a whiff of a few D-1 offers, but off-the-field issues eventually quieted the recruiters' phone calls. In this way, he and Nolan had something in common. A love for the suds. They'd actually met once before when Nolan's company developed a plot of land behind the station when the city finally looked under enough couch cushions to fund the thing. Nolan had shown up to the site a bit more than he usually did at other projects, on account of you never know when you're going to need a couple friendly faces in the force to know your name.

Like today, he thinks. *Not that you did anything wrong or anything, but ...*

Nolan and Jared had shared a beer as they watched Nolan's worker ants maneuver backhoes and Bobcats around the dirt lot.

My truck, he thinks as the big baby-faced dope of a cop mounts his porch.

"Mr. Donovan," Officer Bumbalough says, tipping his hat in respect. "I'm sorry for your loss, sir."

He's going to ask about my truck.

"Thank you . . . Jared, isn't it?"

At this, the officer brightens a bit. "Yes sir! I met you when y'all turned that crabgrass lot into a nice little break area for us." And then, leaning in a bit as if they weren't alone: "Nice place to have a couple cold ones." He adds a stupid wink.

Nolan looks at Officer Bumbalough with reproachful wonder, because it seems this man has already forgotten he's talking to a man who just found his wife dead instead of shooting the shit at the local watering hole.

This man is fatally stupid, he thinks. And then: *All the better. Even though you did nothing wrong.*

As if he can read Nolan's thoughts, he comically straightens up and wipes the dopey grin off his scantily stubbled face.

"Where's your partner?" Nolan glances back at the empty

cruiser. "Assuming you've got one." He's buying time to come up with an excuse for his truck.

"Milsap's sick today. Said he feels like he swallowed a rotten opossum. Cold sweats and all." He takes the painfully stereotypical aviators off, folds them closed, and then hangs them from an unbuttoned pocket on his substantial chest.

He's about to ask about the truck. Nolan has stood from the rocking chair but hasn't yet taken a step in any direction.

"Probably just got a bad hangover. My mom used to call it 'getting the devil out.' Bolton and McGill are on the way."

He takes a step toward Nolan's front door but pauses when Nolan doesn't immediately follow. "You can stay out here if you like, sir. Up to you."

"No, it's all right, I'll come," Nolan says aloud. But thinks to himself, *Is he not going to ask about the fucking truck?*

As Officer Bumbalough reaches for the front door, Nolan has a bit of panic spread through him because he can't remember if he locked the door behind him when he left her alone. But the door opens right up and the big dumb officer steps inside, in a politely clumsy sort of way that's rather endearing. But he quickly turns to Nolan as if he'd just remembered something that could be of importance.

"Hey, by the way. Is your front gate always open? And are you aware that there's a truck sitting at the end of your driveway, kinda half in and half out of the woods up there?"

When his wife—

Ex.

—was noticeably getting closer and closer to the inevitable long walk off the short dock, Nolan began leaving in calculated moments in hopes that the effect would wreak havoc on her unstable little melon and push her over the edge. He wouldn't be there when she did it. It was just them in this sprawling single-level. There couldn't be any witnesses. No piece of evidence or testimony that could possibly throw his plan wonky. That might send *him* over the edge. No, this had to be seamless. A typical, no-funny-business, good old-fashioned suicide. This had to be viewed by the public (by one individual even more so than the dumbass blue suits) as a sad woman's inner cascade of hope that brutally ended in an unannounced crescendo of self-infliction.

So, he'd pick and choose his moments carefully. Sometimes by just a look in her eye he'd know, or at least have an idea, of the dreck mucking up her brain water, and he'd leave. Her eyes would plead to please stay. They'd say that they know their marriage is hogwash, but he's still her husband. They'd plead in big thrumming letters HELP ME, NOLAN.

And he'd leave. It got bad in the last year or so, and he made many trips out that front door, leaving her in her darkest moments to just fucking do it already. A well-worn path began to take place in this part of the plan. Like Nomar Garciaparra's pre-batting ritual in hopes to evoke the baseball gods into good fortune with his superstitious offering.

The suicide god, he'd think. *The suicide god is superstitious, surely. Maybe it's the devil I'm offering.*

He didn't believe in the devil any more than he believed in Santa Clause, but he sure as shit played along with the girls' little shallow-minded elementary hope of an afterlife.

So, he'd do the same thing every time. Telling himself every time he slammed that front door behind him (sometimes her cries being audible through it, and sometimes not) that this is it. This is the time she finally does it. He'd take a deep breath, smile, and head briskly to his truck parked next to the house in its usual spot. He'd pause for a moment at the door handle and wait for a muffled gunshot or perhaps a chair being kicked over (certainly if this were the chosen method of earthly escape, it would take place under the beam running crossways in the foyer, where a strategically placed wooden chair—an extra from the world's largest dust collector they call a dining room table—has been sitting off to one side for months now, waiting to be dragged over by a woman drowning in dread with a bundle of perfectly cut rope found under the sink in one arm)—

And then kicked over.

—which would clearly be heard from the truck just off the side of the porch. Those chairs are heavy, and the flooring in the foyer is a shiny bamboo.

He'd give it a minute, fighting against the yearn to speed up his seconds as he gets more and more excited, then he'd open the door of his double-cab and climb in. The Donovans' driveway is almost a quarter mile of gravel, curving to the right about three-fourths of the way down to meet the big, ominous gate at the mouth. So once he got to the end, he couldn't be seen from the house if she happened to be looking. He'd park half in and half out of the woods (mainly to minimize the possibility of the nigger family he shares the point with, seeing it and logging it as suspicious in their measly little brains), then he'd get out and walk back up.

Don't forget to open the gate for authenticity! he'd remind himself. He couldn't afford to have the ugly little family on the right out there somehow hear the time of death and be able to recall the Donovans' gate being closed at the time. They surely knew by now that he opened it when he left, and left it open until he returned.

If it's closed, scram. If it's open, leave your package on the porch and scram. On occasion, he had parts and things shipped to his house instead of to a site. He liked seeing things first sometimes.

He'd walk back up through the woods, well off the driveway and parallel tree line so as not to be heard if she decided to step out front and get some air. A literal path through the underbrush began to take shape about a month or so ago, like a shortcut game trail.

It is *a game,* he'd sometimes think. *Cat and mouse.* Can he catch her with her head too far in the trap to see another day? But the only game he'd pass on the way back up were a few twitchy squirrels and the occasional crow, watching from a high limb like it knows what he's doing. Nolan would never admit it out loud to anyone, but every time he saw one while walking back up to wait for his wife to kill herself, it'd send a chill from the crack of his sweaty ass all the way up to the greasy, tan skin on the nape of his neck.

He'd reach the old barn, only about a hundred feet from the side of the house but completely blocked from view by the thick foliage. It is here he waits every time. The old window on the side facing the house was broken out by a tree branch in a storm years ago. So he'd grab a beer from the mini-fridge (yes, he had electricity run out to it on account of he actually used to do work in here—

This is *work.*

—and yes, he kept the mini-fridge stocked for these stakeouts), pop the top and sip on it—

Just sip. Can't be drunk if the cops come. When *they come. This one's it, I can feel it!*

—and wait. An old Chevy Nova rusts away under the window, and he'd lean on it on occasion while he waited and listened for his wife to kill herself. He'd remember the dirty brunette he used to fuck in the bench seat back when its old rubber touched road instead of dirt and sawdust.

Rubber . . . Ha! That's something that back seat never saw.

One day a few summers back, Jordy came over and helped him move a table saw in here and asked Nolan about the car. Nolan really hates Jordy, thinks him nothing more than a thick-skulled trailer park mutt with eyes too close together, which probably means his mommy and daddy knew each other long before he busted in her, most certainly not from school and probably from frequenting the same reunions at Old Man Danielson's double-wide.

But he did tell Jordy about the brunette. "Her muff smelled like roadkill, but she fucked hard enough to twist the chassis," he'd said.

What he didn't tell Jordy, or anyone else, was that he was *sure* she was dirty. And instead of going to get checked, he just waited out the first few months with Patricia. Once she never had anything pop up, he figured he was probably good.

I don't believe in the good Lord but thanks anyway for that solid there. And I don't believe in hell, but Patty, I hope you're riding shotgun down that long hill with your head out the window and your hair on fire.

"Yeah, that's my work truck," he tells Bumbalough. "I was about to load some loose limbs and burn 'em." He never mentions the gate. When the officer just keeps staring dumbly into Nolan's eyes, he adds, "Heard the shot and just started running toward the house."

A faint tick at the corner of the big officer's mouth is the only reply. Then he heads toward the bedroom, and Nolan follows.

Jared Bumbalough mentioned one time, and one time

only, that he thought Nolan Donovan was lying to him that day. Or at least not telling full-truth. But this was at a bar, and he said it to two of his even dumber blue-suited brothers while they chased shots with shots and wondered if the cougar who was bellied up to the bar behind them had on any panties or not. It was never mentioned again.

At least, not for a few years.

CHAPTER 23

Cole and Gerome sit silently for what feels like an eternity. Finally, Gerome breaks it.

"What are we going to do now?" There is a gelid undertone to the question. Not quite anger, but close. Very close.

Throughout this short but powerful friendship, Cole has usually been the one with the plan. He's the one who's lived a fairly average life (up until now). Young, good-looking white male. He's a stone's throw from cookie-cutter save for the relocation and the whole no-dad thing. But nowadays, those things are practically the norm.

Gerome, on the other hand, is far from cookie-cutter. He used to be, minus the fact that he is part of that growing yet still-looked-down-upon segment of America called *minorities*, very average. Until he got ran down by a middle-aged man in a red Astro van. Which subsequently changed his life forever. Along with his right leg, Gerome lost most, if not all, sense of hope. Confining himself in his dark room all day, every day. His safe place. Until the kid he's now looking at with the dead lady's final plea in his hand knocked on his front door. That couldn't possibly have been only less than two months ago, could it?

But now, Cole is the one who's unsure. Now that he has the hard evidence in his hands, he's not positive what to do with it. All he knows is that that alarm siren in the back of his brain somewhere is now blaring full blast. And all he can think about is Ellie. What does she have to do with all this? Is he right that she may be in some real danger too, like Nolan's wife was back when she was a living, breathing thing?

Only one way to find out.

"We have to break in," Cole says plainly. Like you would say the postman left something at the door or we're out of milk.

"Break in," Gerome says. "Break in where?"

Cole throws a thumb over his shoulder, toward the front of the bus yard and ultimately toward—

"His *house*?" Gerome stands up from the old seat. Curds of foam from the backing cling to his shoulder. His fake leg clanks against the metal bracket under the seat as he stands. "Are you fucking crazy?" He points to the letter in Cole's hand. "You just read what this guy's capable of, man. He may not have technically killed that lady—"

"Ellie's mom," Cole states.

"Yes, Ellie's mom. That's who it seems to be. But, man, he obviously didn't stop her! And isn't that just as bad? You have to be some kind of twisted to do something like that. Even *if* you didn't like the person."

"That's the point, Gerome." He's folding the letter back, like it has been all this time, and slides it into the brittle envelope. "I'm afraid Ellie's in trouble. And I'll never forgive myself if I don't do something about all this. See as much of him as I can before I go somewhere with it."

Gerome rolls his eyes and puts out his hands in a "just hear me out" gesture. "Okay, first off, I know you're in love with this chick or whatever, dude, and yes, she's fine as hell and seems cooler than the other side of my fucking silk *Star Wars* pillow, but she doesn't even *know* you. You mow her yard, so she's nice to you—"

"There's something there, Gerome. It's not just innocent flirting."

"Yeah, yeah, whatever. You're her little lawn boy who's like nine years younger than her!" His hands are clasped together in a plea gesture. "But the *bigger* issue here is can't we just take this to the cops, man? We don't have to be the heroes! This isn't the Sunday matinee, man—this is real life! The here and the now where heroes die every single day for trying to jump in the box and hit a Randy Johnson fastball. Look, I agree that this is something big. My dreams that scare the shit out of me and show me things I wouldn't believe if this were happening to someone else and they were telling me, the way this Nolan guy seems to certainly be behind most, if not all, of this shit. Hell, even *this* creepy place." He points out through the windows behind Cole. "You can feel something here."

"You can, and I think the reason is this." He holds up the letter.

"But it's not our job to investigate all this, man. We're just a couple kids not even graduated from high school yet! Look, I know you want to impress Ellie and—"

Cole cuts him off. "What are we supposed to say to the cops? You think of that? 'Uh, excuse me, sir, my friend had this dream and we found this note from a lady who killed herself a long time ago. It doesn't say her husband killed her in the note, but she was pretty upset with him. You guys should definitely go arrest him. Oh, and if you could search his house for us too, that'd be great.'" He adds a dopey wink and holds up an "A-okay" sign.

"Okay, look, how about this," Gerome starts. "My mom works with a lady who's got a son that used to be a cop here. She was telling me about him one day when she was just trying to make conversation so I wouldn't go back into my Xbox lair. Apparently, he had an accident and had to quit because he's not physically able to chase people down and munch donuts in his cruiser behind the strip mall anymore. Real bitter about it too. Let's go to him and ask him what to do. Not tell him much, though; just the gist of the letter and how we think something bad is going to happen. See what he says—he'll shoot us straight. From Mom's account, it seemed like he's not a very 'by the book' type of dude. If he thinks they'll listen, then we'll go to the police. If not, we'll search Nolan more thoroughly ourselves, Hardy Boys style."

He puts an arm around Cole, passing some of the cushion curds to his buddy.

"But we don't even know this guy. What says he's gonna tell us anything at all?"

It's a very valid question.

"Man, I'd much rather have an awkward convo with a stranger ex-cop than break into Old Man Donovan's house without being prepared for what we may find."

An even *more* valid answer.

As the boys file off the stifling bus and head toward the broken back fencing of the boneyard with a dead lady's final plea in hand, Cole asks, "What's today?"

"The first, I think, why?" Gerome says, being careful not to put his prosthetic in a snake hole or, hell, a bear trap.

"Because if it's a go, we're getting into his house on the Fourth while the whole town is down at the lake for the fireworks." A brief memory hits him like a slap in the face from a bigger girl. It stings more than hurts. And awakens something deep inside. The flier for the fireworks show in his mailbox rolling and twisting hypnotically in the breeze. And that strange siren it flicked to life back in his head. Only a soft moan then, nothing like the horror-flick shriek it is now. It's there, all right.

It's *been* there. Now he knows why. Nolan put that there. That's why Ellie didn't get one. He's probably handed out a thousand. "He'll be down there too. Networking his money-hungry little ass off, I'm sure."

Gerome says nothing for a few lurching paces, then: "Makes sense. That's soon, though. I don't know if I'm—"

Cole cuts him off as if he were talking to himself. "It has to be then. I'll go talk to Ellie tomorrow, so I'll try to see if she knows anything. I'll make it casual. We'll know for sure then. But if so, it has to be then. It *has* to be soon."

As Gerome clanks over the back slope of the boat mountain toward Cole, he's only a lumbering silhouette as the high sun hangs burning in the sky behind him. A crow dives in from the right, circles silently a few times, and glides off toward the lake.

Almost a thank-you, Cole keeps to himself, not daring to yet bring up what he thinks that bird that isn't quite a bird might be. Or somehow *who* it might be. He's too young for the funny farm.

Cole's down there patiently holding the fence open for him. Gerome taps his leg just like he did the day they met, standing there awkwardly in Gerome's living room while his mother stood back and watched her son show some life for the first time in years, and says, "I'll follow you in that house, man, if that's what it comes to. But let's just hope we don't have to run out of it."

"We won't," Cole says, hoping his certainty passes the smell test.

CHAPTER 24

THE NIGHT OF SUNDAY, JULY 1, BEARS UNEVENTFUL. AND THE boys are thankful for that. They sit in Gerome's dark, dungeon of a room knowing, however, that the lull is certainly temporary. They know that things are soon to ramp up to level ten now that they have the letter, whether they want them to or not. Like a patient living with a stealth bomber that is pancreatic cancer, everything seemingly hunky-dory until that nightmare of a doctor's visit when the news is broken. An evil snowball gets nudged over ever so gently at the top of a hill, gaining speed and collecting bones and other organs until there's nothing left to suck up at all.

So the next day, Monday, July 2, Cole and Gerome mount the brick steps to Ellie's place together, knowing the second they ring the doorbell, that snowball will be pushed.

All downhill from here, Cole thinks as he reaches out and punches the button. Gerome stands back, nervous in his own right. This is the first time he's met the infamous Ellie Porter.

"Let's see what all the fuss is about," he says aloud.

Cole shoots him a look over his shoulder as Ellie pulls the big door open and greets them.

A few minutes into the conversation, and Gerome has decided that she is, in fact, undoubtedly even hotter than he thought before. In a strange way, though. In a girl-next-door sort of way. Gerome smiles over his glass of sweet tea with, literally, the girl next door. But he's not yet completely sold on the fact that she has anything to do with any of this, like Cole is. Someone potentially caught in the crosshairs.

He continues sipping his tea and keeping quiet as Cole does the dirty work. He smoothly transitions from the typical pleasantries to more meaningful conversation. First, it's how each of them is doing, if they are excited for school to start back up and to be making new friends, when she can get him to mow her yard again. At this, Cole had replied that it hadn't nearly been a week yet. To which she was startled and said that she didn't realize (and did she blush a bit at that? Gerome thinks she actually did), that she thought it had been longer. She doesn't get many visitors, so it seems like forever since Cole came by last. Gerome paused with an ice cube clamped between his teeth, looking back and forth at the way they were looking at each other. The cube shattered and sent mini glaciers tinkling down into the bottom of the glass, causing Cole and Ellie to snap out of whatever the hell was going on between them. Gerome looks at Cole and tries to send a message to him. One of the telepathic variety. For he was very wrong. There most certainly *is* something between these two.

Cole uses her "not many visitors" bit to funnel the conversation.

"Speaking of, what are you doing for the Fourth?" He takes the final brackish swig from his own glass, then adds with a quick jab, "Going down to watch the fireworks with Pops?"

"No, I think he mentioned wanting to come here, actually. Said something about a father-daughter date night."

Both boys are pulled up to the living-room side of the long, granite bar, and at this comment, both simultaneously stiffen in their tall chairs.

Gerome thinks she might've noticed. But he couldn't help his reaction. That rang an alarm siren in *his* head, shocking the nerves all the way out to his fingertips into temporary panging paralysis.

Ellie gives the boys a peculiar look. Back and forth, over her own glass of sweet tea, paused an inch below her perfectly smooth lips. She looks at them with questioning eyes—

She definitely noticed, Gerome says to himself.

Stupid, stupid, stupid, Cole thinks.

—but as she opens her mouth to ask why they reacted that way and what they're up to, Gerome achieves the save of all saves.

Only a handful of times that he can remember in his life, post-accident, has he used his handicap to his advantage. Some small and some not. And none of them left him feeling anything at all but slimy.

Once while he was tired and simply didn't feel like helping his mother and little sister carry a big, potted hosta from her car to the backyard (not that he would've been much help anyway, but he certainly could've given a better effort than just calling back from his room that his leg hurt—er, where what's left of his leg meets plastic, just above the knee, but she knew what he meant, actually a fairly common occurrence as one might imagine, when she asked from the living-room end of the hall). Not a huge deal, but he's felt bad since. They struggled mightily. Dropped it once on Kris's toe. She limped for a week.

Another time was while he was in school for the brief period after the sweet little love tap from the Astro van (before the whispers and the stares became too much). The pretty girl in class, he'll never forget her name—Angela Linklatter—was standing haughtily at the front, back to the whiteboard, peering out at the mere mortals as she played with the hem of her dress code–violating skirt and smacked her gum. Always Orbit.

Always spearmint. He'd catch little glimpses of green as it flipped over her tongue between each mash. It was drama class (taught by a crusty old Yankee named Mr. Carrol, who undoubtedly was not going to be the one to send Little Miss Linklatter to the principal's office. He was far too old for such vernal issues, but he also wasn't tucked snuggly against his desk for no reason), and she had to pick a boy to play her boyfriend in a dumb little skit Mr. Carrol drew out on the board in a web of lines and circles that no one knew the meaning for. All the boy had to do was sit in a chair and act cool while his "girlfriend" sat on his lap and chatted with her friends (the first of the "friends" picked out by the winner of the Linklatter sweepstakes as her "boyfriend" and the next "friend" picked by the last one, and so on). See, Angela was running for class president, and God knows a little public charity never hurt anyone's odds at the polls, so Gerome slowly stuck his leg out in the aisle as she scanned the room as if to say "Don't you know I've only got one leg? Don't you feel bad for me?" and tried his damnedest to look as sad and disinterested as possible. He sure as hell didn't want to get up in front of the class, but the anxiety of that notion was blitzkrieged by the yearn to feel the back of Angela Linklatter's bare thigh against the front of his own (even if it was badly atrophied and ugly, hormones are hormones).

She did pick him. She also ended up winning the election later that week.

That one was only a little bit bigger in scale than ditching his mom and sis with the hosta while he sat in front of his TV, and he's not sure he wouldn't have practically begged for the boyfriend part again if given the chance, but the slime was still there.

For only the third time that he can remember using it to

his advantage, Gerome swings his metal leg out and kicks over a vase that had been so eloquently placed at the base of a decorative wall table to his left. The conversation is abruptly broken by a ceramic explosion beneath his feet.

Cole looks at him with an expression of confusion that morphs into a knowing smirk at about the same time laughing lights up the room. (Yes, laughing. No telling how much that vase costs, and she's *laughing*.)

This chick is hard not to like, Gerome surmises as he stands up and brushes off the acting skills he learned once upon a time from a now-ancient perv named Mr. Carrol.

Ellie comes skipping around the corner of the bar to assess the damage with her hands planted firmly against her cheeks in a drastically cute way.

"What have you done, Gerome?" she scolds, clearly acting herself. Her smile wider than ever, and on the verge of laughter again.

Cole thinks this poor girl probably has nothing to laugh at. And no one to laugh with. And what a shame, because this side of her is so positively contagious. He watches her comically wag a finger in Gerome's face. He's laughing too! She's mentioned to him before during one of their talks that she'd love to pursue teaching again, and he wishes that she would. For her. Not for anybody else. He wishes she could crawl out of her stepfather's watchful eye and be her own woman. He wishes that she could see what's going on. He wishes that for her now more than ever as he watches this scene play out, all three of them clearly needing a good laugh. But he can't help but feel that there's something to that watchful eye. Something to the fact that he wants her all alone so badly in this big, quiet house. Sitting here all day, shuffling around, lost in her own thoughts instead of getting out and finding the rest of her life. After the apparent suicide of her mother and then the tragic death of her husband, this is the last thing she should be doing, Cole is old enough to know. In here all day staring at the same silent walls and psychologically wallowing in her pain and sorrow, unable to move on.

Fuck him, Cole thinks. *Fuck Nolan and whatever he's up to. And God help him if he ever hurts this girl.*

She switches to a perfect British accent and belts up to the high ceiling of the living room, "But whyyy? 'Twas my favorite *vase*!" She pronounces vase like "voz." She picks up handfuls of pieces and shakes them in front of Gerome's face like a dog who's shit in the house, showing him what he'd done.

He stifles his own laughing fit and manages to say between breaths, "I'm sorry . . . I really am. It's my leg . . . sometimes it's got a mind of its own. Kicks out of anger or something." He still feels that slime, even through a smile. The charity slime.

A long stone's throw away (maybe if it was a small stone from a big ball player) sits that watchful eye, seeing a black-and-white version of the living room he built through the microscopic lens of a HOSUKU camera hidden in the clock on the mantle under the TV. He sees the purposeful kick from the nigger boy to change the subject. He also later sees and hears (audio in the ones down here unlike the ones upstairs, and still scolding himself for *that* blunder) the rest of their little visit and all the various topics they cover. About an hour. An hour of bullshit with two or three loaded questions intelligently weaved into the conversation.

He now knows that they know. They found the letter. Somehow. He should've tossed that fucking thing and just hoped no one picked through his trash. He feels an alien disdain for the two boys, something like a hatred for a parasite that's suckling off a tit that's meant for someone else. At one point, the conversation turned particularly serious. But things could've gotten much worse had either of them decided not to change the subject after Ellie had said that no, there was no letter after her mother killed herself. Before she knew what they had just hit her with.

As the three of them sit on the long leather couch facing the watchful eye, wavering words laced with rage are spoken aloud to a dark, empty room. Empty save for the monitors and articles of sick pleasure. A soft, green glow reveals a hard face staring into that green. Mouth mumbling unintelligibly as a head and neck creep closer to the glass. A lion sizing up the strength of its enclosure as a couple kids giggle on the other side.

"I know your plan," that hard face says. "And I'll be ready." The swivel chair in front of the monitors flies the short distance across the floor and slams against the wall behind him. The thing with that face stands and screams into the screen, "You will not fuck this up for me!" It breathes heavily and turns toward the door. "Not when my big night is so close. I've waited so long. The Fourth is *still* my night." And just before it steps through the door, it turns back, as if the three people on one of the glowing screens can hear it, and utters a cold sentence through lips that are pulled taut under a pair of dead eyes. Black holes in the greenish gloom. "Let us hope those fireworks are loud."

A haunting laugh follows it out of the small room and into the big, sprawling house.

CHAPTER 25

LATER THAT NIGHT, ABOUT FORTY-EIGHT HOURS BEFORE THE big fireworks show, Cole and Stacey accept a dinner invitation at the Conleys' house. The reason for the small celebration being the return of Gerome's father from the road. A too-long stint that called him up the Eastern Seaboard, eventually all the way to Bangor and then back again, with dozens of loads in a drunkard's line. Kris told Gerome to invite Cole so he can "see who you got your smart mouth from," to which Bree had vehemently nodded in agreement. She had also given Stacey a buzz and invited her as well. She'd told Gerome's father after hanging up that "Stacey is a very sweet woman—you'll like her. A bit of a townie, always running somewhere or busy with something, but very sweet nonetheless."

They now sit at the oval oak-stained table, Gerome and Cole facing Gerome's mother and Bree, and Stacey facing Gerome's father, Glenn. After the first few inevitably awkward minutes, Glenn settled into center stage (to which yes, Cole can clearly see who Gerome had so graciously received his smart mouth from), and the air went thin, easy breezy lemon squeezy. And it was as if all six had called each other friends since about the first Bush. Glenn is a relatively short man, shorter than his son but twice as wide and a hundred times as boisterous. If Gerome is quiet funny, a "dry humor" as some might pin on him, Glenn is a knee-slapping, shoulder-punching kind of guy.

They pass around biscuits and mashed potatoes and converse between chewing. Mrs. Conley asks Stacey how her job is going and about all the what's what and who's who from in town; Glenn asks Cole how many girlfriends he's got, which warrants a quick glance from Gerome before turning his attention back to attempting to cut his steak with a butter knife.

"None, Mr. Conley," Cole replies and pushes out a polite laugh.

"Ah, come on, man! Look at you!" Glenn puts his knife and fork down for the first time since Kris and Bree brought the food to the table. "Wait, wait. Let me guess." He eyes Cole humorously up and down, like a fashion designer with a little dash-mark mustache would. "She's a blonde. That much is obvious. She's *verrrry* pretty." He glances over and sees Kris and Stacey talking to themselves about whatever women talk about, hand gestures and wide eyes, the whole kit and caboodle, and whispers to Cole, "Long legs. She's hot shit, huh?"

Cole waves it off and laughs a little too hard, while Gerome looks like he's trying to hold his breath. Bree puts her utensils down, crosses her arms with fervor, and pouts down at her plate, clearly heartbroken for the first time in her young life.

"I'm not hungry anymore!" she proclaims to anyone who's listening, which turns out to be no one at all.

Half an hour later, Gerome hands his mother his plate. She's running water over the dishes and humming happily to herself. Everyone else is in the dining room. She smiles into the steam rising from down where her hands are working as Glenn tells Stacey one of his go-to "three women in a bar" zings. Bree knows to squeeze her hands to the sides of her head, covering her ears, when Dad breaks out these jokes.

"These done?" Gerome points to the oven where the olfactory orgasm-inducing smell of baked cookies wafts through the cracks.

"Yep, should be," she says. "Go ahead and pull them out if you would." He's reaching for the oven mitt on the counter when she says without looking up, "Don't forget the oven mitt! You'll sear off your fingerprints."

Which might not be such a bad idea on account of there being a good chance I'm going to be slapped with a B and E charge in the near future.

Maybe not. Maybe that ex-cop will tell them to go straight to the feds and back the fuck away, slowly. Which is why he followed his mother into the kitchen. He couldn't give a shit about the cookies, had to force himself to eat the steak, which is his favorite meal. He's currently got the appetite of a rabbit with stomach cancer.

He slides the tray of bubbling sugar balls out of the oven and drops it on the burners above. "Hey, Mom, what'd you say that ex-cop's name was again? The one who had to quit because of the accident?"

She turns off the faucet and pulls off a paper towel from the roll and turns to face him, leaning one hip against the counter.

She's on to me, he thinks quickly. *But what exactly would she be on to?* The rational corner of his mind takes over.

"Well, well, well …" she starts, dabbing one hand and then the other.

She knows. I don't know how she knows, but she knows. And then again, *Knows* what?

But then she says, "I sure thought you weren't listening to me when I told you about that poor man. I was just trying to keep you out of your room, even if it was just for a few minutes longer."

You really need to chill your grits, man.

"I know," he says and smiles wanly.

"But that was back when ..." She pauses, unsure how to finish. Gerome waits, taking his time with the oven mitt. "You weren't as happy. The depression."

He doesn't say anything, so she continues. "I didn't want you to end up like ..."

He only nods so she'll keep going, relaying the information he needs.

"Jared Bumbalough," she says. "Why?"

"I just thought I saw him the other day when Cole was taking us in town to get something for my Xbox." He'd thought about just saying because he'd like to speak with him. Maybe see how he's coping. See if there's anything to learn from someone who has a similar injury. But surely she'd get too excited, go too far into setting them up to chat, make a big deal of it. He didn't want that at all. So he went with this.

She looks at him questioningly, those motherly eyes.

"But do you even know what he looks like?"

No voz to kick over here, dickweed. Keep it together.

"Well, the guy was dragging around his legs and sure looked like an ex-cop to me. I mean, how many of us can there be? You know, people like me?" He places the mitt in its drawer.

She rolls her eyes and turns to grab some clean plates for the cookies.

Good save, two for two today!

"You're too much, son."

"He got into an old pickup, I think—that him?" He prods a little deeper, knowing damn well he never saw a paralyzed man pull himself up into a pickup while he and Cole were making a game run.

"Huh? Oh, I don't know what he drives. But yes, that was

probably him. He's not doing so well according to his mother. Said he's holed up in his little trailer over in that park off
Carlsen. Lakefront. I think that's the name of it. Just sits there
and gets madder and madder at the world around him. He's still
a young guy, you know. So sad."

She puts the stack of plates on the countertop with a little
clatter and hugs Gerome fiercely before he knows what hits him.

"I'm just so glad you're finally better and not still like that,"
she says into his ear. She sounds on the verge of tears and pushes
off before she gets there. "Can't cry in front of the guests like a
crazy lady."

"I am too," he says. "Glad I'm not still like that."

She grabs the plates and heads back for the dining room.
But just before she reaches the opening, she turns back and
says, "You know what, I do know. And I only know because his
mother mentioned one time that she hoped his attempting to
fix it up would light a fire for him. 'A fire in a dark place' is how
she'd worded it. It's an older Camaro. Not a pickup. Put those
cookies on that tray on top of the fridge and bring them in here,
would you, sweetie?"

Then she joins the laughter in the other room.

CHAPTER 26

THEY'D TALKED AT LENGTH ON THE WAY HERE. PASSING HORDES of sparkler-wielding kids in dry lawns left and right, as well as a few teenybopper gangs bombarding rival gangs with bottle rockets. They hadn't been much younger than Gerome and Cole.

But the boys had serious business on their plates tonight. Potentially even *illegal* business. The thought procures the willies in both boys, evenly.

Much can be said in ten minutes, about how long it had taken them to get here. Just a hop, skip, and a jump. And it all had been. They'd run through all potential scenarios based off the possibilities of how this conversation would go.

Gerome had mentioned that he wished they had done this yesterday instead of doing nothing. That way they would've had a whole day to digest whatever is about to happen. Cole had looked at his friend in the passenger seat, staring out the open window as front yards flashed by, lighting up his chestnut forehead in flashes of bright colors, and said, "No, it had to be today. If we'd have sat on it for a day, no matter *what* he said, we would have talked ourselves out of it. But this *has to be* the night if we decide to do it after this. Has to be. It's probably the only chance we'll get to be one hundred percent sure Nolan won't be home. I swung by her house again yesterday when you and the fam went out to lunch. I pushed a little bit more and told her to call or text me if she ever needed me, and gave her my cell number."

"Why the *fuck* did you do that?" He wasn't looking at peoples' yards in passing anymore—he was looking at Cole. He wasn't terribly angry, per se, the way something that surprises you makes you angry, because it didn't surprise him—he was just truly curious as to why he'd do that. That's a big step, and maybe a little reckless in the situation they were currently in.

Maybe, maybe not.

"So she'd have it if anything happens while he's there with her. I'm scared shitless that they're going to be alone."

Gerome interjects, "It's her *dad,* man."

"Step."

"Yes, we agree that he's hiding something or he's capable of something terrible or his demons are the sole reason for the dreams I've had—"

He visibly shudders in his seat, even though the late-afternoon breeze stealing into the cab is a heavy seventy-five degrees.

"—or maybe all of the above. But he's her dad. Do you really think he'd do anything to hurt her?" Again, non-accusatory. Genuine. Scared that one of them may be thinking it.

"No," Cole says plainly. He's gazing *through* the cracked asphalt running under them like a gray river. "I don't. I used to, but I don't think that now. Otherwise, I would've found a way to stop him from coming over tonight somehow. Or maybe I just would've told her everything after she'd said he wanted a father-daughter date night." He pauses. Watches the painted dashes shoot under them like off-target gunfire from one of their warplane games. "But in a way, that's scarier, isn't it?"

Gerome just keeps staring at the side of his buddy's face. He doesn't follow. And that's okay because Cole continues on, monotonously. As if his inner self were making the statement, his body only a fleshy conduit.

"In a way, it's even scarier now. Now that I don't think he'd hurt her. Because maybe that's what all this is about. Maybe the whole time, Nolan *wanted* her."

Gerome doesn't answer, still. Just watches ahead as his brain tries to chew on this new, gristly information. He watches as Cole slows and turns off Carlsen into Lakefront Park.

It's a grid of gravel; each chalky rectangle holds in a shitty trailer and a splash of grass, growing up through rocky, Tennessee hardpan. They proceed down the main drag in a crawl, keeping their eyes peeled for an older Camaro in the dying daylight. Lord knows there aren't any garages, so it shouldn't take long.

If he's even home, Cole thinks, not for the first time since they set off for this place. But based on the loose description from Gerome's mother, he probably will be. Even on a holiday. *Especially* on a holiday.

They inch by a trailer with a pile of beer cans high enough for a kid to drown in on one corner of the front porch. The porch looks like a sneer made of knotty pine, wrapped around the front door and baked a hard white. A piece of pottery that looks maybe like a frog shares the corner with the pile of cans. Some of them look like they'd been there so long they've since began to fade in the summer sun.

Cole and Gerome look at each other and shake their heads, sharing a sad expression. They creep on deeper into the park. As they go, the sound of the tires crunching gravel rocks into dust pushes away the yells coming from a cracked window on the side of the beer-can house with the sneering porch. And it definitely drowns out the steady drone of an army of box fans. Despite the heat, the window had been cracked because the little boy's room had started to smell.

They finally spot the Camaro. Way in the back of the park. Cole pulls up in front of its owner's trailer, half of his tires in gravelly grass and the other half in grassy gravel. They get out and walk cautiously toward the door, slowing as they pass the car. It's an '85 IROC Z28. And by the looks of it, the dude's mother's hopes of it being fixed up have yet to come to fruition. It's a real piece of shit. Its color is a tired teal with a six-inch-thick band of rusted gray running along the bottom of the rocker panels, all the way around the car. A half-assed job of washing off FOR SELL in the top-left corner of the windshield is still visible (yes, "For Sell"). A soapy swirl of window paint remains there with ghost words underneath, baking permanent, forever waiting for someone to come along and finish the job. A thick steering-wheel cover pockmarked with yellowing skulls can be seen through the filmy driver's window. There's a crooked bumper sticker on the back shouting, GodLESS Bless!

"Here goes nothin'," Cole says and knocks on the front door. He closes the screen back and slides backward a step to stand next to Gerome, who's still on the top step of the cinderblock staircase, connecting porch to yard.

Something falls over inside, followed by a muffled curse.

"Hang on!" someone booms. Cole picks up more than just a touch of annoyance. Another noise that Cole deduces as whatever was knocked over now being put right. "Hang on a damn second." This only spoken, not yelled, but Cole realizes he's certainly right about the annoyance riding on those words.

The boys share a nervous look.

Please let this go okay, Cole prays to the back of his eyelids. *Please let this help us somehow.*

The big man who opens the door is clearly a shell of what

he once was. Though no older than Ellie herself, he has the look of someone who's gone through a drastic physical change. And not the good kind like you find on magazine covers or exercise machine infomercials, where stamped in the air are words in all caps like *WOW!* and *AMAZING!* No, the guy looks *atrophied.* Cole supposes he had been. And also notices with a quick glance at the man's legs that they're the culprits. They're not legs that fit this man, but instead two noodles tied to the seat he sits in with nylon straps. It looks like he'd sold his legs and bought a pair that were 75 percent off.

WOW! AMAZING!

"Can I help you boys?" he grunts.

Cole takes a step forward, leaving Gerome on the top step.

"Uh, yes. We came to speak to you about something. I know it's strange, but your mothers"—he points at the man and at Gerome behind him—"know each other, and she had mentioned you to my friend here, once."

He looks at Cole suspiciously, then around him to Gerome. Cole recognizes the hatred in the man's eyes immediately, just a flash before it's gone, and he knows like he knows his own balls that the man in the chair is racist.

One for the away team, I'm afraid, bud.

He's sure Gerome sees it too. Those looks are commonplace for people like him.

But then something interesting happens. The man looks down at Gerome's leg, and his face softens. Only for a second or two. Like a dream upon awakening is just for a moment right there at arm's length but then quickly gone and forgotten, pulled under raging waters of consciousness.

He looks back at Cole and says, "I ain't no faith healer and I sure as hell ain't no role model. I got nothing for ya, kid."

He calls Cole a kid like a granddad would, not someone who's only a handful of years older than him.

"What? No, no, no." Cole looks back at Gerome and then back at the man (who Cole has come to realize is just as cautious, if not more so, than them). "This has nothing to do with his leg."

Actually, his mind side-mouths, *it kinda does.*

The man in the chair again looks at them both, long and hard. Eyes squeezed to slits. Then he finally says, "You boys in trouble?"

Cole supposes they are, but he's not sure what answer will best give them a chance to get the man's opinion. He wishes Gerome would chime in, help him out a bit. But he knows he won't. His racism radar is well-weathered and far more sensitive than Cole's. And it's currently redlining. Gerome's not moving unless the man invites them in. And even then …

"We're in a bit of a jam," Cole finally says.

"A jam." A sly smile creeps across his stubbly face.

Jared? Was that it? They should've planned this out better.

"We just need some advice, that's all. We heard about your situa— that you were once a police officer, and when we got in this jam, we knew we couldn't go to the police just yet. We thought about coming to you first to see what kind of advice you could give us. A bit off-the-record if possible."

The man actually belches out a mouthful of laughter. "Off-the-record, huh?" He slaps his dead legs with both hands, not unlike the way Gerome sometimes does. "There *is* no record anymore. When I got paralyzed, they didn't do shit for me, so fuck 'em."

Cole assumes the police are whom he's fucking. That tight-knit brotherhood of white men in blue suits.

"Hell, come on in," he says and rolls backward into the gloom. "I'll help you boys the best I can."

Cole heads inside, out of the stifling heat, and Gerome follows timidly. He'd sweat dark rings under his arms standing there with his back to the falling sun. It was now just over the tree line. He pictures the workers at the boat dock getting everything ready for the fireworks show a little later. Time is moving fast.

"Love your IROC," Cole lies as he steps inside.

"Thanks," the man says, lighting up. "I'm gonna fix 'er up soon. She's gonna be so loud she'll crack all the windows in this park every time I start 'er up!"

Cole wonders how much one of those conversion kits that allow people to drive with their hands are.

In watching the man talk now and studying his mannerisms (not at all the cautious recluse he was only a few minutes ago, his face completely different), Cole sees this man's mind is about as useful as his ruined body. He's hopelessly stupid.

Thank God, he thinks.

The ex-police officer holds out a sweaty hand to Cole. "Jared Bumbalough," he says proudly. He doesn't offer a hand to Gerome, who follows Cole inside. Only nods at him. "Come sit," he says. "Let's talk about this jam."

The ambiance of Jared Bumbalough's place immediately puts Cole at ease. It reminds him of his hangout back in Ramshackle Row. The air seems murky, choked with dust. Fine particles undulate through thin blades of light piercing through the place. The blankets on the windows doing a pretty good job of holding the midsummer sun at bay. He sits on the couch, and his ass seems to fall forever, Gerome experiencing a similar sensation next to him. But Cole finds it quite easy to focus on what they need, the goal of this drop-in. And he can't help but think the calmness has something to do with how much the inside of this shitty trailer reminds him of his bus. That hideout he'll probably never hide out in again.

So, he falls into the story, not having to belabor at all. Like he's talking to his mother about what all he did today instead of sitting in front of a strange man in the back corner of one of the town's biggest mobile home collections called Lakeview Park (which possesses no view of the lake whatsoever; you'd have to roll your little trash wagon about five miles down Carlsen for that).

He talks for three or four minutes, occasionally looking over at Gerome for a terse, corroborating nod, while Jared sits silent, listening with vacuous intent. He's able not to stray too far off the thought-out path of conversation, leaving out names and places, as well as the unbelievable parts. The dreams. He aims his story toward a target where the only answer could be yes, the police would have enough evidence to pursue, or no, they wouldn't give you boys the time of day if all you've got is an old letter. And he hits center mass.

He finishes, breathing heavily. Either because the sour smell of alcohol mixed with a weightless molasses of dust has done a small number on his lungs, or because he had gotten a little worked up toward the end when talking about Ellie and how they think she could be in some trouble now too (though never naming names). Maybe both.

Jared takes a moment to process. Cole can clearly see dusty gears slowly turning to life behind his stupid eyes. But what finally rides out of his mouth on a cloud of rotten breath confuses the boys immensely.

"I'm not an uncle, ya know."

Cole and Gerome look at each other and then slowly back at Jared. Silent, not picking up what the man in the wheelchair is putting down.

Gerome has a flash of foresight, and, based on his previous visions, he has no reason not to think it true, of Jared pulling out a gun from under one of his dead legs and ordering the boys to spill their guts at gunpoint. Otherwise, he'll "Pump you jizzbags full of fucking lead!" Gerome actually sees this scene play out in his head. It seems like it lasts minutes, but when he swims back to reality, Jared still hasn't expounded on his strange statement.

He's going to kill us, Gerome thinks. *He knows Nolan.* He is far more confident in that second assumption than the first, but he shifts in his place on the couch nonetheless. Trying to get his bad leg under him without being noticed, in case a dive for his life is necessary here soon.

Jared smiles and shakes his head slowly.

Gerome's head again pulses with the deadly knowledge that this man knows Nolan. And when he feels like it's going to explode, when he reaches for Cole's arm, the ex-cop finally continues.

"It's a cop saying, no one wants to turn into an uncle after they stop wearing the badge." He pivots on the left wheel and turns his chair so he's able to reach a Coors resting next to a gray lamp on a fold-up dinner tray. Cole is reminded of the beer mountain on the porch of that trailer they passed and wonders quickly, like the *zing* of a passing bottle rocket, what that person's life must be like behind those walls back there. He thinks it's probably a lot like what's sitting in front of him right now. "Sticking their nose into current police business like it's still their job." He takes a swig—the bottom of the can zaps them with a mincing flash of reflected light on its way up—and exhales through clenched teeth as it burns a path down. One of the blades of light lay at a diagonal across his chest like a seat belt. "But I don't think you've got anything here. If I were to guess, I'd say they'd take the letter from you, thank you both, and tell you they were gonna follow up on it, but as soon as you guys walked out the door, it'd be crumpled up and Kobe'd into the closest can." He whirls his chair in a tight circle and shoots the empty into the trashcan at the end of the kitchen counter behind him and is once again looking at the boys. "Like that. Cops like to think what's done is done, see? They don't want to go back through old business unless they have to. And an old suicide note with not much to say doesn't necessarily require them to 'have to.'" He air quotes this.

Gerome's head drops, and Cole nods at nothing at the realization that the decision has been made. They're breaking into Nolan's place. And they're doing it right after this. Those blades of light have now blurred and dimmed, the one across his chest losing its sharp edges. The sun has almost set.

"Say," Jared says. "What's this guy's name? The guy with the dead wife?"

Cole sees those cogs again behind his eyes. He doesn't much care for them.

"I'd rather not," Cole replies politely, looking away from Jared's face because there's *something* there. He can see the man trying to work something out in his murky mind. Trying to remember something.

Gerome sees it too. He's looking straight into Jared's face and sitting bolt upright on the sagging couch, ready for anything. Gerome thinks he may be trying to figure out whether or not he should let them leave.

Jared smiles, flashing yellow teeth, and says, "Fair enough. You boys ain't snitches, that's for sure. Those kinds are everywhere nowadays. They breed like cock-a-roaches."

Cole swallows back a bubble of laughter at the pronunciation. Then a precarious silence envelops them, as the boys don't know what else to say and Jared is beginning to wonder if that was all the advice they wanted. But that's not all that's going on in his head. There's something tickling some gray part way in the back. Something sounds so familiar about that watered-down version the nigger boy and the talker came here with. But he can't quite reach it. He can't, for the life of him, *remember*. If he just knew the name of the man, maybe that would shine a light on the dark memory hiding back there.

Cole knows there's nothing else for them here. They've gotten the answer they came for. But before they go, Cole wants to know what happened to the man. Something so bad at such a young age. A perverse part of his mind wants to pry, wants to know all the details. "What happened to your legs?"

Jared immediately turns icy, his face flash-frozen into a brittle moue. Cole instantly scolds himself for asking.

What are you doing?

Then another voice.

Should've just thanked him for his time and left, stupid.

Gerome squeezes his lips shut and shoots a look at Cole, silently cussing him for the question. Especially since that question was aimed at someone who's clearly not doing so hot after whatever happened, happened.

Jared visibly peels off that stony layer like the browned exterior of an onion and tries his best at a neutral face. "Got shot in the back by some nig—" He glances at Gerome, who doesn't react at all. He's numb to the word. "By some black guy one day while I was off duty. It was a Sunday." He pronounces this "Sun-dee," like the church crowd at Gibbly's. "I'd just got done playing some basketball at the old courts over off Jefferson. I had parked a block away at that corner store, Moogie's, where they sell the barbecue, and walked down there. Just enjoying the day. I took that path that goes through the woods and comes out at the little playground by the courts."

They'd heard of the path.

"Halfway in, when I couldn't see neither the court behind me or the street yet out in front, someone shot me in the back."

He's looking away from them. Lost in painful recollection. "Never saw him."

Confused, Cole thought about the racial description. He knew Gerome was thinking the same thing.

"Knew he was black 'cause he ran west into the woods." As if he'd read their minds. Probably could see the question on their young faces, not yet able to hide their feelings. Not yet able to not give away their hand. Especially from cops. Even though he'd never put on the uniform again. He is a dumb man, but even a dumb man can sometimes think like a cop. And even rarer can see like one. "Only thing that way is the projects, Jackson Heights and the even blacker Wildberry Place. I probably arrested one of his family members or something. He was probably waiting for me, knew I played down there most Sundays." *Sun-dees.* Then more to himself than to the boys, "You lock one up and you got fourteen cousins wantin' your head."

Cole knows their time is up. He wonders if kicking those old gears to life had also knocked out a few screws. Jared was unconsciously squeezing his thighs while he talked, like he was searching for feeling in there. Though he didn't seem upset. But this somehow unnerved Cole even more.

Their time is up.

"I just remember lying there, looking up at the sky. Church bells were ringing," he said to a spot on the couch between them. He's squeezing his thighs harder now, like he's kneading dried-out flour. Chords stand out in waves on the back of his long, white hands. "I'll find him one day, you know."

Cole takes this opportunity of a somewhat finality of the conversation to stand and start for the door. Gerome is somehow up before he is.

"Thank you for your time, Mr. Bumbalough." This tastes strange coming out of his mouth, because the man is only a handful of years older than himself, but he wants to show respect nonetheless, and he's not sure how else to accomplish that upon leaving. "You've been a big help. You really have. And I'm sure you will find him." But as they file past Jared, who's still strangling his thighs, unbeknownst to him, and staring at that spot on the couch, he shoots a hand up and grabs Cole at the wrist like a cobra strike.

Amid the initial terror, Cole can't help but hear one of his mother's Stacey-isms.

If it had been a snake, your balls would be in your belly! Twisting the old line into a strange version of her own that no one knew the meaning of. The thought is gone almost before it is even there. An inchoate reverie.

His hands are huge, he thinks, looking down. Jared's fingers could comfortably wrap around Cole's thin wrist twice.

"Tell me his name," he says plainly into Cole's face. Cole feels no threat, only sees clearly those cogs turning behind his yellow eyes. The man remembers something.

"I don't know his name," Cole says with a scruple of confusion. Out of the corner of his eye, he sees Gerome already at the door, one hand on the copper-colored knob.

You've got this, Cole thinks, not pulling away at all. *He's a little crazy. But who wouldn't be?*

"If you don't know him, how would I?" he asks Jared.

Jared blinks, and then realizes the mishap. Also apparently realizing he's still squeezing the kid's wrist and probably scaring him to shit, because he drops his hand back into his lap. The other relaxing its grip on his left leg.

"The man from your jam, not the nigger who shot me." He doesn't hold back this time. Maybe he thinks Gerome has already walked out the door behind him. But probably he just doesn't care.

As Jared waits patiently for the answer, Cole has a flash of intuition himself and now knows why Gerome had been so on edge since the conversation started. He didn't think Jared had noticed, but Cole knows Gerome. Cole could feel him coiled and ready to spring off the couch next to him. The reason was that this man knows Nolan. He thinks the ex-cop doesn't quite realize it yet—he's not messing with them, but he's putting something together in his head.

Cole feels the importance of leaving right now hit him like a left hook from Tyson. If this man knows Nolan, then it's possible that he's *friends* with Nolan. In which case, they'd be fucked. Royally.

"I really can't," he blurts. "I'm sorry."

Cole heads for the door, and Gerome opens it, clearly ready himself.

"No cock-a-roaches here," Jared says. Cole turns to look at the back of his head just before shutting the door behind them. Gerome is already lurching out to the Jeep. "I can respect that. I really can." The ex-cop is once again staring at the empty couch. Cole gently closes the door and jogs out into the new night. Sizzles and pops cut through the heavy air in a thousand cannonades.

"I'll think of it," Jared Bumbalough promises the empty trailer. He breaks his gaze, wheels a one-eighty, and pushes off for the fridge. He's thirsty for another one.

CHAPTER 27

CAM IS DEAD. JORDY'S BEEN STARING AT HIS BODY SINCE LONG before the Cherokee rolled by the window real slow. About twenty minutes ago that had been. An anger he'd never felt pierced his soul like a rusted screw, pushing deeper and holding tighter with each crank. He'd been drinking since Sandy left for work a little before eleven this morning. She'd walked out of the bathroom with that damn bombshell bra pushing her tits up over the top of her black-and-green Moneymakers shirt. That thing worked wonders on account of her tits actually looked like tube socks with rocks in the bottom. But she kept working more and more hours and coming home with more and more money. Every now and then walking in and tossing down a ball of cash almost the size of the pretty girls' pots. She hasn't yet asked him why he hasn't gone in to work in days. Simple answer was that they didn't speak much anymore. Like it or not, their sick kid had buried a thick wedge in their already-shaky marriage. Maybe she's scared of him. Possible, but he hadn't yet noticed a timidness when she crawls into bed beside him or when he slides behind her while she's doing her makeup in the bathroom mirror, two places Jordy knew caused a ruffle of lady feathers in those *Lifetime* movies he sometimes momentarily pauses on, when the bitch didn't trust her man anymore. Even when the bitch, herself, was the one stepping out.

She'd said something about having to close again tonight, something about a drink special, something for the Fourth, to which Jordy had replied with a noise that reminded her of a bear that had been poked awake. A bear that had been sleeping for a very long time. A bear that didn't yet know what it was capable of.

But he hadn't been sleeping. In the literal sense. He'd been watching *Judge Judy* and already drinking. He was yelling at some guy who was being sued for stealing something on the show, and Cam had been screaming right along with him from his sick room in the back.

She was tired of the screaming. The sleepless nights. The cries, her cries, that went on and on until she dried up like a slug in salt. Tired of everything. She'd been loading up on hours to get out of the fucking house, not because she cared too much about what bill needed to be paid next or pulling the extra slack since Jordy's recent unemployment. She's just been going through the motions, sharing a trailer with two cardboard cutouts that made noise. One just grunts and the other just screams.

She didn't even think Jordy realized what he'd done when he smashed his phone last week. He'd been putting a frozen pizza in the oven, and that was it. An emotionless tantrum from a man with red-rimmed eyes and deep furrows in his brow. But otherwise emotionless. She'd paused on her way to the bedroom and watched the scene play out, emotionless herself. He's smashed two cell phones now (one only a month or two ago, though that one happened at work), out of anger, but this time it was as if it were simply a reflex. Something he couldn't control. Something he couldn't help. When he never went to get a new one from the little electronics shop in town, Patel's (Mr. Patel knows him well), she knew he wasn't going back to work. She knew he was just going to sit here and drink and watch *Lifetime* and *Judge Judy* and scratch his balls and yell at the TV and wait for Cam's screaming to stop. She was surprised that no one from work had stopped by yet. Even though Jordy had said that Nolan hadn't come in in a week or so before he left. Surprised, nonetheless. Not even a courtesy call. She had a phone, you know? A simple stop on their way home? Nobody?

But she wasn't even sure any of them knew where they lived anyway. Not like they were proud of it. Maybe that old guy Jordy sometimes talked about. Gary, she thinks that's his name. But he probably doesn't care, either. Probably acts nice enough to her husband's face, but when the gettin' gets going, he doesn't give a rat's ass about why Jordy's been out and if everything's okay. And she doesn't blame him one bit.

Barry would've stopped by. Such a shame, what happened to him. He was a nice man with a nice future up ahead. Everyone knew it. He would've found out where they lived and stopped by to make sure everything was all right. But he was gone, and her heart told her that none of the ones still breathing cared much at all about them. They just didn't. They'd probably seen dozens of people come and go, and Jordy is just the next to fade out, however eventual. They simply did their job and went home at the end of the day to their own shitty houses and shitty wives and lives. No room to carry anyone else's shit, you know?

That's where she's at with it all. She's been beaten down. Battered and flash-fried. She's a walking bag of bones and blood with no feelings left to feel. Whittled down to performing her only skill, and that alone. Leaning her tits over a table of scruffy boys and popping her ass from side to side as she saunters through the restaurant with a tray full of beers on one arm and a tray full of wings on the other. Actually much harder than it looks.

When she had left earlier, she did a strange thing and

kissed Jordy on the forehead. He didn't think he'd said anything to her when she did it, though he couldn't quite remember. But when he went and got the sawed-off shotgun out from under his bed, he was thinking about that kiss. Thinking about how it had seemed like a wordless permission. On the way to Cam's bedroom, he had silently thanked a God that he didn't believe in that Bill Hatter hadn't yet blabbed. At least, apparently hadn't. He knew when he took the thing that the chances of Bill not blabbing were slim, being that the thing was illegal (along with everything else in that goody box in the back room of Hatter Tactical) that he stole. Bill would probably want to use his buddies in the force to help get it back before real damage could be done with something he should have never had in his shop in the first place and *real* trouble finds its way to his door. Or maybe he was just scared. Just like Jordy had hoped. Scared to do anything at all even though he knew what was right.

"Until now," he'd said aloud. One white-knuckled hand squeezing the gun's butt and the other clamped on the barrel as he strolled to the sick room at the back of the trailer. Bill hadn't tattled at least until this point, and that's really all that matters, because Jordy doesn't give a shit about what happens to himself after tonight.

Sometime before the sun finally gave up and set, he had walked into Cam's room. Cam was screaming into his pillow, lying on his stomach. He looked like uncooked chicken. He was slimy. A sheen of sweat covered the boy's back in a thin film. He didn't hear his father come up behind him and stand over him, either because of the screaming or the drone of fans (although one of the five had died days ago, it still sat in its spot like a mute watchman)—maybe both.

"I love you, son," Jordy said and brought down the butt of

the shotgun onto the back of Cam's little head before he could turn around at the sound of his dad's voice. The sound reminded Jordy of when he was a teenager and he and his buddies would toss people's pumpkins into the street and watch them splatter.

He'd remained emotionless for a while—just relieved he could end his son's suffering for him. But soon after, the rage came. It didn't slam into him head-on but rather stole through his body, slowly turning him.

He'd yelled at his son's body until he couldn't anymore. He yelled at the man who could've helped him but didn't. The man who had more money than he knew what to do with but didn't give a flying fuck about an employee who had busted his ass for him for years. Cam had just lain there listening as blood leaked from the crater in the back of his head and began pooling at the nape of his neck and dripping onto his Spider-Man pillowcase. The swell of his back no longer hitching sporadically with each laborious breath. Because there was no more breath.

At some point, Jordy had stopped yelling. His rage had turned inward and began festering into a putrid ball of hate he wanted to deliver to someone's doorstep. Someone in particular. He moved in a dream as he took the two shells out of the gun's chamber and began rolling them in the blood of his dead son.

He'd sat down in the chair next to Cam's bed, replaced the shells into the chamber, and snapped it shut.

"The blood of my son will be on your hands," he'd said quietly. Only the fans' single-note melody answered.

Now, outside, a Cherokee's headlights pierce through the dark, passing back by the trailer with the sneering porch. The trailer with a dead boy and a guy who's no longer a dad. It's leaving much faster than it came.

CHAPTER 28

THOSE DUSTY COGS AND GEARS CONTINUE TO GRIND AS HE gulps down his beer, now nothing more than a splash of sour backwash prattling around the bottom of the can. Sometime through *America's Got Talent*, a single name is spit forth, cutting line to the front of his dull brain. Like a lone Everlasting Gobstopper, a mere trinket of cubed, colored sugar, popping out into a polished tray after minutes of giant moving parts pounding and squashing in a white room of Mr. Wonka's factory.

His eyes shoot wide, like a cartoon character. Had the boys still been there, it probably would have resulted in laughter, despite their uncertainty about the ex-cop in the chair.

Jared rolls for the phone and dials his mother's cell. While he's listening to Luke Bryan warble about rain making whiskey, and thus whiskey causing his baby to feel a little frisky, he pulls back a blanket and peers into the night, hoping to see the Cherokee still parked out on the road. But, of course, he doesn't. They walked out his front door a good five minutes ago, maybe more. Unless they were suckin' each other off out there under the stars (which, they didn't come off as funny to him, but nowadays, who the hell knew), they were probably a few miles down Carlsen by now. And that shriveled and wounded piece of him that'll always be a cop whispers which way they're headed.

Across town in her own shitty spot, Jared's mother, Agatha, is popping Cheetos through her rotting teeth and trying not to touch herself to Simon Cowell ripping some wannabe magician a new asshole on *America's Got Talent*. Simon *hates* magicians. She peels her gaze away and peers angrily at her lit-up phone, which tells her it's her son. She knows he's low on groceries and doesn't feel like going anywhere tonight. Can't he just fix that damn Camaro up and go out and get them himself? She reminds herself that the hand-control kit for handicapped drivers is almost three hundred dollars on eBay. Where's he going to get *that* from?

Simon begins speaking again in his patented syrupy British accent that she'd like to pour all over herself, and so she turns back to the TV.

He is in some kind of mood *tonight,* she thinks and does a little shimmy in her chair, wrinkling her nose and giving him her best attempt at a sexy look through the thousand-mile thick glass between them. She doesn't see the "1 New Voicemail" icon pop up on her phone's screen.

"Mom, you need to call that black lady you know." It occurs to him that she may know more than one, so he adds, "The one with the son that's only got one leg." That should narrow it down pretty well. "Tell her that her son and his friend are in trouble." Jared has no idea why this is hitting him so hard. Generally, he could give two turtle shits about what a couple teenagers were getting into, even if it *was* bad news.

He's not an uncle, ya know.

But once those cop cogs begin running true, wonky and slow no longer, every once in a while, they spit out an Everlasting Gobstopper, something to behold. Something to take very seriously. When the name hits him, those feelings he'd felt while searching the man's house that day years ago come rushing back like a hungry flood. A flood with currents ten times stronger than they were then, now pulling him out toward a knowledge hulking in the depths. Something's wrong. *Very* wrong.

He's not sure if he should insert this or wait till she calls back.

You can't wait. There's not much time, that wounded little cop whispers, his brass badge lodged into the skin of his little chest. He's not nearly as stupid as the man he lives inside of.

"It's about a man named Nolan Donovan. Tell her not to let them go near Nolan Donovan." He almost hangs up at that, then adds, "And not to go through with whatever they're planning."

He hangs up and gazes out the window. Flashes from nearby fireworks paint his IROC much cooler colors than it is. He wishes he'd saved up and bought that kit off eBay that lets crips drive with their hands instead of throwing his dwindling drawer of cash at beer and more beer. He'd go after those boys himself. But the thing is three hundred bones. Where's he going to get *that* from?

CHAPTER 29

THE JEEP'S WINDOWS ARE DOWN, AND COLE'S GOT THE accelerator hovering too close to the floorboard. His golden locks, pushed back off his forehead, tussle with each other back between his ears. Gerome is staring longingly at the Cherokee's digital display on the dash. Green letters announcing 8:09 throw soft, ghoulish light on the contents of the cup holders below. Ghostly crumbs and quarters. He's hoping they're not running too late for this. Who knows how long a "father-daughter date" lasts? God knows his dad and Bree have never done such. What is it, dinner and a movie? Netflix and takeout? How fucking creepy is that? He'd been thinking about what Cole had said when they first turned into the trailer park—what seemed like hours ago, but in checking the time, he realized it had only been about thirty minutes. He's thinking about how Cole had said that maybe that's what all this is about. Maybe it *is* about Ellie. Maybe Nolan (her stepdad, he reminds himself) wants her. Not like a kid wants a puppy. No, what if he really *wants* her? Her stepdad. The thought has been catching steam in his head ever since it rolled out of Cole's mouth.

As he stares at those block numbers—8:10, the cause of the gloom—wondering what a father-daughter date means to a creepy fuck like Nolan Donovan and how long such a date might last, Cole's cell buzzes to life between his legs on the seat. The white light meets the clock's glow and wrestles into a friendly merger where their edges touch.

"Hello, Mother," Cole says.

Gerome watches, trying to pick up on the cause of the call based off Cole's replies and facial expressions.

"At GameStop, where we said we'd be."

She asked where we were, Gerome surmises. Continues watching.

"Okay . . . okay." He turns to Gerome and rolls his eyes. Gerome smiles. "Love you too. Okay, bye." He clicks the phone black and tosses it back to the seat.

"Ask where we're at?" Gerome says.

"Yeah, said we've been gone for a while." He looks at the clock. "Eight twelve? Well, I guess we have if we really would've been at GameStop. What'd we leave, like, forty-five minutes ago?"

"Something like that."

"And GameStop is just about five minutes from our houses. We should really run by there and pick something up. Forty-five minutes is a long time to spend in a little game store without leaving with something."

"Cole, I don't know. It's getting late. What if Nolan comes back while we're snooping around the place?"

"I don't think he'll be heading home anytime soon." Gerome sees a glassy look in his friend's eyes. Something he knows he'll have to accept at this point, perhaps. A concession. Gerome also thinks it was probably true that Nolan's night might be more than just dinner and a movie. But it's too strange to say out loud. He already knew it'd taste like bile coming up over his tongue. He keeps quiet.

"He won't try to hurt her," Cole says. To Gerome, it sounds like something someone would say to himself in the mirror. Something he wishes could be spoken into being. "Besides, I'm sure they'll watch the fireworks from her porch.

It'd be a great view from there. It would almost be weirder if he left *before* that."

Gerome hadn't thought of this. He did the math in his head, probably at least another hour before the grand finale. His mind eases a bit. The break-in needed to be quick, though. In and out. This makes him think of something.

"All right, let's run by and get a game or something so when we don't walk in empty-handed, it won't tickle Stacey's spidey senses wrong."

Cole nods in agreement, eyes back on the road pointed toward home.

Gerome goes on: "You run in and grab something, and I'll run in to that CVS next to GameStop and get us some gloves."

Cole looks questioningly at Gerome, eyebrows awaiting explanation.

"What?" Gerome shrugs. "You can't break into someone's house without wearing *gloves*, dude. Haven't you ever watched *Criminal Minds*?"

They allow a laugh. And it feels good. Even though something is really wrong here: the letter, the precognitive dreams, the blackness they can feel even for a man they've never met. If you pull back the curtains and expose the inner workings, they are, after all, human beings. Just two teenage boys riding this dangerously high wave of adventure.

CHAPTER 30

ABOUT THE TIME COLE'S CELL VIBRATES TO LIFE BETWEEN HIS legs, Jordy is getting ready to leave. It's dark now, and the fireworks show will begin within the hour. At least, he hopes. He's lived here long enough to become fairly familiar with the little townie get-together down at the big lake every Fourth, but he's also been out of the loop in recent weeks. A hermit lying in wait. Preparing for *his* SOMETHING BIG. He hasn't been at work to hear the banter between saw-blade songs about who's taking their boy, who's not going this year.

What if it's off this year? What then? His mind flits forward.

It's happened before, though only because of bad weather as far as he knows. He glances out the dead boy's window and sees a bank of twinkling stars across the blackness overhead and smiles a fox's grin. Wouldn't *that* have been some shit luck if he'd have looked out and seen purple thunderheads just beginning to leak rain? His whole plan has been based off the notion that a gunshot would blend right in to the firework barrage, if anyone even heard it at all. Nolan's driveway is long, if he remembers correctly. And there's also a little barn off in the woods to the side of the house. He thinks he'll hole up in there and wait for the show to begin.

But as he's tucking his son to sleep for the final time, pulling some of the sheets up from the foot of the bed for the first time in probably a month, he realizes he'd have gone through with it anyway, even if the show had been canceled. And not just because he'd already killed his son—

Set him free, I put him out of his goddamn misery

—and he'd *have* to; otherwise, Cam's death would be in vain. All for nothing. No, he'd have gone over to Nolan's and done it regardless because that's what he's got coming. Jordy's drunk on a mixture of Budweiser and his SOMETHING BIG. This is *his* chance to stick it to the man. He'd sat and watched Cam suffer for too long; his already pockmarked heart has been turning into nothing more than a beating coal throughout these last couple weeks. A beating coal laced with glowing seams of rage, burning valleys into the thing, all for one man now and a need to fight back for once in his sad little shit show of a life.

He kisses his son on the top of his head, because the bottom is a crimson crater, and sets off for the door. But as his hand touches the handle, he realizes he's forgotten three things. Three very important things. He shakes his head side to side, low and slow, and grunts a drunken giggle. He heads to the fridge and snags a straggler on the bottom shelf, lying on its cylindrical side as if it had been sleeping in the cold, hoping Jordy had forgotten about it.

Almost.

Playing dead, are ya? he thinks. "Ohhh no ya don't." He jams the one for the road down the front pocket of his tattered, plaid button-down. Then Jordy turns and stabs at the keys on the counter, only succeeding in punching them off the other side and onto the floor in a happy little jingle. He walks around, grabs them, and heads for the third and final thing. He doesn't know if he'll need it—probably he won't—but he *does* know that he doesn't care. It's just part of the plan. He's a puppet on a string; his puppeteer looming above is his SOMETHING BIG. He's just doing what he's told. He staggers to the bedroom and drops onto his knees. The beer falls out when he's reaching under the bed for the third thing he'd forgotten.

"I said no ya don't!" He cackles and replaces it in his shirt.

With the keys in one hand and the third thing in the other, he heads out into the busy night. He thought about leaving a note for Sandy and then thought it stupid. What would it say? *"Hope you had a great night at work, sweetie! But hey, don't go in the back bedroom 'cause our boy is dead! Love you!"* He thought turning off the box fans would be enough of a warning. Their noise had become something as normal as eating or breathing, and once he pulled their plugs, he felt the silence violating his ears. He'd thought his head might explode. *Wished* it would explode. She'd *feel* it as much as she'd hear it and know that her son was gone as soon as she stepped through the front door.

But hopefully it wouldn't matter because he'd be back before she returned from work. If he comes back.

He climbs into the truck and slams the door. It's got a clean oval in place of the DONOVAN DEVELOPMENT & BUILDING magnet that's been there for too long. He can't remember when he'd thrown it away. Probably around the same time he dropped his phone.

Haven't had my cell in at least a week, he thinks. It doesn't faze him. He doesn't care. Just simply stating a fact that has just been realized.

He gets Thing Three where it belongs, and the shotgun is resting patiently on the passenger seat. He eyes it with wonder. It's powerful and deadly, but it's on *his* side. To Jordy, it looks like a pit bull told to "stay," beautifully obeying its master.

He smiles and pops open the beer from his pocket, takes a long swig, and drops it in the cup holder with a weighty *thunk!* He hopes it's not his last one but couldn't care less either way, really. The truck roars to life with a single pull of the puppeteer's finger and backs out of the gravel drive onto the gravel road, the main drag of his shitty trailer park community. The truck's shifter slides to Drive, and he heads toward Carlsen.

Toward the lake, the puppeteer whispers from above. Jordy's hair ruffles. *We're heading toward the lake.* Jordy tips an invisible cap and takes another swig through smiling lips. The pit bull in the passenger seat wags his tail in excitement. Jordy rolls the windows down for him.

"There ya go, bud, gotcha window for ya," he says, turning to look out his own.

CHAPTER 31

He's always seemed a bit strange to her. Like he wasn't quite sure what to do with her, how to be around her. A baby tossed in a caveman's arms. Always protective, though. *Overly* protective. A few times even stepping between her and her mother to take her side. Ellie's side. There were a handful of instances during her mother and Nolan's marriage that made her quite uncomfortable, though she never mentioned such things to her mother. She'd finally seemed happy, at least in the beginning. She recalls one day a few summers before her mother killed herself, vividly. Ellie was at their house. She'd brought cookies left over from a camp she had helped with at an elementary school in town. Her mother was out in the garden, and Nolan was in the kitchen with her. She'd been bending over looking for a jar under the counter to put the cookies in, and not having much luck. She'd turned without standing up to ask him where she might find one and saw that he was touching himself to the view of her ass in the sundress. He'd quickly acted as if he'd had a "man itch," and they'd both laughed, anxious to leave the awkward situation in the rearview. She knew what he was doing.

There were only one or two such instances while her mother was alive, but after her death, there have been a handful more. Even in the limited number of times she'd spent time with him. A faint prickle had begun to blossom in her gut in regard to Nolan, but she did her best to squash it. Telling herself he was a lonely man and always has been. Yes, she is his

stepdaughter, but she's only been in his life a fairly small portion
of it. He's not quite sure what to do with her, how to be around
her. Nowadays, a man's entire life could be drastically altered by
a single accusation, the level of truth unimportant. She's careful
with her thoughts, knowing the power they hold. But she also
keeps them alive, every now and then, ever so gently peeking in
that back-corner room in her head and whispering them awake.

This afternoon, he'd been decidedly strange. He'd brought
flowers, shoved them in her face as soon as she'd opened the
door. The bright display of carnations and daisies smelled beautiful, but she couldn't help but feel that prickle of worry despite
it. He had noticed immediately. It must've been all over her
face. And she could've sworn when she said "Oh, you shouldn't
have, Dad!" with all the faux enthusiasm she could muster, he'd
whispered "Don't call me that" under his breath and pushed
past her into the house. It wasn't much more than an exhale
through gently moving lips, but she could've sworn that's what
he had said.

She'd made chicken and potatoes, but he wasn't interested.
He asked to sit in the front room at least until the fireworks
show. Then they'd eat, he said. She was a bit perturbed by this,
because she'd spent the last couple hours preparing the meal and
now it was going to sit on the stove and get cold. However, her
appetite is about the size of an acorn at the moment, pushed
aside by that growing flower of concern in her gut. It's his eyes
above all. The flowers, the comment, the way he seems on edge
about something she's not yet aware of, but his *eyes*. She'd never
seen them so bright. Like a boy on his first date. Another petal
unfolds.

"Okay," she says. "We'll eat after. It'll probably be around
nine by the time they are done." She checks the clock on the

microwave, hands nervously working the flowers down into a long vase. "Depending on whether they start them on time or not. Supposed to be about fifteen minutes from now, but who knows? I'm not terribly hungry yet anyway." She realizes she's rambling and turns away to act like she's looking hard at which part of the bouquet should face the open room. She can feel his eyes on her. He hasn't said anything or moved so much as a muscle. She wonders where his eyes are crawling on the back of her body and knows before the question is even fully formed in her subconscious. She suddenly feels her shorts riding too high on her thighs and her top not quite low enough at the bottom, but she bites her lip and forces herself not to adjust, either. He'd know she was on to him.

Finally, after what seemed like minutes of heavy silence, she turns back around to face him, acting as if she'd finally arranged the flowers how she wanted. She knew he'd be staring at her ass like he was that day years ago. Back when Barry was alive, even though they hadn't quite met yet.

Please don't be touching yourself, she asks the cabinet door through eyes pinched shut. *Please, if he's touching himself, I'll scream.*

But when she steels herself and turns around, perfectly naturally, he's not touching himself. He's stirring the tea in a big blue jug on the counter. The wooden spoon lightly *thunking* the sides on its way around and around. She does notice his other hand shoved into his pocket as if working something back down and wonders if it's an old-man boner until she notices that he seems completely transfixed by the brown whirlpool in the jug. He watches it swirl and just keeps on staring, as if she isn't even there. As if he's lost in his own world and doesn't care at all to go looking for another.

She clears her throat, and he jumps, almost knocking the jug over with the spoon handle.

What is wrong with him? she thinks.

He looks at the clock on the microwave and says, "Come on, let's go watch for them," and turns away toward the front room. It takes her a second to remember who *them* is. The fireworks. She mentally palm-slaps her forehead and scolds herself to relax and follows Nolan into the front room with a glass of tea in each hand. He's already pulled back the curtains and is sitting in the chair with the best view of the street, Cole's house, and where the fireworks will light up the sky beyond. The point they live on is high above the lake, but the fireworks will easily reach above the trees running behind Cole's house. They should be able to see them perfectly.

She sits in a chair across from him. Between them is a polished oak coffee table, and she sets the glasses down there. She thinks this may be the first time she's ever actually used this room—

Except when you're watching Cole push that mower around your yard like the damn neighborhood cougar.

—and joins Nolan's gaze out the big bay window. Two sets of eyes peering into the dark, looking for two different things. She wonders what Cole is getting into tonight.

At the other end of Lakeview Heights, Jordy bonks his truck into the shallow ditch running parallel to Carlsen and throws it into park. He pauses to make sure Thing Three is snuggly in place and grabs the pit bull out of the passenger seat. He hops out into the night and slams the door behind him, scoffing at the slow flow of cars rolling by. Two-thirds of which are turning onto Boatdock Road about a hundred yards in the direction he came from, racing down to the lake and fighting for a last-minute spot to watch the show. *They've* got a family. *They've* got good jobs. *They've* got kids who aren't turning stiff in their Spider-Man sheets back home.

"Fuck 'em," he says to the steady flow of minivans and shiny SUVs. He wonders for the first time if maybe Nolan's down there, then shakes the thought away as fast as it came. He almost surely wasn't. He hadn't been to work for some time either, apparently gone off the deep end like Jordy himself. Same pool, different corners.

"Yeah, we'll see," he mumbles.

He's drowning in the *rich* corner. The same one a lot of these fucks in Navigators and Suburbans will drop into one day. A small town has a special way of doing that to you. Despite your income or quality of life, it can still lull you to sleep, sneak up behind you, and give you a hard shove into the water. And the water's black.

Don't matter either way, he thinks. *Even if he* is *down there for some reason, I'll wait in that old barn for headlights.*

He smiles into the oncoming string of headlights in front of him now. "I've got all the time in the world."

He's got the sawed-off shotgun swinging from his left hand as he's walking toward the stop sign at the end of Lakeview, but none of the passing cars even slow. Maybe it's too dark to see exactly what the strange man is holding; maybe getting little Johnny and June down to the lake is paramount, never mind the nutjob. There is, after all, a gaggle of crazies in this town.

Either way, nobody stops. Jordy cares about as much as a lion cares about those NatGeo photographers in their Land Rovers with hard-ons and clicking cameras as he stalks a sick zebra. He's swimming in booze, riding on the assiduous currents of revenge. He turns left onto Lakeview, disappearing into an

even darker dark. His boots kick pebbles scuttling along the asphalt as he strolls under the trees toward some houses, whistling
that tune by Luke Bryan about whiskey making his baby feel a
little frisky.

CHAPTER 32

IT'S ALMOST 8:30 NOW. SHOWTIME. KIND OF. SHOOTING fireworks off a floating dock is a bit hairier than off solid, dry land. Plus, everyone's late in this town. An 8:30 start time means try to be parked by 8:30; we'll get the show kicking by 8:45 if we're lucky.

They've only been sitting here in the front room for a few minutes, but she's become alarmingly fatigued. It seems a full job just to keep her eyes open and on her stepfather instead of something that should come easily. Speaking of her stepfather, his behavior has changed as well. Still acting odd, but recently he's begun putting a hand on his gut every couple sentences, as if holding something in. It's become more and more frequent in a matter of minutes. Like whatever it was that was trying to get out was wanting to see the fireworks too. She's got a dreamy smile lightly drawn across her face and tells him to go to the restroom. He vehemently shakes his head and shifts in his seat, eyes still searching out the big bay window. She thinks again, not for the first time (or the second or the third) that it's strange he wants to see the fireworks so badly this year. Why he cares so much. Harmless, but strange. She muses some setup, her name in the fireworks or perhaps the arrival of a gift to her doorstep in which he can revel in her excitement of its approach. She smiles as she drifts and again tells him to go and that she'll call to him if they begin while he's still in the restroom. He turns his gaze on her really for the first time since sitting down; he'd been keeping conversation through the side of his mouth with eyes cut out into the dark the entire time.

At some point, her vision runs ragged. Edges of objects seem to swim in space. He looks her up and down, slowly. This time not in a creepy way, but instead as if searching for something. It was a look of someone taking inventory, unabashed either way. Strictly business now. Her eyelids are tied to anchors down around her feet somewhere, but she fights their pull with all she has. She doesn't think she *wants* to fall asleep. Though she can't be sure, can't quite remember. Something is definitely off with Nolan tonight, yes, but he's still her stepfather, the man her mother trusted enough to marry, so Ellie doesn't want to disappoint him. She thought she told him she'd stay awake and keep watch while he uses the restroom, but she can't quite remember *that* anymore either. But after yet another grab of his gut, this time almost doubling him over, she said, "Dad, go! I'll watch for them and yell. Promise." She sees herself say this.

He stands out of the chair, still doubled over, like he's afraid that if he straightens up, whatever he's holding in will come shooting out (an unconscious thought drifts across her eyelids that they hadn't yet eaten what *she* had made so it wasn't *her* fault his stomach is singing the embarrassing tune of the bubbly guts). He looks once more out the window, far to the right, and sweeps his gaze as far as he can over to the left. She watches with another person's eyes as he looks at her phone poking out of the top of her shorts, then to the glass of tea on the little oak table between them. She's parched for more, but it's empty. He makes her promise (*Again?*) to watch for them out the window and yell if she sees *anything*. Even if it's not what she thinks she's looking for.

Did he really say that part? Or did she dream it? Now she already can't remember. All of this happened minutes ago and right now simultaneously. The sequence of events has officially gone wonky, a slapdash handful delivered to her head all at once with no clues as to what came after what. In that handful of things, she hears (*Heard?*) herself say, "Okay, Dad. I'll watch hard." Her mouth moves for her. Those anchors are dragging carpet now, searching for purchase and growing impatient.

He waddles off to the bathroom, but not before telling her again not to call him that. This she was sure of as something real, because even through her blinding haze, that worry flower in her belly reaches wide into full bloom, growing tender and aggravated. Its edges are sharp and hooked, clinging tight now to the corners of her stomach. She thinks for sure this will be enough to keep her awake. But as she stares at the melting ice cubes in the glass in front of her (his only half-empty across from it) and wonders if she can make it to the kitchen to get more, she starts really slipping away. Her vision condenses into a ball, something you can see empty space around, pushed together by the blackness of consciousness's nemesis, until it disappears altogether. Her last thought is if she even has *room* in her belly for more tea, being that that worry flower has gotten so *big*. And if she'd have just held on a minute longer, she'd have seen …

Jordy is outside. The black gate guarding Nolan's property strikes him as nothing short of ominous. An iron shield, nine feet at its highest point where the two doors come together, keeping his former boss's private life tucked safely away in the woods.

Not for long, he thinks.

"I'm about to shake up yer pretty little world, boss man."

Standing in the center of the road, he parts a fleeting breeze. His shirt waggles and flaps up around his neck. He realizes he's left the top couple buttons undone. The gun drops to the asphalt, and the sound reminds Jordy of a little yellow plastic clapper toy he had as a kid. His father was never around to annoy, so his mother had taken the brunt of it, eventually getting fed up and snapping the thing across her knee one morning after burning their eggs. She was sitting at the kitchen table and had her robe hiked up. He remembers that her knee had started bleeding, but he was looking past that at the dark thatch of hair between her splayed legs.

He buttons his shirt, having to pull tight to get the top one to come together, and slowly turns to face Ellie's house.

Nolan's truck is in the driveway. He sees lights on but no movement.

This presents Jordy with a bit of a tizzy. His immediate impulse is to knock on the front door and shoot whoever answers. If it happens to be her, then so be it—at least Nolan would then feel what it's like to lose a kid too, even if his ability to feel *anything* only lasts as long as it takes for Jordy to find him hiding somewhere in that big, beautiful house of hers and pumps that final shell deep into Nolan's gut.

He actually takes an eager step toward her house. High on the idea of a hunt for Nolan somewhere in there. Hopefully she *would* answer, and he'd blow her sexy eyes through the back of her head and then give Nolan to the count of ten.

"No, *twenty*." Eyes wide and wild.

Wouldn't *that* be fun? "Ready or not! Here I come!" he'd say, and listen intently for Nolan scampering around, looking for the best hiding spot like they were just a couple fucked-up kids. He'd sure know a few, being that he built the damn house and all.

Although, I helped. Surely I could think of a few too.

How fun that game would be! Maybe he'd make Nolan

scream like a little girl before he shot him. Scream like . . . well, scream like Cam did for so long.

But after that first eager step toward Ellie's, Jordy's puppeteer yanks him back and aims him at Nolan's gate. He knows that's the right move, going up and waiting in the barn for Nolan to return, just like he would have if Nolan had instead been down at the lake watching the show.

The fireworks! he thinks as he's plodding toward the gate.

"Yes, the fireworks, you dipshit. If you'd have blasted him at Ellie's, the neighbors would've heard the gunshot because the fucking *fireworks* show hasn't started yet," the puppeteer scolds from above. Jordy agrees with a nod and lets the SOMETHING BIG take control. He thinks he actually lifts his feet off the asphalt and glides from the strings attached to his shoulders toward the ominous gate, but in reality, he's just riding on the suds.

The gate is closed, even though he's obviously not home. But that's no problem. At the hinges on either side of the driveway, where the swing arms connect, it's only about six feet high.

"Up we go," someone says. Either him or his puppeteer, he doesn't know who is who. And *that* odd realization happened fast.

Because it's almost showtime, he says in his head.

He tosses the shotgun up and over into the brush, plants a boot on the low hinge, and hoists himself up.

In the bathroom, Nolan is wishing he'd built it farther down the hall so she wouldn't hear what is about to happen. He's got a hand clinching the sink to his right and the other pushed flat onto the textured wall at his left and holds on for dear life as an explosion happens beneath him. He'd seen *Dumb and Dumber* one night many years ago with Ellie's mother and thinks he probably looks a lot like Harry (*Is Harry the dumb one or the dumber one?*) in the bathroom scene after drinking Ex-Lax.

Ellie's mother had cackled through the whole damn thing.

She's probably cackling right now too, that bitch, he thinks. *I hope she has to suck the devil's dick for sunscreen.*

It's been a couple weeks since he's cared enough to show up at one of his jobsites. He's resorted to texting as the only means of communication with his employees. Only a few have asked where he's been, but he'd picked up on their obligatory tones rather quickly, even through messages. Only Morales had seemed sincere at all. But Nolan really couldn't care any less. They had their jobs to do, and that was that. Hell, they were probably tickled pink that the mean old boss man isn't there to breathe fire down their necks. He knows how he is. Again, though, couldn't really care less.

He's been busy, that's all.

Another gurgling explosion from beneath him. He grips the sink tighter and winces at the splash of cold water on the back of his legs.

Hopefully she's out already.

He'd only drank half of his before his stomach started seizing, but Ellie had downed the whole glass. He'd slipped the Rohypnol in the jug of tea while she had her back to him, messing with the flowers. He'd forced his hungry eyes off the delicious swell of her ass in those shorty shorts just long enough to toss a couple capsules in.

The "date-rape drug" it's called. And that's exactly what he intends to do. What he's been waiting on for so long. Like the difference in homemade and store-bought.

"And those two fucks are going to have to watch," he says. He'd shaved for tonight, and his smile stretches so impossibly wide that it pops the top off a tiny scab from a straight razor's cut on his cheek. A crimson pinhead of blood appears in its place.

A final cry from below seems almost violent enough to rattle the prints on the wall. All things considered, he'd done pretty well in his attempt at the quickest immunization to roofies in the history of man. He'd started the day he came up with the plan that tonight was his big night. While everyone in this slap-dick town was down at the dock oohing and aahing at the pyrotechnics, he'd be up here at the point, having his night with her. The one he's wanted for so long. And so badly.

The fliers in the boys' mailboxes were an afterthought. He'd scrambled and made them after overhearing a conversation between the white one (Cole is *that* particular fuck's name) and Ellie. He'd just wanted to increase his odds with the fliers. He knew both families had probably already heard about the fireworks (the black family certainly; they'd been here a couple years, and he thinks the mom works in town), but any little thing that could give him a better shot at having the point to himself on the night of the Fourth, he'd take. He'd gone around the town at night and stapled them to several streetlights and shoved them into many mailboxes till his stack had disappeared. He wanted the whole town down at the dock. His hungry and twisted head fantasizes about somehow blocking off the narrow entrance and seeing how long it'd take his town's people to start killing each other.

Not that it truly matters either way. He's going to finally get what he's been dreaming of for years now, whether his neighbors are home or not. But he'd hoped he and Ellie would have the point to themselves, nonetheless. How *romantic*, huh?

But now he knows their plan.

No one to hear her scream, he thinks as he stands and flushes, pulling up his pants and cinching his belt tight and low to stifle his rising part. *Well, except ...*

"Later, boy," he whispers, patting the old dog on the head to calm him. He turns to the faucet and twists the hot water on.

The bouts of diarrhea, as well as the more sporadic waves of dizziness, have become more and more infrequent with each passing day. Now, usually, only a quick bathroom break stands between him and a return to normalcy. Only a few minutes, then he's back on his game, which he needs desperately right now if his plan is going to come together.

At first, he thought he'd simply slip the Rohypnol in *her* drink when she wasn't looking. That would be the easiest way to go. But while researching, he'd come across an article written by a college student that explained how difficult it actually was to do this without being noticed. He'd also given a list of signs for people to look for when a guy and girl were talking to each other in a bar-type setting. It was bad, but it was enough to change his mind. He knew he'd have a much better chance quickly dumping a handful in the tea jug (which is a mainstay on her kitchen counter) in passing, or when she had her back to him, which is exactly what he'd done. Tonight had to be perfect; there could be no hiccups whatsoever. He'd waited so long. Plus, he knew he could get anything he needed and as much of it as he'd wanted through Morales. So the issue of *how* wasn't an issue at all. And Morales would keep his mouth shut. Nolan learned *that* a couple years ago.

He lathers his hands and stares through some psycho in the mirror, thinking about the sequence of events that are about to play out. This part of the plan was added later, after he'd heard the boys' conversation with Ellie a few days ago. It was just a new wrinkle—the more the merrier as far as he's concerned. If they wanted to try to play heroes, then so be it.

The back door of his house is unlocked. He'd left it that way, knowing that's the way they'd come. If they'd found the letter, they'd come through the back way. Through the old bus yard. But the door to his fun room is certainly not unlocked. He wanted to have the joy of showing the boys around that particular part of his house himself. He's thinking about this with that long smile still stretched across his face as he dries his hands and heads back down the hall toward the front room.

CHAPTER 33

GLENN CAN'T SEE WHAT THE STRANGE MAN IS LOOKING AT, though it seems to be in the direction of his neighbor's house. Ellie, he'd learned, is her name. Her house had been built slightly behind theirs, so he can't see much past her mailbox out the living-room window. It occurs to him that he can see her entire house out Gerome's window, but the idea of taking his eyes off the man in the road tickles him as the wrong move. It doesn't quite set sirens of alarm off in his mind, but they have certainly turned to life. A long, low warble. Like the deep growl of a jungle cat, the sound emanating from the hollow walls of its gut.

The Fourth is a night of celebration; people do things they'd be embarrassed of in the morning. And as a truck driver, he's certainly seen loads of drunkards doing embarrassing shit. What he's looking at now is a mere blip on that radar, but it's very *strange*. He's watched the guy stumble down the street since before he passed Cole's house. There are no streetlights on Lakeview Heights, but the moon is a silver coin in the blank sky, casting a silk blanket over everything beneath. Even in the dark, he can see something swinging from the man's hand. It seems to be the hand opposite from Glenn. Something with some weight to it. A shovel, maybe? It'd have to be one of those short ones.

He'd only meant to glance through the front blinds to see if Gerome and Cole were at Cole's house. Earlier, they'd dissed the idea of joining Bree down at the lake for the fireworks show. Glenn doesn't blame them. Bree has a thing for Cole, as hot and as heavy as a little girl can hold. Joining her would be a disaster. They are teenage boys. They need to do things on their own. Learn the world for themselves. Lord knows he once did. He'd met Gerome's mother while hitchhiking across Tennessee in his early twenties. She was a waitress at an old-school diner he'd stopped at. He'd had the sudden hankering for a dangerously cold root beer float. The place had brushed silver doors and checkered floors, the whole nine. He'll never forget. Oh, the magical eighties.

He'd thought that if the Harper family's Cherokee wasn't there (they'd always parked in the driveway, according to Kris; apparently Stacey still had half the house in boxes scattered about the garage), then the boys probably did what boys do and decided on a whim to go somewhere where their chances of getting laid under the fireworks increased drastically. He'd chuckled silently at the young adult male, testosterone-bulged mind. That was when he'd seen the man.

He's still standing over there, like a man having a casual conversation with a mailbox. He's clearly debating something, torn between two decisions. Which normally wouldn't be anything to gawk at except for the fact that it's full dark and he looks about as sober as a Bering Sea captain's cat. Plus, that *thing* in his hand. What else could that be besides a short-handled shovel?

Kris is in the bathroom. She'd gotten up after their episode of *Scandal* finished. Glenn heard her flush, heard the faucet spray quickly, the bathroom door open and close out in the hall.

When she enters the room, he turns and says, "Hey, hon, come check out Odd Thomas out here." He turns back to look through the blinds. "He's got a shovel or some—" But the guy is climbing the fence to the man's house at the end of the road.

Another octave.

"I don't see anyone," she says, snuggling up beside him and flicking up a single blind for a peek.

Glenn suddenly sees his future. In a matter of decades, they'd turn out to be exactly this, just a couple of old concerned folks peeking out the front blinds, keeping a wide eye on the neighborhood out there.

"Well, he just hopped that guy's fence."

"Oh, Nolan's? Did you say he had a shovel?" She drops the blind back to place with a little plastic *tick* and makes her way back to her favorite spot on the couch.

"Yeah, it looked like it. I don't know what else it could've been." Then, when she says nothing, he adds, "Hon, don't you think that's *weird*? And he looked plastered, swaying on his feet and everything."

Kris chuckles behind him.

"But up and over he went."

He finally turns around to face her, unsure of what's funny. The blinds waggle slowly, then still behind him. He holds his hands to his sides, palms up. "What?"

"I'll tell you who that guy probably was." She's thumbing the remote, scrolling for the next episode of season three. "Nolan's that guy with the building company, remember? Well, word in town is he drinks like a fish and bosses over a bunch of guys with similar interests. Yes, episode six!" She power-clicks a button on the remote and tosses it on the coffee table in front of her. "Guarantee it was one of his drinking buddies from work coming to ring in the day of freedom." She remembers the shovel and adds, "And he probably brought the shovel to bury the dead soldiers!" At this, she cackles maniacally. Empty wine glass on the little table next to the sofa or not, Glenn had always thought it was irresistibly cute how she sometimes cracks herself up, uncaring if anyone else is joining in on her fun.

A smile touches the corners of his previously taut mouth.

She slaps a worn spot in the sofa cushion next to her. "Come sit, hon. Watch with me."

He joins her once more over on the couch, and as the new episode starts, he already begins to forget about the strange man in the road. Weird shit happens on the Fourth, remember?

The fireworks should be starting soon, he thinks as his wife cuddles up next to him, the same way she's been doing for twenty years. Like a koala bear against a big tree in a downpour.

He's quickly lost in the show, but that siren is still whining deep in his head. Like a dog does when he knows there's a bad man outside the door. It's not as sharp—submerged in water or something instead of bouncing off the dry walls of his skull. But it's still there, nonetheless.

CHAPTER 34

COLE'S BLINKER IS THE ONLY NOISE IN THE CAB. A SOFT TOCK on repeat. That and the sound of the motor galloping healthily after the tires bark back onto Carlsen. The realization has set in; there's no need for words. Both Gerome and Cole are running on autopilot as their consciousness wrestles with a big bear called breaking and entering. They've been too long on their little errand run. Gerome got caught in line at CVS, stuck behind a trio of overweight white women wearing matching tanks—the colors were different, but all three bore holes and stains. The one in the back had looked Gerome up and down slowly, uncaring that he was looking directly at her. He was close enough to reach out and poke her upper-arm blubber. It had taken the clerk three "ma'ams" to break her gaze and turn to checkout. "Gimme a pack of Marlboro Lights and this here Meller Yeller, and that'll be it for Gina."

Cole was opening the driver's door to go in and see what Gerome's holdup was when he finally came out. Cole had simply grabbed the first cheap item he saw (a used Halo 2 game), checked out, and bounded back to the car, beating his buddy by minutes.

"What's the deal?" he asked Gerome, who was swinging his fake leg up and over the bottom of the doorframe.

He'd tossed the bag containing two pairs of all-purpose work gloves (the thinnest ones he could find, which was easy when the selection consisted of only about three different kinds) to the floorboard and twisted to buckle in.

"You see Shamu and her two besties come out before me?" He nodded to the trio jamming into a rusty sedan parked in the closest handicapped spot to the door. It conjured up an expression an old preacher once said in an old congregation Cole once sat in, comparing a sin to someone squeezing a bit of toothpaste out of the tube, unable to ever get it back in. They'd looked like the human version of toothpaste trying to somehow slide back into the tube. Or in this case, a Buick. "Yeah, well, the first two couldn't figure out what kind of cigarettes to get, and the one in the back just stared at me like she'd never seen a black person before."

"Probably was wondering why a black kid needed gloves at eight thirty at night," he'd said. "Probably thought you were going to break into someone's house."

He'd thrown it in reverse, commencing silence.

Now they sped down Carlsen, the cab still silent. Cole checked his phone for a text—there was none—and replaced it on the seat between his legs. He'd sent a message to Ellie asking if Nolan was still there while he was waiting for Gerome to come out. He's getting a bit nervous himself. He was *sure* Nolan would stay for the fireworks, giving Cole and Gerome a healthy thirty to forty-five minutes to do their proposed snooping. Cole thinks it better to keep the text to himself. He wants to appear as confident as possible for Gerome, knowing his friend would want to call it off more than he already did if he were under the impression Cole was wavering. Also knowing that Gerome would scold him for sending the text. Ellie would probably (and maybe already *has*) think it a bit odd that Cole was asking. Cole knows they'd have to be fast if they wanted to actually pull this off, but he *had* to find whatever's hiding in Nolan's house. He feels it somewhere deep, like the odd feeling a man gets sometimes when cancer sprouts in his balls, a terrible itch no physical action can scratch. A BB in a cold bowl of Cheerios.

Glowing white tents sporadically emerge from the horizon on both sides, then zoom past. Last-minute firework hubs for last-minute firework fans. People pick through dwindling selections, jittering around the tents like moths flocking around flames.

Their street emerges from the gloom. The deep green Lakeview Heights street sign flashes reflections of oncoming headlights back at them. Traffic noticeably increased the closer they'd gotten to Lakeview, causing Cole to have to feather the gas pedal instead of mash it like he really wanted. He fantasizes smashing through the blundering line of stupid families trying to get to the lake in time to get a good spot. The whole town is here.

They finally manage to reach the road they live on and swing the Cherokee off Carlsen. Neither of them thinks a thing about the truck parked in the ditch. Probably a couple love birds getting off on sucking some face under the colorful explosions soon to start overhead. How romantic.

People do crazy shit on the Fourth. They come by it honestly enough, though. It *is* the day to celebrate freedom, after all. Maybe do something you wouldn't normally do. Cole has a quick vision of *The Purge*, that creepy movie where all crime is legal for one night a year in order to "cleanse" people's souls. He shakes the thought off and begins searching the dark for anything peculiar. Ellie's house appears at the end of the street. Cole notices how closely it's built to Nolan's fence. Not for the first time, he's thought it many times before, but something about it tonight feeds into that wrongness he's trying to grab hold of. All he wants to do is grab it and shake the thing upside down, see what's in its pockets. But it's hiding behind things, well out of Cole's reach at the moment. His mind conjures up an image of a lion keeping his kill close, waiting in the shade till he's hungry enough to finish but watching for any other critters to come slinking out of the shadows to poke around.

"His truck's there," Gerome says, a slight quiver in his words.

It's the first time he's spoken the entire ride. The first time either of them has spoken, in fact.

"See?" he says. "We're good."

Cole was hoping they'd be able to sneak out the back door. That way, the chances of being seen by Ellie and Nolan (if they were, in fact, watching out the front window for the fireworks) would be zero. But that wasn't possible. Stacey is sitting in the living room flipping through prime-time shows instead of doing the same in her room.

Front door it had to be. So be it. They'd simply go out the front, then break right, sticking close to the house, and head for the back fence that way. It would have been too dark for Nolan to see them do whatever they did, but Stacey has the porch light on. Had it not been, they could've performed a nude tango in the front yard and ended the number with a beautifully executed double bird directed right at Nolan, which he probably wouldn't have been able to see. Maybe a little movement in the dark, Cole's pale ass reflecting the moon glow or something, but that'd be it. A floating double orb dancing an adolescent jig. Something soft swimming in the silver light.

But the porch light *is* on; he'd hoped they'd beat it, but the trip had run a bit long and Stacey is a Nazi for that light being on as soon as full dark sets in. It probably didn't matter too much anyway, though, or so they hoped, because if Ellie and Nolan were watching, the boys would be visible only for a brief moment before disappearing around the corner of Cole's house. And even then, it shouldn't seem too suspicious. Just a couple kids heading the long way to the backyard to play some night football or something. Nothing to see here.

"Finally," she says to them, looking away from the TV. "You guys and your games. I spend less time at Wally World getting a whole week's worth of groceries."

"Well, it took us awhile to find what we were looking for," Gerome says, looking down at his feet, not wanting to face Stacey's heat-seeking laser-gaze every mom possesses in order to sniff out and destroy bullshit from unseasoned bullshitters. His shield is thin.

"Do show," she says, genuinely interested.

Cole hands her the bag. As she starts studying the case, Gerome takes this opportunity to continue on to Cole's room with his own bag.

"Haloooo!" she says with faux fortitude, brows furrowed and voice deepened. She turns it over in her hands, checking out the now-obsolete graphics. She doesn't know any better. Cole feels a pang of disappointment. Disappointment in himself. He's pretty close with his mother and loves her very much. Keeping something of this magnitude from her makes him feel sick. A green sickness of inevitable regret. But it's the way it has to be. He can't be honest; he knows she wouldn't let him go.

She's a fun lady, certainly a "cool mom." She's even told Cole a couple stories (usually after a second glass of wine, empty takeout boxes on the coffee table pushed aside) that made red roses bloom on his cheeks, things she did back when *she* was young. But she wouldn't go along with his. He knows that. She'd feel the danger, just like Cole feels it, and she'd put her foot down.

He'd been hoping for one of Gerome's precognitive dreams. Praying, even. The cheap way of already knowing what would happen if they broke in and snooped around. The back-door way through the back door without having to actually be there. But the dreams had stopped as soon as the letter was found. Some esoteric work was done. The single strand of doubt that still clung in Cole's head had been severed. It was clear that *something* needed them to find that letter, and it had used Gerome's reoccurring haunting nightmare of an accident to hijack its way into this realm. He could literally *feel* the relief when they'd found it. The air had been a timid, writhing soup before. Now two points made a straight line again.

The relief of some unknowable grief was powerful, yes, but not quite as strong still as that feeling of impending danger crawling around his skin. He is starting to come to the realization that this might not go quite as smoothly as he'd hoped. But the need to look trumps all, for Cole. It was simply something that had no choice to compete with it. The only line on an otherwise empty page, no keys nor blinking cursor. He has to find out what's putting Ellie in potential danger. Because he knows it's there, and he knows no one else can do it.

He loves her, after all.

After a few moments of inspection, Stacey grows bored and tosses the game back into the bag. She turns back to the TV. "You guys want to watch *America's Got Talent* with me? I know you said earlier you were going to check out some fireworks around here, but it's only on till nine. You guys can catch the last twenty minutes or so, then head out? They always save the best for last, and Simon is *super* pissy tonight." She says all this with her eyes glued to the TV, and Cole is thankful. It's much more difficult to meet her eyes as he lies.

He'd told her before leaving for "GameStop" that they'd be back home in time to stroll down Carlsen and catch some individual front-yard firework shows. He'd said they didn't want to go down to the lake. Too many people.

"Nah, that's all right, Mom. We want to get going before the show down at the lake starts." He doesn't know why he says this. It doesn't make much sense. He never practiced different variations of the lie. He watches the side of her head for confusion at his Freudian slip. But she only laughs at the TV. A sheepdog balances on a tightrope while its owner prances around in a clown getup. He lets out a long, silent exhale.

He turns down the hall and begins walking back toward his room when she asks what was in Gerome's bag. He bites his lip and wheels back around to face her gaze. They are caught. She's going to stomp right into his room and demand to know why they'd bought two pairs of gloves at 8:30 at night and what they planned on doing and did they think she was *really* that stupid? *Did they?!* And he'd crumble and tell her everything and—

She isn't really even looking at him. She's still watching the dog do circus tricks. It has her full attention. He thinks he could probably just mumble something and head down the hall and she wouldn't have even noticed, but he thought it best to risk an answer.

Another lie.

"Gum," he says. Carefully. Watching her. "His breath stinks." Adding this part in hopes that if she is listening, maybe the humor will gently ride away any further questions. People like to end things on a laugh.

But she doesn't laugh. "Okay, sweetie," is all she says. Still not looking away from the TV.

A few moments later, Cole follows Gerome out the front door, pausing briefly to remind Stacey they are walking down Carlsen for a bit and would be back. They're sleeping here tonight, and Gerome's parents had already been told (which they had).

The letter from Ellie's dead mother lay open on Cole's bed. Gerome had pulled it out of its hiding place between *The Tommyknockers* and *The World According to Garp* in Cole's bookshelf. He'd wanted to remind himself why they were doing what they're doing, carefully rereading over each line while Cole was in the bathroom. He'd finished the last line: "Maybe if you were here right now, you could stop me. But would you?" That chilling accusatory plea, when Cole stuck his head in and said it's time to roll, not noticing what Gerome was reading. Gerome pulled his cell phone out of his pocket, a split decision, knowing noisy cell phones always caused bad things to happen to the idiots holding them in horror flicks (also knowing he never uses it anyway, so why risk it), and tosses it on top of the letter, an expensive paperweight, and heads out of Cole's room. He was going to ask Cole if he was bringing his and, if so, was going to remind him to put it on silent, but Cole is already at the end of the hall waiting for him and Stacey is sitting right there. So Gerome jams the gloves into his pockets and keeps his mouth shut, and as soon as he opens the Harpers' front door and steps out into the soft glow of the porch light, his anxious mind has pushed other things forth and he's already forgotten about asking.

CHAPTER 35

ELLIE IS FAST ASLEEP IN HER CHAIR, THE DEEPEST SLEEP SHE'S ever experienced; though she's not aware, no one is here to tell her about it. Her chin is raised high, pointing at a boring print on the wall. Georgia O'Keeffe's *Jimson Weed*. The original, hanging on a white wall 285 miles north in Indianapolis, is the ugly cousin of a radically austere oil piece that hung in the White House at the request of Laura Bush and eventually sold for a cool $44 million.

But she is not Laura Bush, this is not the White House, and the print on the wall isn't quite what the first painting was. Things can happen here. Bad things to good people.

Her mouth agape, she makes a quick, phlegmy hiccup sort of a noise, and a spume of spittle mists from her throat. She'd almost choked to death on her own drool.

What a way to go out, she would think if she were at all present and accounted for. Not quite the resplendent passing of Mrs. O'Keeffe at ninety-eight with pastel still caked under squared-off nails. But she's not. She swims up out of unconsciousness, awakening like someone coming to too early in the post-op room after a major surgery. Nurses scuttling around and plastic clacking off metal. Her arms flail heavily, just a tick up from full-blown slow motion, as she searches this new sand of coherence after a rooted sleep in those murky waters. It had been dark and dreamlike down there; the weight of her depth compressed her chest to no more than a half-inch rise and fall. An attenuate thing.

She tries for awareness, tries so hard that her brain bruises, but she just can't remember. It's that terrifying yet usually brief moment some people experience upon waking from a particularly deep sleep when they can't, for the life of them, remember where they are, why they're there, even *who* they are. Ellie feels this now, only the feeling is drawn out like God is pulling the pixels of life apart for fun, stretching them long ways and jagged, just to see what will happen.

It takes a few moments for the information riding the receptors to make the marathon jog to her brain, telling it that the thing on the table next to her wasn't there before, that someone must've moved it. And then third place tells her through huffing breaths that her stepfather, Nolan, had been here. And that he isn't now. On her own, she puts together that he must've been the one to move her phone. At once, she knows that it had been in her pocket.

Why would he go digging in her pocket while she was asleep?

Why were you asleep? she asks herself.

She's slowly coming to now, like the dial on an old-school radio swimming through the fading static, homing in on some familiar tunes. This fills her with relief. Although the sleep had been beautiful, she's scared of it now. Like it'd pull her back under any second. A big monster six inches under the muddied surface. Close enough to smell. Huge and silent and waiting. Now that she thinks of it, the *weight* is still there; maybe she just *thinks* she's out. Maybe it's a trick. Her vision begins to fizz. Not fade, but fizz. A million snap-crackle-and-pops make up edges of objects around her. Her mind tosses forth an image of that killer whale in the Orlando SeaWorld. Tilikum. The one that killed those trainers. She sees the scene play out. That time that big, beautiful fish decided to play that deadly game of how-long-can-you-hold-your-breath-Mister-Trainer-Man. It had the guy by the ankle, holding tight to status quo. It would rest at the surface of the big pool with the trainer, let him catch his breath, and then suddenly drag him to the bottom, flailing like a flag in the breeze on the way down. After a minute or two, it'd pull him back up to the surface and begin again.

She feels like that trainer probably did, only a false sense of clarity before being dragged back to the bottom of the pool, deep into the dark world. Whereas, he knew he was going to die. You could see the calm acceptance on his face.

Somewhere, she finds the importance of this brief moment of something similar to clarity, but not *quite* it, and hangs it on a nail in front of her thoughts.

Slipping again.

That cold whale has her ankle tight in its toothy mouth. She rolls from her lounging position and reaches for her phone. She feels an odd sensation and droops her head toward it. Her T-shirt had been pulled off one shoulder, along with the bra strap on that side. She can see her nipple clearly, right out in the open. She fixes her shirt and bra and seizes the phone. Hauling it back to her and flopping back into her previous position.

Something is wrong.

Her muscles feel like Play-Doh that's been left out in the sun, porous and brittle. A taste becomes known in her mouth. It had been sleeping on her tongue and in the crevasses of her lips. She smacks her lips, searching for what it is.

Saliva, she thinks. *Not my saliva, though.* It reminds her of college (not all that long ago, at all), waking up after a drunken night of making out with some backup football player carrying a bit of a beer belly already.

Her stomach rolls in place.

What the fuck, she thinks. Her mind too tired for further questions. She feels the muscles of that big animal wading next to her begin to tense, displacing water. It thrums with power. She's about to go back under.

She's not completely certain again where she is or why she's messaging back a boy named Cole. Her thumbs dance slowly on their own, too far away for her to control.

Cole. The boy from across.

She'd been dreaming of him. It was him who had pulled her shirt down and him who had kissed her deeply, and she hadn't minded a bit. She'd been at his mercy.

Only, that had been a dream. That had happened in the deep water, not out here in the air above. Someone else had been here with her.

That third-place neuron reminds her that it had been her stepfather who had been here. Though he didn't seem to be now. For the second time. Shaking its little neuron head, knowing she still didn't understand the meaning of the message, it'd come all these millions of miles to the front of her thoughts for.

She finishes her text to Cole. The boy from across.

Across what?

Her text *from* Cole had been opened already. Previously bold, unread letters sat there in her inbox as lifeless and used as the rest of the threads below. She sees that she has just typed an answer to the question the boy from across asked. "Is Nolan still there?" Her head sifts through the snippets of the dream she'd had down there under all that heavy water, deciphering real from make-believe. It had relayed the information to her thumbs before letting her in on it.

"No," they reply. *"Said he wnt home t o Get something. Hed be back shortly.* ”

She wishes she could stay up here in the clean and let her head do its deciphering, rebuilding her memory one block at a time. No mortar, just wobbly stacks up toward the ceiling. But she can't. The big animal has let her catch her breath long enough and wants to go back down to play.

She hears a great chuff, and mist erupts in a spume around her head, not unlike it had a few moments ago when she awoke. Those thick, yellow teeth clamp harder as the beautiful black fish plunges deep. A beautiful fish back into the beautiful blackness.

With her.

CHAPTER 36

They'd come through the bus yard and down the overgrown path that runs from its front gate to the backyard of Nolan's house. They'd followed the barely visible wheel ruts in the grass, pushed into the earth from maybe fifty trips with heavy loads from the past. They'd paused at the edge of the expanse of backyard. It isn't as big as Cole had expected. They wait behind an ancient maple and peer at the back of the black house in silence, waiting for movement. Lights, noise, anything at all. But of those, there is none.

From the house, at least.

Cole notices the crow. Gerome does not. He still hasn't shared with Gerome what, or who, he thinks that crow might be. It's still too much to even look at. He'll wait that out. It's no longer a coincidence. That thing has been present at every important moment of their journey; he knows what Gerome would say, anyway. Some stat showing the vastness of the crow population in this part of Tennessee; that it would be theoretically impossible for the bird that Cole had seen so many times to be the same one. But Cole knows. Because it's not a *bird*. He recalls the first few times he saw it, picking up on the thing's wrongness almost immediately. It had terrified him. It looked like something wearing a bad costume. But now, he feels almost comforted by its presence. As if it were actually somehow watching out for them instead of planning something malicious behind those dead eyes.

Could be both.

It's perched a rock's toss away on what looks to be a small gravestone. Maybe an old pet. The only source of light back here is from the moon. The crow dances its tipsy jig on top of the small headstone, claws *clickety-clacking*. Gerome hasn't noticed. He's frozen next to Cole, staring at the back of the strange man's house. Cole knows there's nothing to see. He knows Nolan is still with Ellie, waiting for the fireworks.

Which should begin any minute now, he thinks. He pictures a pissed-off Bree down at the dock, her and all her little girly-friends, arms folded over board-flat chests, tapping toes in the gravel in grand displays of displeasure and impatience.

He elbows Gerome. "Let's go."

Gerome simply nods and hands Cole one of the pairs of gloves, then slides his own pair on. They cross the narrow backyard through the silver murk collected from above. Cole takes a final glance back at the thing on the gravestone and tips an invisible cap. It replies with a single, strange little skip. Like it's not yet used to its legs.

'Cause it isn't, he thinks, and turns away, mounting the deck's wooden steps. He slips on his CVS gloves.

Cole is about to wonder why the thing back there hadn't made a sound since he'd noticed it, like it had in many other occasions now, but he knows before the thought is even fully formed. It *knows* to be quiet. That is really all there is to it. Why question an impossibility if it's in your favor? It has to be what Cole thinks it is. *Who* Cole thinks it is. And an old crow it certainly isn't.

They cross the porch on tiptoes (Gerome doing his best) and huddle close to the back door. Cole gives Gerome a nod, just like they'd hastily rehearsed back next to the babbling creek before heading into the back of the bus yard. Gerome returns with his own, though lacking a bit of the zeal he seemed to have earlier in the safety of Cole's room.

Cole pulls out a credit card to pick the tumbler on the back door—plan A. If that didn't work, they'd move to plan B, which meant searching the perimeter of the house for open windows. Something neither of them wanted to do. The credit card trick needed to work. Cole pulls the screen open and slides the card in through the door and the frame, searching for the strike plate, when Gerome puts a hand on Cole's arm.

"Wait," he whispers. He's standing so close to Cole it's like he's trying to keep warm despite the temp hovering in the low eighties and humidity playing with the top of the scale.

"Let's just see," he whispers. Cole can really only see the whites of his friend's eyes and the brightness of his teeth. A thin line of light between his still lips. It reminds Cole of the first incident, the thing that seemed to set all this off. That terrible night they'd fallen asleep in Gerome's room and Cole had awoken to that scream that filled his head and nothing else. Though it came from Gerome's open mouth.

Too open, he remembers.

All he'd really seen were Gerome's teeth around that black hole and his *eyes.* His eyes were golf balls. Brand new, straight from the box. Solid white, because Gerome's pupils were somewhere back in his head checking out his brain. He'd been possessed. Used as a catalyst for whatever it was that pushed its way into his dream that night, pleading for help. At the time, it had caused nothing short of true terror. But now, Cole realizes it wasn't malicious at all, only a misunderstood soul hijacking its way through a grotesque afterlife, desperately trying to be heard. Cole knows it's the same restless soul that is now in that quiet form of a crow behind them. Watching through unknowable eyes of the best it could do.

"Let's just try it first," Gerome says into Cole's ear. He reaches out and turns the knob.

It's open.

The boys look at each other with wide eyes.

Cole steps timidly into the dead, silent house. Gerome follows.

Things are moving quickly now. The great Knower of life scrawls scenes across divine parchment in rapid succession, like the blurring staccato of a semiautomatic. Though Jordy seems immune at the moment. For him, the fabric of time is loaded down with a black sludge. Seconds stretch into long, lazy minutes. Jordy stares out the barn window, watching the quiet house in the woods. Waiting for any sign of Nolan's return. He'll wait as long as he needs, thinking the old fuck may hang around for a bit after the show.

Maybe watch a movie?

He sure as shit hopes not. He hasn't brought any more booze, and he'd already checked the old mini-fridge Nolan used to keep stocked. He was excited when he saw the thing plugged in, but the inside was only keeping cool an ancient baggie of sandwich meat and a Styrofoam cup from McDonald's.

So he sits, waiting.

He's leaning on the hood of the old Nova, the seat of his jeans resting in a sea of filmy dust. He'd pulled the string on the single bulb that hangs above the workbench next to the fridge, and now its low glow touches only the high points of his face. Nose, cheekbones, brows, and lips are all slightly visible, but his eyes remain black as burnt coals. It's enough light. Not that he really needs any, though. He'd sort of flipped it on, on a whim. Maybe some smarter corner of his brain is thinking ahead. What if he trips on a two-by-four and the gun goes off and discharges its pissed-off belly of bullets into *him* instead of who it's supposed to? The same smarter part refuses to turn on the overhead. Four long sodium bulbs stretch silently across the ceiling up there, waiting to light the place up white. He wouldn't want old Nolan to catch a glimpse of a bright window floating back in the woods beside his house. This needs to be an ambush. Not a faceoff. Jordy's a touch drunk, and he knows it. An Old West–style showdown against a sober man might not be in his best interest.

So he sits. Silently waiting for the opportunity. Sawed-off shotgun resting across his thighs as long-dormant dust now dances in front of his eyes, stirred up into the soft light.

Gerome sits in a chair just inside the back door, waiting both for Cole to come back with the all-clear and for his eyes to adjust. He clenches the sides of the seat, ready to bolt if he hears anything loud, as Cole had instructed. He knows his limitations physically, and when Cole whispered that he might want to wait here in case they had to run, he didn't argue. Nothing moves but his eyes, darting back and forth to identify objects as they appear to him. He sees an island, maybe a coffee cup resting on its edge. An old-style stove catty-corner across from him. Porcelain with sweeping curves and feet like those old tubs his mom is always talking about. Slowly, his gaze reaches farther and farther down the dark tunnel in front of him. A hallway. Now it seems to reach all the way to the front door. There are no lights on in the house and no noise whatsoever. Some things take something like shape as the moon glow through the windows is enough now for his eyes to adjust. It's so quiet that Gerome can hear the sticky *click* of the vertebrae high in his neck as he begins to feel okay about moving his head left and right along with his eyes.

Something moves at the end of the hall.

Beads of sweat pop out on the corners of his lips. A plague of gooseflesh flies over his skin, crawling up his thighs and down his back. His balls suck up as high as they can, as if trying to run and hide. Which is exactly what Gerome feels like doing. He feels like tearing his ass off the chair he's glued to and running as fast and as far as a boy with a fake leg through a dark forest could. But he can't move. He tries. He pulls with everything in him, but his body betrays his brain's flight signal.

That's bigger than Cole, he thinks as the thing makes its way up the hall toward him. It's so quiet he's sure it can hear the alarm going off in his head. It's sticking close to one wall, as if trying to remain unseen. He feels like his bladder may burst into his lap any second, but he somehow manages to talk it back. Gerome thinks about calling out, a soft pry into the dark, asking for identification. He thinks the thing may laugh back, though, and if it does, Gerome's body may literally implode. He feels like his muscle fibers are playing a losing game of tug-of-war with his nerves as the thing keeps coming. It's sort of hunkered, bending at the waist in a predatory slink. It certainly can see *him*. Coming straight for him. His hands still clench the sides of the chair, and had the kitchen overhead been on, he'd be humored to see he's squeezing so hard that his knuckles are the same color as—

"Cole," he whispers.

"It's me," Cole says. Crossing the kitchen toward him, checking out the back door one last time before they begin their secondary search for a bad room.

Gerome lets out a bellyful of hot breath, like he'd just broken the surface after a long time under. "Dude, I'm not kidding at all when I say that's the closest I've ever knowingly come to shitting myself."

"Sorry, man," he says, peeking back down the hall. On alert, barely listening to Gerome. "It's creepy as fuck in here."

A little monster of moonlight lay splattered in a rough square at Jordy's feet, illuminating old bolts buried in the dust. They faintly glimmer, reminding him of the night sky through smog. Something he's never seen. Maybe in a movie. The moon's rays steal through the barn window, pushing straight through the yellow gloom of the single bulb above the worktable, in a silver column so thick that Jordy thinks he can knock on it. The moon above is full and has found a clear alley through the overhanging trees to touch the old barn.

He's not sure how long he's been sitting here, leaning on the rusty coupe. Though he's sure it hasn't been all that long. Fifteen, maybe twenty minutes.

At most.

He hasn't so much as moved an inch since planting his ass here; he'd fallen into a sort of trance. He'd forgotten how to blink, though he'd do it every time a noxious burp of Budweiser climbed out of his throat. He stares at his boss's house.

Former.

He doesn't care anymore if the fireworks started or ended or whatever before he comes back. He doesn't care anymore that they're probably far enough back in here that his shotgun blast might not actually be heard anyway (although it'd probably travel across the lake, a blip on the radar for the other richie-riches over on the other side, nothin's gonna ruin *their* night, *nosireee*). The only person who could probably hear would be Ellie, and Nolan's probably tucked her in nice and tight, stroked her golden hair till she started snoring, maybe reached under the sheets and got his fingers a little wet before turning on the nightlight and heading back home. Maybe not. He doesn't care. All he knows is he's going to sit right here with the gun he got from Bill lying across his thighs and watch the dark house through the trees till he sees something. He doesn't think he'd hear Nolan's truck approach, but maybe he would. Either way, he'd probably see the leaves light up on one side of the driveway out there when his headlights came sweeping across as he crawled up toward the house. Yes, he only has a slap-dick view of the east face of the house, along with two windows, but he's pretty sure he'd see headlights.

He's thinking about his son. He's thinking about how badly he wants to put that pain into someone else. His old asshole of a boss, for example. He's thinking about the glory of busting a couple hot shotgun shells into his belly and how that would feel when one of the windows on the side of the house lights up. He doesn't think the light is coming *from* the room attached to the window, but maybe if that room's door were open and a light was flicked on out in the hall or something. It's soft. But it's certainly there.

He doesn't bother wondering why he hasn't seen headlights or heard a truck motor, doesn't bother thinking it odd that Nolan had apparently *walked* back instead of driven.

His feet are moving before he remembers how to move them; out the door and into the woods he goes. Those great fingers of his SOMETHING BIG move the strings attached to Jordy with quick, confident flicks.

As he's walking back out into the night, he *does* look back and wonder whether or not he should've turned off the bulb. Too late now. Not important. What *is* important is his drunken feet are already stumbling back through the underbrush toward the house.

He doesn't dare look up and ask his puppeteer to go back. He doesn't want to see the thing's face.

"This has to be something," Cole whispers, jiggling the knob.

They're standing at a door halfway down the long hall, the only one not at least cracked open. Cole prays it's the door that holds answers behind it. Prays it's a bad room hiding in plain sight. He sure as hell doesn't want to go creeping around the place anymore, this time searching for some sort of trap door or secret passageway in the dark stillness. He also knows they probably don't have time for that. This *has* to be it. In more ways than one. Has to be something worth finding.

It's a plain old knob, a silver sphere with a tiny hole in the center for a pick. No beefy lock system or homemade booby traps—just a regular bedroom or office or whatever it used to be, now serving as some sort of sick bear's lair. Evil hiding behind an inch and a half of particleboard and wooden veneer.

He jiggles the knob a different way, thinking about his old bedroom door in the house he grew up in. He could lock it from the inside, but his mother could always give it a little jimmy and a quick shoulder and pop it ajar. She'd never done it to bust in on him as some moms do, only using the trick a few times when he'd managed to somehow leave the little thumb-turn vertical on the inside, then closing it behind him. No, actually, there was one time she'd used the trick while he was still inside. She was sure he'd died in his sleep because he wasn't answering her calls one morning, only to break in to see him sitting on the short, shingled ledge outside his window trying to feed a Dorito to a circling bird.

He tries the jimmy-punch again, but nothing doing. The latch in there sits deep in the strike plate when it's locked.

"What do you think?" Gerome whispers.

"You don't have to whisper anymore, man. There's no one here but us. That's what I think."

"About the door, asshole," Gerome says back, still whispering but with a touch of confidence in the dark now.

"There's a key somewhere. Go run your hand on top of all the doorframes you can find. That's where people usually leave them. Even if you find one for a different door, it should work. Looks like there's nothing special about this knob."

"Maybe there's nothing special about this room then," Gerome offers.

"There is. I can feel it coming out from under the door."

Gerome can't see Cole's face enough to know if he's speaking literally or in generalities. But he also thinks Cole is right; why else would a man who lives alone have a locked room right here? It has its own sort of gravity.

"Go, man," Cole says, reaching into his pocket. "Look for a pick, and I'll try the card."

Gerome sets off down the hall in his patented step/lurch, pausing at each door he comes to and running a hand over it. He slowly makes his way toward the front of the house, from here knowing he'd be royally fucked if Nolan bursts through the front door. Cole is a good ten long yards away; he'd have plenty of room for a head start out the back door from there. These are the things you think about when you put yourself in positions like this. You weigh the risk against the reward and usually don't have enough time to sit there at the scale to see which wins out. You just pick and go.

He's thinking of this, thinking of what he'd actually do if Nolan *did* come through the front door, only a handful of steps to his right, when an eardrum-bursting *bonggg* sounds off in the darkness behind him. Loud things are even louder in the dark. He wheels around comically, flailing his arms at the would-be attacker looming behind him. He spins on his good leg, his bad one managing to kick over a chair from its quiet position against the wall. It clatters over on its side and slides toward the front door, coming to rest under an overhead beam. A big bold hyphen hanging above the foyer.

"You idiot," Cole says from down the hall. "It's the clock!" He turns back to the lock, sliding the card back through the frame, coming at it from another angle.

"I see that," Gerome says, facing the thing that made him nearly shit his pants. His second close call in a matter of minutes. An oak behemoth on the opposite wall of the hall. He listens to the rest of its old song, obnoxiously singing the time of 8:45 to anyone who'll listen.

Gerome replaces the chair as close to where he thinks it was, sliding it up flush with the wall. But when he does this, he notices one side won't push back all the way against the baseboard. Just a minute detail, but he figures something that small could possibly be noticed by a man like Nolan. He moves the chair an inch or so to one side and looks down behind the thick leg that seemed to have been hitting something.

In a replay of the way they'd found the letter in the bus yard less than a week ago, Gerome swallows down a writhing morsel of fear and guilt and imminence for the next step in all this, and says, "Uh, Cole."

"You got it?" He peers down the dark hallway, sees his friend standing over something. Again, reminding him of someone who's got a snake cornered.

"Unfortunately."

Gerome reaches down and plucks the key from its hiding place along the tall baseboard. For a moment, the scene could've been a painting. Everything completely frozen except for the dust bunnies drifting silently from the sharp edges of the key in Gerome's hand back down in a soft little pile on the hardwood.

CHAPTER 37

COLE HEARS A FAINT CLICK, MUFFLED FROM ITS PLACE DEEP IN the mechanics of the knob, and pushes the door open. It groans a long, scary note as it swings away from the frame. The boys timidly step inside.

Against the wall to their right is a long table. On it, computers sit in formation. Their screens all on, coating everything in the room with a blue-green hue. Not enough to read by, but enough light to see what they're stepping around. A low trunk, longer than the table, lay open against the opposite wall. Cole creeps over to it and peers inside. He sees things he's never seen in real life, only occasionally when stumbling over some strange porn site after one too many clicks. He sees a ball gag (at least, he thinks that's what it's called), whips, chains, a pair of handcuffs. He sees weird things made of black leather and studded with silver spikes, like a fucked-up KISS costume. Everything looks cold and heavy. He sees an open baggie of zip ties and some sort of canister, a tube-like object about eight inches long with what looks like a rubber mouth on one end (he's never seen anything like *that* in those strange pornos, but he can put two and two together). It gets worse as he goes. A coil of rope, something that looks like a small guillotine without the blade, a black mask with only a mouth hole, something that looks like a half-opened metal flower with a hand-crank on the other end.

He feels sick.

His eyes scan the length of the box, up and over rolling hills of tangled and sharp perversion, and eventually fall on something that sucks the air straight from his lungs like a dip in Arctic waters. A pair of legs, naked as far up as he can see, protrudes from behind the far end of the box. Pale feet lay oddly rigid, like cold blocks of once-real things. Heels on carpet, toes pointed up toward the ceiling. He can't speak. He tries, but the only thing that comes out is a terse, breathy hitch. Gerome, checking out the computers behind him, hears only the soft whirr of electrical things keeping screens alive.

Cole remembers how to move his legs and makes his way to the end of the long box. He peers around it, knowing what he'll see slumped against the wall.

And he's right.

Ellie lay there naked from top to bottom. He lets out a short cry and slaps a hand over his mouth. She's bone-white with a tinge of blue. Like she's recently taken her own dip in those icy, Arctic waters, only her dip was skinny and she forgot how to swim. His eyes crawl up her nude body with no excitement whatsoever; only horror and sadness fill every crevice of his being. What had he *done* to her? Cole knows he'll forever be haunted by this summer. He'll forever be tormented by the way things turned out, when the way things should've been (had he figured everything out faster) could have been heroic. Selfishly, this crosses his mind first. Of course it does—it's human nature to want to feel the power that procures being someone that saved someone else. But quickly, the sadness comes flooding back. This poor, beautiful girl. The sadness of what could've been her life, but instead some fucked-up derailment happened and she never found the path again. Soon, blue lights would be splashing the outside of the house and men in dark suits would be carefully picking through the things in here. A busy crime scene. But for now, it's just him and her in here, Gerome forgotten. He is so sorry for not being faster. Sorry for not going to the cops from the start like they should have, even if what they had wasn't much. Those men are paid to sift through bullshit and home in on things that have weight hiding under the water. He was so stupid to think otherwise.

And now a girl is dead.

That's why she never replied to my text, he thinks. A flat, emotionless sentence laced with so much terrible finality that it could bring a whole theater audience to tears. Cole kneels beside the dead woman. The girl he'd barely known but found a way to fall in love with over the course of a summer. He can hear Gerome fidgeting with a keyboard behind him, facing away, unaware of what Cole has stumbled across. What's lying in this room with them. And that's okay. He wants one last moment with Ellie before this place is lit up like an excavation site and crawling with quiet men holding loud walkies. It's very dark in this corner, but he can see that her eyes are closed, almost squinting with anguish.

No, that's not right. Pleasure?

As his eyes adjust more, he sees that yes, in fact, her face is scrunched up, eyebrows high in the middle but sloping down as they go, mouth slack in a small oval. He notices there are no teeth in there, and he thinks no tongue, either.

Something isn't right.

He reaches a shaky finger past her lips and immediately yanks his hand back like she'd tried to bite. But she hadn't. She couldn't. There really *aren't* any teeth in there. No tongue, either. Her lips are stuck in that oval shape.

As if . . .

He runs a hand through her hair and again pulls away, repulsed. It doesn't feel like any hair he'd ever felt. Any *human* hair. It feels like the hair of a—

"Doll," he whispers. Barely audible, even to his own ears. "A fucking sex doll." A little louder this time. He jumps to his feet and backs away, like the thing's strapped with C-4 and mumbling cadenced Arabic. He sees now that it definitely looks just like Ellie, but it's definitely not. The legs and arms look rubbery, not like dead flesh. The body is bluish, yes, but only from the computer glow behind him. He can now even see the creases where the arms and legs meet the torso, allowing the thing to be configured however the owner wants, he assumes. Cole has never been so disgusted in his life, like *he* is the one messing with the thing instead of the sick fuck who was supposed to be a father to her.

He has to literally turn his head away for a moment, thinking he might throw up. Which would be very bad considering the fact that they probably wouldn't have time to clean it up and would have to leave the place with a big, sopping stain of his DNA drying into the carpet in front of the doll that looks like Ellie.

He looks out the window on the wall to his right. A dark sheer lay over it. He looks hard, tries to look *through* it at the trees beyond, just till his head clears a bit. To try to get out of this room for a second. But he can't. It's thin, but not thin enough to see through. Especially at night. He suddenly realizes it odd that Nolan hadn't covered it with something thicker.

In plain sight, he again thinks. Just a monster hiding in plain sight for all the world to see, if they'd just look hard enough.

Either that, or he's fucking crazy.

"Cole. I said, did you say something?" Gerome asks from behind him. "Come look at this, man. You were right. He's watching Ellie from in here. She's on one of the screens right now. She's either asleep or …" His voice trails off. It's hitchy, words a stoked fire of dancing fear. "Wait now . . . she's moving. She's looking around for something. Cole, I don't like this." Silence for a moment. Cole waits for Gerome to continue and for his stomach somersaults to subside. "Okay, she's texting someone it looks like." He turns to Cole. "Do you think she's okay?"

Suddenly a loud *ding* shouts from Cole's pocket.

Little late, hun, he thinks. Also realizing he forgot to put his phone on silent.

Wait, where's …

Gerome reads his thoughts. "Dude, okay, where's Nolan then? She just texted *you,* and I don't see *him,* and why the fuck is your phone not on vibrate?"

Cole returns his gaze to the thing slumped on the floor in front of him, unsure of what to do next. He's about to turn and join Gerome at the computers when he hears a voice that makes his blood run cold, that Arctic water now *inside* him, stealing through clenched veins. He's only heard that voice once. Earlier this summer. It was yelling then, angry with a bunch of workers.

Now it is low, though just as startling. That powerful energy still emanates from those words.

"Not for sale, kiddo."

Cole turns to see a dark figure standing in the doorway. It seems to be looking directly at Cole.

"But I bet you'd sure like to buy her, huh? With your cute little allowance?" An arm reaches out of view from the frame and flicks on the hallway overheads. Nolan Donovan remains a silhouette, though the light from behind him crawls over the edges of his outline, revealing cheeks that grow too large on the sides of his face as an evil sneer stretches toward his ears.

Cole can't move and neither can Gerome. He's stuck to the rolly chair just like he had been stuck to the chair by the back door in what seemed like years ago. And God, how he wishes he could go back to then and turn and run instead of pushing deeper into this man's house.

Nolan steps into the room with them, the light from the computers revealing a pistol hanging from his hand. It's strangely beautiful. Cold, black steel dancing in the blue gloom.

He raises the revolver and points it at Gerome's face. Cole hears him roll backward instinctually, just a foot or so. Then all is silent again. Time has stretched long into a crawl. Cole's eyes never leave Nolan, who's staring straight back at him.

"Toss me your cell phone," Nolan says.

Cole reaches into his pocket and pulls out his phone. He tosses it across the room into Nolan's free hand. Nolan snatches it, clicks the home button, and says, "How precious. You even put a little heart next to her name."

Cole feels as if he's been dry-swallowing cold stones for weeks. His breath catches in his throat and struggles to perform its normal in-and-out function. His hands begin to tremble at his sides. Thankfully, it's probably too dark in the room for Nolan to notice. He definitely doesn't want Nolan to see how terrified he is. The only chance they have is to stay cool and use their heads. Although he presumes the interior of Gerome's head right now probably looks like Walmart on Black Friday: screams and cries, things tearing down aisles, smashing into each other.

Nolan drops Cole's cell to the floor, never taking his eyes off him, and presses the heel of his boot down onto the center of the screen. Not a dramatic smash, but an *efficient* one. He hadn't done it to send a message but simply to do the job of disabling their only chance at a getaway, while also keeping in mind he'd have to come back and pick up all the little pieces later after he'd killed them both and buried them back in the bus yard, like he had the letter. Does he know they'd found that?

Just as Cole is silently praying that Gerome brought *his* cell and is somehow secretly speed-dialing the Putnam County Police Department telekinetically, Nolan shoots down all hope.

"And you, boy," he says, finally turning his gaze to Gerome. Cole hears the purposeful authoritative way he said *boy*, and winces. Outside, Cole thinks he hears a thick branch snap somewhere close to the window. But he's not sure, and there are more pressing needs here and now in front of him. Like how the fuck are they going to survive this situation, for one. How the fuck again are they going to be able to disarm Nolan and somehow make it past him out of the room and ultimately out into the night. Cole thinks briefly that this must be a similar feeling to the people locked up for life. So close to freedom they can smell it but literally will never bask in that playful breeze again. It's a terrifying thought. Maybe they can bull-rush him. Take their chances of him getting a shot off and just hope that if a bullet makes contact with someone's body, it won't hurt so badly that they can't run.

His head is spinning.

His head is the one that conjured up the images of Walmart on Black Friday, not his buddy's.

He suddenly realizes that they *aren't* getting out alive (aside from a miracle stroke cast down from God himself or a brain aneurism in which Nolan drops dead right there in the doorway) because they hadn't planned for this. There's no way to know what the other is thinking, which actions the other was forming in the front of his head, building courage to attempt. They are screaming at each other through dead air. Silent.

"Speak up!" Nolan booms. Cole jumps in place. "I said gimme your goddamn phone, *boy*!"

Gerome clears his throat.

Cole risks a glance over. His heart breaks for Gerome. He's cowering in his chair, staring down the barrel of the gun. A gun held by a murderer with a new, provocative motive. Cole can see the quiescent look in his friend's eyes. He knows he has no chance. He can't even run.

An enormous responsibility sinks in across Cole's shoulders, the weight of the world personified. *He'd* gotten them into this. Gerome didn't want to come, said it was a bad idea, now *he* is the one who had to get them out.

Good luck with that.

"I-I don't have it on me. Left it at his house. Swear to God."

Nolan then switches the barrel stare to Cole and makes his way over to Gerome, who stands out of fright, not boldness. Like a young Gestapo might when the mad little warlord shuffled into the room. The chair rolls backward another foot or so, as if it were scared too.

"Pull out your pockets," Nolan says.

Every fibrous mechanism of movement in Cole's body screams for him to run out the door, beg for the chance to get missed by a bullet, and thus give an opportunity to make it out alive.

But he can't.

He can't leave Gerome here alone with this monster. Plus, he's pretty sure Nolan would easily disable him with an accurate shot if he tried. Hell, even a not-so-accurate shot at this close of range would probably fuck him up royally. So he sits still.

He watches Gerome open out his pockets to prove his phone isn't in them, while Nolan stands at arm's length for a close inspection.

Cole moves his gaze slightly over to the computers along the wall. The one directly behind Gerome shows Ellie in one of the small squares that makes up a collage on each screen. Her small square is a live feed of the front room of her house. The one he didn't think she ever used. All four computers are top-of-the-line, twenty-seven-inch Mac desktops with the deep, detailed clarity of the damn Hope Diamond. So he can clearly see Ellie passed out cold on one of the stiff chairs in there.

He drugged her, he immediately thinks. Then he begins to glance over the other screens, a quartet of technology coming in at about the same price as a gently used Camry. His eyes flick through all the boxes as Nolan pats down Gerome for good measure.

Then it hits him. A cold right-hand cross into his soft, unsuspecting middle.

He knows everything, he realizes. *He knows we found the letter, knows everything Ellie and I ever talked about, even knew we were coming tonight because he was watching when we talked about the Fourth.*

"Where is it?" Nolan says, snapping Cole away from his thoughts.

"I gave it to you," Cole says, assuming he's talking about his cell.

Nolan drops his head, gun still staring Cole in the face, and lets out a laugh. A strange sound with no humor at all. Like he had never tried before and is practicing how. Then his head snaps up, eyes burning black in their sockets, and says, "The note, motherfucker. Where's the note from that wrinkly old bitch my wife turned into?" He waves the gun back and forth, a steel pendulum. "Ah, ah, ah," he warns. "Don't you dare lie to me."

Cole shuts his mouth.

"These are hollow-points in here, kiddo. Exactly five left. One of them went through my wife's head and turned it into green gumbo. Hadn't touched it since I got it back from forensics those years ago. Put it right back in my nightstand, my trusty old Colt." He pats the gun as if it were a dog he'd potty trained. "Four bullets," he continues. "That's two for you, and two for your black buddy."

He thinks hard about his next line, boldly showing his crazy.

"I suppose I'd use the last one on myself after I have my night." He nods toward the computers. Cole knows he's talking about Ellie.

He looks back at Cole and asks, "Don't you know how *long* I've waited?" A genuine question, as if he truly wants an answer. An answer he won't get from a kid whose mouth feels stitched and soldered shut.

And he *was* going to lie. He doesn't know what he was going to say, maybe a denial of ever even finding the letter, even though Nolan certainly knew that they had.

"Where's the letter?" Nolan says calmly. He's planted firmly back in the doorframe. He seems an immovable object. And they're just two teenagers. Not quite qualifying as an unstoppable force.

"It's at my house. It's hidden. No one knows about it but us." Cole immediately curses himself. Telling Nolan no one knows about the letter but them is like saying, "Go ahead and shoot us, your secret goes to our grave, no worries."

Nolan's a step farther back than he was before. His movement hadn't been noticed, but the light from the hall now exposes most of his face. So Cole can see him narrow his eyes in speculation. Deep lines of crow's feet bunch together. Maybe he thinks Cole couldn't have been stupid enough to say that.

"Doesn't matter," he finally says. "I'll get the truth all outta ya one way or another. Truth and nothin' but it." That predatory sneer crawls back across his face. "As for right now, I'm gonna tie you both up in the very same wiring I placed in my Ellie's house in order to keep an eye on her."

"You sick fuck." It comes out before Cole can catch it on his lips. Nolan would raise his pistol now and bury a long bullet deep into his belly, making him suffer at least for a handful of minutes before he bled out all over the floor. But Nolan doesn't do that, only cocks his head to one side and closes his eyes in an attempt to keep the pin of his grenade of a temper in place. At least for now.

His face flattens again, and he carries on. "As I was saying, I'm going to use the extra wire from *my* Ellie's house to tie you both up. Then I will place you both in front of my computers and make you watch what I do to her." He pauses. "I'll find tape for your eyelids!" He says this the same way someone would say they'll make water balloons at a backyard barbecue.

"Especially *you*," he says.

Fuck you, Cole says, this time safely in the confines of his own head.

"Then, after I'm done ..." He visibly shivers at this with excitement, and in that moment, Cole and Gerome both simultaneously think that there is nothing on this earth creepier than an old man shivering with excitement about a young girl. "I'm gonna come back and kill you both." As flat and as casual as someone reading the phone book. "Then I might kill myself. I'm not sure, haven't decided on that part yet. Depends on if I can kill each of you with only two bullets. I mean, of *course* I can, but I want to make it last. I think I'll shoot each of ya in the gut and wait to see who gets all goofy first—won't that be fun? It'll be like a game. Like when I was a boy and we used to tie rubber bands around our little dicks tighter and tighter to see who's went all blue and goofy first." He pauses and thinks. "You boys are lucky though, ya know it? I was planning on shootin' ya right here as soon as the fireworks started. But I think I changed my mind." He nods a little like a bad actor, too dramatic for something so simple. "Yeah, I changed it. Just decided I changed it. I want you to watch. My dick will be harder than an Eskimo turd knowin' y'all are watchin' us fuck. Just like I always used to get a little hard when we'd all whip our little weenies out and wrap rubber bands around them. My friends would make a little fun, but I didn't care."

Then he brightens, as if an idea occurs to him suddenly.

Cole is both amazed and terrified at just how quickly Nolan can switch from one mood to the next. He had to read a book for psych class last year called *Sybil*—had gotten an A on the paper. Now he wonders if this man had similar demons swimming around inside him. How had he functioned in society, especially as a successful business owner?

Hid in plain sight.

"You think she's a screamer?"

Cole is dumbfounded. He couldn't have conjured this scene up had he been toking on the same shit the *SpongeBob* creators passed around the production meetings.

"I've always wondered," he continues. He seems to have gone soft now; the gun lowered a few inches, unbeknownst to him. "I put the wrong cameras in her room, see? Of course!" He slaps himself hard on the forehead with the hand holding the gun. So hard the cylinder shakes in its frame. Both boys flinch, expecting an accidental discharge. "My luck. The only room in the whole fucking house I couldn't hear a thing. The box was misleading, 'clearer' seemed to pertain to sight *and* sound. Bullshit. But by the time I realized it was too late, see, by then, she was all ready to move in and my boys would've gotten a little suspicious had I gone back and tweaked some things on my own for a few more days. And I think some of them *were* suspicious, *were* wondering what I was doing over there so long after it was done. So I said 'Oh, well' and bit the bullet." He shrugs, and the boys wince at the quick movement of the gun. "I can imagine the noises she makes when she plays with herself at night well enough. All women make similar noises, see, like they all get a big noise bank as soon as their little tits start growing and their pussies start sproutin' little lips. Then they choose a few and combine them for their special own little coming noise. Ya know, *their* noise. They're all pretty much the same, though. You'll find out."

He pauses and brightens, slapping his knee with his empty hand. "Wait! No, you won't!" He cackles for at least a ten-count. An eternity in here. Doubles over at the waist. The boys risk a fast glance at each other, looking for strength or calmness or a fucking *plan* in the other's eyes, but neither of them sees any of that.

"Well, I'll letcha hear *her*. I know *you* always wanted that." He nods at Cole, face again quickly switching to stifled rage. "I'll fuck her right there in the front room for ya, won't even carry her up to the bed, so you can hear loud and clear. How 'bout that?" He's walking slowly toward Cole now, eyes prying deep into Cole's soul, finding the fear to latch on to.

Cole stands his ground.

Ridiculously, he's trying to apply the knowledge he learned at Wesley Woods camp back when he was eleven. Around the campfire, after his first-ever kiss, the guy with the guitar told them to *never* run from an approaching bear (among other things that he was in too blissful of a state to comprehend), that you'd immediately be seen as food.

That's why he's not moving now. And maybe that's *not* so ridiculous.

"You never had a chance with her." He keeps coming. Cole wonders how far away from the door he'd have to be for Gerome to make a break for it. Then he remembers that *he* hadn't when he had the chance a moment ago. He knew Gerome wouldn't leave him just like he couldn't leave Gerome. "At least her ex-husband probably had a big dick—he was a big ole boy. What you got? Little peashooter?" Nolan again cackles, but this time quickly pushes it back down. "And you know what? A big body just hits the ground a little harder, that's all. Like a fat fucking sack of potatoes—*splat!*" He slaps his hands in Cole's face, so close he feels the wind tickle his nose. That close. The gun again clatters. Cole can feel the weight of the thing, like it being this close to his head displaces the air immediately around it.

Nolan's farther into the room now than Gerome is, but he never takes his eyes off Cole. Either he knows Gerome won't be stupid enough to try to escape or he knows that if he is, then he has plenty of time to pump a slug into a part of the body of his choice. Gerome would be slow; Cole again feels pity for making him come.

Did Gerome just make a hand gesture?

Cole thinks he catches something out of the corner of his eye, but he doesn't dare cut his eyes away from Nolan.

Nolan puts the end of the barrel between Cole's eyes. Cole's teeth are clenched so tight his jaw muscles cramp painfully. "All it took was a little *push*," Nolan says quietly, barely loud enough for Cole to hear, and shoves him gently in the forehead with the pistol. Cole takes a step back to catch his balance and gathers himself.

Did he kill Ellie's husband too?

"So, yeah!" Nolan says, switching to happy and stepping backward toward the door. He suddenly sounds like someone who'd just delivered a solid pitch to his company's marketing department. "That's what I'll do. Make ya watch, come back, and find out just where I can get that letter. It was to *me*, ya know, no one else. If that takes two bullets apiece, then so be it. Won't matter anymore about shootin' ya during the fireworks. Point-blank muffles most of the report."

He breaks out into a sinister smile. "But not all! It can sure be heard from that barn over there!" He points the gun over Cole's head toward the window. Cole slightly ducks and wonders what the hell he's talking about. "But anyway, gotta save one for myself. Just in case things get a smidge sticky. Hey, if they do, I left everything to my dead dog!"

Cole knows two things now. The headstone out back was from the grave of said dead dog, and this man is stone-cold crazy.

They're never getting out of here.

CHAPTER 38

Jordy had been in the hall for a minute now. He'd heard most of the spiel. Apparently, there are two young guys in there, although he could see only one. A one-legged black kid sat in a chair by a table full of computer monitors. He has the angle. Jordy had taken a step forward when Nolan stepped deeper into the room, out of view, talking to the other one. But the black kid quickly held his hand up, telling him to hold off. Shortly after, Nolan had backed into the doorframe, maybe ten paces in front of him. Maybe. He has no clue who these kids are or why they're here, but judging from the portion of the conversation Jordy caught, they are in deep shit.

The gun is getting heavy in Jordy's hands, and he's ready to use it. This is *his* moment. *His* Something Big. He raises the shotgun and points it at Nolan's back, now seemingly an even bigger piece of shit than Jordy originally thought, after hearing some of those awful things he'd just heard him say.

"Now. You," Nolan says, nodding at Cole. "Go over to that box and pull out the jumble of wires at the bottom. Don't worry, nothing else in there has been used . . . yet."

The next few moments reveal themselves in a series of snapshots, like one of those old picture books you quickly flip through to get the characters to move. Yet somehow everything is simultaneously in slow motion; Cole has time to think between each tiny page flip. No, *think* is not quite right; his mind moves on autopilot, body suddenly being tugged along by the bullish instinct of survival. *Narrate.* That's it. His head talks to him as things happen. As shit hits that proverbial fan.

The shotgun jams. Jordy had his shot and blew it. He'd closed his eyes and pictured his boy playing T-ball, running around the bases with that dumb-luck grin on his face while the ball rolls all the way out to the wall, and pulled the trigger. There was a faint click, and that was it.

Goddammit the bullets the blood on the bullets had blood all over the bullets gummed up the thing.

He has time to curse himself. His favorite movie is *The Hurt Locker*, and in it, his favorite actor, Jeremy Renner, had a soldier clean off their bullets with spit because they were bloody and the gun wouldn't fire. He should've known. But wasn't that just the story of his shitty little life?

You numb fuck, the voice from above scolds as he pops open the chamber to clean off the bullets as quietly as he can. Nolan is right in front of him, but he's talking again and Jordy's drunken mind doesn't think twice, doesn't hesitate the slightest bit; he's a pawn under the strong hand of the puppeteer. A *powerful* pawn. One with hate in his heart and murder dripping deliciously behind his cloudy eyes.

But it all goes bad. His vision swims as he looks down to do something dexterous, like pluck a couple shells from a gun barrel with no sound. He sees two hands and doesn't know which is his. He jabs for a shell and stubs his finger on a hard part next to it.

Gerome can't help but glance past Nolan into the hall with horror. He's talking mainly to Cole, anyway. The man appeared out there a moment ago like he was sent straight from God to save them. A white knight with a big gun. Much bigger than Nolan's. So what if the guy looked like a carny with a pocket full of inositol-laced coke? He's clearly here to shoot Nolan in the back and save their lives, and Gerome already loves him for it. But when he'd raised the gun and nothing happened, Gerome's heart dropped into his stomach like a wet toad, ribbits picking up as the stack of hope gets cut down the middle in an instant. What was, only seconds ago, a beacon of hope is now nothing more than a strange man bent over a gun he's clearly never used, loudly plucking at the chamber and trying to fix whatever is wrong.

The gun slips in his hands. It clatters so loudly Gerome jumps despite watching it fall. Nolan wheels around and fires before he knows who or what he's firing at. The slug hits Jordy in the stomach with a sickening *whump!* He goes flailing backward, hits the opposite wall of the hallway, and falls facedown in a heap of murdered meat.

The clock at the end of the hall bongs dumbly that it's nine.

Cole is hunkered and moving for Gerome as Nolan wheels back around and toward them. The whites of his eyes pulse with spiderwebs of red, and white froth gathers in the corners of his mouth as he booms, *"Jordy? Did you two get Jordy to come kill me?!"* Cole grabs Gerome's hand, who's frozen in shock, and yanks him awake. "I change my mind *back!*" he shrieks. "I'm gonna kill you two right here and now." Cole glances toward the hall from Gerome's position and sees a man lying dead.

Like a fat sack of potatoes, he thinks.

The shot had caused a blast wave so violent in the small room that it renders everyone's ears all but useless. Cole doesn't know he's practically screaming at Gerome, but he is.

Just then, a cannon blast goes off from outside and Nolan's red eyes widen. "They've started," he says, seemingly to himself.

Cole smartly thinks that the dead man in the hall must've come through the back door as well and had left it wide the hell open; otherwise, they couldn't have been able to hear the initial explosion from the show down at the lake through the ear-splitting note currently throbbing through their heads. Cole has Gerome's hand in his. His friend is a life-size dummy of himself, like that thing in the corner behind them, and he knows they're going to have to charge him. It's their only hope.

But just then, Nolan raises his revolver and fires. The shot flies wildly high, and the window behind them explodes outward into a million blades. Cole opens his eyes to see that the man he thought was dead in the hall has Nolan by the leg.

Cole is literally throwing Gerome through the window and out into the side yard without thinking. That bullish survival instinct never second-guesses otherwise arcane decisions.

He's dead now, he thinks as he's jumping out after Gerome and Nolan is blasting another bullet into the hero's back.

Three bullets left, he thinks as he runs. He drags a silent Gerome by the hand into the woods just outside the window. Nolan had mentioned a barn out here. They'd have to hide out and figure out how to get back. No way in the world they'd beat Nolan back to their house with Gerome, especially how he currently is. He *really* needs his buddy to snap out of it. And fast.

Cole has no idea what to do next besides keep pushing through the thick underbrush until a faint light appears ahead of them. Another beacon. Trying times are full of beacons, he's learned. Whether they come through or not.

A window.

"Quiet," Cole whispers directly into Gerome's ear. The ringing starting to fade. Cole knows Nolan is already out the window after them.

A cannonade of explosions continues to pump pastel colors into the black sky above, painting the treetops in greens and reds in craggy flashes as the duo hops fallen limbs and dodges land mines of loud, crunchy leaves below.

CHAPTER 39

AMERICA'S GOT TALENT HAS JUST ENDED, AND KRIS LETS OUT A long yawn as she watches the promo for the next episode. Looks like someone gets the Golden Buzzer! Glenn has hopped up and crept back over to the window, once again peering out. He tells himself if he sees the man out there again that he's going to do something about it. At least ask the guy what the hell he's doing stalking around their seemingly quiet street at night. With a shovel.

But he doesn't see him. He sees nothing of interest other than the Cherokee in the driveway across the street. *They're back,* he thinks, and a queer calm slows his heart in a way only a parent can experience. He's not a worrier, nothing even close to the sort, but strange things happen on nights like tonight; plus, knowing his son and his son's best friend are back safe erases the ever-so-slim possibility that they receive a call from a low voice informing them that their boy had been involved in an accident. People drank and drove on nights like this, and he's not used to his son being out and about in a car, especially one being driven by another teenager.

As he's looking, a golden kernel of fire rises into the sky back behind the opposite tree line. It slows and seems to hover in place for a moment, having forgotten what to do next. Then it remembers its job, realizing all the people flocked together at the lake far below are watching and waiting, though not so patiently anymore, and lets itself fulfill its destiny, exploding into a fantastic display above them. Glenn watches it flower open in long, purple lines that end in brittle points and begin to wilt, sizzling at the tips like a hundred supersize sparklers.

The show has begun.

He remains there, watching through the window. No matter your age, it's difficult to steal yourself away from a fireworks show. He watches one flower open that's the size of an alien mother ship from *War of the Worlds*. Another one shoots up through it and continues higher, exploding into a thousand twisting rockets corkscrewing every which way. They're coming quickly now, anxious to show off. As if they themselves have been perturbed by the delay.

Glenn is vaguely aware of his wife answering her phone on the couch behind him. Not even half listening as the almost entirety of his senses is being commanded by the show in the sky. But when she says "He's at a friend's, and Bree is down at the dock—why?" that paternal warning siren begins its almost sickening warble deep inside him. Low and slow, as if shaking its ancient head in knowing. He continues looking out the window, but all of his senses are now directed behind him at the conversation his wife is having on the couch. He prays it's not a police officer.

"Agatha," she begins, sending cooling relief through him. "Slow down. You're going too fast."

He turns to face her. She covers the bottom of her cell and mouths a mouse's whisper at him. "I work with her. Says her son called and left a message." She pauses and listens for a moment, then covers the phone again and says, "Something about Gerome and Cole and her son. She's going too fast. Sounds like she's got a mouthful of cheese." It would be funny in a different situation, but Glenn's warning siren is picking up steam, so he remains stoic, only watching his wife's face carefully. She's talking to the lady again: "Honey, it's okay, I was watching it too. No, no. It's okay you waited till it was over to check your phone. Agatha, honey, slow down. It's okay." She's speaking like a mother would to her child upon awakening from a dream of running from a big monster. "It's okay you didn't check your phone sooner, sweetie. Yes, I'm sure. Bree had just texted me about the fireworks finally starting right before you called, and Gerome—"

She breaks off and asks Glenn if they're home, pointing the hand she'd used to cover the phone in the general direction of Cole's house.

Glenn nods yes but is beginning to think they aren't. Maybe they're out looking at fireworks. Hadn't Gerome mentioned that they might do that?

"Oh, not Bree, okay, well, yes, Gerome is across the street at a friend's house, honey. Can you tell me why? Slow down and tell me exactly what your son said."

Glenn has been watching her face carefully. He'd prayed that the call wasn't from the cops, and that had been granted. Now he's praying he isn't about to see a look in his wife's eyes as she listens to the woman on the other end of the line that would indicate trouble.

That prayer, however, is left unheard.

He feels a sick ball of slime begin twisting in the pit of his stomach as he watches her face turn from concerned friend, with even a smidge of humor at the edges, to horrified parent.

"She said her son said to tell us not to let Gerome and Cole go near Nolan Donovan." Now pointing in the general direction of the black gate at the end of their street. "And not to let them go through with whatever they're planning." She pauses. "She says they're in trouble." She doesn't bother covering the phone.

Fear mounts in the coming moments for Stacey too. She'd been watching *America's Got Talent* also; it's a staple among middle-class moms, like the never-aging *Wheel of Fortune*. But she had immediately risen from the couch upon its conclusion and carried a hamper full of fresh whites down the hall to the master, when she'd heard a cell phone ring in Cole's room. It tickled her interest for some reason. More than it should have. So she put the hamper on her bed and flipped it over so it vomited its clean contents across her comforter, then went back to investigate. She didn't know *what* she was investigating. She already knew both Gerome and her son didn't depend on their cells in order to function like most kids she's seen—and thank God for that. So it's not strange in the slightest that one of them had left theirs. But something gently nudged her on, back into the hall, and turned her into Cole's room.

Maybe it was that thing she'd felt when they left earlier. She'd been fully entrenched in her show, but something had been off in Cole's answers. She trusted him completely, so she hadn't acknowledged it. Only continued watching TV and hoped he didn't notice her perplexity, however slight it was. She wanted *him* to know that she trusts him. She'd hoped all his life that that was good enough parenting.

There's a letter lying open on the bed, held down by a cell phone. She presumes it's the one that had just finished ringing, although she's unsure which boy it belongs to. She hadn't seen much of either to know which is which. The letter looks old. Folded three ways for quite some time and written in pen like a chicken had dipped its claws in blue ink. She slowly sits on the end of the bed next to it, attention undivided.

A few moments later, her own cell clatters to life in her

pocket. She lays the note back down on the bed, wipes her eyes, and pulls it out. She feels faint from reading the note, a rickety raft in choppy waters. It had called up from the dark a deep-seated feeling of sadness for the woman who'd written it. A woman who'd found herself in that thing that marriage sometimes reveals its ugly self to be. A vacuous partnership where lists are prevalent but love itself is fallow. A business decision. Her head spins as the questions of why this letter is in her son's room begin to sink in their rotten teeth. She wipes her eyes again.

She tells Gerome's mother that the boys had left when she was asked the question if they were there. Then she listens to the reply that sends those already-choppy waters into a frothy frenzy. She hears everything Gerome's mother says, but as she talks, she feels herself starting to slip. It's as if everything she's hearing is coming through earholes that have squeezed to pinheads. She feels far-off. The voice through the phone gets weaker and weaker, even though the woman on the other end has gotten louder and louder, almost crying out in fear at the end when she tells Stacey that Glenn is going over there to that Nolan Donovan's place. He's already left, and she is so scared. He'd seen a strange man earlier, and she is just so scared.

Stacey ended the call and let the cell fall to her side in a hand made of lead. She feels herself go and has enough strength at the end to send her weight backward instead of forward onto the floor. She faints, out cold, landing flat on her back on Cole's bed. The letter from the sad woman lies beside her, patiently waiting for her to wake while Cole's little library stands guard against the wall.

CHAPTER 40

FURIOUS IS AN UNDERSTATEMENT. NONE OF THIS IS PART OF HIS plan. Ellie will only be out for another forty-five minutes or so, depending on how much she drank. He has to be back there before then; he'd need to give her more sleepy medicine so he can do all the things he's dreamed of doing with her since the day they met. Letting the boys go just isn't an option; they'd go straight for help, and he'd be through. He's not afraid of being caught. He's afraid that he'd be caught before he has his night. He's got to find those two fucks before *they* can find someone to tell about the big bad man in the woods. Him. In which case his little father-daughter date would be cut short, ever so rudely interrupted by a couple pistol-wielding members of the Putnam County Police Department. And that just won't do.

That thought brings Nolan to his next problem. He's got his *own* gun in case the boys in blue jump out of the bushes, yes, but there are only three bullets left. There's a box of ammo somewhere in the house, but he hasn't the slightest clue where. He truly hadn't touched the gun since getting it back from the police and putting it back in the nightstand where his ex-wife had found it. He hadn't just said that to the white kid to try to scare him. Other things, but not that.

He doesn't have time to go back and look.

As he creeps through the woods out toward the old barn, guided by a glowing square in the gloom like the wise men following the North Star—

Three wise bullets, he thinks. *Have to be very wise with them.*

—he silently cusses that piece-of-shit Jordy for trying to save the day and wasting two of Nolan's valuable rounds. Each bullet takes with it a few clicks of power, lowering the gaudy level of status quo he possesses.

How had he known? Did the two fucks befriend the trailer-trash piece of shit when Jordy used to mow Ellie's yard? Was that when all this had started? Like a bitch befriending another bitch simply because they're both exes to the same asshole? Had they started a little "Fuck Nolan" club behind his back and conspired against him, waiting for this night to strike?

"Had Jordy *blabbed*?" he asks the gently grabbing branches.

He doesn't think so; he'd seen the look in his eyes before putting one in the guy's gut. He'd shown up with a sawed-off shotgun wanting all the glory. Probably jammed because he packed it with the wrong-size shells. Guys like him could never be heroes. He is—

was

—a bottom-feeder for a reason. Because he can't handle the big time. He'd taken center stage, tapped the mic, and proceeded to choke on his own phlegm.

Nolan chuckles as the barn grows large.

His mind tells him that drunks like Jordy *always* blabbed, especially about something big. Nolan reminds his mind that he himself is a drunk and he himself hasn't blabbed about what keeps him up at night. The good kind of "keep up at night." He reminds his mind also that, actually, it doesn't particularly matter. That as long as none of the three had called the police, he's golden. He knows the boys in the barn don't have cells (anymore) and the man lying facedown back in the hall has two holes too many, leaking out all his smelly air.

Besides, as long as he can put a bullet in Fuck Number One and Fuck Number Two here in the next few minutes, everything will be back on track. He realizes he's calmed considerably on his tramp through the woods; as the explosions over the lake to his left grow louder, his pulse grows lighter. He's going to kill them both—

Wise bullets.

—and go back and grab some things from his goody box and sneak back over to Ellie's. He's so close to the barn now, he can see individual slats. He's laughing. Laughing so loudly that the guys inside can hear his approach through the cracks.

"Wise bullets," he says to the trees.

Then he'd still have one left in the end, along with a decision of what to do with it. If things go bad, he'd just use it on himself. If they didn't, he'd leave it be. Or use it on *her.* Or he'd give her a chance to join him in Mexico.

Slim. His mind tells him. Yes, probably very.

Morales has everything ready to go for him, and Nolan has already paid him in full. Not the first time Morales had made a healthy chunk of green for a big favor from Nolan. Nolan has been siphoning cash from the business for a long time. By now, he has a nice little pot to run away with and live off of for the rest of his life. Enough to stir slowly until he dies down there on a beach somewhere with a margarita in one hand and syphilis hopefully in his shorts. The contents of the pot will cool after a decade or two but should never grow completely cold. It'd never run out.

He's got options. Hopefully.

An idea occurs to him as he approaches the barn door. He can put *two* in the white boy: one in the gut and the other about twelve inches lower. And if Ellie doesn't want to come, he'll just drug her a third time and choke her while they fuck. He'd envisioned choking her hard hundreds of times with him on top, them under the sheets. Only this time, he won't let go until her lips turn blue and her eyes lose life. Then he'd just keep on fucking her till his dick split open like some of those rock stars' stories.

He pauses at the barn door. The pistol hangs from his hand, a part of him now. Till the end. The old wood flashes with colors, pulsating beautifully like those strange jellyfish on *Animal Planet* a million miles under the surface, and is timed perfectly with the low booms he can feel in his chest, acting as palpitations for his already-pounding heart and giving a euphoric feeling of irregularity deep inside him.

He stands there for a moment. It's almost hypnotic, the barn. He watches as his pulse begins to slow. There's a strange transition. He's no longer running. No longer chasing. He's simply a man with a plan and seeing to it. Guiding it along like dumb cattle into a big pen.

He lets out a belch of long, terrible laughter, not bothering for stealth, and flings open the old door. It's big (big enough to drive a car through) and hits the side of the barn so hard that skeins of dust tumble down from the ceiling in puffs that no one can see. The little bulb above the worktable is off now. Too late, though.

Stupid kids, he thinks as he steps inside.

Between firework blasts, Nolan inhales greatly and booms, "HEEEY, KIDS!"

Cole and Gerome had stumbled in only a few minutes before. They'd sat in a stew of sawdust and cobwebs behind some machine the size of a box freezer against the wall. They heard Nolan coming up to the barn and laughing like someone who'd taken advantage of a back door left unlocked at the loony bin, when Cole realized the bulb above the table next to them was still on. He'd shot out from his place next to Gerome and flicked it off and dove back in, ramming Gerome hard with his shoulder by accident. Gerome didn't make a sound. The window to their right is broken, and Cole could both hear and see a dark silhouette slink by, coming for the big door at the end. Cole had peeked out at the door, looking over the old car sitting in front of them, and waited for it to open.

He didn't have to wait long.

Cole had turned to Gerome and whispered so softly he could only be heard from a distance close enough to kiss. "He's coming in. He knows we're in here. If I say run, you run as fast as you possibly can, man. For the bus yard." He'd peeked up and over again, then came back down face-to-face. "It's a long way to the front gate, and he'd catch up while we're trying to get over. I have a feeling it's closed, and he's the only one who can open it." Cole didn't know this for certain, but he's right.

Gerome leaned in the rest of the way, just a tiny distance, and for a split second, Cole thought he *was* going to kiss him. Plant a big ole farewell smackeroo right on his lips, but he keeps going all the way to Cole's ear. And in an even lower tone than Cole had used, Gerome said, "I want that car."

That's when the barn door burst outward and slammed against the outside wall.

Cole is trembling.

He peeks over the edge of the machine and sees the shadow man swaying in the open doorway. The night behind him is a painted portrait of thick tree trunks and tangled underbrush, the artist not being able to make up her mind on what color to leave it.

Cole knows Nolan can't see him. At least until his eyes adjust. He's watching for movement. But then in an instant, the doorway is empty. He's inside the barn with them. Cole's balls try to push their way up into the safety of his belly at the idea of Nolan slinking around somewhere in the shadows. Can he see them? Gerome is hunkered low; he's been watching Cole closely for what to do and when to do it.

Cole spots him. He sees a low shadow moving from right to left along the perimeter, pausing every few feet. Sooner or later, he'd make his way to where they sit. They can't be here when that time comes. Cole knows that Nolan knows this barn and knows all its hiding spots. He probably built the damn thing. He knows that Nolan would know to look behind the long, low machine. That there'd be room enough for two teenage boys to snuggle into. In which case, he'd proceed to blow their heads off.

Cole grabs Gerome's arm.

Strings of color flash in the dust through some of the bigger cracks between slats. But Cole thinks they can sneak over them unnoticed. The fireworks show is a giant's racing heartbeat now, almost a slow machine gun of booms, each rattling his bones and bouncing through his head like lead Super Balls. It's time to move.

Cole drags Gerome out and pulls him into the open. He feels like he's holding onto that life-size Ellie doll, dragging it across the dusty floor behind him. He's scared to look back.

Cole notes the thick shaft of pulsing light coming in through the window to their right. He thinks if they get down on all fours, they'd be blocked by the old car; once they're through it, they can pop up and run along the side of the barn opposite of where Nolan should be now and slide out the barn door unnoticed.

They're almost to the front of the car. They can feel its presence in the dark more than they can see it, and by the shaft of light, Cole knows they're close. Gerome yanks Cole to a dead stop. Cole slowly turns and peers out into the open barn but sees nothing. He looks harder and realizes that, yes, he actually sees nothing moving. Which means *Nolan* isn't moving. Which means, terrifyingly, he sees *them.*

Gerome suddenly lurches past Cole, now dragging *him* by the arm, and sends them both tumbling behind the rusty Nova a split second before a gunshot sounds in the dark. It's a painful backhand slap to the ears. The car's passenger mirror explodes in a shower of sparks and glass, giving them their own personal miniature firework. Cole lands on Gerome hard in the dirt between the driver's door and the wall. Gerome's face is in the light from the window, looking back up at Cole. "I knew I liked this car," he mouths. Then big and serious, "*Run!*"

He doesn't have to say it twice. They're up and moving quickly through the dark, running along the driver's side of the car and out the door, bursting into the underbrush in a dead sprint as Nolan trips over something and lets out a string of profanities that'd make Captain Ahab blush.

They have a head start, but not much of one.

Not enough, either, Cole thinks. He's going to try his hardest to get Gerome back safely. Or die in the process. It's his fault they're in this mess, after all. All his and no one else's. Even though he was right about Nolan, he was wrong about putting it into their hands and not the authorities'. He should've listened to Gerome. Hindsight is always twenty-twenty. But he hadn't, and now there's a very real and very good chance both of them are going to be hunted down and slaughtered out in the bus yard.

They burst out of the woods into the glassy grass and race along the side of Nolan's house toward the bus yard, going only as fast as Gerome's prosthetic allows him.

Not fast enough, is all he can think over and over, running terrified loops in his head as they run from the man with a gun like a common nightmare that had somehow slipped undetected across the threshold of reality and chosen them to ruin.

Their footfalls hit hard, a staccato of thumps through brittle grass. With each step, Cole braces for a bullet in the back.

They make it safely to the roll-open door at the bus yard's entrance with no sign of Nolan. Everything around them lights up with each boom from above, their only means by which to see. Cole knows Nolan should be right behind them, at least coming up through the overgrown pathway. He should be close enough to hear.

But he's not. A prickle of skepticism sprawls over him, though he pushes on. Are they being tricked? All Cole knows is that they have to beat him through the yard and out the back corner of the fence. The going will be tough with Gerome, but he lurches behind furiously. Head down and arms piston punching into the warm air. Oddly silent, save for the horselike *thump THUMP, thump THUMP* and the air tearing in and out of his open mouth. Cole turns and waits for Gerome to pass through, then rolls the door shut behind him. The lazy old tire is half-flat and takes its time getting there. It bangs against the frame.

CHAPTER 41

Jordy rolls over on his back in the hallway, expecting to feel a puddle of warmth embrace him. But he doesn't. The floor under him is hard and cold. He's not bleeding at all. He lies there, staring up at the cream-colored swirls of texture on the ceiling above. He'd lay here forever if he could, but the puppeteer won't allow *that*. The puppeteer is running the show now, remember? Had been ever since the boy slipped away in his smelly little Spider-Man bed back in the trailer. *His puppeteer* is the one who'd kept him alive to finish the job. *His puppeteer* is the one who told Jordy not to forget Thing Three, even though *he* thought it'd be pointless. Turns out *his puppeteer* was right, the bulletproof vest had saved his life and given him another opportunity to finish the job he botched the first time.

Two shots at close range had done quite a lot of damage. Especially the one to the back. His breathing is a thick whistle, like he's trying to inhale and exhale around a Coke can, and he doesn't know how many ribs a human has, but whatever the number is, is probably the same number he's got broken.

But he's alive.

He's yanked up by unsympathetic strings. He finds his feet and stands on them, leaning against the wall so he doesn't fall back onto the floor. He feels like someone had switched on a buzz saw and set it down on the soft tissue inside his head. It runs along the ground in there, chewing gutters of goo until it runs out of cord, then bounces crazily like a deranged pit bull at the end of its chain.

Pit bull, he thinks. He looks down at the shotgun on the ground, only to remember that it's jammed. His boy's blood. He kicks it aside, not out of anger, but petulance. He'd have to do this without it somehow. Just how, he doesn't know. But maybe *his puppeteer* does.

His feet stagger as he makes his way to the back door. He's not so much being pulled now as he is being *called* toward something. He feels his SOMETHING BIG out there behind the house somewhere. It's almost radioactive; his skin prickles and his head swims as he gets closer. He's out the back door and struggling across the porch, heading toward whatever is waiting for him. A zombie following its rotten nose toward virgin meat.

He pauses at the edge of the porch for guidance—just a man checking out the back lawn under the fireworks show. The booms in the sky pause for a moment, gathering themselves for the next bundle to send up. Jordy listens, seeing nothing out of the ordinary at the moment.

Then he hears it.

A faint bang, metal on metal, through the trees. A gate closing? He's not sure, but it gets him moving. A solacing sound, quiet reassurance prodding him onward. The puppeteer had cut the strings and ran ahead, leaving the next part of the plan all in Jordy's hands. He'd have all the glory.

He steps off the back porch and lumbers toward a small opening in the tree line. It takes shape as his eyes adjust. The next batch of bright booms is sent up. He imagines hundreds of people down at the lake, not far at all from where he stands, gawking up at the sky. But his head is down, scanning the ground for things that might trip him. He doesn't want to fall, because he can't imagine trying to get back up on his own. That buzz saw had finally begun losing juice. It gives only a half-hearted little yank on its orange rubber chain every now and then. He sure doesn't want to send it back into hysterics. Plus, his chest feels like a big bag of gravel. So many things jutting wrongly in there.

As he passes through the tree line toward whatever lay beyond, an old pathway begins to emerge. Old wheel ruts are visible down at his feet. He chooses one and pushes on. Awful is a disgusting understatement when it comes to how he feels at the moment. He feels like he'd already begun to settle into death when he was violently yanked back to the upright side. Worse than his hundred worst hangovers combined. He feels too heavy, his limbs aren't working right. He thinks about taking off the vest and tossing it aside, freeing up a little weight to help him walk. But he quickly thinks better of it. The vest had kept two bullets *out*, yes, but he has a feeling it's now keeping more than a few things *in*. He can't afford to shed it, only letting out a loose bag of guts behind it or letting a dozen ribs rupture things the rest of the way in there, only to die out here in the woods.

What the hell kind of bullets ...

So close to his SOMETHING BIG.

He leaves it on and keeps walking. After a minute or two, a tall fence appears up ahead. It's menacing in the dark. It's chain-linked, topped with barbed wire. He sees what made the sound he heard back on the porch. A big gate sits heavily on a saggy tire. The gate's end had hit the frame. It sits closed. He walks up to it, sees no locks, and rolls it open a couple of feet. It takes a great heave from his battered body, as the tire had apparently given up on moving many summers ago. Once he's got a couple of feet of clearance, he slides through, not bothering with closing it back. He doesn't know why, but it doesn't seem to matter.

The fireworks flash wide spotlights on an old junkyard in front of him. He waits patiently for whatever he's supposed to do next.

CHAPTER 42

IT TAKES WHAT SEEMS LIKE LONG MILES TO REACH THE BACK corner, but they're finally there. They can see the boat mountain in the flashes. Pure joy steals over them as they allow themselves to believe they've made it. Cole had repeatedly checked over his shoulder as they'd ran through the yard, weaving between dead giants and skipping around particularly high thickets of grass, not wanting to catch a corner of a rusty old tool on the way through. The whole yard is a hip-high sea of matted weeds. Even Ramshackle Row had grown a lot of the way up. Cole glances down the long tunnel, a place to feel far away in a time that now seems so long ago. He lets Gerome start up the boats first. The fireworks are extremely loud back here; they're but a few hundred yards from the lake, so Cole doesn't hear the little squeal that escapes Gerome as he reaches the top of the pile. Cole does see him come to a dead stop, though, standing up there like a plagued yardbird, the first of his people to make it up and over the blockade only to be ruined by what he saw. Or rather, the dereliction of the sight he *thought* he'd see.

Cole is staring at the back of his friend's head, but judging by his body language, Gerome's eyes are wide in their sockets, staring at something down there on the other side. Something in the corner, waiting for them in the dark. Cole knows it's Nolan. Somehow. All at once, the blissful joy he'd felt, the feeling a mouse must have when the metal bar snaps shut a millisecond late and it runs off into the dark with a crumb of cheese in its cheek, is sucked dry. He literally feels it go, making room for the fear to flood back in.

It never really left.

It rises to the insides of his ears and whispers a sinister question: Did he *really* think he was getting out of here alive?

Cole's head tells him to run. To run hard for the front gate and never look back. So what if he heard a couple gunshots as he fled? *Someone* had to survive this. *Someone* had to tell the proper people that this man is a monster and that he is going to strike again if given the chance. *Someone* had to see their parents again. If both boys die, Nolan will win. Which means Nolan's prize will be Ellie—at least for a night—but despite Cole's age, it's not lost on him how much a nightmarish night with someone as sick as Nolan could affect a girl for the rest of her life, especially one already as fragile as Ellie. Cole can't let that happen.

He had actually taken a soft step backward, ready to turn and burn. Gerome is an ice statue on top of the boats. A dead man frozen in splashes of color. Cole takes another soundless step back and wonders if maybe Nolan thought they'd separated. But just then, Nolan becomes visible beside Gerome. They're two creatures from different planets, both claiming a strange, fiberglass hill under beautiful colors above. They look a part of a post-apocalyptic painting from the eighties.

Cole's blood chokes his veins, his heart saying *fuck it* for a moment. He sees Nolan say something into Gerome's ear, then steps back and waits for a reply. When he gets none, Nolan puts the barrel into Gerome's side and shoves him backward, toward Cole. Gerome's fake leg lodges into a splintery hole and sends him tumbling back down the way he'd come. He hits the bottom, and dust flies around Cole's feet in a perturbed cloud, then quickly settles. Cole helps Gerome to his feet but keeps his eyes on Nolan. A thick, dark figure coming down toward them. Each passing second of hesitation exponentially diminishing any chance at escaping. Green-and-blue fireworks blossom behind him as Cole cranes upward, watching.

Did he *really* think they were getting out of here alive?

The walk back toward the front seems even longer than before. Nolan keeps close behind with the gun pointed forward as they go. No one speaks. The boys are prisoners who'd gotten caught trying to escape. They'd been outsmarted by the guard and are being led back to resume their endless punishment. The fireworks carry on overhead. Their blithe show of appreciation. Surely they'd soon end. Cole thinks it'd been twenty or so minutes now since the initial boom. Though he's not positive. Time has a funny way of rolling open when pushed by fear, like a ball of yarn down a staircase toward a landing it could not see. Twenty is just a shot in the dark.

Nolan doesn't have to say anything for them to know where they're going. As they march toward the front of the yard, the new bus comes into view. He begins to speak. His voice hitches with excitement as he stalks close behind them. They feel like they're being led down death row, chaperoned by the lunatic guard who'd finally been given the shot to switch on the deadly current in the small room at the end of the hall.

"I'm gonna make you boys watch."

Cole winces at the words as he walks. Maybe it has something to do with the emphasis he'd placed on the word *make*. He thinks of that box full of terrible things. He thinks of the leather straps, the silver spikes. He thinks of the rope and medieval-looking devices. He thinks of the zip ties and wonders if Nolan still has them. He's not well versed in such intimacies, but he certainly hadn't gotten the feeling the things were for fun when it came to this guy behind them. Things that could do a certain sadistic job, and do it very efficiently and effectively, slamming straight past the typical stopping point of teasing or playfulness.

"I'm gonna make you boys watch," he says again. The first time he'd said it, it had the flat inflection of someone stating the obvious. This time, though, is a bit louder, someone agreeing with an unpopular yet growing opinion. A fist shooting upward out of a crowd.

"I'm gonna make you boys *watch*!" He yells it now, a lunatic behind them in the dark. One with a gun. Their feet shuffle heavily beneath them.

"You. *You're* going to watch." Cole feels something punch his shoulder blade. Had he thrown a rock? Cole glances at Gerome, who returns the mirror-image look of hopelessness, of unthinkable sadness and irrevocable terror.

They're walking toward the front corner. Diagonally away from that long-ago getaway called Ramshackle Row in the back. The trio walks around the front of an old city bus; its rounded brushed-silver snout and low oval headlights give it a look of longing. The old wipers are stuck together at the center of the windshield like droopy eyebrows. It feels sorry for them. Cole wishes with everything in him he could somehow board that bus, fire it to life, and bounce straight out of this nightmare. Leaving nothing behind but a trail of blue smoke and the devil's unfulfilled desires.

But Cole *does* see a trail of blue smoke. He thinks he's seeing things. It wafts up from the exhaust pipe of the yellow school bus that had been backed in. The ass end is clear from their vantage point, but neither Gerome nor Nolan seem to notice. They're walking toward the same gate the thing's nose is pointing at, coming at it from a wide angle. The fireworks are too loud to hear if the engine is rumbling, but Cole thinks it must be. Why else would smoke be coming from it? It's a faint string, almost undetectable, though all the bus's lights are off. Save for the smoke, it looks just as dead as all the others. Cole glances over at Gerome, who's watching the weeds pass his feet. He doesn't dare look back at Nolan, but by the way he hadn't stopped mewling under his breath, the things they're going to have to watch him do to Ellie, Cole doesn't think he's noticed either. He's mumbling, too, about there still being time and that they weren't going to see the sun.

Cole suddenly has a sickening thought come forth. What if Nolan was the one who fired the bus up? Somehow doing it on the way out to beat them to the corner. They had been running as hard as they could on the first pass, so maybe they hadn't noticed. Maybe Nolan is planning on driving them somewhere.

But cool logic overrides those notions. One, if he was planning on driving them somewhere, why in the hell would he take a bus? And two, more importantly, there was just no way Nolan had enough time to board the bus, start it, and then proceed to beat them to the back corner when they had a fairly good head start. He'd been in the barn still when the boys burst out into his side yard. It was impossible.

But how did he beat us to the back corner? He must've known where we were going and ran straight down the fence line as soon as he left the barn.

He watches that ribbon dance quietly upward.

Who started the bus then?

Cole doesn't know, but as he walks for the front gate, he risks a few more glances at the new bus, a long black sub under murky water. The colors from above touch only its rounded roof, not venturing any farther down its sides. He scans those sides, looking for anything strange, and sees nothing. They walk a few more paces, and as they come to the front of the thing, he looks over again while Nolan is wailing on behind them and Gerome is a robot marching toward a new task, and is there someone …

Someone behind the wheel.

He snaps his head forward and hopes to God Nolan hadn't noticed. Cole's mind flits to the dead guy back in the hall. Who had *that* guy been and why had he been *here* too? Cole hadn't thought about it enough in the last few minutes.

Not like you've had much time, bud.

But still, there's something there. He had clearly been here to kill Nolan.

Or to save you.

Not as likely. No one knew they were here. Plus, the guy seemed pretty dead set on the guy behind them. Too bad his gun jammed. He'd botched his shot.

Nolan's mad cackles of evil promises give way to an eerily slow number as they walk farther away from the man in the bus. One Cole had heard before, maybe in a movie.

"They're gonna hang me in the mornin', before the night is done."

There's a pause in the explosions, laying a light blanket of pseudo silence down here in the yard, the low grumble of the engine now far enough behind them that Cole can only barely hear it because he knows what he's listening for. Though a loud caw fills the void pretty well also.

"They're gonna hang me in the mornin', we'll never see the sun."

Everyone falls silent as the gate grows large in front of

them. Their feet crunch, like they're trekking through knee-deep snow instead of thickets of leaves and tangled weeds. They'd be almost directly in front of the new bus now, and Cole fights the urge to look back. To see if someone is staring back at them through the front glass. He beats it. Something tells him he better let that go, to just do as he's told and listen hard. So he does.

He keeps moving. He keeps quiet.

CHAPTER 43

Jordy's in the new bus. He'd hotwired it because that's what he had been told to do. He'd found the wiring for the lights and ripped them out because that's what he'd been told to do. He'd done it in the dark. Could've probably done it with his eyes closed. He'd done eleven long months in county back in the day for hotwiring (before all but one of the DUIs and the felony assault). He'd done it many times but only got caught once. All it takes. Luckily, he'd been as drunk as Cooter Brown so the Beamer he thought he was stealing was actually a 1993 Miata valued at under fifteen hundred dollars, therefore punishable as a misdemeanor. And *therefore*, why he did eleven months instead of a couple years.

In the manufactured time the inmates were allotted for the jail's version of life, and sometimes during the other times they were supposed to be asleep in their little hard white cells, Jordy had often wondered why he'd done it. Why had he hotwired so many cars? He never took them to chop shops to get handed bags of cash—he'd just drive around till he got bored and park it in an alley or at a strip mall and walk home. Eleven long months in the pen and the sporadic times since then thinking of why and not being able to decipher that simple question into a real answer.

But now, as he sits behind the big wheel of an old school bus somewhere out behind his boss's house, as ghosts of schoolchildren bang the walls and scream on behind him, the answer hits him. It had all been preparation for tonight. This was his

CHAPTER 43

purpose. This *is* his purpose. His SOMETHING BIG won't let him fail. The glory will be too good. He'd do the job quickly. He knows it has to be done fast, but he doesn't know *how* he knows. Just that is has to be.

His answer comes into view off to his left.

The two boys who had been in Nolan's house are trudging toward the front gate. Nolan follows them with his gun. Jordy can barely see Nolan's mouth moving rhythmically, like he's singing or chanting. Quick images of different facial features in each flash of a colorful strobe light.

Jordy glances ahead at the gate and wonders if he'd made a mistake by leaving it partway open. No one seems to notice. The three of them begin to funnel toward it, the tall weeds on either side condensing into a bottleneck at the mouth. To Jordy, the weeds look like motionless soldiers standing guard.

He throws a salute and squeezes the thin steering wheel so hard his knuckles crack. He thinks of his boy. He says Cam's name aloud to the empty cockpit and mashes the gas.

The bus's engine roars, and he jumps forward.

"*This is for you, Cam!*" he screams at the top of his lungs as the bus tears across the dirt, closing the short distance between its nose and the three guys with each bounce. He feels no pain.

"*This is for both of us!*" He aims the big yellow nose straight for Nolan, who is directly behind the two boys now, as they are almost at the yard's entrance, and directly *in front* of Jordy. He keeps the pedal pinned to the grimy floorboard. Jordy's main focus is Nolan, but if he has to take out the other two in the process just to get him, if they're a package deal of victims, he'd just have to live with that.

Or die with it.

Nolan notices first, and that's okay because it's too late now anyway not to get hit. The wheel is trying its damnedest to buck loose from Jordy's grip, but he keeps it centered as the speedo crawls and closes the gap between thirty and forty. The whole scene since the bus started moving had only lasted eight or nine seconds, but to Jordy, it'd felt like minutes. It's as if his puppeteer had grabbed a giant jar of molasses and dumped it out over everything for the upright ants to have to move through.

Jordy doesn't know he'd been screaming until Nolan fires a shot. He doesn't hear it—either it falls into line with the big booms from above, or he's screaming loud enough to swallow it quietly. But Jordy sees the flash from the end of the pistol in the dark ahead. It's the last thing that lifelong downfall that was his brain registers before the bullet tears through the windshield— only a single hole surrounded by long lightning bolts of cracks running away from it, and then his head. The slug goes straight through Jordy's right eye and leaves an exit wound the size of a softball in the back of his skull. Brains fly three rows back, splattering empty seats to join crumbly boogers and moldy gum from the ghost kids.

The bus is only about twenty feet from impact when Nolan shoots him dead, and when he does, it hits a low rut in the grass. The wheel flings from Jordy's already-dead hands, causing the bus to jump in the same direction, saving all three of their lives. Its front-left bumper sideswipes Nolan and Cole, sending them flying backward toward the gate. Nolan lands hard and tumbles in the dirt till he comes to rest only about five feet from the entrance. Cole flies sidelong into the weed soldiers standing guard off to the side. He lay facedown and motionless, feet protruding from the line of weeds like the Wicked Witch's poked out from under the house.

Gerome is the only one who isn't hit. Call it luck or call it learned survival instincts from previous meetings with speeding vehicles, but either way, he'd dove clear of the big, yellow death snout just before impact. He rolls over and watches it continue past them. The driver had cut the wheel just after Nolan's gun went off, sending the bus over on its side just after it hit the other two and ultimately sliding to a stop against the tall fence to the right of the entrance. The chain-link bows outward but doesn't give. The grinding slide on its side had slowed the behemoth tremendously. It looks like a walrus caught in a fishing net. The engine races, and blue smoke pounds out of the exhaust pipe and spreads high in the air. The huge drive shaft spins furiously, reminding Gerome of those stupid people who hop on floating logs to see how fast they can roll them with their feet. The front tires whir loudly, begging to be flipped upright so it can leave. The driver is still on the gas in there somehow.

Gerome gets up and takes inventory for the second time in his life after an incident with a motor vehicle. But very much unlike the last time, he hadn't a scratch as far as he could tell. Cole, however, looks dead. He's facedown about ten feet to his right. All he can see is his friend's legs sticking out, and they aren't moving. He takes one step toward him and hears a groaning from ahead. He looks up and sees Nolan lying at the entrance, rolling around and holding his side. Gerome can see in the flashes that he still somehow has the gun.

One bullet left, Gerome thinks. This is vital information. Gerome knows Nolan has to use it on him. He'd killed the man in the bus, it seems, the guy who wanted Nolan dead maybe even more than Nolan wants *them* dead, and Cole is probably dead too. Even if he's not, Gerome knows Nolan won't waste his last bullet to finish the job. Gerome has a choice.

As he stands there in the funnel of weeds, watching Nolan

roll around and groan, he realizes he can either jump in the tall
grass with Cole and play dead (this would certainly end in him
not having to *play* the role of dead kid as soon as Nolan gets to
his feet and finds him still breathing), or he can run. For the
third time tonight, he's blessed with a substantial head start in
a chase by a monster with a gun. Maybe third time really is the
charm.

Even though Gerome has already decided to bolt for the
hole in the back corner, his decision is quickly made terrifyingly
final as Nolan turns his head and sees him. He stops rolling;
he stops making noise from the pain in his side. He lay there
staring at Gerome in the fireworks' flashes and raises his pistol. Gerome turns and runs as fast as he can. He has the brief
thought pass through his head as he goes that if he somehow
survives, he won't be able to move tomorrow with all this
running. He's done more of it tonight than in the long years
since the accident combined. His arms pump at his sides as he
lurches through the tall grass, praying to God with each step not
to trip on something. He tries to stick to the path they'd taken
only a handful of minutes before, trying to remember where the
things that could snag a shoe hid in the grass below. He hears
the bus's engine fade as he pushes deeper. He hears the booms
from above that had become background noise. He doesn't hear
someone running behind him and doesn't dare look back to see.

The grand finale begins out over the lake as Gerome runs
through the boneyard. They are sending up everything they
have left in a flurry of cannon blasts, saving the best for last.
Gerome knows soon all will be silent, and if he were not already
through the back fence by that time, he'd be fucked royally. He
won't be able to move quietly enough after that to get away. He
zigzags around long buses sitting dead in the dark. He doesn't

want to join them. His breath tears in and out of his mouth in great chuffs as he goes. Above, the blasts are mashed together in a long note of earsplitting boom. He wonders if Nolan had used that last shot and he just hadn't heard it.

His mind tells him no, that he'd be saving it for the right moment.

Gerome listens as hard as he can, trying to focus his ears behind him for any clues as to the whereabouts of the monster. But the fireworks are just too loud. He's sweating profusely, but gooseflesh pushes through as he remembers his dream. He'd been chased out of this very bus yard by the very thing that's chasing him now. That dark figure with holes for eyes. The monster hiding in the shadows, working unnoticed by everyday life.

He runs on, listening hard, but it's useless. He just has to get to the back fence before the grand finale finishes—that's all there is to it. He's well over halfway now, and even though he gets closer with each step, the crow sitting on a bus in Ramshackle Row still can't be heard. It'd been cawing all night, doing all it could do to help. But its voice is running thin; it's losing volume with each painful squawk. Not unlike the kids screaming bloody murder at the show down at the dock. It's losing its voice. Soon it'll be mute, no matter how hard it pushes its words out. Like a human, not like the thing it appears to be.

CHAPTER 44

Glenn had walked around the back of the house because checking out the front had gotten him nowhere. The door was locked, and all exterior lights were cut off, so he'd jumped off the stone porch and began checking windows as he went. The smooth river-rock gravel quibbled beneath his boots. But all the windows had been locked as well, so he'd mounted the back porch and began toward the back door when he noticed that it was ajar. His pulse kicked up a notch as he neared it. He saw his hand reach out to meet it, coming up from the bottom of his field of vision like a first-person horror film. The boards beneath him creaked against his weight with each step. He's being too loud. Even though the fireworks were still booming out beyond the backyard, if someone were waiting in the dark behind the door, they'd hear his approach clearly. He thinks they might even be able to hear the thuds of blood through his veins over the fireworks.

He sure could.

His heartbeat had slowly increased in both speed and volume inside his head since he'd hopped the big gate at the end of the drive. The walk up had been hell. A father's worst fear became more real with each step, as no sign of either the boys or the strange man who had hopped the same gate earlier presented itself.

Glenn is a strong man, more mentally than physically, but he can certainly hold his own in a fight; however, as he pulled back the same screen that had been shut in a dead lady's face those years ago, sending her over the edge for the last time, and pushed open the back door and saw the innards of someone else's kitchen splashed with seemingly the only light on the entire property, the one halfway down the long hall, he quite literally began to shake in his boots. Something was wrong, certainly with the drunk in the road and the owner of this house, Nolan, but he prayed those were the only two people here. He prayed Gerome and Cole weren't a part of this mess, whatever it was.

He could smell it in the air. Trouble has stink, you know, and the place *reeked*. He took one step into the kitchen, and that's when he heard it. If he'd have been farther inside, he might've missed it. The fireworks might've drowned it out. The door was still open behind him, and through the perforated screen, he heard a huge commotion out beyond the backyard, somewhere through the trees. A heavy crash and roll. No screaming, nothing else at all.

He turned and went back through the door he'd just came in, sort of thankful to be out of the house as he walked with purpose toward that noise he'd heard. He crossed the backyard in a fast walk, someone trying for some exercise but not ready to run. He didn't need his vision jumbled; it was already dark enough. He also didn't want to be heard. He wanted to reveal himself to whoever was back in the woods in a complete surprise. The unrivaled element.

It occurs to him that he probably should've brought a weapon. His pulse is thumping so hard now that his vision blurs briefly with each beat. As he passes through the tree line and is spilled out into a pathway, for the first time in his life, he thinks he might have a heart attack.

He's in a tunnel of black, barely big enough to drive a car

through. Something from a nightmare. He forces himself to focus, tries his best to bury his own fears deep in the dirt of his gut for his boy. If Gerome is in some sort of trouble back here, he could only imagine how scared *he* must be. Maybe it's this thought rattling around his head, or maybe it's simply because the grand finale commenced then, silencing his hard heartbeats in his ears (which seemed to breed speed if you allowed yourself to pay attention to how alarmingly fast those beats were happening), but either way, he focuses on the job at hand. He knows he has to find Gerome and Cole, if they're even here to find.

They're okay, he lies to himself.

The leaves chatter among themselves at his sides as he makes his way down the path. He'd heard nothing since the commotion. Although the only thing that *could* be heard now is the machine-gun blasts of color above him. Swords of color slash at the ground all around him, but for the most part, the overhanging trees keep all light from above at bay.

Ahead, the path opens up to meet a tall chain-link fence, but he's still too far away to see anything through it. He just needs the grand finale to finish before reaching it. He literally can't hear himself think, and that is a problem. He pushes a little closer to one side of the pathway. Leaves gently swipe across his left shoulder, telling him to stop while he still has the chance, but he can't hear them. He slows his power-walking pace to a stroll, trying to time the end of the fireworks show with his arrival at the big fence. It's taller than the gate out front and seems to be laced with razor wire across the top. Large forms begin to take shape as he gets closer, though he still can't make out any details. The grass inside the gate is as tall as a man; something huge is up against the fence out to the left. He speeds up a step.

But that fence gives him a terrible feeling. The razor wire

on top is a threat. As he reaches it, he sees that the door is the kind you roll and it's open a bit. Enough for him to fit through if he turns sideways. So he does and slides inside, not being able to help the image in his head of the boys possibly flying through the same gap sometime before. The finale is still booming ridiculously overhead, but he can't wait any longer. This place reeks of trouble far worse than the house did.

He's standing in the mouth of tall weeds; they run off to the right and the left. What he sees in both of those lines turns his blood cold. A massive school bus lay on its side to his left, its top nestled against the chain-link. To his right, legs stick out of the weeds. The colorful flashes aren't enough light to be able to tell whose legs they are at this distance. He runs for them, completely unaware he's screaming. The fireworks blossom in beautiful arrays over him, playing to the last of the *oohs* and *aahs* from the large crowd down there. The show has reached its ending.

Silence falls as he reaches the legs sticking out of the weeds. He isn't screaming anymore. He thinks they belong to Cole when he gets close enough to touch. He pushes through and rolls the boy over.

He's right.

But Cole isn't dead; he's coming to. Glenn gently pats his face until he opens his eyes. He glances back at the bus. Its motor is running, and Glenn surmises the driver has been pushed against the gas pedal in the crash. He looks back into Cole's face, putting two and two together.

He's been hit, but by the looks of it, he hasn't received any external damage. At least as much as he can see out here in the dark. Glenn is sure the boy has at least a whopper of a concussion. He's probably been knocked out cold on impact, unconsciously relaxing his body as it flew to the side, surely saving at least a few bad breaks. Hey may have had a couple, but after the quick once-over, he sees nothing out of place, nothing poking through the skin or all wonky.

He is a lucky boy.

"Mr. Conley?" Cole asks, his voice sharpened with confusion. It isn't much more than a whisper, like a boy awakening from a bad dream, so Glenn leans in to hear better. The bus's engine is loud; Glenn can hear the big driveshaft tumbling in a blur underneath it over there.

"Who's in the bus, Cole?" He puts a hand on each of Cole's shoulders.

Cole pauses for a moment, as if he's forgotten. Then it comes to him.

"The other guy," Cole says. He thinks he'd have to say more but is surprised to see that Mr. Conley seems to already know who "the other guy" is. "He shot him. Nolan." Cole winces at a thunderclap in his head as he tries to sit up in the grass. Glenn holds him still. He *thinks* the boy probably only had a concussion, but internal damage is a very real possibility. As if he heard Glenn's thoughts: "I'm okay. Just clipped me."

Clipped by a school bus, Glenn thinks. *Jesus, what is going on back here?*

"Nolan shot the guy, and he swerved." He makes a funny face; a strange realization hits him. "Saved our lives, I guess."

Glenn gets him back on track.

"Where's Gerome, Cole?" He darts his eyes around their perimeter. "Did you see anything after you got hit?" He knows the answer is no—Cole had been knocked out—but he has to ask. He has to search for *something* that will point him in the right direction.

Cole shakes his head. Almost invisible in the dark. The moon glow doesn't penetrate through the tall weeds where Cole lay. This time, he succeeds in sitting up, with the help of Glenn. Glenn allows it this time too—he needs answers. He needs them now. Cole looks around, surveying the scene of the crash like a man who'd decided to visit a childhood classroom.

"Did you pass them? Either of them?"

Glenn says no.

"How long ago have the fireworks been finished?"

Glenn replies, "A minute or two at most."

Cole looks at Glenn. Man to man. From his seated position, Cole's eyes have burning white dots in them. A reflection of the full moon as he cranes up at Glenn who is leaning over him, hands on knees. "He's hiding in here then," Cole says. "He knows he can't beat Nolan in a footrace." Cole's head begins to swim, and he has to lie back down. "The back corner. Go straight back, and once you hit the fence, turn right and follow it till you get to the corner."

Glenn is standing now. Cole is speaking normally so he can be heard over the bus's half roar. "There's a hole in the fence. Maybe they went through it. But I bet Gerome's hiding on a bus on Ramshackle Row."

"On *what*?" Glenn asks, raring to go, but these details are paramount and he knew it. He'll be Ray Charles in a corn maze without them.

"Ramshackle Row. You'll see the sign once you get to the corner. Couple down on the right. I bet he's in that one. Door slides open. My old hang …"

Cole seems like he is starting to swim in and out of consciousness again, so Glenn turns to run.

"Mr. Conley."

Glenn turns back, only seeing the boy's feet sticking out of the weed line like he'd found him.

"Be careful. He's got one bullet left."

Glenn runs straight back like Cole had told him. He doesn't have to ask *who* has one bullet left. Nolan has the gun. He shot the driver of the bus and now is after his son. Why, though, he does not know. He prays to God he'll get the opportunity to sit down with Gerome after this and get the story straight.

The engine fades as he runs. He fights the urge to sprint back, climb in the overturned school bus, and pry the dead man's foot off the gas. The idea that a dead guy is still making a very real noise sickens him. But he doesn't have time for that. As he runs, he tells himself he'll ask Gerome after all this what the hell *that* guy is doing here too.

He runs through a field of old rusty buses. One thing tumbles through his head now, trying to punch its way out: Find your son. Have to find him and save him from the man with the gun.

Cole hears Glenn run off until his footfalls dissipate under the sound of the sideways engine.

Why is the bus still running? he thinks.

A migraine rocks him hard in the dirt. He squeezes his temples and looks up at a full moon over the trampled-down weeds where Glenn had been beside him. It hangs low, staring back at him.

"One more bullet," he whispers.

CHAPTER 45

THE FIREWORKS END JUST AS HE HITS THE GROUND ON THE back side of the boat mound. All falls silent. He hears faint cheers riding on the breeze blown up over the point. He hears nothing behind him. He's not sure whether that's good or bad, but that doesn't much matter because he's here. He made it. Now he just has to get through and along the creek bed back to Cole's. He remembers how hard it was scaling the fence in Cole's backyard, but he'll cross that bridge when he arrives there. He can't move as quickly as Nolan, true, but he has the advantage of knowing the way. Nolan will just be running in the dark. Assuming he chooses the right direction, he still won't know where to peel off and hit Cole's backyard.

Gerome's hope is a catching pile of dry logs, but when he goes to push the chain-link aside and step through, someone dumps a bucket of water on his hope's fire. It lets out a great, defeated hiss.

There are two zip ties on the end of the ripped chain-link and around the corner support post. They are perfectly placed apart; he can't slide through over them or squeeze under them. When Gerome had climbed to the top of the boats the last time they thought they were home free, he'd seen Nolan immediately. He had been standing motionless, covering the mended fence with his body. He'd climbed straight up toward Gerome, never allowing a good look around him. He hadn't wanted them to know they couldn't escape this way if they'd somehow gotten away from him again.

Gerome realizes that Nolan would know exactly where he would be headed. He turns and crashes over the boats. There's no time now for quiet. He somehow reaches the other side without falling and runs for Cole's bus. It's the only place he can think to go. He lurches past the Ramshackle Row sign and turns onto the bus, squeezing through the half-open door, never pausing to listen. He hadn't seen Nolan get all the way up on his feet back at the front gate, didn't give him enough time to, but he knows he had. He could *feel* him closing in as he ran around the old buses. He had to have been arriving at the boat pile any moment now. Gerome doesn't dare peek out the door to see, though; he finds his way to the makeshift bed halfway down the bus Cole used a lifetime ago and sits down behind the seat in front of it. He peeks up and over toward the front of the bus, knowing it's too dark in there for Nolan to see him immediately if he boards.

Gerome prays to God that man doesn't find his way onto this bus. He wouldn't have anything to do, no way to defend himself. What would he do—throw a miniature fan at him? Maybe his heart will just explode before Nolan finds him. He'd check each seat on the way down until he found Gerome lying dead with blood oozing from his ears. He'd much rather go out that way than be shot.

His wide eyes search assiduously for movement at the front. His hands are pushed hard against the back of the seat as drips of sweat squirm out from under his palms and run down the textured faux leather. His heart is pounding so loudly that he's sure Nolan can hear it out there. Gerome knows he's got to be at the boats now—not so much that he's *heard* anything of note, per se, but the silence isn't solid anymore. Small sounds here and there break the long drone of nothingness up into segments. He's outside, looking down Ramshackle Row with his back to the boats. He'd hear Gerome's heart like a beacon in the night. He'd follow it, taking him straight here. Then he'd deliver a hot bullet into his brain.

Now Gerome *does* hear something out there. It's not just a break in the silence. It's Nolan. And he's *talking* for Chrissakes. Gerome can't gather the words, but the tone is a terrible *mewling*. Probably telling Gerome to come out, come out, wherever he is. He feels as if he may explode. His bones vibrate, and his innards churn with the need to run, the need to survive. But he has nowhere to go. He's a sitting duck in an antique bus, waiting for the Big Bad Wolf to find him. All he can hope for is that Nolan will lose interest after peeking through the first few buses and head back out into the yard.

But Gerome knows that won't happen. This bus is one of the few that someone can actually get into. That's why Cole had chosen it. Nolan's voice grows louder as he gets closer. It's a normal talking voice, but Gerome can now make out most of what he's saying out there. His words thrum through the otherwise dead air. Gerome thinks now that this is actually the most scared he's ever been in his life. Even more so now than the other terrible situations they'd been through tonight. Each scene topping the last.

"I know you're in here," Nolan says normally. A terrible truth. A lunatic talking to himself right outside his hiding place. Gerome isn't even sure how close Nolan is now; he wasn't 100 percent positive Nolan is looking at *his* bus or just standing somewhere near it. Either way, his time is almost up.

He sits down ever so gently on the seat bed. He closes his hand around one of the fans, a stupid thing, but the only thing he *can* do.

Just then, a heavy foot falls onto the first step up front, hitting hard, meaning to scare its only passenger. It certainly works. Gerome catches a yell high in his throat just before it bursts past his squeezed lips. This is it. He closes his eyes and waits for the end.

Instead of the end, what comes is a racket. A furious *whoosh* of wing flaps accompanied by a scream of surprise. Gerome looks over the seat and sees Nolan swatting a bird from his head, a madman reeling in the bus's doorway. The big black bird is repeatedly dive-bombing and letting out an awful noise each time it jabs at Nolan's face. A raspy caw is forced out angrily with each swoop from the thing. Gerome gets to his feet as the pair wrestles out into the tall grass between the bus's rows. He doesn't know what to do. Should he take the chance while he actually *has* a chance and run for it? Nolan surely still has his gun; he hasn't yet wasted that last round on the black bird. Or should he stay put? Had Nolan been bluffing? Did he even have any idea whether Gerome is on this bus or not?

He's stuck.

He'd done a good bit of freezing in big moments tonight, and here he is again. America, your hero. They say you learn who you really are in life-or-death situations. He's learned so far that he's apt to just turn to stone.

He hears what sounds like wet slaps. It sounds like the bird is popping Nolan's eyeballs with its mangy beak. What sort of bird *is* this? Was there a nest somewhere that Nolan got caught too close to? They are a tornado of flaps and whacks out there; cries of pain pierce the hot air.

Gerome waits where he is, pleading for that final gunshot, the last bullet. In which case, he'd burst out of the bus and make a mad dash for the front of the field, hoping like hell that the bird-thing will keep its attention on Nolan.

Maybe it is *popping his eyeballs,* Gerome thinks. He pictures Nolan choking on the black goo dripping down into his mouth from his deflated eyes. Black goo mixed with the runnels of blood oozing from multiple puncture wounds from the bird-thing's long, mean beak.

"Goddammit, get the F—" Nolan screams. His voice cracks with a mixture of pain and rage. "*Get off meeee!*"

Just then, Gerome hears a thick smack. Nolan's connected with the bird finally, flinging it off him. He sounds like he'd just ran a 5K. He hears nothing form the bird. Gerome shrinks back down behind the seat, hoping with everything he has that he hasn't squandered his one opportunity to escape. He hears Nolan get to his feet, a rustle, then a pair of *thumps.* Dignified stomps. He winds up and hawks a loud loogie.

He spit on it.

Maybe the bird is just knocked silly and it's going to get back up in its own version of a rustle and dignified bird-stomp and attack Nolan again and this time he wouldn't waste his chance. He'd run like hell and wind up and sock Nolan in the jaw as hard as he could on the way by. He'd break his hand trying to knock him out. He swears he would.

Just another chance.

He listens for the bird. Listens for *anything.* But there is nothing. Nothing from Nolan, either. No footsteps. No more heavy breathing. Nothing. Gerome shrinks further, once again finding the small fan he'd had before, reaching out behind him in the dusty blackness.

Nolan sees someone. Someone has come to save Gerome. He stands up and creeps toward the front of the bus, keeping his eyes locked on the fold-open door.

"Come on," Nolan says out there. Gerome can tell he's looking the other way; his voice runs off the other direction. "I see you over there. I thought for sure your ass was dead, boy."

Cole.

Gerome hurries quietly to the front of the bus as Nolan begins walking toward the back corner. He steals himself down the two steps and slides one eye around the open door's frame. It's darker than dark, but his eyes adjusted long ago. It seems they'd spent years trying to survive this night. He sees Nolan walking away from him, only about fifteen or twenty feet from where he stands. He'd probably come up for a look too soon. It's a big risk considering the metal thing strapped to his nub of a leg is seemingly designed perfectly for making obnoxious clanks and clunks off unseen things in the dark. But he can't let Cole fight alone. Especially since Nolan still has that one slug left, patiently waiting for the sweet taste of teenage brain. He sees the gun swinging at the end of Nolan's arm as he walks toward Cole at the front of Ramshackle Row. Above the gun, Nolan's bare arm is pockmarked with dark polka dots. Gerome surmises that'd been the arm Nolan had put over his face to fight off the black bird, taking the brunt of the damage offered up by that sharp beak and even sharper talons.

Nolan is thirty feet away now, walking with a hard limp like a man who'd gone through a long night of unaccustomed physical activity. His old-man strength keeps him moving with strong purpose, saving the pain for later. Gerome looks around and sees no sign of the bird. Maybe it'd just been knocked out after all. His house has sliding-glass doors that open to a small back deck, and sometimes birds will fly into them, seeing the reflection of the woods behind the house. He'd learned to wait a few minutes to see if the bird came to before scooping it up in the shovel and tossing it through the tree line. Sometimes they'd wiggle back to life like they'd been flash-frozen and sat out on the scalding deck to thaw. He'd seen his fair share of jays and robins come back to life but never a black bird. Or crow, raven, whatever the thing is. It's big. Its open wings had filled the space of the doorway and seemed to go on past it on either side.

Gerome steps out into the night, still not seeing Cole. He can't see that far in the dark, adjusted eyes or not. Part of him waits for a barrage of wings and swipes of vicious talons as he stands there in the open, a step outside Cole's bus. He's in the exact same spot Nolan had been when he was attacked.

But the attack never comes. The tall grass sways in the breeze up from the big lake. The row of buses on either side sits quietly—big giants just there to watch. Nolan keeps talking as he walks, threatening the life of the person hiding against the front of the first bus up there like a pussy. Gerome begins to follow, doing his best stalking Indian impression, thinking hard before each step like his life depends on it. Because it certainly does. He can't imagine how Nolan could have seen Cole all the way up there; he can barely make out Nolan's form in the murky darkness. All he can figure is that Cole had tried to sneak up when he saw Nolan fighting the bird and then quickly retreated when Nolan threw it off.

Not quick enough, Gerome thinks. But maybe this is their best chance here and now, one coming at him each way, a surprise attack. As he walks, picking up speed now because Nolan is almost to the front, he tries to think of what he'd do when he gets to him. Would he wind up and go for the knockout shot to the jaw from behind? He'd never punched anyone before, and he'd always feared that if the day came when he actually *had* to, the person would simply wear it without so much as a flinch and begin to laugh in his face. He'd had faith a moment ago. But now, not so much.

Maybe he should go straight for the gun, let Cole do the boxing. He takes long strides now, gaining confidence and making up the distance. Broken bus windows pass his left ear in whooshes of warmer air seeping out from within them. He's less than a bus-length behind Nolan, who'd slowed substantially, clearly wanting Cole to come the rest of the way. The gun hangs at his side, an Old West standoff. Gerome keeps the same pace. The grass is a bit softer the closer he walks to the buses. It hadn't been out in the open all day, every day baking to a crisp like its neighbors only a few feet away, more toward the middle of the alley. His feet hit softly, and his sleeve skims faded, cracked paint as he goes. He hopes Cole has something good. If not, Gerome will have to hit Nolan from behind before he can pull the trigger. He doesn't even want to think about that.

Suddenly Gerome sees a big sign with legs step out from the front of the first bus. Cole's plan is to bum-rush Nolan, hoping the sign will stop the bullet.

"Jesus," Gerome whispers. Audible, but only loud enough to reach the short distance to his own ears.

The following sequence of events unfolds in rapid succession before Gerome is completely ready for them to. But that's become the norm tonight, now hasn't it? Nolan had stopped completely and raised the revolver, aiming center mass at the sign. Gerome breaks into a full sprint, making up the remaining half a dozen yards or so in long strides. He doesn't even think about his prosthetic, simply acting out of the primal impulse of survival, thus resulting in a smooth gait he'd been capable of for years. The ability buried deep below heavy fear and sticky doubts. His best friend is about to be gunned down.

Cole is running too. Running straight at a man with a gun in his hand. Gerome thinks in a split second between frames that there's no way in hell he would've been brave enough to do that.

Then, from the darkness to his right, a large, heavy object is heaved at Nolan. Gerome is only a yard or so behind him when the thing hits, gathering for a transition between full sprint and a lunge at Nolan's back. It flies past Gerome's head and wallops Nolan in the side of his face. Gerome's adrenaline-drunk brain thinks stupidly in that moment that someone from somewhere had thrown a black sack of potatoes. He can't hold up. He puts a shoulder into Nolan's lower back just as the gun goes off. His last bullet. The black sack of potatoes skids to a stop under the bus to their left, just behind the front passenger tire. Gerome sees in the moon glow that the sack has wings. As his head rings like a small room full of big gongs, he realizes what it is. The same bird from before.

Cole had shoved the sign forward through the air at Nolan right before he reached him, making up the last couple feet between them, knowing the last shot was coming and it was all he could do to increase his chances. It hung in the air like a big metal feather before he collided with it hard, giving a shoulder with as much *oomph* behind it as Gerome had on the other end. For a split second there, Nolan was sandwiched. He let out a huge *ooof!* before falling to the ground.

They are a pile in the weeds, arms and legs flailing, going for the gun like it still has bullets. Gerome stands to deliver a kick to Nolan's head, which is currently in a tight headlock from Cole, when he realizes the arms around Nolan's neck are black. Something thumps against his metal leg. Metal on metal. He looks down and almost jumps out of fright to see the big crow at his feet. Its beak is wide open, struggling to hold the rubber handle while the metal blades lay up against his bionic shinbone.

The shears.

He has no time to try to decipher what the flying fuck this thing is or what it's doing here. Nolan and the guy he'd thought was Cole were fighting a grown-man fight in the weeds to his right. Gerome picks up the shears, blades pointing down, and approaches the tussling pair. Eyes are being gouged, punches thrown, threats from both guys. Nolan sees Gerome and flings the heavy sign as hard as he can off of them, an attempt to knock him over. Gerome jumps aside as it lands facedown on the big crow. He hears it squash under the weight of the thing. A muffled splat from a gelid bag of bones. It gives a final cry from its flattened body. A dusty sound. Gerome will later lie in bed and try to talk himself out of the thought that it sure sounded like very human words that escaped from underneath that sign.

He tells himself in this moment that it's his *own* mind telling him what he has to do, his *own* mind that had whispered "Kill him" from somewhere within. Not from under the sign. But from within.

So he tells himself.

And so he does.

Nolan's white head shines bright in the light from the full moon, an ivory globe hitching in the darkness at his feet. The black man is doing his best to keep Nolan's hands from shooting out and grabbing Gerome's leg, who stands there in a daze like a boy deciding whether or not to dive into the deep end.

"*Do it now!*" someone screams. He doesn't know whether the words come from the crushed crow, his own head, or the man wrestling Nolan who sounded a lot like his dad, but he listens.

He watches that glowing orb of Nolan's head twitch back and forth, back and forth as he struggles in the strong arms of his father. He has the pattern down. Gerome closes his eyes just as Nolan shrieks, "Fuck you, you fucking ni—"

And that's it.

The blades go farther than he thought they would. Only half of them still visible, protruding from just above Nolan's left ear.

Glenn shoves the dead body off him before blood drips on his face. It slumps into the weeds to the side. Gerome can still see his bald head down deep. It sits lolled over on top of a loose body. The garden tool that had slipped from Cole's backpack many moons ago sticks out in a rusty "Y." Blood gathers at its base.

Gerome stares at the strange sight in awe, looking at the gruesome result of an act he didn't think he was capable of. Before he knows it, he's wrapped in a strong embrace. His father is crying, and Gerome begins to cry right along with him. He allows himself to be held steady by his father. He is safe now. A feeling he'd never take for granted again as long as he had air in his lungs.

"Thank you, Dad," Gerome says into Glenn's shoulder. Saving other questions such as "How did you know to come for me?" for later.

Glenn takes a step back, remembering something crucial. His hands search his midsection frantically. After a moment, he looks back at Gerome and says, "He missed, kid. He missed 'cause you got to him first. Thank *you*." Gerome glances over at the sign lying flat in the grass by the bus. *Almost* flat. His father hugs him again, even harder this time. Gerome says nothing of the bird. Had that *really* happened? Or was that something his mind had thought up, a vision put forth by which to give hope that he could fight Nolan and come away alive, that he could take on that challenge? A little helper back here in the spooky bus yard. He stares over at the sign through tears with his hands at his sides as his father squeezes him under the big moon.

He wants to go over and lift up one side of the Ramshackle Row sign, peek under it. He wants to prove to himself that he'd seen what he'd seen. It'd saved both his life when Nolan was about to find him cowering in Cole's bus *and* his father's life when it had bashed Nolan in the side of the head, sending his final bullet astray. But before he can go look, his dad is ushering him away.

"We gotta go get Cole," Glenn says. They take a wide loop around the body in the weeds. Like it just might slide the shears out from its dead head and continue to chase. Holding them high above its head. Its head with a big hole over one ear, drooling blood onto its shoulder. Gerome can actually *hear* the testicle-tingling sound of metal against bone.

He allows himself to be led on. Stride for stride with his dad toward the front of the yard for the final time that night and forever after it.

Gerome thinks of the words he'd heard when the garden shears were presented at his feet. "Kill him." That's all he can think about as he walks on next to his dad, their shoulders touching, toward the front. That thing that looked like a crow had told Gerome to "Kill him." So he had.

He stifles the crazy thought as best as he can while he gets farther and farther away from where it all happened. They are close to the front now, and with each step, it'd lost a little muster, magic fading. And that's good. *He* killed Nolan, help or not.

The man in his head says nothing.

Quick crunches from below them are the only sounds, save for the growing warble of a school bus engine. Gerome floods his head with thoughts of his friend. He hadn't asked his dad if Cole was okay. He couldn't find the words and was too afraid of the reply they'd require to look for them.

EPILOGUE

THAT GRUESOME NIGHT IS A GROWING MEMORY. THEY'D DONE something stupid, taking things into their own hands to expose the monster that hid in plain sight. And they'd almost gotten killed in the process. Gerome hasn't had a night terror since, but the events that unfolded on the night of the Fourth replay themselves in his head over and over in quiet moments. Moments when his mind is clear and inviting. In the tender, waning moments before sleep, in the shower while steam twists up and around him, forming the face of the man he'd killed, and in the car line. The place he now sits.

He inches forward, tosses it in park, and closes his eyes. The movie he's now seen a thousand times starts in the dark. He's missed most of it; it's already almost over. He sees the heap of flesh and bones that was Nolan hunched in the grass with that garden tool poking from his head (after a brief investigation into the incident, he was cleared of all wrongdoing, and most of the town knew all the details of that night, even down to the items in the box and the hidden cameras, and especially that terrible letter, by a couple weeks after), he sees him and his father finding Cole, who was hurt but alive in the grass by the entrance (turns out he'd had a slightly cracked pelvis and a pretty severe concussion, non-life-threatening injuries, but he was stuck in front of his TV for weeks), he hears the engine of the school bus fade as they walk through the gate and begin the long journey back to his house, pausing only to let his dad run back into the house and find the remote for the big gate while the two mothers greeted them with terrified faces from the other side, each with arms crossed and hands frantically rubbing opposite elbows. He'd sat Cole down, who he'd been carrying, and ran in. He found it quickly, said it was on the island in the kitchen next to a pyramid of coffee mugs that had the name of Nolan's business wrapped around them. They later learned that that's who the driver of the bus had worked for, though the other details varied depending on who you spoke to. It was the general consensus of the town that the toxicology report found Jordy dangerously above the legal limit, that he'd worn a bulletproof vest that night, which saved his life the first time he was shot but unfortunately did nothing to stop the shot that did him in (in *Call of Duty*, you get double points for shots like that one), and that his son had passed away earlier that night, possibly sending him into full-blown drunken hysterics. Though why he chose to go at such great lengths to take it out on his boss, nobody knew. Some people simply credited the very familiar "disgruntled employee" situation that everyone has seen on the news too many times. But some others thought differently, a little deeper. Maybe he'd had an inkling too, one similar to the boys'. An inkling that Nolan was a monster that needed to get what he had coming for a long time.

Someone punches a horn behind him. Gerome opens his eyes and creeps a couple car-lengths forward and throws it into park again. The big engine bumbles under the hood, the speedo impatiently taps the peg next to zero. He closes his eyes again and sees the three of them join the two moms out on Lakeview Heights from Nolan's long driveway, Cole draped over his dad's thick arms like a giant baby. He'd made Glenn take him to Ellie before heading back to their house. Glenn was about to assign one of the moms with running up there and seeing if the girl was okay, but after taking one look into Cole's eyes, he didn't give a single rebuttal. He simply turned up her drive and hurried toward the front door with Cole bouncing in his arms. If it was painful, Cole didn't make it known. His eyes were locked on the door. It had been left unlocked; Nolan had been sure he'd be right back. Ellie was half-awake. She'd looked like a drunk trying to keep the room from spinning long enough to stand up. She'd said only one thing when the three burst into the front room: "Cole."

Gerome creeps up again, almost to the side entrance of the school now. The side the cool kids come out (as cool as a kid being picked up by another kid could be). Cole rode the bus most days, but every now and then, Gerome picked him up in the car Ellie gave him. It'd taken awhile to get it out of the old barn, and even longer for him and his dad to get it running and fairly fixed up (high on the priority list was finding a new side mirror since the original had been blown off by Nolan back in the barn that night). But he loves the thing. Sometimes he clanks down the steps of his garage and flicks on the fluorescents overhead and just stares at the long, thin grille bookended by circle headlights. It says Chevy Nova from a mile away. Ellie had gotten everything of her stepfather's, despite what he'd told the boys in the bad room. That he'd left everything to a dead dog out back named Dozer. She sold the house as well as the company. Cole said she told him one time not long after, that one of Nolan's workers tried to buy it from her for dirt-cheap. He was a Mexican man, could barely speak any English, but wanted to purchase a business worth more than ten times the value of his own house. She'd almost accepted, simply because she didn't give a damn about the money and she wanted nothing from her stepdad. She wanted it gone. She told Cole that she told the man no because she didn't like the way he looked at her. Like he knew more about her than she herself did, she'd said. The denial had turned out fruitful, because only about a week or so later, a bigger business from a bigger, neighboring town looking to expand swooped in and swallowed it, making it theirs for a hefty check.

Gerome pulls up to the wide concrete path connecting the road to the side doors of Cookeville High School just as Cole is walking out. He walks with a bit of a limp, but Ellie's there close at his side. To steady him, of course. Nothing more. The passenger's door opens and cool October air rushes in. Cole plops down with a wince and plants a quick kiss on the lips waiting for him in a pucker. She'd bent inside the car so none of the students would see. Her nametag dangles from her cotton blouse as she pretends to help him get situated.

"Hi, Gerome," she says through a smile that stops time. "Nice ride." Something she says every time she sees him in it. A cute joke that's theirs and theirs alone.

She closes the door and saunters back toward the side doors. She has papers to grade. She's teaching again. Well, subbing for now, but it's good enough. She's at Cookeville at least for the next couple months, until Mrs. Quebedeaux has her baby boy. Cole says the students are quite pleased, "like replacing Fat Amy with Jen Aniston" one of the guys had said. Cole doesn't have her, but he knows she's certainly the talk of the guy's locker-room and between-class circles.

If they only knew.

Cole slaps Gerome hard on the leg, his real leg, and tells him to quit staring. Ellie's hips roll under her pencil skirt as she climbs the steps just before the door. That girl's been through five lifetimes of tragedy, but her confidence grows every day.

They watch till she disappears into the school.

Maybe it's me, Cole thinks as they pull away from the curb and head for the main drag. *Maybe I'm why.*

Both boys are smiling as golden beams of warm sunlight lay across their arms. A beautiful clash with the cool air swirling in through the open windows.

Gerome turns onto Carlsen as "Under the Bridge" seeps from the Nova's speakers. The Red Hot Chili Peppers are a favorite of Cole's. His '90s jams are starting to rub off on Gerome. He'd had his dad rig up an aux cord in the old car so they can plug in their phones and listen to music. Usually Cole's, considering he and Ellie text day and night while Gerome's still mostly lays dry on his nightstand. And that's all right.

Cole sees a flash of black high in the trees as they tear down the two-lane blacktop. He thinks of the crow. He thinks about it a lot. Usually wondering why he hadn't seen it since that night. Though he's kept these thoughts to himself. They talk about anything and everything, Cole and Gerome, but the events of that night lay in a back room somewhere, dusty and untouched. Talking about it would be slipping the thin sheets off the horrible things that sit heavily underneath. Neither of them wants that.

He closes his eyes and lets the sharp air scream past his ears.

As Anthony Kiedis bleeds another long chorus of haunting bars through the new Pioneers, Gerome tells Cole to look ahead. A rusty bullet, splashed with teal, rumbles toward them. It's an IROC Z28. As the gap closes, Cole sees a big hand sitting atop a thick steering wheel dotted with little yellow skulls. It's only a flash, but the boys know. They remember. The two drivers lift a couple fingers from their wheels as they pass. A cool wave—an appreciation for the other's ride.

As the Camaro disappears around the bend behind them,

Cole and Gerome look at each other and smile. No words are needed.

Gerome looks back at the pavement rushing under the Nova's hood like a hard river, and Cole back out his window, eyes once again closed in the breeze. Gerome pushes the gas a little harder. The needle flutters around sixty, and he holds it there. He holds it there all the way home.

ACKNOWLEDGMENTS

To my dad, who gave me a book of scary stories to read during a road trip when I was nine. For me, it started there. For that and for everything else you've given me, I love you.

To my mom, whose voracious reading rubbed off on me at an early age. I was thinking about you most when writing this, hoping it would be something you couldn't put down. For the gift of love for literature and the gift of life, I love you.

Finally, to the select few whom I felt comfortable enough to show some of the first drafts of this manuscript to: thank you for not breaking face and doing your best to show me that you actually thought it was good. Each of your reactions helped push me onward. You know who you are.

ABOUT THE AUTHOR

DANE OWEN HAS BEEN SCRIBBLING STORIES AND POEMS FOR AS long as he can remember, but *Ramshackle Row* is his debut novel. He wears many hats and enjoys a wide array of things, from personal training to physics, yet his passion for writing supersedes all. He is an avid space lover and prides himself on asking the questions most people are afraid to ask. In a perfect world, you'd either find him on a beach somewhere or huddled up in a funky book nook with a warm cup of coffee. He lives in Cookeville, Tennessee, with his dog, Mister.

CONNECT WITH THE AUTHOR

instagram.com/dane_owen_
DaneOwenAuthor.com

LEAVE A REVIEW

If you enjoyed reading *Ramshackle Row*,
will you consider writing a review on your platform of choice?
Reviews help indie authors find more readers.

Made in the USA
Las Vegas, NV
22 March 2022